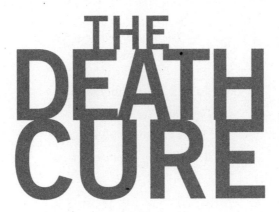

ALSO BY JAMES DASHNER

The Maze Runner
The Scorch Trials

The 13th Reality series
The Journal of Curious Letters
The Hunt for Dark Infinity
The Blade of Shattered Hope

THE DEATH CURE

JAMES DASHNER

Delacorte Press

Text copyright © 2011 by James Dashner
Jacket art copyright © 2011 by Philip Straub

Visit us on the Web! randomhouse.com/teens

Educators and librarians, for a variety of teaching tools, visit us at randomhouse.com/teachers

Library of Congress Cataloging-in-Publication Data
Dashner, James.
The death cure / James Dashner. — 1st ed.
p. cm.
Sequel to: The Scorch trials.
Summary: As the third Trial draws to a close, Thomas and some of his cohorts manage to escape from WICKED, their memories having been restored, only to face new dangers as WICKED claims to be trying to protect the human race from the deadly FLARE virus.
ISBN 978-0-385-73877-4 (hc) — ISBN 978-0-375-89612-5 (ebook)
ISBN 978-0-385-90746-0 (glb) [1. Survival—Fiction. 2. Science fiction.] I. Title.
PZ7.D2587De 2011
[Fic]—dc23
2011022236

The text of this book is set in 11-point Bembo.

Printed in the United States of America

10 9 8 7 6 5 4 3 2 1

First Edition

This book is for my mom—
the best human to ever live.

CHAPTER 1

It was the smell that began to drive Thomas slightly mad.

Not being alone for over three weeks. Not the white walls, ceiling and floor. Not the lack of windows or the fact that they never turned off the lights. None of that. They'd taken his watch; they fed him the exact same meal three times a day—slab of ham, mashed potatoes, raw carrots, slice of bread, water—never spoke to him, never allowed anyone else in the room. No books, no movies, no games.

Complete isolation. For over three weeks now, though he'd begun to doubt his tracking of time—which was based purely on instinct. He tried to best guess when night had fallen, made sure he only slept what felt like normal hours. The meals helped, though they didn't seem to come regularly. As if he was meant to feel disoriented.

Alone. In a padded room devoid of color—the only exceptions a small, almost-hidden stainless-steel toilet in the corner and an old wooden desk that Thomas had no use for. Alone in an unbearable silence, with unlimited time to think about the disease rooted inside him: the Flare, that silent, creeping virus that slowly took away everything that made a person human.

None of this drove him crazy.

But he stank, and for some reason that set his nerves on a sharp wire, cutting into the solid block of his sanity. They didn't let him shower or bathe, hadn't provided him with a change of clothes since he'd arrived or anything to clean his body with. A simple rag would've helped; he

1

could dip it in the water they gave him to drink and clean his face at least. But he had nothing, only the dirty clothes he'd been wearing when they locked him away. Not even bedding—he slept all curled up, his butt wedged in the corner of the room, arms folded, trying to hug some warmth into himself, often shivering.

He didn't know why the stench of his own body was the thing that scared him the most. Perhaps that in itself was a sign that he'd lost it. But for some reason his deteriorating hygiene pushed against his mind, causing horrific thoughts. Like he was rotting, decomposing, his insides turning as rancid as his outside felt.

That was what worried him, as irrational as it seemed. He had plenty of food and just enough water to quench his thirst; he got plenty of rest, and he exercised as best he could in the small room, often running in place for hours. Logic told him that being filthy had nothing to do with the strength of your heart or the functioning of your lungs. All the same, his mind was beginning to believe that his unceasing stench represented death rushing in, about to swallow him whole.

Those dark thoughts, in turn, were starting to make him wonder if Teresa hadn't been lying after all that last time they'd spoken, when she'd said it was too late for Thomas and insisted that he'd succumbed to the Flare rapidly, had become crazy and violent. That he'd *already* lost his sanity before coming to this awful place. Even Brenda had warned him that things were about to get bad. Maybe they'd both been right.

And underneath all that was the worry for his friends. What had happened to them? Where were they? What was the Flare doing to their minds? After everything they'd been subjected to, was this how it was all going to end?

The rage crept in. Like a shivering rat looking for a spot of warmth, a crumb of food. And with every passing day came an increasing anger so intense that Thomas sometimes caught himself shaking uncontrollably before he reeled the fury back in and pocketed it. He didn't want it to go away for good; he only wanted to store it and let it build. Wait for the right time, the right place, to unleash it. WICKED had done all this to him. WICKED had taken his life and those of his friends and were using them for whatever purposes they deemed necessary. No matter the consequences.

And for that, they would pay. Thomas swore this to himself a thousand times a day.

All these things went through his mind as he sat, back against the wall, facing the door—and the ugly wooden desk in front of it—in what he guessed was the late morning of his twenty-second day as a captive in the white room. He always did this—after eating breakfast, after exercising. Hoping against hope that the door would open—actually *open,* all the way—the whole door, not just the little slot on the bottom through which they slid his meals.

He'd already tried countless times to get the door open himself. And the desk drawers were empty, nothing there but the smell of mildew and cedar. He looked every morning, just in case something might've magically appeared while he slept. Those things happened sometimes when you were dealing with WICKED.

And so he sat, staring at that door. Waiting. White walls and silence. The smell of his own body. Left to think about his friends—Minho, Newt, Frypan, the other few Gladers still alive. Brenda and Jorge, who'd vanished from sight after their rescue on the giant Berg. Harriet and Sonya, the other girls from Group B, Aris. About Brenda and her warning to him after he'd woken up in the white room the first time. How had she spoken in his mind? Was she on his side or not?

But most of all, he thought about Teresa. He couldn't get her out of his head, even though he hated her a little more with every passing moment. Her last words to him had been *WICKED is good,* and right or wrong, to Thomas she'd come to represent all the terrible things that had happened. Every time he thought of her, rage boiled inside him.

Maybe all that anger was the last string tethering him to sanity as he waited.

Eat. Sleep. Exercise. Thirst for revenge. That was what he did for three more days. Alone.

On the twenty-sixth day, the door opened.

CHAPTER 2

Thomas had imagined it happening, countless times. What he would do, what he would say. How he'd rush forward and tackle anyone who came in, make a run for it, flee, escape. But those thoughts were almost for amusement more than anything. He knew that WICKED wouldn't let something like that happen. No, he'd need to plan out every detail before he made his move.

When it *did* happen—when that door popped open with a slight puffing sound and began to swing wide—Thomas was surprised at his own reaction: he did nothing. Something told him an invisible barrier had appeared between him and the desk—like back in the dorms after the Maze. The time for action hadn't arrived. Not yet.

He felt only the slightest hint of surprise when the Rat Man walked in—the guy who'd told the Gladers about the last trial they'd been forced on, through the Scorch. Same long nose, same weasel-like eyes; that greasy hair, combed over an obvious bald spot that took up half his head. Same ridiculous white suit. He looked paler than the last time Thomas had seen him, though, and he was holding a thick folder filled with dozens of crinkled and messily stacked papers in the crook of one elbow and dragging a straight-backed chair.

"Good morning, Thomas," he said with a stiff nod. Without waiting for a response, he pulled the door shut, set the chair behind the desk and took a seat. He placed the folder in front of him, opened it and started flipping through the pages. When he found what he'd been looking for he stopped and rested his hands on top. Then he flashed a pathetic grin, his eyes settling on Thomas.

When Thomas finally spoke, he realized that he hadn't done so in weeks, and his voice came out like a croak. "It'll only be a good morning if you let me out."

Not even a flicker of change passed over the man's expression. "Yes, yes, I know. No need to worry—you're going to be hearing plenty of positive news today. Trust me."

Thomas thought about that, ashamed that he let it lift his hopes, even for a second. He should know better by now. "*Positive* news? Didn't you choose us because you thought we were intelligent?"

Rat Man remained silent for several seconds before he responded. "Intelligent, yes. Among more important reasons." He paused and studied Thomas before continuing. "Do you think we *enjoy* all this? You think we *enjoy* watching you suffer? It's all been for a purpose, and very soon it will make sense to you." The intensity of his voice had built until he'd practically shouted that last word, his face now red.

"Whoa," Thomas said, feeling bolder by the minute. "Slim it nice and calm there, old fella. You look three steps away from a heart attack." It felt good to let such words flow out of him.

The man stood from his chair and leaned forward on the desk. The veins in his neck bulged in taut cords. He slowly sat back down, took several deep breaths. "You would think that almost four weeks in this white box might humble a boy. But you seem more arrogant than ever."

"So are you going to tell me that I'm not crazy, then? Don't have the Flare, never did?" Thomas couldn't help himself. The anger was rising in him until he felt like he was going to explode. But he forced a calmness into his voice. "That's what kept me sane through all this— deep down I know you lied to Teresa, that this is just another one of your tests. So where do I go next? Gonna send me to the shuck moon? Make me swim across the ocean in my undies?" He smiled for effect.

The Rat Man had been staring at Thomas with blank eyes throughout his rant. "Are you finished?"

. "No, I'm not finished." He'd been waiting for an opportunity to speak for days and days, but now that it had finally come, his mind went empty. He'd forgotten all the scenarios he'd played out in his mind. "I . . . want you to tell me everything. Now."

"Oh, Thomas." The Rat Man said it quietly, as if delivering sad news to a small child. "We didn't lie to you. You *do* have the Flare."

Thomas was taken aback; a chill cut through the heat of his rage. Was Rat Man lying even now? he wondered. But he shrugged, as if the news were something he'd suspected all along. "Well, I haven't started going crazy yet." At a certain point—after all that time crossing the Scorch, being with Brenda, surrounded by Cranks—he'd come to terms with the fact that he'd catch the virus eventually. But he told himself that for now he was still okay. Still sane. And that was all that mattered at the moment.

Rat Man sighed. "You don't understand. You don't understand what I came in here to tell you."

"Why would I believe a word that comes out of your mouth? How could you possibly expect me to?"

Thomas realized that he'd stood up, though he had no memory of doing so. His chest lurched with heavy breaths. He had to get control of himself. Rat Man's stare was cold, his eyes black pits. Regardless of whether this man was lying to him, Thomas knew he was going to have to hear him out if he ever wanted to leave this white room. He forced his breathing to slow. He waited.

After several seconds of silence, his visitor continued. "I know we've lied to you. Often. We've done some awful things to you and your friends. But it was all part of a plan that you not only agreed to, but helped set in place. We've had to take it all a little farther than we'd hoped in the beginning—there's no doubt about that. However, everything has stayed true to the spirit of what the Creators envisioned— what *you* envisioned in their place after they were . . . purged."

Thomas slowly shook his head; he knew he'd been involved with these people once, somehow, but the concept of putting anyone through what he'd gone through was incomprehensible. "You didn't answer me. How can you possibly expect me to believe anything you say?" He recalled more than he let on, of course. Though the window to his past was caked with grime, revealing little more than splotchy glimpses, he knew he'd worked with WICKED. He knew Teresa had, too, and that they'd helped create the Maze. There'd been other flashes of memory.

"Because, Thomas, there's no value in keeping you in the dark," Rat Man said. "Not anymore."

Thomas felt a sudden weariness, as if all the strength had seeped out of him, leaving him with nothing. He sank to the floor with a heavy sigh. He shook his head. "I don't even know what that means." What was the point of even having a conversation when words couldn't be trusted?

Rat Man kept talking, but his tone changed; it became less detached and clinical and more professorial. "You are obviously well aware that we have a horrible disease eating the minds of humans worldwide. Everything we've done up till now has been calculated for one purpose and one purpose only: to analyze your brain patterns and build a blueprint from them. The goal is to use this blueprint to develop a cure for the Flare. The lives lost, the pain and suffering—you knew the stakes when this began. We all did. It was all done to ensure the survival of the human race. And we're very close. Very, very close."

Memories had come back to Thomas on several occasions. The Changing, the dreams he'd had since, fleeting glimpses here and there, like quick lightning strikes in his mind. And right now, listening to the white-suited man talk, it felt as if he were standing on a cliff and all the answers were just about to float up from the depths for him to see in their entirety. The urge to grasp those answers was almost too strong to keep at bay.

But he was still wary. He knew he'd been a part of it all, had helped design the Maze, had taken over after the original Creators died and kept the program going with new recruits. "I remember enough to be ashamed of myself," he admitted. "But living through this kind of abuse is a lot different than planning it. It's just not right."

Rat Man scratched his nose, shifted in his seat. Something Thomas said had gotten to him. "We'll see what you think at the end of today, Thomas. We shall see. But let me ask you this—are you telling me that the lives of a few aren't worth losing to save countless more?" Again, the man spoke with passion, leaning forward. "It's a very old axiom, but do you believe the end can justify the means? When there's no choice left?"

Thomas only stared. It was a question that had no good response.

The Rat Man might have smiled, but it looked more like he was sneering. "Just remember that at one time you believed it did, Thomas." He started to collect his papers as if to go but didn't move. "I'm here to tell you that everything is set and our data is almost complete. We're on the cusp of something great. Once we have the blueprint, you can go boo-hoo with your friends all you want about how *unfair* we've been."

Thomas wanted to cut the man with harsh words. But he held back. "How does torturing us lead to this blueprint you're talking about? What could sending a bunch of unwilling teenagers to terrible places, watching some of them die—what could that possibly have to do with finding a cure for some disease?"

"It has everything in the *world* to do with it." Rat Man sighed heavily. "Boy, soon you'll remember everything, and I have a feeling you're going to regret a lot. In the meantime, there's something you need to know—it might even bring you back to your senses."

"And what's that?" Thomas really had no idea what the man would say.

His visitor stood up, smoothed the wrinkles out of his pants and adjusted his coat. Then he clasped his hands behind his back. "The Flare virus lives in every part of your body, yet it has no effect on you, nor will it ever. You're a member of an extremely rare group of people. You're *immune* to the Flare."

Thomas swallowed, speechless.

"On the outside, in the streets, they call people like you Munies," Rat Man continued. "And they really, really hate you."

CHAPTER 3

Thomas couldn't find any words. Despite all the lies he'd been told, he knew that what he'd just heard was the truth. When placed alongside his recent experiences, it just made too much sense. He, and probably the other Gladers and everyone in Group B, was immune to the Flare. Which was why they'd been chosen for the Trials. Everything done to them—every cruel trick played, every deceit, every monster placed in their paths—it all had been part of an elaborate experiment. And somehow it was leading WICKED to a cure.

It all fit together. And more—this revelation pricked his memories. It felt familiar.

"I can see that you believe me," Rat Man finally said, breaking the long silence. "Once we'd discovered there were people like you—with the virus rooted inside, yet showing no symptoms—we sought out the best and the brightest among you. This is how WICKED was born. Of course, some in your trial group are *not* immune, and were chosen as control subjects. When running an experiment you need a control group, Thomas. It keeps all the data in context."

That last part made Thomas's heart sink. "Who isn't . . ." The question wouldn't come out. He was too scared to hear the answer.

"Who isn't immune?" Rat Man asked, eyebrows raised. "Oh, I think they should find out before you, don't you? But first things first. You smell like a week-old corpse—let's get you to the showers and find some fresh clothes." With that he picked up his file and turned to the door. He was just about to step out when Thomas's mind focused.

"Wait!" he shouted.

His visitor looked back at him. "Yes?"

"Back in the Scorch—why did you lie that there'd be a cure at the safe haven?"

Rat Man shrugged. "I don't think it was a lie at all. By completing the Trials, by arriving at the safe haven, you helped us collect more data. And because of that there *will* be a cure. Eventually. For everyone."

"And why are you telling me all this? Why now? Why did you stick me in here for four weeks?" Thomas motioned around the room, at the padded ceiling and walls, at the pathetic toilet in the corner. His sparse memories weren't solid enough to make any sense of the bizarre things that had been done to him. "Why did you lie to Teresa about me being crazy and violent and keep me in here all this time? What could possibly be the point?"

"Variables," Rat Man answered. "Everything we've done to you has been carefully calculated by our Psychs and doctors. Done to stimulate responses in the killzone, where the Flare does its damage. To study the patterns of different emotions and reactions and thoughts. See how they work within the confines of the virus that's inside you. We've been trying to understand why in you, there's no debilitating effect. It's all about the killzone patterns, Thomas. Mapping your cognitive and physiological responses to build a blueprint for the potential cure. It's about the cure."

"What *is* the killzone?" Thomas asked, trying to remember but drawing a blank. "Just tell me that and I'll go with you."

"Why, Thomas," the man replied. "I'm surprised being stung by the Griever didn't make you recall at least that much. The killzone is your brain. It's where the virus settles and takes hold. The more infected the killzone, the more paranoid and violent the behavior of the infected. WICKED is using your brain and those of a few others to help us fix the problem. If you recall, our organization states its purpose right in its name: World in Catastrophe, Killzone Experiment Department." Rat Man looked pleased with himself. Almost happy. "Now come on, let's get you cleaned up. And just so you know, we're being watched. Try anything and there'll be consequences."

Thomas sat, attempting to process everything he'd just heard. Again, everything rang true, made sense. Fit in with the memories that had come back to him in recent weeks. And yet his distrust of Rat Man and WICKED still sprinkled it all with doubt.

He finally stood, letting his mind work through the new revelations, hoping they'd sort themselves into nice little stacks for later analysis. Without another word, he walked across the room and followed the Rat Man through the door, leaving his white-walled cell behind.

Nothing stood out about the building in which he found himself. A long hallway, a tiled floor, beige walls with framed pictures of nature— waves crashing on a beach, a hummingbird hovering beside a red flower, rain and mist clouding a forest. Fluorescent lights buzzed overhead. Rat Man led him through several turns and finally stopped at a door. He opened it and gestured for Thomas to go in. It was a large bathroom lined with lockers and showers. And one of the lockers was open to show fresh clothes and a pair of shoes. Even a watch.

"You have about thirty minutes," Rat Man said. "When you're done, just sit tight—I'll come back for you. Then you'll be reunited with your friends."

For some reason, at the words *friends,* Teresa popped into Thomas's mind. He tried calling out to her again with his thoughts, but there was still nothing. Despite his ever-growing disdain for her, the emptiness of her being gone still floated like an unbreakable bubble within him. She was a link to his past and, he knew without any doubt, had once been his best friend. It was one of the only things in his world that he was sure of, and he had a hard time letting go of that completely.

Rat Man nodded. "See you in a half hour," he said. Then he pulled the door open and closed it behind him, leaving Thomas alone once more.

Thomas still didn't have a plan other than finding his friends, but at least he was one step closer to that. And even though he had no idea what to expect, at least he was out of that room. Finally. For now, a hot shower. A chance to scrub himself clean. Nothing had ever sounded so good. Letting his cares slip away for the moment, Thomas took off his nasty clothes and got to work making himself human again.

CHAPTER 4

T-shirt and jeans. Running shoes—just like the ones he'd worn in the Maze. Fresh, soft socks. After washing himself from top to bottom at least five times, he felt reborn. He couldn't help but think that from here on things would improve. That he was going to take control of his own life now. If only the mirror hadn't reminded him of his tattoo—the one given to him before the Scorch. It was a permanent symbol of what he'd been through, and he wished he could forget it all.

He stood outside the door to the bathroom, leaning against the wall, arms folded, waiting. He wondered if the Rat Man would come back—or had he left Thomas to wander the place, begin yet another Trial? He'd barely begun the line of thinking before he heard footsteps, then saw the weaselly man's white form turn the corner.

"Well, aren't you looking spiffy?" the Rat Man commented, the edges of his mouth crawling up his cheeks in an uncomfortable-looking smile.

Thomas's mind raced with a hundred sarcastic answers, but he knew he had to play it straight. All that mattered at the moment was gathering as much information as he could and then finding his friends. "I feel fine, actually. So . . . thanks." He plastered a casual smile on his own face. "When do I get to see the other Gladers?"

"Right now." Rat Man was all business again. He nodded back toward the way he'd come and gestured for Thomas to follow him. "All of you went through different types of tests for Phase Three of the Trials.

We'd hoped to have the killzone patterns mapped out by the end of the second phase, but we had to improvise in order to push further. Like I said, though, we're very close. You'll all be full partners in the study now, helping us fine-tune and dig deeper until we solve this puzzle."

Thomas squinted. He guessed his Phase Three had been the white room—but what about the others? As much as he'd hated his trial, he could only imagine how much worse WICKED could have made it. He almost hoped he never found out what they had devised for his friends.

Finally Rat Man arrived at a door. He opened it without hesitating and stepped through.

They entered a small auditorium and relief washed over Thomas. Sitting scattered among a dozen or so rows of seats were his friends, safe and healthy-looking. The Gladers and girls of Group B. Minho. Frypan. Newt. Aris. Sonya. Harriet. Everyone seemed happy—talking, smiling and laughing—though maybe they were faking, to some extent. Thomas assumed they'd also been told things were almost over, but he doubted anyone believed it. He certainly didn't. Not yet.

He looked around the room for Jorge and Brenda—he really wanted to see Brenda. He'd been anxious about her ever since she'd vanished after the Berg picked them up, worried that WICKED had sent her and Jorge back to the Scorch like they'd threatened to—but there was no sign of either one. Before he could ask Rat Man about them, however, a voice broke through the din, and Thomas couldn't stop a smile from spreading across his face.

"Well, I've been shucked and gone to heaven. It's Thomas!" Minho called out. His announcement was followed by hoots and cheers and catcalls. A swell of relief mixed with the worry clawing in Thomas's stomach and he continued to search the faces in the room. Too overcome to speak, he just kept grinning until his eyes found Teresa.

She'd stood up, turned from her chair on the end of the row to face him. Black hair, clean and brushed and shiny, draped over her shoulders and framed her pale face. Her red lips parted into a huge smile, lighting up her features, making her blue eyes glow. Thomas almost went to her but stopped himself, his mind clouded with vivid memories of what she'd done to him, of what she'd said about WICKED being good even after everything that had happened.

Can you hear me? he called out with his mind, just to see if their ability had come back.

But she didn't respond, and he still didn't feel her presence inside him. They just stood there, staring at each other, eyes locked for what seemed like a minute but could only have been a few seconds. And then Minho and Newt were by his side, slapping him on the back, shaking his hand, pulling him into the room.

"Well, at least you didn't bloody roll over and die, Tommy," Newt said, squeezing his hand tightly. His tone sounded grumpier than usual, especially considering they hadn't seen each other in weeks, but he was in one piece. Which was something to be thankful for.

Minho had a smirk on his face, but a hard glint in his eyes showed that he'd been through an awful time. That he wasn't quite himself yet, just trying his hardest to act like it. "The mighty Gladers, back together again. Good to see ya alive, shuck-face—I've imagined you dead in about a hundred different ways. I bet you cried every night, missing me."

"Yeah," Thomas muttered, thrilled to see everybody but still struggling to find words. He broke away from the reunion and made his way to Teresa. He had an overwhelming urge to face her and come to some kind of peace until he could decide what to do. "Hey."

"Hey," she replied. "You okay?"

Thomas nodded. "I guess. Kind of a rough few weeks. Could—" He stopped himself. He'd almost asked if she'd been able to hear him trying to reach out to her with his mind, but he didn't want to give her the satisfaction of knowing he'd done it.

"I tried, Tom. Every day I tried to talk to you. They cut us off, but I think it's all been worth it." She reached out and took his hand, which set off a chorus of mocking jabs from the Gladers.

Thomas quickly pulled his hand from her grasp, felt his face flush red. For some reason, her words had made him suddenly angry, but the others mistook his action for mere embarrassment.

"Awwww," Minho said. "That's almost as sweet as that time she slammed the end of a spear into your shuck face."

"True love indeed." This from Frypan, followed by his deep bellow of a laugh. "I'd hate to see what happens when these two have their first *real* fight."

Thomas didn't care what they thought, but he was determined to show Teresa that she couldn't get away with everything she'd done to him. Whatever trust they'd shared before the trials—whatever relationship they'd had—meant nothing now. He might find a sort of peace with her, but he resolved right then and there that he would only trust Minho and Newt. No one else.

He was just about to respond when Rat Man came marching down the aisle clapping his hands. "Everybody take a seat. We've got a few things to cover before we remove the Swipe."

He'd said it so casually, Thomas almost didn't catch it. The words registered—*remove the Swipe*—and he froze.

The room stilled and the Rat Man stepped up onto the stage at the front of the room and approached the lectern. He gripped the edges and repeated the same forced smile from earlier, then spoke. "That's right, ladies and gents. You're about to get all your memories back. Every last one of them."

CHAPTER 5

Thomas was stunned. Mind spinning, he went to sit by Minho.

After struggling for so long to remember his life, his family and childhood—even what he'd done the day before he woke up in the Maze—the idea of having it all back was almost too much to comprehend. But as it sank in, he realized that something had shifted. Remembering everything didn't sound good anymore. And his gut confirmed what he'd been feeling since the Rat Man had said it was all over—it just seemed too easy.

Rat Man cleared his throat. "As you were informed in your one-on-ones, the Trials as you've known them are over. Once your memories are restored, I think you'll believe me and we can move on. You've all been briefed on the Flare and the reasons for the Trials. We are extremely close to completing our blueprint of the killzone. The things we need—to further refine what we have—will be better served by your full cooperation and unaltered minds. So, congratulations."

"I ought to come up there and break your shuck nose," Minho said. His voice was terrifyingly calm considering the threat in his words. "I'm sick of you acting like everything is peachy—like more than half of our friends didn't *die*."

"I'd love to see that rat nose smashed!" Newt snapped.

The anger in his voice startled Thomas, and he had to wonder what awful thing Newt had been through during Phase Three.

Rat Man rolled his eyes and sighed. "First of all, each of you has been warned of the consequences should you try to harm me. And rest assured, you're all still being watched. Second, I'm sorry for those you've lost—but in the end it'll have been worth it. What concerns me, though, is that it seems that nothing I say is going to wake you people up to the stakes here. We're talking about the survival of the human race."

Minho sucked in a breath as if to begin a rant, but he stopped short, closed his mouth.

Thomas knew that no matter how sincere Rat Man sounded, it had to be a trick. Everything was a trick. Yet nothing good could come of their fighting him at this point—with words or with fists. The thing they needed most for the time being was patience.

"Let's all just slim it," Thomas spoke evenly. "Let's hear him out."

Frypan spoke up just as Rat Man was about to continue. "Why should we trust you people to . . . What was it called? The Swipe? After everything you've done to us, to our friends—you want to remove the Swipe? I don't think so. I'd rather stay stupid about my past, thank you very kindly."

"WICKED is good," Teresa said out of the blue, as if talking to herself.

"What?" Frypan asked. Everyone turned to look at her.

"WICKED is good," she repeated, much louder, turning in her seat to meet the others' gazes. "Of all the things I could've written on my arm when I first woke up from my coma, I chose those three words. I keep thinking about it, and there has to be a reason for that. I say we just shut up and do what the man says. We can only understand this with our memories back."

"I agree!" Aris shouted, much louder than seemed necessary.

Thomas was quiet as the room broke into arguments. Mostly between the Gladers, who sided with Frypan, and the members of

20

Group B, who sided with Teresa. There couldn't possibly be a worse time for a battle of wills.

"Silence!" Rat Man roared, pounding his fist on the lectern. He waited for everyone to quiet down before he continued. "Look, no one's going to blame you for the mistrust you feel. You've been pushed to your physical limits, watched people die, experienced terror in its purest form. But I promise you, when all is said and done, none of you will look back—"

"What if we don't want to?" Frypan called out. "What if we don't want our memories back?"

Thomas turned to look at his friend, relieved. It was exactly what he'd been thinking himself.

Rat Man sighed. "Is it because you really have no interest in re-membering, or is it because you don't trust us?"

"Oh, I can't *imagine* why we wouldn't trust you," Frypan replied.

"Don't you realize by now that if we wanted to do something to harm you, we'd just do it?" The man looked down at the lectern, then back up again. "If you don't want to remove the Swipe, don't do it. You can stand by and watch the others."

A choice or a bluff? Thomas couldn't tell by the man's tone but nonetheless was surprised by his response.

Again the room was silent, and before anyone else could speak, Rat Man had stepped away off the stage and was walking toward the door at the back of the room. When he reached it, he turned to face them again. "You really want to spend the rest of your lives having no memory of your parents? Your family and friends? You really want to lose the chance to hold on to at least the few good memories you may have had before all this began? Fine with me. But you might never have this opportunity again."

Thomas considered his decision. It was true that he longed to re-member his family. He'd thought about it so many times. But he *did* know WICKED. And he wasn't going to let himself fall into another trap. He'd fight to the death before letting those people tinker with his brain again. How could he believe any memory they replaced anyway?

And there was something else bothering him—the flash he'd felt when the Rat Man had first announced that WICKED would re-move the Swipe. Besides knowing that he couldn't just accept anything WICKED called his memories, he was scared. If everything they'd been insisting was true was in fact true, he didn't want to face his past even if he could. He didn't understand the person they said he was before. And more, he didn't like him.

He watched as the Rat Man opened the door and left the room. As soon as he was gone, Thomas leaned in close to Minho and Newt so only his friends could hear him. "There's no way we do this. No way."

Minho squeezed Thomas's shoulder. "Amen. Even if I did trust those shanks, why would I *want* to remember? Look what it did to Ben and Alby."

Newt nodded. "We need to make a bloody move soon. And when we do, I'm going to knock a few heads to make myself feel better."

Thomas agreed but knew they had to be careful. "Not *too* soon, though," he said. "We can't screw this up—we need to look for our best chance." It had been so long since Thomas had felt it, he was surprised when a sense of strength began to trickle through him. He was reunited with his friends and this was the end of the Trials—for good. One way or another, they were done doing what WICKED wanted.

They stood up and, as a group, made their way to the door. But as Thomas put his hand on the knob to pull it open, he stopped. What he was hearing made his heart sink. The rest of the group was still talking, and most of the others had decided to get their memories back.

Rat Man was waiting outside the auditorium. He led them down several turns of the windowless hallway until they finally reached a large steel door. It was heavily bolted and looked to be sealed against outside air. Their white-clad leader placed a key card next to a square recess in the steel, and after a few clicks, the large slab of metal slid open with a grinding sound that reminded Thomas of the Doors in the Glade.

Then there was another door; once the group had filed into a small vestibule, the Rat Man closed the first door and, with the same card, unlocked the second. On the other side was a big room that looked like nothing special—same tile floors and beige walls as the hallway. Lots of cabinets and counters. And several beds lined the back wall, each with a menacing, foreign-looking contraption of shiny metal and plastic tubes in the shape of a mask hanging over it. Thomas couldn't imagine letting someone place that thing on his face.

Rat Man gestured toward the beds. "This is how we're going to remove the Swipe from your brains," Rat Man announced. "Don't worry, I know these devices look frightening, but the procedure won't hurt nearly as much as you might think."

"*Nearly as much?*" Frypan repeated. "I don't like the sound of that. So it *does* hurt, is what you're really saying."

"Of course you'll experience minor discomfort—it *is* a surgery," Rat Man said as he walked over to a large machine to the left of the beds. It had dozens of blinking lights and buttons and screens. "We'll be removing a small device from the part of your brain devoted to long-term memory. But it's not as bad as it might sound, I promise." He started pressing buttons and a buzzing hum filled the room.

"Wait a second," Teresa said. "Is this going to take away whatever's in there that lets you control us, too?"

The image of Teresa inside that shed in the Scorch came to Thomas. And of Alby writhing in bed back at the Homestead. Of Gally killing Chuck. They were all under WICKED's control. For the slightest moment Thomas doubted his decision—could he really allow himself to remain at their mercy? Should he just let them do the operation? But then the doubt vanished—this was about mistrust. He refused to give in.

Teresa continued. "And what about . . ." She faltered, looked at Thomas.

He knew what she was thinking. Their ability to talk telepathically. Not to mention what came with it—that odd sense of each other when things were working, almost as if they were sharing brains somehow. Thomas suddenly loved the idea of losing that forever. Maybe the emptiness of having Teresa not there would disappear too.

Teresa recovered and continued. "Is everything going to be out of there? *Everything?*"

Rat Man nodded. "Everything except the tiny device that allows us to map your killzone patterns. And you didn't have to say what you're thinking because I can see it in your eyes—no, you and Thomas and Aris won't be able to do your little trick anymore. We did turn it off temporarily, but now it'll be gone forever. However, you'll have your long-term memory restored, and we won't be able to manipulate your minds. It's a package deal, I'm afraid. Take it or leave it."

The others in the room shuffled about, whispered questions to each other. A million things had to be flying through everyone's heads. There was so much to think about; there were so many implications. So many reasons to be angry at WICKED. But the fight seemed to have drained from the group, replaced by an eagerness to get it all over with.

"That's a no-brainer," Frypan said. "Get it? No-brainer?" The only response he got was a groan or two.

"Okay, I think we're just about ready," Rat Man announced. "One last thing, though. Something I need to tell you before you regain your memories. It'll be better to hear it from me than to . . . remember the testing."

"What're you talking about?" Harriett asked.

Rat Man clasped his hands behind his back, his expression suddenly grave. "Some of you are immune to the Flare. But . . . some of you aren't. I'm going to go through the list—please do your best to take it calmly."

CHAPTER 6

The room lapsed into silence, broken only by the hum of machinery and a very faint beeping sound. Thomas knew he was immune—at least, he'd been told he was—but he didn't know about anyone else, had actually forgotten about it. The sickening fear he'd felt when he'd first found out came flooding back.

"For an experiment to provide accurate results," the Rat Man explained, "one needs a control group. We did our best to keep the virus from you as long as we could. But it's airborne and highly contagious."

He paused, taking in everyone's gazes.

"Just bloody get on with it," Newt said. "We all figured we had the buggin' disease anyway. You're not breaking our hearts."

"Yeah," Sonya added. "Cut the drama and tell us already."

Thomas noticed Teresa fidgeting next to him. Had she already been told something, also? He figured that she had to be immune like him—that WICKED wouldn't have chosen them for their special roles otherwise.

Rat Man cleared his throat. "Okay, then. Most of you are immune and have helped us gather invaluable data. Only two of you are considered Candidates now, but we'll go into that later. Let's get to the list. The following people are *not* immune. Newt . . ."

Something like a jolt hit Thomas in the chest. He doubled over and stared at the floor. Rat Man called out a few more names, but none Thomas knew—he barely heard them over the dizzying buzz that seemed to fill his ears and fog his mind. He was surprised at his own reaction, hadn't realized just how much Newt meant to him until he heard the declaration. A thought occurred to him—earlier the Rat Man had said that the control subjects were like the glue that kept the project's data together, made it all coherent and relevant.

The Glue. That was the title given to Newt—the tattoo that was etched in his skin even now, like a black scar.

"Tommy, slim yourself."

Thomas looked up to see Newt standing there with his arms folded and a forced grin on his face. Thomas straightened back up. "Slim myself? That old shank just said you're not immune to the Flare. How can you—"

"I'm not worried about the bloody Flare, man. I never thought I'd still be alive at this buggin' point—and living hasn't exactly been so great anyway."

Thomas couldn't tell if his friend was serious or just trying to seem tough. But the creepy grin still hadn't left Newt's face, so Thomas forced a smile onto his own. "If you're cool with slowly going crazy and wanting to eat small children, then I guess we won't cry for you." Words had never felt so empty before.

"Good that," Newt responded; the smile disappeared, though.

Thomas finally turned his attention to the rest of the people in the room, his head still dizzy with thoughts. One of the Gladers—a kid named Jackson who he'd never gotten to know very well—was staring into space with blank eyes, and another was trying to hide his tears. One of the girls of Group B had red, puffy eyes—a couple of her friends were huddled around her, trying to console her.

"I wanted to get that out of the way," Rat Man said. "Mainly so I could tell you myself and *remind* you that the whole point of this operation has been to build toward a cure. Most of you not immune are in the early stages of the Flare, and I have every confidence that you'll be taken care of before it goes too far. But the Trials required your participation."

"And what if you don't figure things out?" Minho asked.

Rat Man ignored him. He walked over to the closest bed, then reached up and put a hand on the odd metallic device hanging from the ceiling. "This is something we're very proud of here—a feat of scientific and medical engineering. It's called a Retractor, and it will be performing this procedure. It'll be placed on your face—and I promise you'll still look just as pretty when everything is done. Small wires within the device will descend and enter your ear canals. From there they will remove the machinery in your brain. Our doctors and nurses will give you a sedative to calm your nerves and something to dull the discomfort."

He paused to glance around the room. "You will fall into a trancelike state as the nerves repair themselves and your memories return, similar to what some of you went through during what you called the Changing back in the Maze. But not nearly as bad, I promise. Much of that was for the purpose of stimulating brain patterns. We have several more rooms like this one, and a whole team of doctors waiting to get started. Now, I'm sure you have a *million* questions, but most of them will be answered by your own memories, so I'm going to wait until after the procedure for any more Q and A."

The Rat Man paused, then finished, "Give me just a few moments to make sure the medical teams are ready. You can take this time to make your decisions."

He crossed the room, the swish-swishing of his white pants the only sound cutting the silence, and disappeared through the first steel door, closing it behind him. Then the room erupted with noise as everyone started talking at once.

Teresa came over to Thomas, and Minho was right behind her. He

28

leaned in close to be heard over the buzz of frantic conversations. "You shanks know more and remember more than anybody else. Teresa, I've never made a secret of it—I don't like you. But I want to hear what you think anyway."

Thomas was just as curious to hear Teresa's opinion. He nodded at his former friend and waited for her to speak. There was still a small part of him that foolishly expected her to finally speak out against doing what WICKED wanted.

"We should do it," Teresa said, and it didn't surprise Thomas at all. The hope inside him died for good. "It feels like the right thing to me. We need our memories back so we can be smart about things. Decide what to do next."

Thomas's mind was spinning, trying to put it all together. "Teresa, I know you're not stupid. But I also know you're in love with WICKED. I'm not sure what you're up to, but I'm not buying it."

"Me neither," Minho said. "They can manipulate us, play with our shuck brains, dude! How would we even know if they're giving us back our own memories or shoving new ones inside us?"

Teresa let out a sigh. "You guys are missing the whole point! If they can control us, if they can do whatever they want with us, *make* us do anything, then why would they even bother with this whole charade of giving us a choice? Plus, he said they'd also be taking out the part that *lets* them control us. It feels legit to me."

"Well, I never trusted you anyway," Minho said, shaking his head slowly. "And certainly not them. I'm with Thomas."

"What about Aris?" Newt had been so quiet, Thomas hadn't even noticed that he'd walked up behind him with Frypan. "Didn't you say he was with you guys before you came to the Maze? What does he think?"

Thomas scanned the room until he found Aris talking to some

29

of his friends from Group B. He'd been hanging out with them since Thomas had arrived, which Thomas figured made sense—Aris had gone through his own Maze experience with that group. But Thomas could never forgive the boy for the part he'd played in helping Teresa back in the Scorch, luring him to the chamber in the mountains and forcing him inside.

"I'll go ask him," Teresa said.

Thomas and his friends watched as she walked over, and she and her group started whispering furiously to each other.

"I *hate* that chick," Minho finally said.

"Come on, she's not so bad," Frypan offered.

Minho rolled his eyes. "If she's doing it, I'm not."

"Me neither," Newt agreed. "And I'm the one who supposedly has the bloody Flare, so I have more stake in it than anybody. But I'm not falling for one more trick."

Thomas had already settled on that. "Let's just hear what she says. Here she comes."

Her talk with Aris had been short. "He sounded even more sure than us. They're all for it."

"Well, that settles it for me," Minho answered. "If Aris and Teresa are for it, I'm against it."

Thomas couldn't have said it better himself. Every instinct he had told him Minho was right, but he didn't voice his opinion aloud. He watched Teresa's face instead. She turned and looked at Thomas. It was a look he knew so well—she expected him to side with her. But the difference was that now he was suspicious about why she wanted it so badly.

He stared at her, forcing his own expression to remain blank—and Teresa's face fell.

"Suit yourselves." She shook her head, then turned and walked away.

Despite everything that had happened, Thomas's heart lurched in his chest as she retreated across the room.

"Ah, man," Frypan's voice cut in, jarring Thomas back. "We can't let them put those things on our face, can we? I'd just be happy back in my kitchen in the Homestead, I swear I would."

"You forget about the Grievers?" Newt asked.

Frypan paused a second, then said, "They never messed with me in the kitchen, now, did they?"

"Yeah, well, we'll just have to find you a new place to cook." Newt grabbed Thomas and Minho by the arms and led them away from the group. "I've heard enough bloody arguments. I'm not getting on one of those beds."

Minho reached over and squeezed Newt's shoulder. "Me neither."

"Same here," Thomas said. Then he finally voiced what had been building inside him for weeks. "We'll stick around, play along and act nice," he whispered. "But as soon as we get a chance, we're going to fight our way out of this place."

CHAPTER 7

Rat Man returned before Newt or Minho could respond. But judging by the looks on their faces, Thomas was sure they were on board. One hundred percent.

More people were piling into the room, and Thomas turned his attention to what was going on. Everyone who'd joined them was dressed in a one-piece, somewhat loose-fitting green suit with WICKED written across the chest. It struck Thomas suddenly how thoroughly every detail of this game—this *experiment*—had been thought out. Could it be that the very name they'd used for their organization had been one of the Variables from the beginning? A word with obvious menace, yet an entity they were told was good? It was probably just another poke to see how their brains reacted, what they felt.

It was all a guessing game. Had been from the very beginning.

Each doctor—Thomas assumed they were doctors, like Rat Man had said—took a place next to one of the beds. They fidgeted with the masks that hung from the ceiling, adjusting the tubes, tinkering with knobs and switches Thomas couldn't see.

"We've already assigned each of you a bed," Rat Man said, looking down at papers on a clipboard he'd brought back with him. "Those staying in this room are . . ." He rattled off a few names, including Sonya and Aris, but not Thomas or any of the Gladers. "If I didn't call your name, please follow me."

The whole situation had taken on a bizarre taint, too casual and run-of-the-mill for the seriousness of what was going on. Like gangsters yelling out roll call before they slaughtered a group of weeping traitors. Thomas didn't know what to do but go along until the right moment presented itself.

He and the others silently followed Rat Man out of the room and down another long, windowless hallway before stopping at another door. Their guide read from his list again, and Frypan and Newt were included this time.

"I'm not doing it," Newt announced. "You said we could choose and that's my bloody decision." He exchanged an angry look with Thomas that seemed to say they better do something soon or he'd go crazy.

"That's fine," Rat Man replied. "You'll change your mind soon enough. Stay with me until we've finished distributing everyone else."

"What about you, Frypan?" Thomas asked, trying to hide his surprise at how easily the Rat Man had relented with Newt.

The cook suddenly looked sheepish. "I . . . think I'm going to let them do it."

Thomas was shocked.

"Are you crazy?" Minho asked.

Frypan shook his head, bearing himself up a little defensively. "I want to remember. Make your own choice; let me make mine."

"Let's move along," Rat Man said.

Frypan disappeared into the room, hurrying, probably to avoid any more arguments. Thomas knew he had to let it go—for now, he could only worry about himself and finding a way out. Hopefully he could rescue everyone else once he did.

Rat Man didn't call for Minho, Teresa and Thomas until they were standing at the final door, along with Harriet and two other girls from Group B. So far Newt had been the only one to say no to the procedure.

"No thanks," Minho said when Rat Man gestured for everyone to enter the room. "But I appreciate the invitation. You guys have a good time in there." He gave a mock wave.

"I'm not doing it, either," Thomas announced. He was beginning to feel the rush of anticipation. They had to take a chance soon, try something.

Rat Man stared at Thomas for a long time, his face unreadable.

"You okay, there, Mr. Rat Man?" Minho asked.

"My name is Assistant Director Janson," he replied, his voice low and strained, as if it was hard work to stay calm. His eyes never left Thomas. "Learn to show respect for your elders."

"You quit treating people like animals and maybe I'll consider it," Minho said. "And why are you goggling at Thomas?"

Rat Man—Janson—finally turned his gaze to Minho. "Because there are many things to consider." He paused, stood straighter. "But very well. We said you could choose for yourselves, and we'll stand by that. Everyone come inside and we'll get things started with those willing to participate."

Again, Thomas felt a shiver pass through his body. Their moment was coming. He knew it. And by the expression on Minho's face, he knew it, too. They gave each other a slight nod and followed Rat Man into the room.

It looked exactly like the first one, with six beds, the hanging masks, all of it. The machine that evidently ran everything was already humming and chirping. A person dressed in the same green clothes as the doctors in the first room stood next to each bed.

Thomas looked around and sucked in a breath. Standing next to a bed at the very end of the row, dressed in green, was Brenda. She looked way younger than everyone else, her brown hair and face cleaner than he'd ever seen them back in the Scorch. She gave him a quick shake of her head and shifted her gaze to Rat Man; then, before Thomas knew what was happening, she was running across the room. She grabbed Thomas and pulled him into a hug. He squeezed back, completely in shock, but he didn't want to let go.

"Brenda, what are you doing!" Janson yelled at her. "Get back to your post!"

She pressed her lips against Thomas's ear, and then she was whispering, so quietly he could barely hear her, "Don't trust them. Do *not* trust them. Only me and Chancellor Paige, Thomas. Ever. No one else."

"Brenda!" the Rat Man practically screamed.

Then she was letting go, stepping away. "Sorry," she mumbled. "I'm just glad to see he made it through Phase Three. I forgot myself." She walked back to her post and turned to face them once again, her face blank.

Janson scolded her. "We hardly have time for such things."

Thomas couldn't look away from her, didn't know what to think or feel. He already didn't trust WICKED, so her words put them on the same side. But why was she working with them, then? Wasn't she sick? And who was this Chancellor Paige? Was this just another test? Another Variable?

Something powerful had swum through his body when they'd hugged. He thought back to how Brenda had spoken in his mind after he'd been put into the white room. She'd *warned* him things were going to get bad. He still didn't understand how she'd been able to do that—was she really on his side?

Teresa, who'd been quiet since they left the first room, stepped up to him, interrupting his thoughts.

"What's she doing here?" she whispered, the spite evident in her voice. Every little thing she did or said now bothered him. "I thought she was a Crank."

35

"I don't know," Thomas muttered. Flashes of all that time he'd spent with Brenda in the broken city filled his head. In a strange way, he missed that place. Missed being alone with her. "Maybe she's . . . just throwing me a Variable."

"You think she was part of the show, sent to the Scorch to help run things?"

"Probably." Thomas hurt inside. It made sense that Brenda could've been part of WICKED from the beginning. But that meant she'd lied to him, over and over. He wanted so badly for something to be different about her.

"I don't like her," Teresa said. "She seems . . . devious."

Thomas had to force himself not to scream at Teresa. Or laugh at her. Instead, he spoke to her calmly. "Go let them play with your brain." Maybe her distrust of Brenda was the best indication that he *should* trust Brenda.

Teresa gave him a sharp look. "Judge me all you want. I'm just doing what feels right." Then she stepped away, awaiting the Rat Man's instructions.

Janson assigned the willing patients to beds while Thomas, Newt, and Minho hung back and observed. Thomas glanced at the door, wondered if they should make a run for it. He was just about to nudge Minho when the Rat Man spoke up as if he'd read Thomas's mind.

"You three rebels are being watched. Don't even think about trying anything. Armed guards are on their way as we speak."

Thomas had the unsettling idea that maybe someone *had* read his mind. Could they interpret his actual *thoughts* from the brain patterns they were so studiously collecting?

"That's a bunch of klunk," Minho whispered when Janson returned his attention to getting people settled on the beds. "I think we should take our chances, see what happens."

Thomas didn't answer, looked over at Brenda instead. She was staring at the floor, seemingly deep in thought. He found himself missing her terribly, feeling a connection he didn't quite understand. All he wanted was to talk to her alone. And not just because of what she'd said to him.

The sound of rushed footsteps came from the hallway. Three men and two women burst into the room, all of them dressed in black, with gear strapped to their backs—ropes, tools, ammunition. They were all holding some sort of bulky weapon. Thomas couldn't stop staring at the weapons—they tugged at some lost memory he could just barely put his finger on, but at the same time it was like seeing them for the first time. The devices shimmered with blue light—a clear tube in the middle was filled with shiny metallic grenades that crackled and fizzed with electricity—and the guards were pointing them at Thomas and his two friends.

"We waited too bloody long," Newt snapped in a low, harsh whisper.

Thomas knew an opportunity would present itself soon. "They would've caught us out there anyway," he answered quietly, his lips barely moving. "Just be patient."

Janson walked over to stand beside the guards. He pointed at one of the weapons. "These are called Launchers. These guards will not hesitate to fire them if any of you cause trouble. The weapons won't kill you, but trust me when I say that they'll give you the most uncomfortable five minutes of your life."

"What's going on?" Thomas asked, surprised at how little fear he felt. "You just told us we could make this choice ourselves. Why the sudden army?"

"Because I don't trust you." Janson paused, seeming to choose his words carefully. "We hoped you would do things voluntarily once your memories were back. It would just make things easier. But I never said we don't still need you."

"What a surprise," Minho said. "You lied again."

"I haven't lied about a thing. You made your decision, now live with the consequences." Janson pointed at the door. "Guards, escort Thomas and the others to their rooms, where they can dwell on their mistakes until tomorrow morning's tests. Use whatever force is necessary."

CHAPTER 8

The two female guards lifted their weapons even higher, the wide, round muzzles pointed at the three boys.

"Don't make us use these," one of the women said. "You have zero room for error. One false move and we pull the trigger."

The three men swung the straps of their Launchers over their shoulders, then moved toward the defiant Gladers, one per boy. Thomas still felt an odd calmness—coming in part from the deep determination to fight until he couldn't anymore—and a sense of satisfaction that WICKED needed five armed guards to watch three teenagers.

The guy who grabbed Thomas's arm was twice as thick as he was, powerfully built. He walked briskly through the door and into the hallway, pulling Thomas along after him. Thomas looked back to see another guard half drag Minho across the floor to follow, and Newt was right behind them, struggling to no avail.

The boys were hauled down corridor after corridor, the only sounds coming from Minho—grunts and shouts and curses. Thomas tried to tell him to stop—that he was only making it worse, that he was probably going to get shot—but Minho ignored him, fighting tooth and nail until the group finally stopped in front of a door.

One of the armed guards used a key card to unlock the door. She pushed it open to reveal a small bedroom with two sets of bunk beds and a kitchenette with a table and chairs in the far corner. It certainly wasn't what Thomas had been expecting—he'd pictured the Slammer back in the Glade, with its dirt floor and one half-broken chair.

"In you go," she said. "We'll have some food brought to you. Be glad we don't starve you for a few days after the way you've been acting. Tests tomorrow, so you better get some sleep tonight."

The three men pushed the Gladers into the room and swung the door closed; the click of the lock engaging echoed through the air.

Immediately all the feelings of captivity Thomas had endured in the white-walled prison came flooding back. He crossed the floor to the door and twisted the knob, pulled and pushed with all his weight. He pounded on it with both fists, screaming as loudly as he could for someone to let them out.

"Slim it," Newt said from behind him. "No one's coming to bloody tuck you in."

Thomas whirled around, but when he saw his friend standing in front of him, he stopped. Minho spoke before he could put words together.

"I guess we missed our chance." He plopped down on one of the bottom bunks. "We'll be old men or dead before your magical moment comes rolling along, Thomas. It's not like they're going to make a big announcement: 'Now would be an excellent time to escape, because we'll be busy for the next ten minutes.' We've gotta take some chances."

Thomas hated to admit that his friends were right, but they were. They all should've made a run for it before those guards showed up. "Sorry. It just didn't feel right yet. And once they had all those weapons in our faces, it seemed kind of pointless to waste the effort trying anything."

"Yeah, well" was all Minho said. Then, "You and Brenda had a nice little reunion."

Thomas took a deep breath. "She said something."

Minho sat up straighter on the bed. "What do you mean she said something?"

"She told me not to trust them—to only trust her and someone named Chancellor Paige."

"Well, what's her buggin' deal anyway?" Newt asked. "She works for WICKED? What, was she just a bloody actress down in the Scorch?"

"Yeah, sounds like she's no better than the rest of them," Minho added.

Thomas just didn't agree. He couldn't even explain it to himself, much less to his friends. "Look, I used to work for them, too, but you trust me, right? It doesn't mean anything. Maybe she had no choice, maybe she's changed. I don't know."

Minho squinted as if he was thinking but didn't respond. Newt just sat down on the floor and folded his arms, pouting like a little kid.

Thomas shook his head. He was sick of puzzling everything out. He walked over and opened the small fridge—his stomach was rumbling with hunger. He found some cheese sticks and grapes and divvied them up, then practically shoved his portion down his throat before drinking a full bottle of juice. The other two gobbled theirs as well, no one saying a word.

A woman showed up soon after with plates of pork chops and potatoes, and they ate that, too. It was early evening, according to Thomas's watch, but he couldn't imagine being able to fall asleep. He sat down in a chair, facing his friends, wondering what they should do. He was still feeling a little chagrined, like it was his fault that they'd yet to try anything, but he didn't offer any ideas.

Minho was the first one to speak since the food had come. "Maybe we should just give in to those shuck-faces. Do what they want. One day we'll all sit around, fat and happy."

Thomas knew he didn't mean a word of it. "Yeah, maybe you can find a nice pretty girl who works here, settle down, get married and have kids. Just in time for the world to end in a sea of lunatics."

Minho kept at it. "WICKED's going to figure out this blueprint business and we'll all live happily ever after."

"That's not even funny," Newt said grumpily. "Even if they did find a cure, you saw it out there in the Scorch. It's gonna be a buggin' long time before the world can ever get back to normal. Even if it can—we'll never see it."

Thomas realized he was just sitting there, staring at a spot on the floor. "After everything they've done to us, I just don't believe any of it." He couldn't get past the news about Newt—his friend, who'd do anything for someone else. They'd given him a death sentence—an incurable disease—just to watch what would happen.

"That Janson guy thinks he has it all figured out," Thomas continued. "He thinks it all comes down to some sort of greater good. Let the human race kick the bucket, or do awful things and save it. Even the few who are immune probably wouldn't last long in a world where ninety-nine-point-nine percent of people turn into psycho monsters."

"What's your point?" Minho muttered.

"My point is that before they swiped my memory, I think I used to buy all that junk. But not anymore." And the one thing that terrified him now was that any returning memories might make him change his mind about that.

"Then let's not waste our next chance, Tommy," Newt said.

"Tomorrow," Minho added. "Somehow, some way."

Thomas gave each of them a long look. "Okay. Somehow, some way."

Newt yawned, making the other two do the same. "Then we better quit yapping and get some buggin' sleep."

CHAPTER 9

It took over an hour of staring into the dark, but Thomas eventually fell asleep. And when he did, his dreams were a slew of scattered images and memories.

A woman, sitting at a table, smiling as she stares across the wood surface, directly into his eyes. As he watches her she picks up a cup of steaming liquid and takes a tentative sip. Another smile. Then she says, "Eat your cereal, now. That's a good boy." It's his mom, with her kind face, her love for him evident in every crease of her skin as she grins. She doesn't stop watching over him until he eats the last bite, and she takes his bowl over to the sink after tousling his hair.

Then he's on the carpeted floor of a small room, playing with silvery blocks that seem to fuse together as he builds a huge castle. His mom is sitting on a chair in the corner, crying. Thomas knows instantly why. His dad has been diagnosed with the Flare, is already showing signs of it. This leaves no doubt that his mom also has the disease, or will soon. The dreaming Thomas knows that it won't be long before doctors realize his younger self has the virus but is immune to its effects. By then they'd developed the test that recognizes it.

Next he's riding his bike on a hot day. Heat's rising from the pavement, just weeds on both sides of the street, where there used to be grass. He has a smile on his sweaty face. His mom watches nearby, and he can see that she's savoring every moment. They head to a nearby pond. The water is stagnant and foul-smelling. She gathers rocks for him to toss into the murky depths. At first he throws them as far as possible; then he tries to skip them the way his dad showed him last summer. He still can't do it. Tired, their strength sapped from the stifling weather, he and his mother finally head home.

Then things in the dream—the memories—turn darker.

He's back inside and a man in a dark suit is sitting on a couch. Papers in his hand, a grave look on his face. Thomas standing next to his mom, holding her hand. WICKED has been formed, a joint venture of the world's governments—those that survived the sun flares, an event that took place long before Thomas was born. WICKED's purpose is to study what is now known as the killzone, where the Flare does its damage. The brain.

The man is saying that Thomas is immune. Others are immune. Less than one percent of the population, most of them under the age of twenty. And the world is dangerous for them. They're hated for their immunity to the terrible virus, are mockingly called Munies. People do terrible things to them. WICKED says they can protect Thomas, and Thomas can help them work to find a cure. They say he's smart—one of the smartest who have been tested. His mom has no choice but to let him go. She certainly doesn't want her boy to watch as she slowly goes insane.

Later she tells Thomas that she loves him and is so glad that he'll never go through what they witnessed happen to his dad. The madness took away every ounce of what made him who he was—what made him human.

And after that the dream faded, and Thomas fell into a deep void of sleep.

* * *

A loud knocking woke him early the next morning. He'd barely gotten up on his elbows when the door opened and the same five guards from the day before came in with Launchers raised. Janson stepped into the room right after them.

"Rise and shine, boys," the Rat Man said. "We've decided to give you your memories back after all. Like it or not."

CHAPTER 10

Thomas was still groggy from sleep. The dreams he'd had—the memories of his childhood—clouded his mind. He almost didn't catch what the man had said.

"Like hell you are," Newt responded. He was out of his bed, fists clenched at his sides, glaring at Janson.

Thomas couldn't remember ever seeing such fire in his friend's eyes. And then the full force of the Rat Man's words snapped Thomas out of his fog.

He swung his legs around to the floor. "You told us we didn't have to."

"I'm afraid we don't have much of a choice," Janson replied. "The time for lies is over. Nothing's going to work with you three still in the dark. I'm sorry. We need to do this. Newt, of everyone, you will benefit the most from a cure, after all."

"I don't care about myself anymore," Newt responded in a low growl.

Thomas's instincts took over then. He knew that this was the moment he'd been waiting for. It was the final straw.

Thomas watched Janson carefully. The man's face softened and he took a deep breath, as if he sensed the growing danger in the room and wanted to neutralize it. "Look, Newt, Minho, Thomas. I understand how you must feel. You've seen some awful things. But the worst part is over. We can't change the past, can't take back what has happened to you and your friends. But wouldn't it be a waste to not complete the blueprint at this point?"

"Can't take it back?" Newt shouted. "That's all you have to say?"

"Watch yourself," one of the guards warned, pointing a Launcher at Newt's chest.

The room fell silent. Thomas had never seen Newt like this. So angry—so unwilling to put on a calm front, even.

Janson continued. "We're running out of time. Now let's go or we'll have a repeat of yesterday. My guards are willing, I assure you."

Minho jumped down from the bunk above Newt's. "He's right," he said matter-of-factly. "If we can save you, Newt—and who knows how many others—we'd be shuck idiots to stay in this room a second longer." Minho shot Thomas a glance and nodded toward the door. "Come on, let's go." He walked past Rat Man and the guards into the hallway without looking back.

Janson raised his eyebrows at Thomas, who was struggling to hide his surprise. Minho's announcement was so strange—he had to have some sort of plan. Pretending to go along with things would buy them time.

Thomas turned away from the guards and Rat Man and gave Newt a quick wink that only he could see. "Let's just listen to what they want us to do." He tried to sound casual, sincere, but it was one of the hardest things he'd done yet. "I worked for these people before the Maze. I couldn't have been totally wrong, right?"

"Oh, please." Newt rolled his eyes, but he moved toward the door, and Thomas smiled inwardly at his small victory.

"You'll all be heroes when this is over," Janson said as Thomas followed Newt out of the room.

"Oh, shut up," Thomas replied.

Thomas and his friends followed the Rat Man down the mazelike corridors once again. As they walked, Janson narrated the journey as if he were a tour guide. He explained that the facility didn't have many windows because of the often fierce weather outside, and the attacks from roaming gangs of infected people. He mentioned the severe rainstorm the night the Gladers been taken from the Maze, and how the group of Cranks had broken through the outer perimeter to watch them board the bus.

Thomas remembered that night all too well. He could still feel the bump of the tires running over the woman who'd accosted him before he boarded the bus, how the driver didn't even slow down. He could hardly believe that had happened only weeks ago—it felt like it'd been years.

"I really wish you'd just shut your mouth," Newt finally spat. And the Rat Man *did,* but he never wiped the slight grin off his face.

When they reached the area they'd been in the day before, the Rat Man stopped and turned to address them. "I hope you will all cooperate today. I'm expecting nothing less."

"Where is everybody else?" Thomas asked.

"The other subjects have been recovering—"

Before he could finish Newt had pounced, grabbing the Rat Man by the lapels of his white suit coat and slamming him against the nearest door. "Call them subjects again and I'll break your bloody neck!"

Two guards were on Newt in an instant; they pulled him away from Janson and threw him to the floor, aiming their Launchers at his face.

"Wait!" Janson yelled. "Wait." He composed himself and straightened his wrinkled shirt and jacket. "Don't disable him. Let's just get this over with."

Newt slowly got to his feet, arms raised. "Don't call us subjects. We're not mice trying to find the cheese. And tell your shuck friends to calm down—I wasn't gonna hurt you. Much." His eyes fell on Thomas, questioning.

WICKED is good.

For some inexplicable reason, those words popped into Thomas's mind. It was almost as if his former self—the one who'd believed that WICKED's objective was worth any depraved action—was trying to convince him that it was true. That no matter how horrible it seemed, they must do whatever it took to find a cure for the Flare.

But something was different now. He couldn't understand who he'd been before. How he could have thought any of this was okay. He'd changed forever ... but he had to give them the old Thomas one last time.

"Newt, Minho," he said quietly, before the Rat Man could speak again. "I think he's right. I think it's time we did what we're *supposed* to do. We all agreed to it just last night."

Minho broke into a nervous smile. Newt's hands balled into fists.

It was now or never.

CHAPTER 11

Thomas didn't hesitate. He swung his elbow backward into the face of the guard behind him just as he kicked the knee of the one in front. Both fell to the floor, stunned, but recovered quickly. Out of the corner of his eye Thomas saw Newt tackle a guard to the ground; Minho was punching another. But the fifth—a woman—hadn't been touched, and she was raising her Launcher.

Thomas dove for her, knocked the end of the weapon toward the ceiling before she could press the trigger, but she brought it around and smashed it into the side of his head. Pain exploded in his cheeks and jaw. He was already off balance, and crumpled to his knees, then flat onto his stomach. He put his hands under him to get up, but a crushing weight fell on his back, slamming him to the hard tile and knocking the breath from his lungs. A knee dug into his spine and he felt hard metal press against his skull.

"Give me the word!" the woman yelled. "A.D. Janson, give me the word! I'll fry his brain."

Thomas couldn't see the others, but the sounds of scuffling had already stopped. He knew that meant their mutiny had been short-lived, all three of them subdued in less than a minute. His heart ached with despair.

"What are you people thinking!" Janson roared from behind Thomas. He could only imagine how enraged the man's weasy face must look. "You really think three . . . *children* can overpower five armed

50

guards? You kids are supposed to be geniuses, not idiotic . . . delusional *rebels*. Maybe the Flare has taken your minds after all!"

"Shut up!" Thomas heard Newt scream. "Just shut your—"

Something muffled the rest of his words. Imagining one of the guards hurting Newt made Thomas tremble with rage. The woman pressed her weapon even harder against his head.

"Don't . . . even . . . think about it," she whispered in his ear.

"Get them up!" Janson barked. "Get them up!"

The guard pulled Thomas to his feet by the back of his shirt, keeping the business end of the Launcher pressed against his head. Newt and Minho were being held at Launcher-point as well, and the two free guards were training their weapons on the three Gladers.

Janson's face burned red. "Completely ridiculous! We absolutely *will not* allow this to happen again." He spun on Thomas.

"I was just a kid," Thomas said, surprising himself.

"Excuse me?" Janson asked.

Thomas glared at the Rat Man. "I was a *kid*. They brainwashed me into doing those things—into helping." That was what had been eating away at him since the memories had started coming back. Since he'd been able to start connecting the dots.

"I wasn't there in the beginning," Janson said in a level voice. "But you yourself approved me for this job after the original founders were purged. And you should know, I've never seen someone, child or adult, as driven as you were." He smiled and Thomas wanted to rip his face off.

"I don't care what you—"

"Enough!" Janson yelled. "We'll do him first." He gestured at one of the guards. "Get a nurse down here. Brenda's inside—she's been insisting that she wants to help. Maybe he'll be easier to deal with if she's the technician working with him. Take the others to the waiting room—I'd

51

like to do them one at a time. I need to go check on another matter, so I'll meet you there."

Thomas was so upset that he didn't even register Brenda's name. Another guard joined the one behind him and they each took hold of an arm.

"I won't let you do it!" Thomas screamed, a hysteria rising up in him. The thought of learning who he'd been terrified him. "There's no way you're putting that thing on my face!"

Janson ignored him and spoke directly to the guards. "Make sure she sedates him." Then he started walking away.

The two guards pulled Thomas toward the door, his feet dragging behind him. He struggled, tried to free his arms, but their hands were like iron manacles, and he finally gave up to conserve his strength. The realization hit him that he might have lost the fight. His only hope was Brenda.

Brenda stood next to a bed inside the room. Her face was stony. Thomas searched her eyes, but she was impossible to read.

His captives yanked him farther into the room. He couldn't understand why Brenda was there, helping WICKED do this. "Why are you working for them?" His voice sounded weak to his ears.

The guards spun him around.

"Better to just keep your mouth shut," Brenda answered. "I need you to trust me like you did back in the Scorch. This is for the best."

He couldn't see her, but there was something in her voice. Despite what she'd said, she sounded warm. Could she be on his side?

The guards pulled Thomas to the last bed in the row. Then the female guard released him and aimed her Launcher at him while the man held Thomas against the edge of the mattress.

"Lie down," the guard said.

"No," Thomas growled.

The guard swung back and slapped Thomas across the cheek. "Lie down! Now!"

"No."

The man lifted Thomas by the shoulders and slammed him onto the mattress. "This is going to happen, so you might as well not fight it." The metallic mask with its wires and tubes hung above him like a giant spider waiting to smother him.

"You're not putting that thing on my face." Thomas's heart raced dangerously now, the fear he'd been holding at bay rushing in, beginning to take away any calm that could help him figure a way out of this.

The male guard took both of Thomas's wrists and pressed them to the mattress as he leaned forward with all his weight to make sure Thomas didn't go anywhere. "Sedate him."

Thomas forced himself to calm down, save his energy for one last effort to escape. He almost hurt at seeing Brenda; he'd grown closer to her than he'd realized. If she helped force him to do this, it would mean she was the enemy as well. It was too heartbreaking to even consider.

"Please, Brenda," he said. "Don't do it. Don't let them do this."

She stepped close to him and gently touched his shoulder. "Everything's going to be okay. Not everyone is out to make your life miserable—you'll thank me later for what I'm about to do. Now quit your whining and relax."

He still couldn't read her for the life of him. "That's it? After everything back in the Scorch? How many times did we almost die in that city? All we went through, and you're just gonna abandon me?"

"Thomas . . ." She trailed off, not bothering to hide her frustration. "It was my job."

"I heard your voice in my head. You warned me that things were about to get bad. Please tell me you're not really *with* them."

"When we made it back to HQ after the Scorch, I got into the telepathy system because I wanted to warn you. Prepare you. I never expected us to become friends in that hell."

On some level, just hearing that she'd felt that way, too, made things more manageable, and now he really couldn't stop himself. "Do *you* have the Flare?" he asked.

She answered in quick, short bursts. "I was acting. Jorge and I are immune—we've known it for a long time. It's why they used us. Now be quiet." Her eyes flickered over to the guard.

"Get on with it!" the male guard suddenly shouted.

Brenda gave the man a stern look but didn't say anything. Then she gazed at Thomas and surprised him with a slight wink. "Once I inject the sedative, you'll be asleep in seconds. Do you *understand*?" She stressed that last word, then subtly winked again. Luckily the two guards were focused on their prisoner and not her.

Thomas was confused, but hope ran through his body. She was up to something.

Brenda moved to the counter behind her and started preparing what she needed, and the guard continued to lean all of his weight on Thomas's wrists, cutting off the circulation. Sweat beaded on the man's forehead, but it was clear he wasn't letting go until Thomas was unconscious. The female guard stood just beside him, her Launcher aimed at Thomas's face.

Brenda turned back around, a syringe in her left hand, its nozzle pointing up, her thumb on the trigger. A yellowish liquid showed in the small window on the side. "Okay, Thomas. We're going to do this really fast. Are you ready?"

He nodded at her, not sure what she meant but determined to be prepared.

"Good," she replied. "You better be."

CHAPTER 12

Brenda smiled and moved toward Thomas, then tripped on something and stumbled forward. She caught the bed with her right hand, but she fell in such a way that the syringe's nozzle landed on the forearm of the guard gripping Thomas's wrist. She instantly pushed the trigger with her thumb, releasing a quick, sharp hiss, before he jerked himself away.

"What the hell!" the man shouted, but his eyes were already glazed.

Thomas acted instantly. Now free from those iron fists, he pushed down on the bed and swung his legs in an arc toward the female guard, who was just coming to her senses after a brief moment of frozen shock. One foot connected with her Launcher and the other with her shoulder. She let out a yell, which was closely followed by the smack of her head hitting the floor.

Thomas scrambled after the Launcher, grabbed it before it slid out of reach and aimed it at the woman, who was holding her head in her hands. Brenda had run around the bed and grabbed the man's weapon, and she pointed it at his limp body.

Thomas gasped for air, his chest heaving as adrenaline throbbed through his body. He hadn't felt so good in weeks. "I knew you—"

Before he could finish, Brenda fired her Launcher.

A high-pitched sound pierced the air, increasing in volume for a split second before the gun discharged and kicked, making Brenda jerk backward. One of the shiny grenades shot out, slammed into the woman's chest and exploded, sending tendrils of lightning arcing across her body. She began to twitch uncontrollably.

Thomas stared, stunned at what the Launcher did to a person and amazed that Brenda had shot it without hesitation. If he had needed further proof that Brenda wasn't totally committed to WICKED, he'd just seen it. He looked at her.

She returned his gaze, the slightest of smiles on her face. "I've been wanting to do something like that for a long time. Good thing I convinced Janson to assign me to you for this procedure." She bent over and took the unconscious man's key card, slipped it into her pocket. "This'll get us in anywhere."

Thomas had to resist the urge to pull her into a hug.

"Come on," he said. "We have to get Newt and Minho. Then everybody else."

They sprinted through a couple of twists and turns in the hallways, Brenda leading. It reminded Thomas of the time she'd led him through the underground tunnels in the Scorch. He urged her to hurry—he knew that more guards could show up at any second.

They reached a door, and Brenda swiped the key card to open it; a brief hiss sounded, and then the slab of metal swung open. Thomas burst through with Brenda close on his heels.

The Rat Man was sitting in a chair but sprang to his feet, his expression quickly twisting to a look of horror. "What in God's name are you doing?"

Brenda had already fired two grenades at the guards. A man and a woman dropped to the ground, convulsing in a cloud of smoke and tiny lightning bolts. Newt and Minho tackled the third guard; Minho grabbed his weapon.

Thomas trained his Launcher on Janson and put his finger on the trigger. "Give me your key card, then get on the ground, hands on your head." His voice was steady but his heart was racing.

"This is complete lunacy," Janson said. He handed his card to Thomas. He spoke quietly, seeming amazingly calm under the circumstances. "You have zero chance of getting out of this complex. More guards are already on their way."

Thomas knew their odds were bad, but it was all they had. "After what we've been through, this is nothing." He smiled as he realized it was true. "Thanks for the training. Now, another word and you'll get to experience—how did you put it? 'The worst five minutes of your life'?"

"How can—"

Thomas pulled the trigger. The high-pitched sound filled the room, followed by the launch of a grenade. It hit the man's chest and exploded in a brilliant display of electricity. He screamed as he fell to the ground, convulsing, smoke streaming off his hair and clothing. The room filled with an awful smell—a stench that reminded Thomas of the Scorch, when Minho was struck by lightning.

"That can't feel good," Thomas said to his friends. He sounded so calm to his own ears that it disturbed him. As he watched their nemesis twitch, he was almost ashamed for feeling no guilt. Almost.

"It supposedly won't kill him," Brenda said.

"That's a shame," Minho replied. He stood after tying up the uninjured guard with his belt. "The world would've been better off."

Thomas turned his attention from the twitching man at his feet. "We're leaving. Now."

"I'll bloody drink to that," Newt said.

"That's exactly what I was thinking," Minho added.

They all turned to look at Brenda. She lifted her Launcher in her arms and nodded. She looked ready for a fight.

"I hate these people just as much as you," she said. "I'm in."

For the second time in the last few days, Thomas was filled with that foreign feeling of happiness. Brenda was back. He glanced at Janson. The crackling static was beginning to die. The man's eyes were closed and he'd finally stopped moving, but he was still breathing.

"I don't know how long a blast from one of these lasts," Brenda said, "and he's definitely going to wake up angry. We better get out of here."

"What's the plan?" Newt asked.

Thomas didn't have a clue. "We'll make it up as we go."

"Jorge's a pilot," Brenda offered. "If we can somehow make it to the hangar, to his Berg . . ."

Before anyone could respond, shouts and footsteps sounded in the hall.

"They're coming," Thomas said. The reality of their situation hit him again—no one was going to let them just waltz out of the building. Who knew how many guards they'd have to get past.

Minho ran to the door and took a stance right next to it. "They'll all have to come through right here."

The sounds from the hallway were getting louder—the guards were close.

"Newt," Thomas said. "You get on the other side of the doorway. Brenda and I'll shoot the first couple who come through. You guys catch the rest from the sides, then get out into the hallway. We'll be right behind you."

They took their positions.

CHAPTER 13

Brenda's expression was a strange mixture of anger and excitement. Thomas readied himself next to her, gripping the Launcher tightly in his hands. He knew it was a gamble to trust Brenda. He'd been tricked by nearly everyone in this organization; he couldn't underestimate WICKED. But she was the only reason they'd gotten this far. And if he was going to bring her along, he couldn't doubt her anymore.

The first guard arrived, a man dressed in the same black gear as all the others, but with a different type of weapon—smaller and sleeker—held tightly in front of him. Thomas fired, watched the grenade connect with the man's chest; it sent him reeling backward, twitching and convulsing in a web of lightning.

Two more people—a man and a woman—were right behind him with Launchers raised.

Minho acted before Thomas could. He grabbed the woman by the shirt and yanked her toward him, then swung her across his body and slammed her into the wall. She got off a shot, but the silvery grenade shattered harmlessly on the ground and sent a short burst of crackling energy along the tiled floor.

Brenda fired at the man, hitting him in the legs; tiny jagged bolts of electricity shot up his body and he screamed, falling back into the hallway. His weapon fell to the floor.

Minho had disarmed the woman and forced her to kneel. He now held a Launcher aimed at her head.

A fourth man came through the door, but Newt knocked his weapon away and punched him in the face. He collapsed to his knees, holding a hand up to his bloodied mouth. The guard looked up as if to say something, but Newt stepped back and shot him in the chest. At such close range the ball made a terrible popping sound as it exploded against the man. A wretched squeal escaped his throat as he fell to the floor, writhing in a web of pure electricity.

"That beetle blade's watchin' every bloody thing we do," Newt said. He nodded toward something at the back of the room. "We've got to get out of here—they're just going to keep coming."

Thomas turned to see the little robotic lizard crouched in place, red light beaming. Then he looked back at the doorway, which was empty. He faced the woman. The muzzle end of Minho's weapon hovered just inches from her head.

"How many of you are there?" Thomas asked her. "Are there more coming?"

She didn't respond at first, but Minho leaned forward until his gun was actually touching her cheek.

"There're at least fifty on duty," she said quickly.

"Then where are they?" Minho asked.

"I don't know."

"Don't lie to me!" Minho shouted.

"We . . . Something else is going on. I don't know what. I swear."

Thomas looked at her closely and saw more than just fear in her expression. Was it frustration? She seemed to be telling the truth. "Something else? Like what?"

She shook her head. "I just know that a group of us were called to a different section, that's all."

"And you have no idea why?" Thomas threw as much doubt into his voice as possible. "I have a hard time believing that."

"I swear it."

Minho grabbed her by the back of the shirt and pulled her to her feet. "We'll just take the nice lady here as a hostage, then. Let's go."

Thomas stepped in front of him. "Brenda needs to lead—she knows the way around this place. Then me, then you and your new friend, then Newt in the rear."

Brenda hurried to stand beside Thomas. "I still don't hear anybody, but we can't have long. Come on." She peeked into the hallway, then slipped out of the room.

Thomas took a second to wipe his sweaty hands on his pants, then gripped the Launcher and followed her. She turned right. He heard the others fall in behind him; a quick glance showed that Minho's captor was running along, too, looking none too happy with the threat of an electric bath just inches away.

They reached the end of the initial hallway and made a right without stopping. Their new path looked exactly the same as the last, a beige alley stretching before them for at least fifty feet before it ended in a set of double doors. Somehow the scene made him think of that last stretch of the Maze right before the Cliff, when he, Teresa, and Chuck had run for the exit while everyone else battled the Grievers to keep them safe.

As they neared the doors, Thomas pulled the Rat Man's key card out of his pocket.

Their hostage yelled to him. "I wouldn't do that! I bet there're twenty guns waiting to burn you alive on the other side." But something about her tone sounded desperate. Could it be that WICKED had become overconfident and lax in their security? With only twenty or thirty teenagers left, surely they didn't have more than one security person for each of their subjects—if even that many.

Thomas and his friends had to find Jorge and the Berg, but they also had to find everyone else. He thought of Frypan and Teresa. He wasn't going to leave them behind just because they'd chosen to get their memories back.

He skidded to a stop in front of the doors and turned to face Minho and Newt. "We've only got four Launchers, and we better believe that there are more guards on the other side of those doors waiting for us. Are we up for this?"

Minho stepped up to the key card panel, dragging the guard with him by the shirt. "You're going to open this for us so we can focus on your buddies. Stand right there and don't do anything until we say. Don't mess with me." He swiveled toward Thomas. "Start shooting as soon as the doors crack."

Thomas nodded. "I'll crouch. Minho, you lean over my shoulder. Brenda to the left and Newt to the right."

Thomas got down and stuck the point of his weapon right where the doors met in the center. Minho hovered above him, doing the same. Newt and Brenda got in position.

"Open on three," Minho said. "And guard lady, you try anything or run away, I guarantee one of us will get you. Thomas, you count off."

The woman pulled out her key card but said nothing.

"One," Thomas began. "Two."

He paused, allowed himself a moment to suck in a breath, but before he could yell the last number an alarm started blaring and the lights went out.

CHAPTER 14

Thomas blinked rapidly, trying to adjust to the darkness. The alarm rang in shrill, deafening bursts.

He sensed Minho stand up, then heard him shuffling about. "The guard's gone!" his friend shouted. "I can't find her!"

As soon as he said the last word, that sound of power charging filled the gaps between the whines of the alarm, followed by the pop of a grenade exploding against the ground. The bolts of electricity lit up the room; Thomas saw a shadowy figure running away from them back down the hall, gradually disappearing in the gloom.

"My fault," Minho muttered, barely audible.

"Get back in position," Thomas said, fearing what the alarm might mean. "Feel for the crack where the doors open. I'll use the Rat Man's key card. Be ready!"

He felt around on the wall until he found the right place, then swiped the card; there was an audible click, and one of the doors began to swing inward.

"Start shooting!" Minho shouted.

Newt, Brenda and Minho began to launch grenades through the doorway into the darkness. Thomas carefully got into position and followed suit, shooting into the fray of dancing electricity that now crackled on the far side of the doors. It took a few seconds between rounds, but soon they had created a blinding display of light and explosions. There was no sign of people anywhere, no answering fire.

Thomas let his gun drop to his side. "Stop!" he yelled. "Don't waste any more ammunition!"

Minho let one last grenade fly, but then they all stood and waited for some of the energy to die down so they could safely enter the room.

Thomas turned to Brenda, speaking loudly to be heard over the noise. "We're a little short on memories. Do you know anything that'll help us? Where is everyone? Why the alarm?"

She shook her head. "I have to be honest—something definitely feels off."

"I bet this is another one of their bloody tests!" Newt yelled. "All of this is meant to happen and we're being analyzed all over again."

Thomas could barely hear himself think, and Newt wasn't helping.

He held his Launcher up and walked through the doorway. He wanted to get somewhere safer before the light from the grenade blasts disappeared entirely. From the shallow pool of his few returned memories, he knew he'd grown up in this place—he just wished he could remember the layout. He realized again how important Brenda was to their freedom. Jorge, too—if he was willing to fly them out of there.

The alarm stopped.

"What—" Thomas had started too loud, and quieted himself. "What now?"

"They probably got sick of their ears bleeding from the noise," Minho answered. "Just because they turned it off doesn't mean anything."

The glow from the electric bolts had disappeared, but the room on this side of the doorway had emergency lights that cast everything in a red haze. They stood in a large reception area with couches and chairs and a couple of desks. Nobody was in sight.

"I've never seen one person in these waiting rooms," Thomas said, the space suddenly familiar. "The whole place is empty and creepy."

"It's been a long time since they allowed visitors here, I'm sure," Brenda responded.

"What's next, Tommy?" Newt asked. "We can't just stand here all day."

Thomas thought for a second. They had to find their friends, but ensuring that they had a way out seemed the first priority.

"Okay," he said. "Brenda, we really need your help. We need to get to the hangar and find Jorge, get him prepping a Berg. Newt and Minho—you guys can stay with him for backup and Brenda and I will search the place for our friends. Brenda—do you know where we can stock up on weapons?"

"Weapons depot's on the way to the hangar," Brenda said. "But it's probably guarded."

"We've seen worse," Minho offered. "We'll start firing till they drop or we drop."

"We'll cut through 'em all," Newt added, almost with a growl. "Every last one of those buggers."

Brenda pointed down one of two hallways that branched off the reception room. "It's that way."

Brenda led Thomas and his friends through turn after turn, the dull red emergency beacons lighting the way. They met no resistance, though every so often a beetle blade skittered by, click-clacking across the floor as it scurried along. Minho tried firing a shot at one of them, missing badly and almost scorching Newt, who yelped and wanted to fire back, judging by the look on his face.

After a good fifteen minutes of jogging, they reached the weapons depot. Thomas stopped in the hallway, surprised to find the door swung wide open. From what he could see, the shelves inside seemed fully stocked.

"That does it," Minho said. "No more doubt."

Thomas knew exactly what he meant. He'd been through too much not to. "Someone's setting us up," he muttered.

"Has to be," Minho added. "Everyone suddenly disappears, doors are unlocked, weapons sitting here for us. And they're obviously observing us through those shuck beetle blades."

"Definitely fishy," Brenda added.

At her voice, Minho turned on her. "How do we know *you're* not in on it?" he demanded.

She answered in a weary voice. "All I can say is that I swear I'm not. I have no idea what's happening."

Thomas hated to admit it, but what Newt had hinted at earlier—that this whole escape so far might be nothing but an orchestrated exercise—was looking more and more likely. They'd been reduced once again to mice, scuttling about in a different kind of maze. Thomas hoped so badly that it wasn't true.

Newt had already wandered into the weapons room. "Look at this," he called.

When Thomas entered the room Newt was pointing to a section of empty wall space and shelves. "Look at the dust patterns. It's pretty obvious that a bunch of stuff was taken recently. Maybe even within the last hour or so."

Thomas inspected the area. The room was pretty dusty—enough to make you sneeze if you moved around too much—but the spots Newt pointed out were completely clean. He was dead on.

"Why is that so important?" Minho asked from behind them.

Newt turned on him. "Can't you figure something out yourself for once, you bloody shank!"

Minho winced. He looked more shocked than angry.

"Whoa, Newt," Thomas said. "Things suck, yeah, but slim it. What's wrong?"

"I'll tell ya what's bloody wrong. You go all tough-guy without a plan, leading us around like a bunch of chickens lookin' for feed. And Minho can't take a bloody step without askin' which foot he should use."

Minho had finally recovered enough to get ticked. "Look, shuck-face. You're the one acting like a genius because you figured out some guards took weapons from the *weapons* room. I thought I'd give you the benefit of the doubt, act like maybe you'd discovered something deeper than that. Next time I'll pat you on the freaking back for stating the obvious."

Thomas looked back at Newt in time to see his friend's expression change. He seemed stricken, almost teary.

"I'm sorry," Newt murmured, then turned and walked out of the room.

"What was *that*?" Minho whispered.

Thomas didn't want to say what he was thinking: that Newt's sanity was slowly being eaten away. And luckily he didn't have to—Brenda spoke up. "You guys *were* missing his point."

"Which was?" Minho asked.

"There had to have been two or three dozen guns and Launchers in this section, and now they're all gone. Very recently. In the last hour or so, like Newt said."

"Yeah?" Minho prodded, just as it clicked for Thomas.

Brenda held her hands out as though the answer should be obvious. "Guards only come here when they need a replacement or want to use something besides a Launcher. Why would they *all* need to do that at the same time? *Today?* And Launchers are so heavy, you can't fire them if you're carrying another weapon, too. Where are the weapons they would have left behind?"

CHAPTER 15

Minho was the first to offer an explanation. "Maybe they knew something like this might happen, and they didn't want to kill us. From the looks of it, unless you get it right in the head, those Launcher things just stun you for a while. So they all came and got those to use with their regular guns."

Brenda was shaking her head before he even finished. "No. It's standard for them to carry Launchers at all times—so it doesn't make sense that they'd all come at once to get a new one. Whatever you think about WICKED, it's not their goal to kill as many people as possible. Even when Cranks break in."

"Cranks have *broken in* here before?" Thomas asked.

Brenda nodded. "The more infected there are, the more past the Gone, the more desperate they get. I really doubt the guards—"

Minho interrupted her. "Maybe *that's* what happened. With all those alarms going off, maybe some Cranks broke in and took whatever weapons were here, stunned people, then started eatin' their shuck bodies. Maybe we've only seen a few guards because the rest of 'em are dead!"

Thomas had seen Cranks past the Gone, and the memories haunted him. Cranks who had lived with the Flare infection so long that it had eaten away at their brains until they were completely insane. Almost like animals in human form.

Brenda sighed. "I hate to say it, but you might be right." She thought

68

a moment. "Seriously. That would explain it. *Someone* came in here and took a bunch of weapons."

An icy chill filled Thomas. "If that's it, our problems are a whole lot worse than we thought."

"Glad to see the guy not immune to the Flare isn't the only one with a brain that still works."

Thomas turned to see Newt at the door.

"Next time just explain yourself instead of getting all snippy," Minho said, his voice empty of compassion. "I didn't think you'd lose it so fast, but glad you're back. We might need a Crank to sniff out these other Cranks if they really broke in."

Thomas winced at the cutting remark, looked at Newt for his reaction.

The older boy wasn't happy—that was clear by his expression. "You never have known when to shut your hole, have ya, Minho? Always gotta have the bloody last word."

"Shut your shuck face," Minho replied. His voice was so calm for a second that Thomas could have sworn Minho was losing it himself. The tension in the room was almost palpable.

Newt slowly walked over to Minho and stopped in front of him. Then, quick as a striking snake, he punched him in the face. Minho staggered back and slammed into the empty weapons rack. Then he rushed forward and tackled Newt to the ground.

It all happened so fast, Thomas couldn't believe it. He ran over and started pulling at Minho's shirt. "Stop!" he screamed, but the two Gladers continued flailing at each other, arms and legs everywhere.

Brenda stepped up to help and she and Thomas eventually got solid-enough grips to yank Minho to his feet, his fists still swinging wildly. A stray elbow smacked Thomas in the chin, sending a burst of rage through him.

"How stupid can you get?" Thomas yelled, pinning Minho's arms behind his back. "We're running from at least one enemy, maybe two, and you guys are gonna brawl?"

"He started it!" Minho snapped, spit spraying on Brenda.

She wiped her face. "What are you, eight years old?" she asked.

Minho didn't answer. He struggled to free himself for a few more seconds before giving up. Thomas was sickened by the whole thing. He didn't know which was worse: that Newt seemed to be slipping already or that Minho—the one who should have been able to control himself—was acting like such a slinthead.

Newt got to his feet, gingerly touching a red spot on his cheek where Minho must've connected. "It's my fault. Everything's just tickin' me off. You guys figure out what we should do—I need a buggin' break." And at that he turned and walked out of the room again.

Thomas blew out a breath of frustration; he let go of Minho and adjusted his own shirt. They didn't have time to dwell on petty arguments. If they were going to get out of there, they had to pull together and work as a team. "Minho—find a few more Launchers for us to bring, and then get a couple of the pistols on that shelf over there. Brenda, can you fill up a box with as much ammo as possible? I'll go get Newt."

"Sounds good," she replied, already looking around. Minho didn't say a word, just started searching the racks.

Thomas went out into the hall; Newt had taken a seat on the ground about twenty feet away and was leaning back against the wall.

"Don't say a bloody word," he grumbled when Thomas joined him.

Great start, Thomas thought. "Listen, something weird's going on—either WICKED is testing us or we've got Cranks running around this place killing people left and right. Whatever it is, we need to find our friends and get out of here."

"I know." That was it. Nothing else.

70

"Then get up and come back in there to help us. You were the one all frustrated, acting like we didn't have time to mess around. And now you want to sit out here in the hall and pout?"

"I know." The same response.

Thomas had never seen Newt like this. The guy looked utterly hopeless, and the sight of it hit Thomas with a wave of despair. "We're all going a little craz—" He stopped; he couldn't possibly say anything worse. "I mean . . ."

"Just shut it," Newt said. "I know something's started in my head. I don't feel right. But you don't need to worry your buggin' panties off. Give me a second and I'll be fine. We'll get you guys out of here and then I can deal."

"What do you mean, get *you guys* out?"

"Get *us* out, whatever. Just give me a bloody minute."

The world of the Glade seemed like eons ago. Back there, Newt had always been the calm, collected one—and now here he was pulling the group apart at the seams. He seemed to be saying that it didn't matter if he escaped himself as long as everyone else did.

"Fine," Thomas answered. He realized the only thing he could do was treat Newt the same as he always had. "But you know we can't waste any more time. Brenda's gathering ammo. You'll need to help her carry it to the Berg hangar."

"Will do." Newt quickly stood from his spot on the ground. "But first I have to go get something—it won't take me long." He started walking away, back toward the reception room.

"Newt!" Thomas shouted, wondering what on earth his friend was up to. "Don't be stupid—we have to move. And we need to stick together."

But Newt kept going. He didn't even turn to look at Thomas. "Just go get the stuff! This'll only take a couple of minutes."

Thomas shook his head. There was nothing he could do or say to bring back that reasonable guy he knew. He spun and headed for the weapons room.

Thomas, Minho and Brenda gathered everything they could possibly carry between the three of them. Thomas had one Launcher strapped to each shoulder in addition to the one in his hands. He'd stuck two loaded pistols in his front pockets and several ammo clips in each back pocket. Minho had done the same, and Brenda held a cardboard box full of the bluish grenades and more bullets, her Launcher resting on top.

"That looks heavy," Thomas said, gesturing to the box. "You wanna—"

Brenda cut him off. "I can manage until Newt gets back in here."

"Who knows what that guy is up to," Minho said. "He's never acted like this before. Flare's eatin' his brain already."

"He said he'd be back soon." Thomas was tired of Minho's attitude—he was only making it worse. "And watch what you say around him. The last thing we need is you setting him off again."

"Do you remember what I told you in the truck, back in the city?" Brenda asked Thomas.

The sudden change in conversation surprised him, and her bringing up the Scorch surprised him even more. It only called attention to the fact that she'd lied to him.

"What?" he asked. "You mean some of the things you said were true?" He'd felt so close to her that night. He realized he was hoping she'd say yes.

"I'm sorry I lied about why I was there, Thomas. And about how I told you I could feel the Flare working on my mind. But the rest was true. I swear it." She paused, looking at him, pleading in her eyes. "Anyway, we talked about how increased levels of brain activity actually quicken the pace of destruction—it's called cognitive destruction. That's why that drug—the Bliss—is so popular with the people who can afford it. The Bliss slows brain function. It lengthens the time before you go bat crazy. But it's really expensive."

The idea of people living in the world who were not part of an experiment or holing up in abandoned buildings like he'd seen in the Scorch seemed unreal to him. "Do people still function—live their lives, go to work, whatever—when they're drugged out?"

"They do what they need to do, but they're much more . . . relaxed about it. You could be a fireman rescuing thirty children from an inferno, but you won't stress if you happen to drop a few of them into the flames along the way."

The thought of such a world terrified Thomas. "That's just . . . sick."

"I gotta get me some of that stuff," Minho muttered.

"You're missing the point," Brenda said. "Think of the hell Newt has been through—all the decisions he's had to make. No wonder the Flare is moving so fast in him. He's been stimulated too much—way more than the average person living their life day to day."

Thomas sighed, that sadness he'd felt earlier gripping his heart again. "Well, there's nothing we can do about it until we get somewhere safer."

"Do about what?"

Thomas turned to see Newt in the doorway again, then closed his eyes for a moment, pulled himself together. "Nothing, never mind—where'd you go?"

"I need to talk to you, Tommy. Just you. It'll only take a second."

What now? Thomas wondered.

"What's this crap?" Minho asked.

"Just cut me some slack. I need to give something to Tommy here. Tommy and no one else."

"Whatever, go for it." Minho adjusted the straps of the Launchers on his shoulders. "But we need to hurry."

Thomas stepped into the hall with Newt, scared to death of what his friend might say and how crazy it might sound. The seconds were ticking away.

They walked a few feet from the door before Newt stopped and faced him, then held out a small sealed envelope. "Stuff this in your pocket."

"What is it?" Thomas took it and turned it over; it was blank on the outside.

"Just put the bloody thing in your pocket."

Thomas did as he was told, confused but curious.

"Now look me in the eyes." Newt snapped his fingers.

Thomas's stomach sank at the anguish he saw there. "What is it?"

"You don't need to know right now. You *can't* know. But you have to make me a promise—and I'm not messing around here."

"What?"

"You swear to me that you won't read what's inside that bloody envelope until the time is right."

Thomas couldn't imagine waiting to read it—he started to pull the envelope out of his pocket, but Newt grabbed his arm to stop him.

"When the time is right?" Thomas asked. "How will I—"

"You'll bloody know!" Newt answered before Thomas could ask. "Now swear to me. Swear it!" The boy's whole body seemed to tremble with every word.

"Fine!" Thomas was beyond worried about his friend now. "I swear I won't read it until the time is right. I swear. But why—"

"Okay, then," Newt interrupted. "Break your promise and I'll never forgive you."

Thomas wanted to reach out and shake his friend—to pound the wall in frustration. But he didn't. He stood unmoving as Newt turned away from him and walked back toward the weapons room.

CHAPTER 16

Thomas had to trust Newt. He had to do this for his friend, but curiosity burned inside him like a brushfire. He knew, though, that he had no time to waste. They had to get everyone out of the WICKED complex. He could talk to Newt more in the Berg—if they could get to the hangar and convince Jorge to help them.

Newt came back out of the weapons room hefting the box of ammo by himself, followed by Minho, then Brenda, carrying another couple of Launchers with pistols stuffed in her pockets.

"Let's go find our friends," Thomas said. Then he headed back the way they'd come, and the others fell in line behind him.

They searched for an hour, but their friends seemed to have disappeared. Rat Man and the guards they'd left behind were gone, and the cafeteria and all the dorms, bathrooms and meeting rooms were empty. Not a person or a Crank in sight. Thomas was terrified that something horrible had happened and they had yet to come across the aftermath.

Finally, after seemingly having searched every nook and cranny of the building, something occurred to him. "Were you guys allowed to move around while they had me locked in the white room?" he asked. "Are you sure we haven't missed anywhere?"

"Not that I know of," Minho responded. "But I'd be shocked if there weren't some hidden rooms."

Thomas agreed but didn't think they could afford to spend any more time searching. Their only choice was to move on.

Thomas nodded. "Okay. Let's zigzag our way to the hangar, keep looking for them as we go."

They'd been walking for quite some time when Minho abruptly froze. He pointed to his ear. It was hard to see because the hallway was only dimly lit by red emergency lights.

Thomas stopped along with the others, tried to slow his breathing and listen. He heard it immediately. A low moaning sound, something that made Thomas shiver. It was coming from a few yards ahead of them, through a rare window in the hallway that looked into a large room. From where Thomas stood, the room seemed completely dark. The glass from the window had been shattered from the inside—shards littered the tiled floor below it.

The moan sounded again.

Minho held a finger to his lips, then slowly and carefully set down his two extra Launchers. Thomas and Brenda followed suit while Newt placed his box of ammo on the ground. The four of them gripped their weapons, and Minho took the lead as they crept slowly toward the noise. It sounded like a man trying to wake up from a horrible nightmare. Thomas's apprehension grew with every step. He was scared of what he was about to discover.

Minho stopped, his back against the wall, right at the edge of the window frame. The door to the room was on the other side of the window, closed.

"Ready," Minho whispered. "Now."

He pivoted and aimed his Launcher into the dark room just as Thomas moved to his left side and Brenda to his right, weapons held ready. Newt kept watch at their backs.

Thomas's finger hovered above the trigger, ready to squeeze it at an instant's notice, but there was no movement. He puzzled over what he was seeing inside the room. The red glow from the emergency lights didn't reveal much, but the whole floor appeared to be covered in dark mounds. Something that was slowly moving. Gradually his eyes adjusted and he began to make out the shapes of bodies and black clothing. And he caught sight of ropes.

"They're guards!" Brenda said, her voice cutting through the silence.

Muffled gasps escaped from the room, and finally Thomas could see faces, several of them. Mouths gagged and eyes open wide in panic. The guards were tied up and laid out on the floor from head to toe, side by side, filling up the entire room. Some of them were still, but most were struggling in their restraints. Thomas found himself staring, his mind searching for an explanation.

"So this is where they all are," Minho breathed.

Newt leaned in to get a look. "At least they're not all hangin' from the bloody ceiling with their tongues sticking out like last time."

Thomas couldn't agree more—he remembered that scene all too vividly, whether it had been real or not.

"We need to question them and find out what happened," Brenda said, already moving for the door.

Thomas grabbed her before he had time to think. "No."

"What do you mean no? Why not—they can tell us everything!" She wrenched her arm out of his grip but waited to see what he had to say.

"It might be a trap, or whoever did this could come back soon. We just need to get out of this place."

"Yeah," Minho said. "This isn't up for debate. I don't care if we have Cranks or rebels or gorillas running around this place—these shuck guards aren't our worry right now."

Brenda shrugged. "Fine. Just thought we could get some information." She paused, then pointed. "Hangar's that way."

After gathering up their weapons and ammunition, Thomas and the others jogged down hallway after hallway, all the while on the lookout for whoever had overpowered all those guards. Finally Brenda stopped at another set of double doors. One of them stood slightly ajar, and a breeze flowed through, ruffling her scrubs.

Without being told, Minho and Newt took up position on either side of the doorway, Launchers at the ready. Brenda grabbed the handle of the door, pistol aimed into the opening. There were no sounds coming from the other side.

Thomas gripped his Launcher tighter, the back end pressed against his shoulder, muzzle aimed forward. "Open it," he said, his heart racing.

Brenda swung the door wide and Thomas charged through. He swept his Launcher left and right, turning in a circle as he moved forward.

The massive hangar looked like it was built to hold three of the enormous Bergs, but only two stood in their loading spots. They loomed like giant squatting frogs, all scorched metal and worn edges, as if they'd flown soldiers into a hundred fiery battles. Other than a few cargo crates and what looked like mechanics' stations, the rest of the area was nothing but open space.

Thomas pushed on, searching the hangar as the other three spread out around him. Not one thing stirred.

"Hey!" Minho shouted. "Over here. Someone's on the . . ." He didn't finish, but he had stopped next to a large crate and had his weapon trained on something behind it.

Thomas was the first one at Minho's side and was surprised to see a man lying hidden from view on the other side of the wooden box, groaning as he rubbed his head. There was no blood showing through his dark hair, but judging from the way he struggled to sit up, Thomas bet he'd been hit pretty hard.

"Careful there, buddy," Minho warned. "Nice and easy, no sudden movements or you'll smell like burnt bacon before you know it."

The man leaned on an elbow, and when he dropped his hand from his face, Brenda let out a small cry and rushed forward to him, pulling him into a hug.

Jorge. Thomas felt a rush of relief—they'd found their pilot and he was okay, if a little banged up.

Brenda didn't seem to quite see it that way. She searched Jorge for injuries as her questions poured out. "What happened? How'd you get hurt? Who took the Berg? Where is everyone?"

Jorge groaned again and gently pushed her away. "Calm your pants, *hermana*. My head feels like it's been stomped by dancin' Cranks. Just give me a sec while I get my wits back together."

Brenda gave him some space and sat down, her face flushed, her expression anxious. Thomas had a million questions of his own, but he understood well what it felt like to be knocked in the head. He watched Jorge as he slowly got his bearings, and remembered how he'd once been scared of this guy—been terrified of him. The images of Jorge fighting Minho inside that wreck of a building in the Scorch would never leave his mind. But eventually, like Brenda, Jorge had realized that he and the Gladers were on the same side.

Jorge squeezed his eyes shut and opened them a few more times, then started talking. "I don't know how they did it, but they took over the compound, got rid of the guards, stole a Berg, flew out of here with another pilot. I was an idiot and tried to get them to wait until

I could find out more about what's going on. Now my head's paying for it."

"Who?" Brenda asked. "Who are you talking about? Who left?"

For some reason Jorge looked up at Thomas when he answered. "That Teresa chick. Her and the rest of the subjects. Well, all of them except you *muchachos*."

CHAPTER 17

Thomas staggered a step or two to his left and caught himself on the heavy crate for support. He'd been thinking that maybe Cranks had attacked after all, or that some other group had infiltrated WICKED, taken Teresa and the others. Rescued them, even.

But Teresa had led an *escape*? They'd fought their way out, subdued the guards, flown away in a Berg? Without him and the others? There were so many elements to the scenario, and none of them would come together in his mind.

"Shut your traps!" Jorge shouted over the din of questions from Minho and Newt, and Thomas jolted back to the present. "You're driving nails through my head—just . . . quit talking for a minute. Somebody help me get up."

Newt grabbed the man's hand and pulled him to his feet. "You better start explaining what bloody happened. From the beginning."

"And be quick about it," Minho added.

Jorge leaned back onto the wooden box and folded his arms, still wincing with every movement. "Look, *hermano,* I already told you I don't know much. What I said happened is what happened. My head feels like—"

"Yeah, we get it," Minho snapped. "You have a headache. Just tell us what you know and I'll find you some shuck aspirin."

Jorge let out a little laugh. "Brave words, boy. If I remember right, you're the one who had to apologize and beg for your life back in the Scorch."

Minho's face scrunched up and reddened. "Well, it's easy to be tough when you have a bunch of lunatics with knives protecting you. Things are a little different now."

"Would you stop!" Brenda said to both of them. "We're all on the same side."

"Just get on with it," Newt said. "Talk so we buggin' know what we need to do."

Thomas was still in shock. He stood listening to Jorge and Newt and Minho, but it felt like he was watching something on a screen, like it wasn't happening in front of him. He'd thought Teresa couldn't be more of a mystery to him. Now this.

"Look," Jorge said. "I spend most of my time in this hangar, okay? I started hearing all kinds of shouts and warnings over the com, then the silent-alarm lights started blinking. I went out to investigate and just about had my head blown off."

"At least it wouldn't hurt anymore," Minho muttered.

Jorge either didn't hear the comment or just ignored it. "Then the lights went out and I ran back in here to find my gun. Next thing I know, Teresa and a bunch of your hooligan friends come running in here like the world's about to end, hauling old Tony along to fly a Berg. I dropped my lousy pistol when seven or eight Launchers were aimed at my chest, then I begged them to wait, explain things to me. But some chick with blond hair whacked me in the forehead with the butt of her gun. I passed out, woke up to see your ugly faces staring down at me and a Berg gone. That's all I know."

Thomas took it all in but realized none of the details mattered. Only one thing about the whole affair stood out, and not only did it confuse him, it hurt him to face it.

"They left us behind," he almost whispered. "I can't believe it."

"Huh?" Minho asked.

"Speak up, Tommy," Newt added.

Thomas exchanged long glances with both of them. "They left us behind. At least we went back and looked for them. They left us here for WICKED to do whatever they want with us."

They didn't respond, but their eyes revealed that they'd been thinking the same thing.

"Maybe they *did* search for you," Brenda offered. "And couldn't find you. Or maybe the firefight got too nasty and they had to leave."

Minho scoffed at that. "All the guards are freaking tied up in that room back there! They had plenty of time to come look for us. No way. They left us."

"On purpose," Newt said in a low voice.

None of it sat right with Thomas. "Something's off. Teresa's been acting like WICKED's number one fan lately. Why would she escape? It has to be some kind of trick. Come on, Brenda—you told me not to trust them. You have to know something. Talk."

Brenda was shaking her head. "I don't know anything about this. But why is it so hard to believe that the other subjects would have the same idea we did? To escape? They just did a better job of it."

Minho made a noise that sounded like a wolf growling. "Insulting us is something I wouldn't do right now. And use the word *subjects* again and I'll smack you, girl or no girl."

"You just try it," Jorge warned. "Smack her and it'll be the last thing you do in this life."

"Could we stop the macho games for a bit?" Brenda rolled her eyes. "We need to figure out what comes next."

Thomas couldn't shake how much it bothered him that Teresa and the others—Frypan, even!—had left without them. If his group had been the ones to tie all the guards up, wouldn't they have searched until they found their other friends? And why had Teresa *wanted* to leave? Had her memories brought back something she hadn't expected?

"There's nothing to bloody figure out," Newt said. "We get out of here." He pointed at a Berg.

Thomas couldn't have agreed more. He turned to Jorge. "You're really a pilot?"

The man grinned. "Damn straight, *muchacho*. One of the best."

"Why'd they send you to the Scorch, then? Aren't you valuable?"

Jorge looked at Brenda. "Where Brenda goes, I go. And I hate to say it, but heading for the Scorch sounded better than staying here. I looked at it like a vacation. Turned out a little rougher than I—"

An alarm started blaring, the same whining scream as before. Thomas's heart jumped—the noise seemed even louder in the hangar than it had been in the hall, echoing off the high walls and ceiling.

Brenda looked with wide eyes at the doors they'd come through, and Thomas turned to see what had caught her attention.

At least a dozen of the black-clad guards were pouring through the opening, weapons raised. They started firing.

CHAPTER 18

Someone grabbed the back of Thomas's shirt and yanked him hard to the left; he stumbled and fell behind the cargo box just as the sounds of glass shattering and electricity crackling filled the hangar. Several arcs of lightning threaded around and over the crate, singeing the air. They'd barely winked out before a round of bullets thudded against the wood.

"Who let 'em loose?" Minho yelled.

"Hardly think it bloody matters right now!" Newt shouted back.

The group crouched low, their bodies pressed against each other tightly. It seemed impossible that they could fight back from such a position.

"They'll flank us any second," Jorge called out. "We need to start shooting back!"

Despite the wild attack going on around them, the statement struck Thomas. "I guess you're with us, then?"

The pilot looked at Brenda, then shrugged. "If she's helping you, then so am I. And if you haven't noticed—they're trying to kill me, too!"

A surge of relief edged through Thomas's terror. Now they just had to make it onto one of those Bergs.

The onslaught had paused momentarily, and Thomas could hear shuffling footsteps and short barked commands. If they were going to gain an advantage, they needed to act quickly.

"How do we do this?" he asked Minho. "You're in charge this time."

His friend gave him a sharp look but nodded curtly. "Okay, I'll fire right, Newt fires left. Thomas and Brenda, you fire over the box. Jorge, you scout a way for us to get to your shuck Berg. Shoot anything that moves or wears black. Get ready."

Thomas knelt facing the box, ready to jump to his feet on Minho's signal. Brenda was right next to him, with two pistols instead of a Launcher. Her eyes were on fire.

"Planning to kill somebody?" Thomas asked.

"Nah. I'll aim for their legs. But ya never know, maybe I'll hit high by accident."

She flashed him a smile; Thomas was liking her more and more.

"Okay!" Minho shouted. "Now!"

They made their moves. Thomas stood, lifting his Launcher up and over the box. He fired without risking a good look, and once he heard the grenade explode he popped up to search for a specific target. A man was creeping toward them from across the room, and Thomas aimed, fired. The grenade burst into lightning as it hit the man's chest, throwing him to the ground in a fit of spasms.

Gunfire and screams filled the air of the hangar, along with the staticky sound of electricity. Guard after guard fell, clutching their wounds—mostly in their legs, as Brenda had promised. Others bolted for cover.

"We've got them running!" Minho yelled. "But it won't last long— they probably didn't realize we had weapons. Jorge, which Berg is yours?"

"That one." Jorge pointed toward the far left corner of the hangar. "That's my baby. It won't take long to get her ready to fly."

Thomas turned to where Jorge had indicated. The Berg's large hatch door, which he remembered from the group's escape out of the Scorch, lay open and rested on the ground, waiting for passengers to run up its metal slope. Nothing had ever looked so inviting.

Minho shot another grenade. "Okay. First everyone reload. Then

Newt and I'll cover while Thomas, Jorge and Brenda run to the Berg. Jorge, you get her fired up while Thomas and Brenda cover for us from behind that hatch door. Sound like a plan?"

"Can the Launchers hurt the Berg?" Thomas asked. Everyone was jamming additional ammo into their weapons and pockets.

Jorge shook his head. "Not much. Those beasts are tougher than a Scorch camel. If they miss us and hit my ship, all the better. Let's do this, *muchachos!*"

"Then go go go!" Minho yelled without giving any warning. He and Newt started launching grenades like crazy, volleying them all along the open area in front of their waiting Berg.

Thomas felt a mad rush of adrenaline. He and Brenda took up position on the left and right of Jorge and they sprinted away from the protection of the cargo box. A flurry of firing weapons filled the air, but there was so much electricity and smoke that it was impossible to aim at anyone. Thomas shot his weapon as best he could while running, as did Brenda. He swore he could feel bullets blowing past him, barely missing. Launcher grenades exploded in a crash of glass and light to their right and left.

"Run!" Jorge shouted.

Thomas pushed himself to go faster, his legs burning. Daggers of lightning shot across the floor from all directions; bullets pinged against the metal walls of the hangar; smoke twirled like fingers of fog in odd places. It all became a blur as he focused on the Berg, now only a few dozen feet away.

They'd almost made it when a Launcher grenade smashed against Brenda's back; she screamed and fell, her face smacking the concrete floor as electricity spiderwebbed over her body.

Thomas skidded to a stop as he cried out her name, then dropped to the ground to make himself a smaller target. Tendrils of lightning-like electricity snaked across Brenda's body, then dwindled to smoky wisps as they raced out along the floor. Thomas lay on his stomach several feet away, dodging the errant streaks of white heat as he searched for a way to get closer.

Newt and Minho had obviously seen the disastrous turn of events and given up on the plan. They were running toward him as they continued firing. Jorge had made it to the Berg and disappeared up the hatch, but he came out again, shooting a different kind of Launcher; its grenades exploded into spouts of raging fire when they made contact. Several of the guards screamed as they erupted in flames, and the others pulled back a little because of the new threat.

Thomas waited anxiously on the ground next to Brenda, cursing his inability to help. He knew he had to wait for the electricity to die down before he could grab her and start dragging her to the Berg, but he didn't know if there was time. Her face had gone completely white; blood dripped from her nose and drool trickled from her mouth as her limbs spasmed and her torso seemed to bounce in place. Her eyes were frozen wide with shock and terror.

Newt and Minho reached him, dropped to the ground.

"No!" Thomas shouted. "Keep going to the Berg. Take cover behind the hatch door. Wait until we start moving, then cover us. Fire like crazy till we get there."

"Just come on already!" Minho yelled back. He grabbed Brenda by the shoulders, and Thomas's breath caught as his friend winced—several jagged bolts of lightning arced up his arms. But the energy had weakened considerably and Minho was able to stand and begin pulling her along behind him.

Thomas hooked his arms under Brenda's shoulders, and Newt picked up her legs. They backed their way toward the Berg. The hangar was a world of noise and smoke and flashing light. A bullet grazed

Thomas's leg: a hot score of pain, then oozing blood. An inch difference and he might've been hobbled for life or bled to death. He let out a furious scream and imagined everyone in black as the one who'd shot him.

He stole a glance at Minho; the boy's face was strained with the effort of dragging Brenda. Thomas harnessed his furious surge of adrenaline and took a risk, lifted his Launcher up from beneath him with one hand, firing in random directions as he used the other to help pull Brenda across the floor.

They reached the foot of the hatch door. Jorge immediately dropped his huge weapon and slid down the ramp to grab one of Brenda's arms. Thomas released his hold on her shirt and let Minho and Jorge yank her up into the ship, her heels thumping against the raised traction molding.

Newt started firing his weapon again, releasing grenades left and right until he ran out of ammunition. Thomas shot once more and his Launcher emptied as well.

The guards in the hangar clearly knew that their time was about to run out, and a horde of them sprinted for the ship and opened fire once again.

"Forget reloading!" Thomas shouted. "Let's go!"

Newt turned and scrambled up the ramp. Thomas was right behind him. His head had just crossed the threshold when something thumped and cracked against his back. In an instant he felt the burning power of a thousand bolts of lightning strike him at once; he fell backward and tumbled end over end until he landed on the floor of the hangar, his whole body convulsing and his vision going dark.

CHAPTER 19

Thomas's eyes were open, but he couldn't see anything. No, that wasn't it. Brilliant lights arced in lines across his field of vision, blinding him. He couldn't blink, couldn't close his eyelids to block it. Pain washed over his body; his skin felt like it was melting right off his muscle and bones. He tried to scream, but it was as if he'd lost all control of his functions—his arms and legs and torso shook no matter how hard he strained to stop them.

The crackle and pop of electricity filled his ears, but soon another noise took over. A deep, thrumming hum that pounded his ears and rattled his head. He was barely on the edge of consciousness, felt himself slipping in and out of an abyss that wanted to swallow him. But something in him knew what that sound was. The engines of the Berg had started up, the thrusters burning their blue flames.

He immediately thought they were leaving him. First Teresa and the others, now his closest friends and Jorge. He couldn't take any more betrayal. It hurt too much. He wanted to scream, all while needles of pain bit every inch of his body and the burning smell overwhelmed him. No, they wouldn't leave him behind. He knew it.

Gradually his vision started to clear, and the white-hot charges of heat diminished in strength and number. He blinked. Two, then three figures dressed in black stood over him, weapons pointed at his face. Guards. Would they kill him? Drag him back to the Rat Man for more tests? One of them spoke, but Thomas couldn't hear the words; static buzzed in his ears.

All of a sudden the guards were gone, tackled by two figures that seemingly flew through the air. His friends, had to be his friends. Through a haze of smoke Thomas could see the ceiling of the hangar far above him. The pain had mostly gone away, replaced by a numbness that made him wonder if he could move. He shifted to his right, then rolled to his left, then leaned up on an elbow, woozy and weak. A last few trickles of electricity skittered over his body and disappeared into the cement. The worst was over. He hoped.

He shifted again, looked back over his shoulder. Minho and Newt were each straddling a guard, beating the living klunk out of them. Jorge stood in between the Gladers, shooting his fiery Launcher in all directions. Most of the guards must've given up or been disabled—otherwise Thomas and the others wouldn't have made it even this far. Or maybe, Thomas thought, the guards were pretending, putting on an act, like everyone else in the Trials.

He didn't care. He just wanted out of this place. And escape was right in front of him.

With a groan he shifted to his belly, then pushed himself up onto his hands and knees. Breaking glass, the crackle of lightning, the booms of weapons firing and pings of bullets hitting metal filled the air around him. If someone shot him now, there was nothing he could do about it. He could only drag himself toward the Berg. The ship's thrusters hummed as they charged; the whole thing vibrated, shaking the ground underneath him as well. The hatch door was only a few feet away. They needed to get on the ship.

He tried to yell something back at Minho and the others, but only a gurgling groan came out. On his hands and knees like a wounded dog, he started crawling forward as quickly as his body would allow—he had to fight for every ounce of strength within. He reached the lip of the ramp, pulled himself over it, inched up the slope. His muscles ached and nausea climbed out of his stomach. The noises of battle pounded his ears, put his nerves on edge; something could hit him at any second.

He made it halfway. Turned to look at his friends. They were backing toward him, all three now firing. Minho had to stop and reload, and Thomas just knew he'd get shot or blasted with a grenade. But his friend finished and started up again. The three of them reached the bottom of the hatch door, so close now.

Thomas tried to speak again; now he *sounded* like a wounded dog.

"That's it!" Jorge yelled. "Grab his butt and drag him in!"

Jorge ran up the ramp past Thomas and disappeared inside. Something clicked loudly, and then the ramp started to swing upward, its hinges groaning. Thomas realized he'd collapsed, his face resting against the raised metal traction pads beneath him, yet he couldn't remember when it had happened. He felt hands pull at his shirt, felt himself lifted through the air. Then he slammed back down just inside the hatch door as it sealed shut and the locks engaged.

"Sorry, Tommy," Newt muttered in his ear. "Could've been a bit more gentle, I 'spect."

Though he was close to unconsciousness, an indescribable joy lifted Thomas's heart—they were escaping WICKED. He let out a weak grunt in an attempt to share that with his friend. Then he closed his eyes and passed out.

CHAPTER 20

Thomas woke to see Brenda's face staring down at him. She looked worried. Her skin was pale and marked with streaks of dried blood, and there was black soot on her forehead and a bruise forming on her cheek. As if her wounds reminded him, he suddenly felt the sting of his own across his whole body. He had no idea how those Launcher grenades worked, but he was happy he'd only been hit once.

"I just got up myself," Brenda said. "How do you feel?"

Thomas shifted to lean on his elbow and winced at the sharp pain in his leg where he'd been grazed by the bullet. "Like a bucket of klunk."

He lay on a low cot inside a large cargo hold that currently held nothing but a bunch of mismatched furniture. Minho and Newt were taking well-deserved naps on a couple of ugly couches, blankets covering their bodies and tucked in under their chins. Thomas had a sneaking suspicion that Brenda had done that—they looked like little kids, all snuggly and warm.

Brenda had been kneeling next to his cot; she now stood up and took a seat on a frumpy armchair a few feet away. "We slept for almost ten hours."

"Serious?" Thomas couldn't believe it—it seemed like he'd just dozed off. Or *passed out* was probably more accurate.

Brenda nodded.

"We've been flying that long? Where are we going, the moon?" Thomas swung his legs out and sat on the edge of the cot.

"No. Jorge got us a hundred or so miles away, then landed in a big clearing. He's actually snoozing, too. Can't have a tired pilot."

"I can't believe we both got shot by Launchers. I liked it a lot better being the one who pulled the trigger." Thomas rubbed his face and let out a big yawn. Then he examined some of the burns on his arms. "Do you think these will leave scars?"

Brenda laughed. "Of all the things to worry about."

He couldn't help but smile. She was right. "So," he started, then continued, slowly. "It sounded great to escape from WICKED when we were back there, but . . . I don't even know what the real world . . . It's not all like the Scorch, is it?"

"No," she replied. "Only the regions between the Tropics are a wasteland—everywhere else has extreme swings of climate. There are a few safe cities we could go to. Especially being immune—we could probably find jobs pretty easily."

"Jobs," Thomas repeated, as if the word were the most foreign thing he'd ever heard. "You're already thinking about getting a job?"

"You do plan to eat, don't you?"

Thomas didn't answer, felt the heavy weight of reality. If they were truly going to escape into the real world, they had to start living like real people. But was that even possible in a world where the Flare existed? He thought of his friends.

"Teresa," he said.

Brenda pulled back a little in surprise. "What about her?"

"Is there a way to find out where she and the others went?"

"Jorge already did—checked the Berg tracking system. They went to a city called Denver."

Thomas felt a prick of alarm. "Does that mean WICKED'll be able to find us?"

"You don't know Jorge." She had a mischievous grin on her face.

"He can manipulate the system like you wouldn't believe. We should be able to stay a step ahead of them for a little while, at least."

"Denver," Thomas said after a moment. The name sounded weird in his mouth. "Where's that?"

"Rocky Mountains. High elevation. One of the obvious choices for a quarantine zone because the weather's recovered pretty quickly there since the sun flares. As good a place as any to go."

Thomas didn't care so much about the location, he just knew that he had to find Teresa and the others, be reunited. He wasn't quite sure *why* yet, and he certainly wasn't ready to discuss it with Brenda. So he stalled for time.

"What's it like there?" he finally asked.

"Well, like most big cities, they're pretty ruthless about keeping the Cranks out, and the residents have to be tested for the Flare randomly and often. They actually have another town set up on the opposite side of the valley where they send the newly infected. Immunes get paid a lot of money to take care of them even though it's extremely dangerous. Both places are heavily guarded."

Even with some of his memories back, Thomas didn't know a whole lot about the population that was immune to the Flare. But he remembered something the Rat Man had told him. "Janson said that people really hate the Immunes—call them Munies. What did he mean by that?"

"When you have the Flare, you know you're going to go crazy and die. It's not a matter of *if* but *when*. And as hard as the world has tried, the virus always finds its way through the cracks of the quarantines. Imagine knowing that and then knowing that the Immunes are going to be okay. The Flare does nothing to them—they don't even transmit the virus. Wouldn't *you* hate the healthy?"

"Probably," Thomas said, glad he was on the immune side of things.

Better to be hated than sick. "But wouldn't it seem valuable to have them around? I mean, knowing they can't catch the disease."

Brenda shrugged. "They're definitely used—especially in government and security roles—but the others treat them like trash. And there's way more people who aren't immune. That's why the Munies get paid so much to be guards—otherwise they wouldn't go through it. A lot of them even try to hide their immunity. Or go work for WICKED, like Jorge and I did."

"So did you guys meet before going there?"

"We met in Alaska, after we'd found out we were immune. There was a gathering place for people like us—kind of a hidden camp. Jorge became like an uncle to me, and he swore to be my guardian. My dad had already been killed, and my mom pushed me away once she caught the Flare."

Thomas leaned forward, elbows on knees. "You told me WICKED killed your dad. And yet you still went and volunteered to work for them?"

"Survival, Thomas." A dark look passed over her face. "You don't know how good you had it growing up under WICKED's wing. Out in the real world, most people will do anything to survive one more day. Cranks and Immunes have different problems, yeah, but it's still about surviving. Everybody wants to live."

Thomas didn't respond, didn't know what to say. All he knew of life was the Maze and the Scorch and the splotchy memories of his childhood with WICKED. He felt empty and lost, like he didn't really belong anywhere.

A sudden pain squeezed his heart. "I wonder what happened to my mom," he said, surprising himself.

"Your mom?" Brenda asked. "You remember her?"

"I've had a few dreams about her. I think they were memories."

"What came back? What was she like?"

"She was . . . a mom. You know, she loved me, cared about me, worried about me." Thomas's voice cracked. "I don't think anyone's done that since they took me away from her. It hurts to think of her going crazy, to think of what might've happened to her. What some crazy bloodthirsty Crank might've . . ."

"Stop it, Thomas. Just stop." She took his hand and squeezed, which helped. "Think how happy she'd be, knowing you're still alive, still fighting. She died knowing that you were immune, and that you'd have a chance to actually grow old, no matter how crappy the world is. Plus, you're totally wrong."

Thomas had been staring at the floor, but at that he looked up at Brenda. "Huh?"

"Minho. Newt. Frypan. All your friends care and worry about you. Even Teresa—she really did do all those things in the Scorch because she thought she had no choice." Brenda paused, then added in a quiet voice, "Chuck."

The pang Thomas was feeling in his chest tightened. "Chuck. He . . . he's . . ." He had to stop a second to compose himself. When it came down to it, Chuck was the most vivid reason that he despised WICKED. How could any good come from killing a kid like Chuck?

He finally continued. "I watched as that kid died. In his last few seconds there was pure terror in his eyes. You can't do that. You can't do that to a person. I don't care what anyone tells me, I don't care how many people go crazy and die, I don't care if the whole shuck human race ends. Even if that was the only thing that had to happen to find the cure, I'd still be against it."

"Thomas, relax. You're going to squeeze your own fingers off."

97

He didn't remember letting go of her hand—he looked down to see his own hands gripping each other tightly, the skin completely white. He eased off and felt the blood rush back to them.

Brenda nodded solemnly. "I changed for good back in the Scorch city. I'm sorry for everything."

Thomas shook his head. "You don't have a single reason more than I do to apologize. It's all just one big screwed-up mess." He groaned and lay back down on the cot, staring at the metal grid of the ceiling.

After a long pause, Brenda finally spoke again. "Ya know, maybe we can find Teresa and the others. Join up. They broke out, which means they're on our side. I think we should give them the benefit of the doubt—maybe they had no choice but to leave without us. And it's no surprise at all that they went where they did."

Thomas shifted to look at her, daring to hope she was right. "So you think we should go to . . ."

"Denver."

Thomas nodded, suddenly certain and loving the feel of it. "Yeah, Denver."

"But your friends aren't the only reason." Brenda smiled. "There's something even more important there."

CHAPTER 21

Thomas stared at Brenda, eager to hear what she had to say.

"You know what's in your brain," she said. "So what's our biggest concern?"

Thomas thought about it. "WICKED tracking us or controlling us."

"Exactly," Brenda said.

"And?" Again, impatience filled his gut.

She sat back down across from him and leaned forward on her knees, rubbing her hands together in excitement. "I know a guy named Hans who moved to Denver—he's immune like us. He's a doctor. He worked at WICKED until he had a disagreement with the higher-ups about the protocols surrounding the brain implants. He thought what they were doing was too risky. That they were crossing lines, being inhumane. WICKED wouldn't let him leave, but he managed to escape."

"Those guys need to work on their security," Thomas muttered.

"Lucky for us." Brenda grinned. "Anyway, Hans is a genius. He knows every little detail about the implants you guys have in your heads. I know he went to Denver because he sent me a message over the Netblock right before I was dropped into the Scorch. If we can get to him, he'll be able to take those things out of your heads. Or at least disable them. I'm not sure how it works, but if anyone can do it, he can. And he'd do it gladly. The man hates WICKED as much as we do."

Thomas thought for a second. "And if they control us, we're in big trouble. I've seen it happen at least three times." Alby struggling against an unseen force in the Homestead, Gally being controlled with the knife that hit Chuck, and Teresa straining to speak to Thomas outside the shack in the Scorch. All three among his most disturbing memories.

"Exactly. They could manipulate you, make you do things. They can't see through your eyes or hear your voice or anything like that, but we need to get you fixed. If they're close enough to have you under observation and if they decide it's worth the risk, they'll try it. And that's the last thing we need."

It was a lot to sort out. "Well, it looks like we have plenty of reason to go to Denver. We'll see what Newt and Minho think when they wake up."

Brenda nodded. "Sounds good." She got to her feet and moved closer, then leaned in and kissed Thomas on the cheek. Goose bumps broke out down his chest and arms. "Ya know, most of what happened in those tunnels was *not* an act." She stood and looked at him for a moment, quietly. "I'm going to wake up Jorge—he's sleeping in the captain's quarters."

She turned and walked away, and Thomas sat there, hoping his face hadn't flushed bright red when he remembered her being close to him in the Underneath. He put his hands behind his head and lay back on the cot, trying to process everything he'd just heard. They finally had some direction. He felt a smile crack his face, and not just because he'd been kissed.

Minho called their meeting a Gathering, just for old time's sake.

By the end of it, Thomas had a headache, the pain throbbing so badly he thought his eyeballs might pop out. Minho played devil's advocate on every single issue and for some reason gave Brenda dirty looks the entire time. Thomas knew that they needed to go over things from every possible angle, but he wished Minho would give Brenda a break.

In the end, after an hour of arguing and going back and forth and coming full circle a dozen times, they decided—unanimously—to go to Denver. They planned to land the Berg at a private airport with the story that they were Immunes looking for a government transport job. Luckily the Berg was unmarked—WICKED didn't advertise when it went out into the real world, apparently. They'd be tested and branded as immune to the Flare, which would allow them access to the city proper. All except Newt, who—because he was infected—would have to stay on the Berg until they figured something out.

They ate a quick meal; then Jorge went off to pilot the ship. He said he was well rested and he wanted everyone else to take a nap since it would take a few more hours to reach the city. After that, who knew how long it would be before they found a place to stay for the night.

Thomas just wanted to be alone, so he used his headache as an excuse. He found a little reclining chair in an out-of-the-way corner and curled up in it, his back to the open area behind him. He had a blanket, and he pulled it up and around him, feeling cozier than he had in a long time. And even though he was scared of what might come, he also felt a sense of peace. Maybe they were finally close to breaking the bonds of WICKED forever.

He thought about their escape and all that had happened along the way. The more he went through it, the more he doubted that any of it had been orchestrated by WICKED. Too much had been done on the spur of the moment, and those guards had fought furiously to keep them there.

Finally sleep took him from all of these thoughts, and he dreamed.

He's only twelve years old, sitting in a chair facing another man, who looks unhappy to be there. They're in a room with an observation window.

"Thomas," the sad man begins. "You've been a little . . . distant lately. I need you to come back to what's important. You and Teresa are doing well with your telepathy, and things are moving forward nicely by all estimations. It's time to refocus."

Thomas feels shame, and then shame at being ashamed. It confuses him, makes him want to run away, back to his dorm. The man senses it.

"We won't leave this room until I'm satisfied with your commitment." The words are like a death sentence handed down by a heartless judge. "You'll answer my questions, and the sincerity better bleed from your pores. Do you understand?"

Thomas nods.

"Why are we here?" the man asks.

"Because of the Flare."

"I want more than that. Elaborate."

Thomas pauses. He has felt a sense of rebellion lately, but he knows that once he recounts all the things this man wants to hear, it will dissipate. He'll fall back into doing what they ask of him and learning what they set before him.

"Go on," the man pushes.

Thomas lets it all out in a rush—word for word, as he memorized it long ago. "The sun flares pummeled the earth. Security in many government buildings was compromised. A man-made virus engineered for biological warfare leaked from a military center for disease control. That virus hit all the major population centers and spread rapidly. It became known as the Flare. The surviving governments put all their resources into WICKED, who found the best and the brightest of those who were immune. They began their plans to stimulate and map the brain patterns of all known human emotions and study how we operate despite having the Flare rooted inside our brains. The research will lead to . . ."

He keeps going and he doesn't stop, breathing in and out with the words that he hates.

The dreaming Thomas turns and runs away, runs to the darkness.

CHAPTER 22

Thomas decided he needed to tell everyone more about all the dreams he was having. About what he suspected were memories coming back to him.

As they sat down for the second Gathering of the day, he made them all swear to keep their mouths shut until he was finished. They'd grouped the chairs near the cockpit of the Berg so Jorge could hear it all. Thomas then began to tell them about each dream he'd had—memories of his life as a kid, being taken by WICKED when they found out he was immune, his training with Teresa, all of it. When he got out all that he could remember, he waited for a response.

"I don't see what that has to do with anything," Minho said. "Just makes me hate WICKED even more. Good thing we left, and I hope I never have to see Teresa's shuck face again."

Newt, who'd been irritable and distant, spoke for the first time since they'd sat down for the Gathering. "Brenda's a bloody princess compared to that know-it-all."

"Um . . . thanks?" Brenda replied with an eye roll.

"When did you change?" Minho blurted out.

"Huh?" Brenda replied.

"When did you become so shuck crazy against WICKED? You've worked for them, you did all those things they wanted you to do in the Scorch. You were all ready to help them put that mask on our face and

103

mess with us all over again. When and how did you come so strongly over to our side?"

Brenda sighed; she looked tired, but her words came out laced with some anger. "I have *never* been on their side. Never. I've always disagreed with how they operate—but what could I ever do on my own? Or even with Jorge? I've done what I needed to do to survive. But then I lived through the Scorch with you guys and it made me realize . . . well, it made me realize that we have a chance."

Thomas wanted to change the subject. "Brenda, do you think WICKED'll start forcing us to do things? Start messing with us, manipulating us, whatever?"

"That's why we need to find Hans." She shrugged. "I can only guess what WICKED will do. Every other time I've seen them control someone with the device in their brain, that person has been close and under observation. Since you guys are running and they have no way of seeing exactly what you're doing, they might not want to risk it."

"Why not?" Newt asked. "Why don't they just make us stab ourselves in the leg or chain ourselves to a chair until they find us?"

"Like I said, they're not close enough," Brenda answered. "They obviously *need* you guys. They can't risk you getting hurt or dying. I bet they have all kinds of people coming after you. Once they get close enough to observe, then they might start doing things to mess with your head. And I have a pretty good feeling they will—which is why getting to Denver is a must."

Thomas's mind had already been made up. "We're going and that's that. And I say we wait a hundred years before we have another meeting to talk about stuff."

"Good that," Minho said. "I'm with you."

That was two out of three. Everyone looked at Newt.

"I'm a Crank," the older boy said. "Doesn't matter what I bloody think."

"We can get you into the city," Brenda said, ignoring him. "At least long enough to have Hans work on your head. We'll just be really careful to keep you away fr—"

Newt stood up in a blur of speed and punched the wall behind his chair. "First of all, it doesn't matter if I have the thing in my brain—I'm gonna be past the buggin' Gone before too long anyway. And I don't wanna die knowing I ran around a city of healthy people and infected them."

Thomas remembered the envelope in his pocket, a thing he'd almost forgotten about until now. His fingers twitched to pull it out and read it.

No one said anything.

Newt's expression darkened. "Well, don't hurt yourselves tryin' to talk me into it," he finally growled. "We all know WICKED's fancy cure is never gonna work, and I wouldn't want it to. Not much to live for on this piece-of-klunk planet. I'll stay on the Berg while you guys go into the city." He turned and stomped away, disappearing around the corner to the common area.

"That went well," Minho muttered. "Guess the Gathering is over." He got up and followed his friend.

Brenda frowned, then focused on Thomas. "You're—we're—doing the right thing."

"I don't think there is a right or wrong anymore," Thomas said, hearing the numbness in his own voice. He desperately wanted sleep. "Only horrible and not-quite-so-horrible."

He got up to join the other two Gladers, fingering the note in his pocket. What could it possibly say? he wondered as he walked out. And how would he ever know when the right time to open it had come?

CHAPTER 23

Thomas hadn't had much time to think about what the world outside of WICKED's control would be like. But now that they were actually going to face it, his nerves lit up with anticipation and butterflies filled his stomach. He was about to enter uncharted territory.

"You guys ready for this?" Brenda asked. They stood outside the Berg, at the foot of the cargo door ramp, just a hundred feet or so in front of a cement wall with big iron doors.

Jorge let out a snort. "I forgot what an inviting place they have here."

"You sure you know what you're doing?" Thomas asked him.

"Just keep your mouth shut, *hermano,* and leave things to me. We're using our real first names with fake last names. All they'll really care about in the end is that we're immune—they'll love putting us on record. We won't have more than a day or two before they hunt us down to do something for the government. We're valuable. And I can't stress it enough—Thomas, you need to keep that yapper of yours closed."

"You too, Minho," Brenda added. "Got it? Jorge created fake documents for all of us, and he lies like a master thief."

"No kidding," Minho muttered.

Jorge and Brenda headed toward the doors with Minho close behind. Thomas hesitated. He looked up at the wall—it reminded him of the Maze, and a quick flash of the horrible memories of that place went through his mind, particularly the night when he'd tied Alby in the thick ivy and hidden from the Grievers. He was thankful that these walls were bare.

The walk to the exit seemed to take forever, the huge wall and doors growing taller and taller as the group approached them. When they finally made it to the foot of the immense doors, an electronic buzz sounded from somewhere, followed by a female voice.

"State your names and your business."

Jorge answered very loudly. "I'm Jorge Gallaraga, and these are my associates, Brenda Despain, Thomas Murphy and Minho Park. We're here for some information gathering and field testing. I'm a certified Berg pilot. I have all the necessary paperwork with me, but you can check it out." He pulled a few data cards from his back pocket and held them up to a camera in the wall.

"Hold, please," the voice directed. Thomas was sweating—he was sure the lady would sound an alarm any second now. Guards would come rushing out. They'd send him back to WICKED, to the white room, or worse.

He waited, mind racing, for what felt like several minutes before a series of clicks rattled the air, followed by a loud thunk. Then one of the iron doors swung outward, its hinges squealing. Thomas peered through the widening crack and was relieved to see that the narrow alley on the other side was empty. At the end stood another huge wall with another set of doors. Those doors looked more modern, though, and several screens and panels were set into the cement to their right.

"Come on," Jorge said. He walked through the open door as if he did it every day. Thomas, Minho and Brenda followed Jorge down the alley to the outer wall, where he stopped. The screens and panels Thomas had seen from the other side were complex up close. Jorge pressed a button on the largest and began to enter their fake names and identification numbers. He typed in a few other pieces of information, then fed their data cards into a large slot.

The group waited quietly as a few minutes passed, Thomas's anxiety growing with every second. He tried not to show it, but he suddenly felt like this had been a huge mistake. They should've gone somewhere else less secure, or tried to break in to the city somehow. These people were going to see right through them. Maybe WICKED had already sent out calls to be on the lookout for fugitives.

Slim it, Thomas, he told himself, and for half a second he worried he'd said it out loud.

The lady's voice came back. "Papers are in order. Please move to the viral testing station."

Jorge stepped to the right and a panel on the wall opened. Thomas watched as a mechanical arm came out of it. It was a strange device with what looked like eye sockets. Jorge leaned forward and pressed his face to the machine. As soon as his eyes were lined up to the sockets a small wire snaked out and pricked his neck. There were several hisses and clicks; then the wire retracted back into the device and Jorge stepped away.

The entire panel rotated back into the wall and the device Jorge had used disappeared, replaced by a new one that looked just like it.

"Next," the lady announced.

Brenda exchanged an uneasy glance with Thomas, then stepped up to the machine and leaned into it. The wire pricked her neck, the device hissed and clicked and it was over. She moved away, taking a very noticeable breath of relief.

"It's been a long time since I've used one of those," she whispered to Thomas. "They make me nervous, like I'm suddenly not gonna be immune anymore."

Once again the lady said, "Next."

Minho went through the procedure. Finally it was Thomas's turn.

He walked over to the testing panel as it rotated again, and as soon as the new apparatus appeared and locked into place, he leaned forward and placed his eyes where they were supposed to go. He braced himself for the pain of the wire, but he hardly noticed the prick on his neck before it was gone. All he saw inside the machine were a few flashes of light and color. He felt a puff of air that made him squeeze his eyes shut; when he opened them again everything was dark.

After a few seconds, he stepped back and waited for whatever was supposed to happen next.

The lady finally spoke again. "You've all been cleared of VCT and confirmed immune. You do realize that the opportunities for your kind are vast here in Denver. But don't advertise it too much out on the streets. Everyone here is healthy and virus-free, but there are many who still don't take kindly to Immunes."

"We're here for a few simple tasks and then we'll be heading out again. Probably in a week or so," Jorge said. "Hopefully we can keep our little secret a . . . secret."

"What's VCT?" Thomas whispered to Minho.

"You think I know?"

"Viral Contagion Threat," Brenda answered before Thomas could ask her. "But keep it down. Anyone who doesn't know that will seem suspicious here."

Thomas opened his mouth to say something but was startled by a loud beep as the doors began to slide open. Another hallway was revealed, its walls made of metal. There was another set of closed doors at the end of it. Thomas wondered just how long this would go on.

"Enter the detector one at a time, please," the woman directed. Her voice seemed to follow them to this third hallway. "Mr. Gallaraga first."

Jorge entered the small space and the doors slid shut behind him.

"What's the detector?" Thomas asked.

"It detects stuff," Brenda replied curtly.

Thomas wrinkled his face at her. Faster than he expected, an alarm buzzed again and the doors opened. Jorge was no longer there.

"Ms. Despain is next," their now-bored-sounding announcer said.

Brenda nodded at Thomas and entered the detector. A minute or so later and it was Minho's turn.

Minho looked at Thomas, a serious expression on his face. "If I don't see you on the other side," he said in a sappy voice, "remember that I love you." Snickering at Thomas's eye roll, he went through the doors and they closed.

Soon the lady called for Thomas to enter.

He stepped inside and the doors closed behind him. A rush of air hit him as several low beeps sounded; then the doors in front of him slid open and there were people everywhere. His heartbeat picked up, but he spotted his waiting friends and relaxed. He was struck by all the activity around him as he joined them. A bustling crowd of men and women—many of whom clutched rags to their mouths—filled a huge atrium topped with a glass ceiling far above, letting in loads of sunshine. Through one corner he could see the tops of several skyscrapers—though these looked nothing like the ones they'd come across in the Scorch. They were brilliant in the sunlight. Thomas was so stunned by everything there was to look at, he almost forgot how nervous he'd been only a moment before.

"Wasn't so bad, was it, *muchacho*?" Jorge asked.

"I kinda liked it," Minho said.

Thomas was utterly wowed; he couldn't stop craning his neck to take in the large building they'd entered. "What is this place?" he finally got out. "Who are all these people?" He looked to his three partners, waiting for an answer—Jorge and Brenda looked embarrassed to be

110

with him. But Brenda's expression changed abruptly, melting into something like sadness.

"I keep forgetting that you've lost your memories," she murmured, then opened her arms to gesture around herself. "It's called a mall—basically it runs along the entire wall surrounding the city. It's mainly shops and businesses."

"I've just never seen so many . . ." His voice trailed off. A man in a dark blue jacket was approaching them, his gaze set on Thomas. And he didn't look very happy.

"Hey," Thomas whispered, nodding toward the stranger.

The man reached them before anyone could respond. He gave the group a curt nod and announced, "We know some people escaped from WICKED. And judging by the Berg you came in on, I'm guessing you're a part of that group. I highly recommend you accept the advice I'm about to give you. You have nothing to be afraid of—we're only asking for help and you'll be protected when you arrive."

He handed Thomas a slip of paper, spun on his heel and walked off without another word.

"What in the world was that all about?" Minho asked. "What does it say?"

Thomas looked down and read it. "It says, 'You need to come meet me immediately—I'm with a group called the Right Arm. Corner of Kenwood and Brookshire, Apartment 2792.'"

A lump formed in Thomas's throat when he saw the signature at the bottom of the slip of paper. He looked up at Minho, sure his face had gone pale. "It's from Gally."

CHAPTER 24

It turned out that Thomas didn't need to do any explaining. Brenda and Jorge had started working for WICKED in plenty of time to know who Gally was, how he'd been an outcast of sorts in the Glade, how he and Thomas had become bitter rivals because of Gally's memories from the Changing. But all Thomas could think of was the angry boy throwing the knife that killed Chuck, that made the boy bleed to death on the ground as Thomas held him.

Then he had lost it—had beaten Gally until he thought he'd killed him. A surprising amount of relief filled him when he realized that maybe he hadn't—*if* this note was really from Gally. As much as he'd hated the guy, Thomas didn't want to be a murderer.

"It can't possibly be him," Brenda said.

"Why not?" Thomas asked; the relief began to wash away. "What happened to him after we were taken away? Did he . . ."

"Die? No. He spent a week or so in the infirmary, recovering from a broken cheekbone. But that was nothing compared to the psychological damage. They *used* him to kill Chuck because the Psychs thought the patterns would be valuable. It was all planned. They forced Chuck to move in front of you."

Any anger Thomas had felt toward Gally shifted to WICKED, feeding his ever-growing hatred for the organization. The guy had been a complete slinthead, but if what Brenda said was true, he was only

WICKED's instrument. It made Thomas even angrier at them to hear that it wasn't a mistake that Chuck had been killed instead of him.

Brenda continued. "I heard that one of the Psychs designed the interaction to be a Variable not just for you and the Gladers who witnessed it, but . . . but also for Chuck during his last few moments."

For one short but frightening instant, Thomas thought rage would overcome him—that he'd grab some random stranger from the crowd and beat the klunk out of him like he'd beaten Gally.

He sucked in a breath and ran a shaking hand through his hair. "Nothing surprises me anymore," he forced out through clenched teeth.

"Gally's mind couldn't handle what he'd done," Brenda said. "He went completely nuts and they had to send him away. I'm sure they figured no one would ever believe his story."

"So why do you think this can't be him?" Thomas asked. "Maybe he got better, found his way here."

Brenda shook her head. "Look, anything's possible. But I saw the guy—it was like he had the Flare. He was trying to eat chairs and spitting and yelling and ripping his own hair out."

"I saw him, too," Jorge added. "He got past the guards one day. He ran through the halls naked, screaming at the top of his lungs about beetles in his veins."

Thomas tried to clear his mind. "I wonder what he means by the Right Arm."

Jorge answered. "There are rumors about them all over the place. It's supposed to be an underground group bent on taking down WICKED."

"Even more reason to do what the note says," Thomas said.

Brenda's face showed doubt. "I really think we should find Hans before anything else."

Thomas held up the piece of paper and shook it. "We're going to see Gally. We need someone who knows the city." More than that, though, his gut told him that it was where they should start.

"What if this is some kind of trap?"

"Yeah," Minho said. "Maybe we should think about this."

"No." Thomas shook his head. "We can't try to outguess them anymore. Sometimes they do things just to make me do the opposite of what they think I think they think I want to do."

"Huh?" the three of them asked at the same time, confusion transforming their faces.

"From now on I do what feels right," Thomas explained. "And something tells me we need to go to this place and see Gally—at least to find out if it's really him. He's a connection to the Glade, and he has every reason in the world to be on our side."

The others stared at him with blank faces, as if they were trying to come up with further arguments.

"Good that," Thomas said. "I'll take all those looks as yeses. I'm glad to see you all agree with me. Now, how're we gonna get there?"

Brenda let out an exaggerated sigh. "Ever heard of a cab?"

After a quick meal in the mall, they caught a cab to drive them into the city. When Jorge handed the driver a card to pay with, Thomas worried again about WICKED tracking them. As soon as they got settled in their seats, he asked Jorge about it in a whisper so the driver couldn't hear.

Jorge only gave him a troubled look.

"You're worried because Gally knew we were coming, right?" Thomas guessed.

Jorge nodded. "A little. But the way that man introduced himself, I'm just hoping that word of an escape leaked out and this Right Arm group's been looking for us since. I've heard they're based here."

"Or maybe it has something to do with Teresa's group coming here first," Brenda offered.

Thomas didn't feel very comforted. "You sure you know what you're doing?" he asked Jorge.

"We'll be fine, *muchacho*. Now that we're here, WICKED will have a hell of a time catching up to us. It's easier than you think to blend in, in a city. Just relax."

Thomas didn't know if there was much chance of that, but he did lean back in his seat to look out the window.

The ride through Denver completely took his breath away. He remembered the hovering vehicles from his childhood—unmanned, weaponized police vehicles everyone had called cop machines. But so much was like nothing he'd ever seen before—the huge skyscrapers, the brilliant displays of holographic advertising, the countless people—he really had a hard time believing it was real. Some small part of him wondered if his optic nerves were being manipulated by WICKED somehow, if it was all yet another simulation. He wondered if he'd lived in a city like this before, and if he had, how he could possibly have forgotten the splendor of it all.

As they drove through the crowded streets, it occurred to him that maybe the world wasn't so bad off after all. Here was an entire community, thousands of people going about their everyday lives. But the drive continued, and gradually details he hadn't noticed began to come into focus. And the longer they drove, the more unsettled Thomas grew. Almost everyone he saw looked uneasy. They all seemed to be avoiding each other—and not just to be polite. They seemed to take obvious measures to stay clear of anyone else. Just like back at the mall, many of them wore masks or held rags that covered their mouth and nose as they walked.

Posters and signs littered the walls of the buildings, most torn or obscured with spray paint. Some warned of the Flare and spelled out precautions; others talked about the dangers of leaving the cities, or what to do if you came across an infected person. A few had terrifying pictures of Cranks way past the Gone. Thomas spotted one poster with a close-up of a tight-faced woman with her hair pulled back, with the slogan CHANCELLOR PAIGE LOVES YOU across the bottom.

Chancellor Paige. Thomas immediately recognized the name. She was the one Brenda had said they could trust—the only one. He turned to ask Brenda about it, but paused. Something told him to wait until they were alone. As they drove, he noticed posters showing her likeness, but most of them were covered with graffiti. It was hard to tell what the woman really looked like beneath the devil horns and silly mustaches.

Some type of security force patrolled every street in great numbers—there were hundreds of them, all wearing red shirts and gas masks, a weapon in one hand and in the other a smaller version of the viral testing device Thomas and his friends had looked into before entering the city. The farther they got from the outside barrier wall, the dirtier the streets became. Trash was everywhere, windows were broken and graffiti decorated almost every wall. And despite the sun glinting off windows high above, a darkness had settled over the place.

The cab turned in to an alley, and Thomas was surprised to see that it was deserted. The cab pulled up and stopped at a cement building that rose at least twenty stories high, and the driver popped Jorge's card out of the slot and handed it back to him, which Thomas took as his sign to exit the car.

Once they were all out and the cab had driven away, Jorge pointed to the closest staircase. "Number 2792 is right there, on the second floor."

Minho whistled, then said, "Looks real homey."

Thomas agreed. The place was far from inviting, and the drab gray bricks covered in graffiti made him nervous. He didn't want to walk up those steps and find out who was waiting inside.

Brenda gave him a push from behind. "Your idea, you lead."

He swallowed hard but didn't say anything, just walked over to the stairs and slowly climbed them, the other three falling in behind. The cracked and warped wooden door of apartment 2792 looked like it had been put there a thousand years ago, only a few scant remnants of faded green paint remaining.

"This is crazy," Jorge whispered. "This is completely crazy."

Minho snorted. "Thomas kicked the klunk out of him once, he can do it again."

"Unless he comes out with guns blazing," Jorge countered.

"Would you guys shut up?" Thomas said—his nerves were shot. Without another word he reached out and knocked on the door. A few agonizing seconds later it opened.

Thomas could tell immediately that the black-haired kid who answered was Gally from the Glade. No doubt about it. But his face was badly scarred, covered in raised lines like thin white slugs. His right eye looked permanently swollen, and his nose, which had been big and slightly deformed *before* the Chuck incident, was markedly crooked.

"Glad you came," Gally said in his raspy voice. "Because the end of the world is upon us."

CHAPTER 25

Gally stepped back and opened the door wider. "Come in."

Thomas felt a rush of guilt at seeing what he'd done to Gally. He had no idea how to act or what to say. He just nodded and forced himself to enter the apartment.

It was a dark but tidy room with no furniture, and it smelled like bacon. A yellow blanket had been hung over the large window, giving the place an eerie glow.

"Have a seat," Gally said.

All Thomas could think of was finding out how the Right Arm had known he was in Denver and what they wanted, but instinct told him he had to play by their rules before he could get answers. They sat down on the bare floor, he and his friends in a line with Gally facing them like a judge. Gally's face looked awful in the dim light, and his swollen right eye was bloodshot.

"You know Minho," Thomas said awkwardly. Minho and Gally gave each other a curt nod. "This is Brenda and Jorge. They're from WICKED but—"

"I know who they are," Gally interrupted. He didn't sound mad, just kind of numb. "Those shucks at WICKED gave me my past back. Without asking, I might add." His gaze focused on Minho. "Hey, you were real nice to me in our last Gathering. Thanks for that." The sarcasm was thick.

Thomas shrank at the memory—Minho throwing Gally to the floor, threatening him. He'd forgotten about it.

"I'd had a bad day," Minho responded, his expression making it impossible to tell if he was serious or even the tiniest bit sorry.

"Yeah, well," Gally said. "Let bygones be bygones, right?" His snicker made it clear he meant anything but.

Minho might not have had regrets, but Thomas did. "I'm sorry about what I did, Gally." He held the other boy's gaze with his own as he said it. He wanted Gally to believe him, to know that he understood that WICKED was their shared enemy.

"*You're* sorry? I killed Chuck. He's dead. Because of me."

Hearing him say that brought Thomas no relief, only sadness.

"It wasn't your fault," Brenda said, her tone soothing.

"That's a bunch of klunk," Gally said stiffly. "If I had any kind of guts I could've stopped them from controlling me. But I let them do it to me 'cause I thought I'd be killing Thomas, not Chuck. Not in a million years would I have let myself murder that poor kid."

"How generous of you," Minho said.

"So you wanted me dead?" Thomas asked, surprised at the boy's honesty.

Gally scoffed. "Don't get all whiny on me. I hated you more than I'd ever hated anybody in my life. But what happened in the past doesn't matter one lick anymore. We need to talk about the future. About the end of the world."

"Wait a second there, *muchacho,*" Jorge said. "First off, you're going to tell us every little thing that's happened since you got shipped out of WICKED till you ended up sitting right where you're sitting."

"I wanna know how you knew we were coming," Minho added. "And when. And who was that weird dude who delivered the message to us?"

Gally snickered again, which actually made his face look even scarier. "I guess being with WICKED doesn't exactly fill someone with trust, now, does it."

"They're right," Thomas said. "You've got to tell us what's going on. Especially if you want our help."

"Your *help*?" Gally asked. "I don't know if I'd put it that way. But I'm sure we have the same goals."

"Listen," Thomas said. "We need a reason to trust you. Just talk."

After a long pause, Gally began. "The guy who gave you the note is named Richard. He's a member of a group called the Right Arm. They have people in every city and town left on this crappy planet. Their whole mission is to bring down our old friends—to use WICKED's money and influence for things that actually matter—but they don't have the resources to disrupt an organization so huge and powerful. They want to act, but they're still missing some information."

"We've heard of them," Brenda said. "But how'd you get involved?"

"They have a couple of spies in the main complex at WICKED, and they got to me, explained how if I faked going crazy, I'd be sent away. I would've done anything to get out of that place. Anyway, the Right Arm wanted an insider who knew about how the building functions, the security systems, that kind of klunk. So they attacked my escort car and took me. Brought me here. As for how I knew you were coming, we got an anonymous message over the Netblock. I assumed you guys sent it."

Thomas looked to Brenda for an explanation, but all he got from her was a shrug.

"So it wasn't you," Gally said. "Then maybe it was someone at headquarters sending out an alert, trying to set up bounty hunters or whatever. Point is, once we knew about it, from there it was just a matter of hacking into the airport system to see where a Berg had shown up."

"And you brought us here to talk about taking down WICKED?"

Thomas asked. Even the remote possibility of such a thing filled him with hope.

Gally nodded slowly and deliberately before he spoke. "You make it sound so easy. But yeah, that's about the gist of it. We've got two big problems on our hands, though."

Brenda was clearly impatient. "What? Just let it out."

"Slim it, girl."

"What problems?" Thomas pushed.

Gally shot Brenda a glare, then looked back at Thomas. "First of all, word is that the Flare is running rampant through this whole shuck city and that all kinds of corruption is going on to hide it because the ones who are sick are government bigwigs. They're hiding the virus with the Bliss—it slows down the Flare so people who have it can blend in with everyone else, but the virus keeps spreading. My guess is it's the same all over the world. There's just no way to keep that beast out."

Thomas felt a fear in his gut. The idea of a world overwhelmed by hordes of Cranks was terrifying. He couldn't imagine how truly awful things could get—being immune wouldn't amount to much when that happened.

"What's the other problem?" Minho asked. "As if that one wasn't bad enough."

"People like us."

"People like us?" Brenda repeated, a confused look on her face. "You mean Immunes?"

"Yeah." Gally leaned forward. "They're disappearing. Being kidnapped or running away, vanishing into thin air—no one knows. A little birdie told me that they're being gathered and sold to WICKED so they can continue the Trials. Start all over if they have to. Whether that's true or not, the population of immune people in this city and others has been halved in the last six months, and most of them are disappearing without a trace. It's causing a lot of headaches. The city needs them more than people even realize."

Thomas's anxiety went up a notch. "Don't most people hate the Munies—isn't that what they call us? Maybe they're being killed or something." He hated the other possibility that was occurring to him: that WICKED might be kidnapping them and putting them through exactly what he'd been through.

"I doubt that," Gally said. "My little birdie is a reliable source, and this reeks of WICKED to the core. These problems make a bad combination. The Flare is all over the city even though the government claims it's not. And the Immunes are disappearing. Whatever's happening, there isn't gonna be anyone left in Denver. Who knows about other cities."

"So what does this have to do with us?" Jorge asked.

Gally looked surprised. "What, you don't care that civilization is about to come to an end? The cities are crumbling. Pretty soon it's just going to be a world of psychos who want to eat you for supper."

"Of course we care," Thomas answered. "But what do you want us to do about it?"

"Hey, all I know is that WICKED has one directive—to find a cure. And it's pretty obvious that's never gonna happen. If we had their money, their resources, we could use it to *really* help. To protect the healthy. I thought you'd want that."

Thomas did, of course. Desperately.

Gally shrugged when no one responded. "We don't have much to lose. We might as well try something."

"Gally," Thomas said, "do you know anything about Teresa and a bunch of other people who also escaped today?"

Gally nodded. "Yeah, we found them, too—gave them the same message I'm giving you. Who did you think my little birdie was?"

"Teresa," Thomas whispered. A flash of hope sparked within him—

she must have remembered all that stuff about WICKED when they'd removed the Swipe. Could the operation have made her change her tune? Was her insistence that "WICKED is good" finally a thing of the past?

"That's right. She said she couldn't agree with them starting the cycle all over again. Said something about hoping to find you, too. But there's one more thing."

Thomas groaned. "That doesn't sound so good."

Gally shrugged. "Never does these days. One of our people out looking for your group came across a strange rumor. Said it was somehow related to all these people escaping from the WICKED headquarters. I'm not sure if they could track you or not, but it looks like they probably could've guessed you'd come to Denver anyway."

"Why?" Thomas asked. "What's the rumor?"

"There's a huge bounty out for a guy named Hans who used to work there, lives here now. WICKED thinks you came here for him, and they want him dead."

CHAPTER 26

Brenda stood up. "We're leaving. Now. Come on."

Jorge and Minho got to their feet, and as Thomas joined them, he knew Brenda had been right earlier. Finding Hans had to be priority one now. He had to get the tracking device out of his head and, if they were after Hans, they had to get to him first. "Gally, do you swear everything you told us is true?"

"Every bit." The Glader hadn't moved from his position on the floor. "The Right Arm wants to take action. They're planning something even as we speak. They need information about WICKED, though, and who better to help us than you? If we can get Teresa and the others, too, that'd be even better. We need every warm body we can get."

Thomas decided to trust Gally. Maybe they'd never liked each other, but they had the same enemy, which put them on the same team. "What do we do if we want in?" he finally asked. "Do we come back here? Go somewhere else?"

Gally smiled. "Come back here. Any time before nine or so in the morning, for another week. I should be around. I don't think we'll make any moves before then."

"Moves?" Thomas was itching with curiosity.

"I've told you enough. You want more, you come back. I'll be here."

Thomas nodded, then held out a hand. Gally shook it.

"I don't blame you for anything," Thomas said. "You saw what I'd done for WICKED when you went through the Changing. I wouldn't have trusted me, either. And I know you didn't want to kill Chuck. Just don't plan on hugs every time I see you."

"The feeling's mutual."

Brenda was already at the door waiting for him when he turned to go. Before Thomas left, though, Gally squeezed his elbow. "Time's running out. But we can do something."

"We'll be back," Thomas said, then followed his friends. Fear of the unknown no longer controlled him. Hope had found its way in and taken hold.

They didn't find Hans until the next day.

Jorge got them into a cheap motel after they'd purchased some clothes and food, and Thomas and Minho used the room's computer to search the Netblock while Jorge and Brenda made dozens of calls to people Thomas had never heard of. After hours of work, they finally found an address through someone Jorge called "a friend of a friend of an enemy's enemy." By that time it was late and they all crashed for the night; Thomas and Minho were stuck sleeping on the floor while the other two got the twin beds.

The next morning they showered, ate, and put on their new clothes. Then they got a cab and went straight to the place they'd been told Hans lived—an apartment building in only slightly better shape than Gally's. They climbed to the fourth floor and knocked on a gray metal door. The lady who answered kept saying she'd never heard of any Hans, but Jorge kept pushing. Then a gray-haired man with a wide jaw peeked over the woman's shoulder.

"Let them in," he said in a gravelly voice.

A minute or so later, Thomas and his three friends were sitting around a rickety table in the kitchen, all their focus on the gruffly distant man named Hans.

"It's good to see you're okay, Brenda," he said. "You, too, Jorge. But I'm not in the mood to catch up. Why don't you just tell me what you want."

"I think you know the main reason we're here," Brenda replied, then nodded toward Thomas and Minho. "But we also just heard that WICKED has put a bounty on your head. We need to hurry and do this, and then you need to get out of here."

Hans seemed to shrug off that last part, looking at his two potential customers. "You've still got the implants, do ya?"

Thomas nodded, nervous but determined to get this over with. "I only want the controlling device out. I don't want my memories back. And I want to know how this operation works first."

Hans wrinkled his face in disgust. "What kind of nonsense is this? Who's this weak-kneed coward you brought to my place, Brenda?"

"I'm not a coward," Thomas said before she could respond. "I've just had too many people in my head."

Hans threw up his hands, then slapped the table. "Who said I'd do anything to your head? Who said I liked you enough for that?"

"Are there any nice people in Denver?" Minho muttered.

"You folks are about three seconds from being thrown out of my apartment."

"Everyone just shut up for a second!" Brenda shouted. She leaned toward Hans and spoke in a quieter voice. "Listen, this is important. *Thomas* is important, and WICKED will do just about anything to get their hands on him. We can't risk them getting close enough to start controlling him or Minho."

Hans glared at Thomas, scrutinized him like a scientist examining a specimen. "Doesn't look important to me." He shook his head and stood up. "Give me five minutes to prep," he said, then disappeared through a side door without further explanation. Thomas could only wonder if the man recognized him. If he knew what Thomas had done for WICKED before the Maze.

Brenda sat back in her chair and let out a sigh. "That wasn't so bad."

Yeah, Thomas thought, *the bad part's coming up.* He was relieved that Hans was going to help them, but as he looked around he got more and more nervous. He was about to let a stranger mess with his brain in a dirty old apartment.

Minho snickered. "You look scared, Tommy."

"Don't forget, *muchacho,*" Jorge said. "You're doing this, too. That gray-haired grandpa said five minutes, so get ready."

"The sooner, the better," Minho replied.

Thomas rested his elbows on the table, his head—which had begun to throb—in his hands.

"Thomas?" Brenda whispered. "You okay?"

He looked up. "I just need to—"

The words caught in his throat as a sharp pain sliced down his spine. But just as quickly as it had come, it was gone. He sat up in the chair, startled; then a spasm sent his arms out straight and his legs kicked, twisting his body so that he slid off the chair and collapsed to the floor, shaking. He yelled when his back slammed into the hard tile, and struggled to get control of his jerking limbs. But he couldn't. His feet slapped the floor; his shins banged against the legs of the table.

"Thomas!" Brenda yelled. "What's wrong?"

Despite his loss of bodily control, Thomas's mind was clear. He could see out of the corner of his eye that Minho was next to him on the ground trying to calm him and Jorge was frozen in place, eyes wide.

Thomas tried to speak, but only drool came out of his mouth.

"Can you hear me?" Brenda yelled, bending over him. "Thomas, what's wrong!"

Then his limbs abruptly stilled, legs straightening and coming to a rest, his arms falling limp at his sides. He couldn't make them move. He strained with the effort, but nothing happened. He tried to speak again, but no words formed.

Brenda's expression changed to something close to horror. "Thomas?"

He didn't know how, but his body started moving even though he wasn't telling it to. His arms and legs shifted, he was getting to his feet. It was as if he'd become a puppet. He tried to scream but couldn't.

"You okay?" Minho asked.

Panic clenched inside Thomas as he kept doing things against his will. His head twitched, then turned toward the door through which their host had disappeared. Words started spilling from his mouth, but he had no idea where they came from.

"I can't . . . let you . . . do this."

CHAPTER 27

Thomas fought desperately against it, straining to get control of his muscles. But something foreign had taken over his body.

"Thomas, they've got you!" Brenda yelled. "Fight it!"

He watched helplessly as his own hand pushed her face away, sent her tumbling to the floor.

Jorge moved to protect her but Thomas reached out and punched him in the chin with a quick jab. Jorge's head snapped back; a little spray of blood shot from his lip.

Again the words were forced from Thomas's mouth. "I can't . . . let you . . . do this!" By that time he was screaming, the effort hurting his throat. It was like his brain had been programmed with that one sentence and he couldn't say anything else.

Brenda had gotten back to her feet. Minho stood dazed, his face a mask of confusion. Jorge was wiping the blood off his chin, his eyes lit with anger.

And a memory bubbled up in Thomas. Something about a fail-safe programmed into his implant to prevent it from being removed. He wanted to shout at his friends, tell them to sedate him. But he couldn't. He started moving toward the door in lurching steps, shoving Minho out of the way. As he half stumbled past the kitchen counter, his hand reached out and grabbed a knife sitting by the sink. He gripped the handle, and the harder he tried to drop it, the more tightly his fingers clenched.

"Thomas!" Minho shouted, finally breaking out of his stupor. "Fight it, man! Get those shuck people out of your head!"

Thomas turned to face him, held the knife up. He hated himself for being so weak, for not being able to master his own body. Once again he tried to speak—but nothing. All his body would do now was whatever it took to prevent his implant from being removed.

"You gonna kill me, slinthead?" Minho asked. "Gonna throw that thing just like Gally did to Chuck? Do it, then. Throw it."

For one second Thomas was terrified that that was exactly what he'd do, but instead his body turned back around to face the opposite direction. Just as he did, Hans came through the doorway, and his eyes widened. Thomas guessed Hans was his main target—that the fail-safe would attack whoever was attempting to remove his implant.

"What the hell is this?" Hans asked.

"I can't ... let you ... do this," Thomas replied.

"I was worried about this," Hans murmured. He turned to the group. "You guys get over here and help!"

Thomas pictured the internal workings of the mechanism in his brain as minuscule instruments operated by minuscule spiders. He fought them, clenched his teeth. But his arm started to rise, the knife gripped tightly in his balled fist.

"I ca—" Before he could finish, someone slammed into him from behind, knocking the knife from his hand. He crashed to the floor and twisted to see Minho.

"I'm not letting you kill anybody," his friend said.

"Get off me!" Thomas yelled, not sure if they were his own words or WICKED's.

But Minho had pinned Thomas's arms to the ground. He hovered over him, heaving to catch his breath. "I'm not getting up until they let your mind go."

Thomas wanted to smile—but his face couldn't follow even a simple command. He felt the tension in every single muscle.

"It won't stop until Hans fixes him," Brenda said. "Hans?"

The older man knelt down next to Thomas and Minho. "I can't believe I ever worked for those people. For *you*." He almost spat the word, looking directly at Thomas.

Thomas watched all this, powerless. His insides boiled with the desire to relax—to help Hans do what he needed to do. Then something ignited inside him, making his midsection arch upward. His body bucked and fought to free his arms. Minho pressed down, tried to get his legs in position to sit on Thomas's back. But whatever was controlling Thomas seemed to release adrenaline inside him; his strength overcame Minho's and he threw the boy off.

Thomas was on his feet in an instant. He grabbed the knife off the floor and dove toward Hans, lashing out with the blade. The man deflected it with his forearm, a red gash appearing there as the two of them collided and rolled across the floor, struggling against each other. Thomas did everything he could to stop himself, but the knife kept slashing as Hans kept dodging it.

"Get him!" Brenda yelled from somewhere close.

Thomas saw hands appear, felt them grabbing his arms. Somebody gripped him by the hair and yanked back. Thomas screamed in agony, then slashed blindly with the knife. Relief flooded through him—Jorge and Minho were gaining control, pulling him off Hans. Thomas crashed onto his back and the knife was knocked from his grip; he heard it clatter across the floor as someone kicked it to the far side of the kitchen.

"I can't let you do this!" Thomas yelled. He hated himself even though he knew he had no control.

"Shut up!" Minho shouted back, now in his face as he and Jorge fought against Thomas's attempts to get free. "You're crazy, dude! They're making you crazy!"

Thomas desperately wanted to tell Minho that he was right—Thomas didn't really believe what he was saying.

Minho turned and yelled at Hans. "Let's get that thing out of his head!"

"No!" Thomas shouted. "No!" He twisted and flailed his arms, battled them with ferocious strength. But the four of them proved too much. Somehow they ended up with one person holding tightly to each of his limbs. They lifted him from the floor, carried him out of the kitchen into a short hallway and down its length as he kicked and squirmed, knocking several framed pictures off the walls. The sound of shattering glass followed them.

Thomas screamed once, then again, over and over. He had no more strength to resist the internal forces—his body fought against Minho and the others; he said whatever WICKED wanted him to. He'd given up.

"In here!" Hans shouted over him.

They entered a small, cramped lab with two instrument-filled tables and a bed. A crude-looking version of the mask they'd seen back at WICKED hung over the empty mattress.

"Get him on the bed!" Hans yelled. They slammed Thomas down onto his back, where he continued to struggle. "Get this leg for me—I need to knock him out."

Minho, who had been holding the other leg, now grabbed both legs and used his body to press them against the bed. Thomas's thoughts immediately went back to when he and Newt had done this same thing to Alby when he'd woken up from the Changing back in the Glade Homestead.

There was the clatter and clanging of Hans going through a drawer, searching for something; then he was back.

"Hold him as still as possible!"

Thomas erupted in one last flurry of effort to get free, screaming at the top of his lungs. An arm sprang loose from Brenda's grip and he smacked Jorge in the face with his fist.

"Stop it!" Brenda yelled as she reached for it.

Thomas arched his torso again. "I can't . . . let you do this!" He had never felt such frustration.

"Hold him still, dammit!" Hans shouted.

Somehow Brenda got his arm again, leaned against it with her upper body.

Thomas felt a sharp prick in his leg. It was such an odd thing to be fighting against something so violently and yet wanting it to happen so completely.

When the darkness started to take him and his body stilled, he finally regained control of himself. At the very last second he said, "I hate those shucks." And then he was out.

CHAPTER 28

Lost in the dark haze of drugs, Thomas dreamed.

He is fifteen years old, sitting on a bed. The room is dark except for the amber glow of a lamp on the desk. Teresa is there—she has pulled a chair out and is sitting close to him. Her face is haunted—a mask of misery.

"We had to do this," she says quietly.

Thomas is there but isn't there. He doesn't remember the details of what happened, but he knows his insides feel like rot and filth. He and Teresa have done something horrible, but his dreaming self can't quite grasp what it was. A ghastly thing that is no less repulsive because they were told to do it by the people they did it to.

"We had to do it," she repeats.

"I know," Thomas responds in a voice that sounds as dead as dust.

Two words pop into his head: *the Purge*. The wall blocking him from the memory thins for a moment and a dreadful fact looms on the other side.

Teresa starts talking again. "They wanted it to end this way, Tom. Better to die than spend years going crazier and crazier. They're gone now. We had no choice, and no better way to make it happen. It's done and that's that. We need to get the new people trained and keep the Trials going. We've come too far to let it fall apart."

For a moment Thomas hates her, but it's fleeting. He knows she's trying to be strong. "That doesn't mean I have to like it." And he doesn't. He has never hated himself with such intensity before.

Teresa nods but says nothing.

The dreaming Thomas tries to invade the mind of his younger self, explore the memories in that unfettered space. The original Creators, Flare-infected, purged and dead. Countless volunteers to take their place. The two ongoing Maze Trials, running strong over a year in, with more results every day. The slowly but surely building blueprint. Training for the replacements.

It's all there for the taking. For the *remembering*. But then he changes his mind, turns his back on it all. The past is the past. There is only the future now.

He sinks into a dark oblivion.

Thomas woke up groggy and with a dull ache behind his eyes. The dream still throbbed in his skull like a pulse, though its details had grown fuzzy. He knew enough about the Purge, about its being the shift from the original Creators to their replacements. He and Teresa had had to exterminate the entire staff after an outbreak—they'd had no choice, were the only ones left who were immune. He swore to never think about it again.

Minho was sitting in a chair nearby, his head lolling as he snored in fitful sleep.

"Minho," Thomas whispered. "Hey. Minho. Wake up."

"Huh?" Minho opened his eyes slowly and coughed. "What? What's going on?"

"Nothing. I just want to know what happened. Did Hans get the thing switched off? Are we fixed?"

Minho nodded through a big yawn. "Yeah—both of us. At least, he said he did. Man, you wigged out big-time. You remember all that?"

"Of course I do." A wave of embarrassment made his face flush hot. "But it was like I was paralyzed or something. I kept trying, but I couldn't stop whatever was controlling me."

"Dude, you tried to slice my you-know-whats off!"

Thomas laughed, something he hadn't done in a long time. He welcomed it happily. "Too bad I didn't. Could've saved the world from future little Minhos."

"Just remember you owe me one."

"Good that." He owed them all.

Brenda, Jorge, and Hans walked in, all three of them looking serious, and the smile fell from Thomas's face.

"Gally stop by and give you guys another pep talk?" Thomas asked, forcing a lighthearted tone to his voice. "You look downright depressed."

"When did you get so cheerful, *muchacho*?" Jorge responded. "A few hours ago you were stabbing at us with a knife."

Thomas opened his mouth to apologize—to explain—but Hans shushed him. He leaned over the bed and flashed a little light into both of Thomas's eyes. "Looks like your head's clearing up pretty well. The pain should be gone soon—your operation was a little worse because of that fail-safe."

Thomas turned his attention to Brenda. "Is it fixed?"

"It worked," she said. "Judging from the fact that you're not trying to kill us anymore, it's deactivated. And . . ."

"And what?"

"Well, you shouldn't be able to talk to or hear from Teresa or Aris again."

Thomas might've felt a pang of sadness at that even the day before, but now he felt only relief. "Suits me fine. Any sign of trouble yet?"

She shook her head. "No, but they can't take any chances—Hans and his wife are going to leave, but he wanted to tell you something first."

Hans had stepped back to stand by the wall, probably to give them a little space. He came forward now, his eyes downcast. "I wish I could go with you and help, but I have a wife, and she's my family. She's my first concern. I wanted to wish you luck. I hope you can do what I don't have the courage to try."

Thomas nodded. The change in the man's attitude was marked— maybe the recent incident had reminded him of what WICKED was capable of. "Thanks. And if we can stop WICKED, we'll come back for you."

"We'll see about that," Hans murmured. "We'll see about a lot of things."

Hans turned and walked back to his position by the wall. Thomas was sure that the man carried around many dark memories in his mind.

"What next?" Brenda asked.

Thomas knew they didn't have time to rest. And his mind was set on what they needed to do. "We find our other friends, convince them to join us. Then we go back to Gally. The only thing I've accomplished in life is to help set up an experiment that failed and tormented a bunch of kids. It's time to add something else to that list. We're going to stop the entire operation before they do it to new Immunes all over again."

Jorge spoke for the first time in a while. "We? What're you saying, *hermano*?"

Thomas shifted his gaze to the man, his resolve solidifying. "We have to help the Right Arm."

No one said anything.

"Okay," Minho finally said. "But first let's get something to eat."

CHAPTER 29

They went to a coffee shop nearby, recommended by Hans and his wife.

Thomas had never been in such a place before. At least, not that he remembered. Customers lined up at the counter, getting coffee and pastries, then heading for a table or back out the door. He watched as a nervous older woman kept lifting her surgical mask to sip her hot drink. One of those red-shirted guards stood at the door, randomly testing people for the Flare with his handheld device every couple of minutes or so; an odd metal apparatus covered his own mouth and nose.

Thomas sat with Minho and Brenda at a table in the back corner while Jorge went to get food and drinks. Thomas's eyes kept coming back to a man, maybe thirty-five or forty years old, who sat at a nearby bench in front of a large window onto the street. He hadn't touched his coffee since Thomas and his friends had arrived, and steam no longer rose from the cup. The man just hunched over, elbows on knees, hands loosely clasped, staring at a spot on the other side of the shop.

There was something disturbing about the look on his face. Blank. His eyes were almost floating in their sockets, and yet there was a hint of pleasure there. When Thomas pointed it out to Brenda, she whispered that the guy was probably on the Bliss and would be jailed if he got caught. It gave Thomas the willies. He hoped the man would leave soon.

Jorge returned with sandwiches and steaming cups of coffee and the four of them ate and drank in silence. Thomas knew they all realized the urgency of their situation, but he was grateful to rest and get some strength back.

They finished up and were getting ready to leave, but Brenda remained in her seat. "Would you guys mind waiting outside for a few minutes?" she asked. Her look made it obvious that she meant Jorge and Minho.

"Excuse me?" Minho responded, his tone exasperated. "More secrets?"

"*No*. Nothing like that. I promise. I just need a moment. I want to tell Thomas something."

Thomas was surprised but curious. He sat back down. "Just go," he said, addressing Minho. "You know I won't keep anything from you. And she knows it, too."

His friend grumbled, but finally went with Jorge, and the two of them stood out on the sidewalk near the closest window. Minho flashed Thomas a goofy grin and waved, his sarcasm making it obvious he wasn't exactly happy. Thomas waved back, then focused on Brenda.

"So? What's this all about?" he asked.

"I know we need to hurry, so I'll be really quick. We haven't had time to be alone, and I just want to make sure you know that what happened in the Scorch wasn't an act. I was there on a job, I was there to help things play out, but I *did* grow close to you and it *did* change me. And there are a few things I think you deserve to know. About me, about Chancellor Paige, about—"

Thomas held his hand up to cut her off. "Please just stop."

She pulled back, a look of surprise on her face. "What? Why?"

"I don't *want* to know anything. Not one more thing. All I care about is what we're going to do from here out, not stuff about my past or yours or WICKED's. Nothing. And we need to move."

"But—"

"No, Brenda. I mean it. We're here and we have a goal and that's all we need to focus on. No more talking."

She held his gaze without saying anything, then looked down at her hands resting on the table. "Then all I'll say is I know you're doing the right thing, going in the right direction. And I'll keep helping as best I can."

Thomas hoped he hadn't hurt her feelings, but he meant what he'd said. It was time to let go, even though she was obviously itching to tell him something. As he searched for a response, his eyes wandered back to the odd man on the bench. He'd pulled something Thomas couldn't see out of his pocket and was pressing it against the crook of his right elbow. He closed his eyes in a long blink, looking a little dazed when they opened again. His head slowly drifted backward until it rested on the window.

The red-shirted Flare tester stepped into the café and Thomas leaned over to get a better look. Red Shirt walked toward the bench where the drugged-out man was still resting peacefully. A short woman moved along next to the tester, whispering into his ear and fidgeting nervously.

"Thomas?" Brenda asked.

He put a finger to his lips, then nodded toward the potential confrontation. She turned in her seat to see what was going on.

Red Shirt kicked the toe of the guy on the bench, who flinched and looked up. The men started exchanging words, but Thomas couldn't hear what they were saying over the bustle and buzz of the crowded coffee shop. The man who'd been relaxing there suddenly looked scared.

Brenda turned back to Thomas. "We need to get out of here. Now."

"Why?" The air seemed to have thickened, and Thomas was curious about what was going to happen.

Brenda was already standing. "Just come on!"

She turned and walked briskly toward the exit, and Thomas finally moved to follow her. He'd just risen from his chair when Red Shirt pulled out a gun and pointed it at the man on the bench, then leaned in to place his testing device on the man's face. But the man swatted it away and rushed forward, tackling the tester. Thomas stared, frozen in shock, as the gun skittered away and disappeared under a counter. The two men crashed into a table and slammed to the floor.

Red Shirt started yelling; his voice sounded almost robotic coming through the protective metal mask covering his mouth and nose. "We've got an infected! Everyone evacuate the building!"

The place turned into pandemonium, screams filling the air as everyone fled toward the only exit.

CHAPTER 30

Thomas wished he hadn't hesitated. He should've run when he'd had the chance. A pack of bodies pressed forward, blocking the door. Brenda wouldn't have been able to come back even if she'd tried. Thomas was stuck at the table, watching in stunned silence as the two men struggled on the floor, punching and grabbing and trying to gain the advantage.

Thomas realized that though it was possible he could get hurt by the fleeing crowd, he really had nothing to worry about. He was immune. The rest of the people in the shop had freaked out knowing the virus was so close. And understandably—odds were at least one of them had caught it. But as long as he could stay out of the way of the commotion, he was probably safe right where he was.

Someone pounded on the window and Thomas turned to see Brenda next to Minho and Jorge on the sidewalk—she was motioning frantically for him to get out. But Thomas wanted to watch what was happening.

Red Shirt had finally pinned the man to the ground. "It's over! They're already on their way," he shouted, again in that creepy mechanized voice.

The infected man stopped struggling, burst into lurching sobs. It was then that Thomas realized the crowd had fully evacuated and the coffee shop was empty except for the two men and Thomas. An eerie silence settled on the place.

Red Shirt glanced at him. "Why're you still here, kid—got a death wish?" The man didn't let Thomas answer, though. "If you're gonna stick around, make yourself useful. Find me the gun." He turned his attention back to the man he'd restrained.

Thomas felt like he was in a dream. He'd seen a lot of violence, but this was different somehow. He went to fetch the gun from under the counter where it had disappeared. "I'm . . . I'm immune," he stammered. He got down on his knees and reached, straining until his fingers found the cool metal. He pulled the gun out and walked over to Red Shirt.

The man didn't offer any thanks. He took his gun and jumped back to his feet, pointing the weapon at the infected man's face. "This is bad, really bad. Been happening more and more—you can tell when someone's drugged out on the Bliss."

"So it *was* the Bliss," Thomas murmured.

"You knew?" Red Shirt asked.

"Well, he's looked weird ever since I got here."

"And you didn't say anything?" The skin around the guard's mask almost matched the color of his shirt. "What's wrong with you?"

Thomas was taken aback by Red Shirt's sudden anger. "I . . . I'm sorry. I didn't really know what was going on."

The infected man had curled up into a ball on the ground and was sobbing. Red Shirt finally stepped away from him and looked sternly at Thomas. "You didn't *know*? What kind of . . . Where are you from?"

Now Thomas *really* wished he had run. "I'm . . . my name's Thomas. I'm nobody. I just . . ." He searched for something to say—to explain himself. "I'm not from around here. Sorry."

Red Shirt turned the gun on him. "Sit down. Sit down right there." He flicked the gun toward a nearby chair.

"Wait! I swear I'm immune!" Thomas's heart thudded in his chest. "That's why I—"

"Sit your butt down! Now!"

Thomas's knees gave out and he plopped into the chair. He glanced toward the door and his chest loosened a bit when he saw Minho standing there, with Brenda and Jorge right behind him. But Thomas didn't want his friends involved—didn't want to chance getting them hurt. He quickly shook his head to tell them to stay out of it.

Red Shirt ignored the people in the doorway, concentrating purely on Thomas. "If you're so sure about being a Munie, then you won't mind testing to prove it, now, will you?"

"No." The idea actually relieved him—maybe the man would let him go once he realized he was telling the truth. "Do it, go ahead."

Red Shirt holstered his gun and stepped up to Thomas. He retrieved his device and leaned forward to put it on Thomas's face.

"Look into it, eyes open," the man said. "It'll only take a few seconds."

Thomas did as he was told, wanting to get it over with as quickly as possible. He saw the same flash of colorful lights he'd seen at the city gates, felt the same puff of air and prick in his neck.

Red Shirt took the device back, looked at the readings on a small screen. "Well, what do ya know? You're a damn Munie after all. You care to explain to me how you came to be in Denver and how you don't know squat about the Bliss or how to spot a user when you see one?"

"I work for WICKED." It came out before he'd really thought it through. He just wanted to get out of there.

"I believe that crap about as much as I believe this guy's drug problem has nothing to do with the Flare. You keep your butt glued right there or I'll start shooting."

Thomas swallowed. He wasn't so much scared as he was mad at himself for having gotten into such a ridiculous situation. "Okay," he said.

But Red Shirt had already turned around. His help had arrived—four people covered from head to toe with a thick green plastic, except for their faces. Their eyes were fitted with big goggles, and beneath those was a mask like the one Red Shirt wore. Images flashed through Thomas's mind, but the one that stuck was the most complete memory— the time he'd been taken from the Scorch after his bullet wound had gotten infected. Everyone on that Berg had been wearing the same type of gear as these four people.

"What in the world?" one of them said, his voice also mechanized. "You caught two of 'em?"

"Not really," Red Shirt replied. "Got us a Munie, thinks he wants to sit around and see the show."

"A Munie?" The other man sounded like he couldn't believe what he'd heard.

"A Munie. He stayed put when everyone else jackrabbited out of here, claims he wanted to see what happened. To make it worse, he says he suspected our future Crank here was on the Bliss and didn't tell anyone, just went on drinking his coffee like all was right with the world."

Everyone looked over at Thomas, but he was speechless. He just shrugged.

Red Shirt stepped back as the four protected workers surrounded the still-sobbing infected man, lying curled up on his side on the ground. One of the newcomers had a thick blue plastic object gripped in both hands. It had an odd nozzle on the end, and the guy was pointing it at the man on the ground as if it were a weapon. Its purpose seemed ominous, and Thomas searched his memory-depleted mind to work out what it could possibly be but came up empty.

"We need you to straighten out your legs, sir," the lead worker said. "Keep your body still, don't move, try to relax."

"I didn't know!" the man wailed. "How was I supposed to know?"

"You knew!" Red Shirt yelled from the side. "No one takes the Bliss just for kicks."

"I like the way it feels!" The pleading in the man's voice made Thomas feel incredibly sorry for him.

"Plenty of cheaper drugs than that. Quit lying and shut your mouth." Red Shirt waved a hand as if swatting a fly. "Who cares. Bag the sucker."

Thomas watched as the infected man curled up even tighter, gripping his legs to his chest with both arms. "It's not fair. I didn't know! Just kick me out of the city. I swear I'll never come back. I swear. I swear!" He broke into another agonizing series of lurching sobs.

"Oh, they'll put you out, all right," Red Shirt said, glancing over at Thomas for some reason. It looked as if he was smiling behind the mask—his eyes shone with something like glee. "Keep watching, Munie. You're gonna like this."

Thomas suddenly hated Red Shirt as much as he'd ever hated anyone. He broke eye contact and returned his focus to the four suited people, now crouching as they inched closer to the poor guy on the floor.

"Straighten out your legs!" one of them repeated. "Or this is gonna hurt something awful. Straighten them. Now!"

"I can't! Please just let me leave!"

Red Shirt stomped over to the man, pushing one of the workers out of the way, then leaned over and placed the end of his gun against the sick man's head. "Straighten your legs, or I'll put a bullet in your brain and make it easier on everybody. Do it!" Thomas couldn't believe the guard's complete lack of compassion.

Whimpering, eyes filled with terror, the infected man slowly let go of his legs and extended them, his whole body shaking as he lay flat on the ground. Red Shirt stepped out of the way, sliding his gun back into its holster.

The person with the odd blue object immediately moved so that he stood behind the man's head, then placed the nozzle so it rested on the crown of his skull, pressing it into his hair.

"Try not to move." It was a woman, and if anything, her voice, filtered through her mask, sounded even creepier to Thomas than the mens'. "Or you'll lose something."

Thomas barely had time to wonder what that meant before she pressed a button and a gel-like substance shot out of the nozzle. It was blue and viscous but moved quickly, spreading over the man's head, then down around his ears and face. He screamed, but the sound was cut off as the gel washed over his mouth, down to his neck and shoulders. The substance hardened as it moved, freezing into a shell-like coating that Thomas could see through. In a matter of seconds, half the infected man's body was rigid, wrapped in a tight sheet of the stuff, which seeped into every crevice of his skin and wrinkle of his clothing.

Thomas noticed that Red Shirt was looking at him, and he finally met the guard's gaze.

"What?" Thomas asked.

"Quite the show, huh?" Red Shirt replied. "Enjoy it while it lasts. When this is over, you're coming with me."

CHAPTER 31

Thomas's heart sank. There was something sadistic in Red Shirt's eyes, and he looked away, focused back on the infected man just as the blue gel reached his feet and solidified around them. The guy now lay completely motionless, wrapped in the hard, plasticky coating. The woman with the gel gun stood up, and Thomas saw that it was now nothing but an empty bag. She folded it up and stuffed it into a pocket in her green coverall.

"Let's get him out of here," she said.

As the four workers reached down and lifted up the infected man, Thomas's eyes flickered back to Red Shirt, who was watching the others carry off their captive. What in the world had he meant that Thomas would be going with him? Where? Why? If the man hadn't had a gun, Thomas would have run.

When the others had made their way out the door, Minho appeared again. He was just about to step inside when Red Shirt pulled out his weapon.

"Stop right there!" the man yelled. "Get out!"

"But we're with him." Minho pointed to Thomas. "And we need to go."

"This one's not going anywhere." He paused, as if something had just occurred to him. He looked at Thomas, then back at Minho. "Wait a second. Are you guys Munies, too?"

148

Panic flared in Thomas, but Minho was fast. He didn't hesitate, just bolted.

"Stop!" Red Shirt yelled, sprinting for the doorway.

Thomas lurched over to the window. He saw Minho, Brenda, and Jorge just as they made it across the street and disappeared around a corner. Red Shirt had stopped right outside the coffee shop; he gave up on the others and came back in. With his gun pointed at Thomas.

"I ought to shoot you in the neck and watch you bleed out for what your little friend just did. Better thank God above that Munies are so valuable, or I'd do it just to make myself feel better. Been a crappy day."

Thomas couldn't believe that after all he'd been through, he was stuck in such a stupid situation. He wasn't scared, only frustrated. "Well, it hasn't been so great for me, either," he muttered.

"You'll bring me a good hunk of cash. That's all there is to it. And just for the record, I don't like you. I can tell by just lookin' at ya."

Thomas smiled. "Yeah, well, the feeling's mutual."

"You're a funny guy. Just full of laughs. We'll see how you feel by the time the sun goes down tonight. Come on." He gestured to the door with his weapon. "And trust me, I'm out of patience. Try anything and I'll shoot you in the back of the head and tell the police that you were acting like an infected and ran. Zero-tolerance policy. Won't even get questioned about it. Not so much as a raised eyebrow."

Thomas stood there, sorting through his options. The irony wasn't lost on him. He'd escaped WICKED only to be held at gunpoint by an average everyday city worker.

"Don't make me say it again," Red Shirt warned.

"Where are we going?"

"You'll find out in time. And I'll be one rich sucker. Now get moving."

Thomas had been shot twice already and knew how badly it hurt. If he didn't want to go through it again, it looked like going with the guy was his only option. He glared at the man, then walked toward the door. When he reached it, he stopped.

"Which way?" Thomas asked.

"Go left. We'll walk nice and easy for about three blocks, then another left. I've got a car waiting for us there. Do I need to warn you again what'll happen if you try something?"

"You'll shoot an unarmed kid in the back of the head. Got it, crystal clear."

"Oh, man, I hate you Munies. Start walking." He pressed the tip of the gun into Thomas's spine and Thomas headed down the street.

They made it to the end of the third block and turned left without saying a word to each other. The air was stifling, and sweat had moistened every last inch of Thomas's body. When he reached up to wipe his forehead, Red Shirt whacked him in the head with the butt of the gun.

"Don't do that," the man said. "I might get nervous and put a hole in your brain."

It took every ounce of Thomas's willpower to stay silent.

The street was abandoned and there was trash everywhere. Posters—some warning about the Flare, others images of Chancellor Paige—covered the lower portion of the buildings' walls, and everything was spray-painted, layer on top of layer, by the looks of it. When they reached an intersection and had to stop to wait for a few passing cars, Thomas focused on an unmarked poster right next to him—a new one, he guessed from its lack of graffiti. He read the words of warning.

Public Service Announcement
!!! Stop the Spread of the Flare !!!
Help stop the spread of the Flare. Know the symptoms before you
infect your neighbors and loved ones.

The Flare is the virus Flarevirus (VC321xb47), a highly contagious,
manmade infectious disease that was accidentally released during the
chaos of the sun flare catastrophe. The Flare causes a progressive,
degenerative illness of the brain, resulting in uncontrolled movements, emotional disturbances and mental deterioration. The result
has been the Flare pandemic.

Scientists are conducting late-stage clinical trials, but there is
no standard treatment for the Flare at this time. The virus is generally
fatal, and can be spread through the air.

At this time citizens must unite to prevent further spread of this
pandemic. By learning how to recognize yourself and others as Viral
Contagion Threats (VCTs) you will take the first step in the battle
against the Flare.*

*Any suspicious subjects should be reported to the authorities immediately.

It went on to talk about a five- to seven-day incubation period and
the symptoms—how such things as irritability and trouble with balance
were early warning signs, followed by dementia, paranoia and severe
aggression later on. Thomas had witnessed them all firsthand, having
crossed paths with Cranks on more than one occasion.

Red Shirt gave Thomas a slight shove and they continued walking.
As they made their way, Thomas couldn't stop thinking about the poster's dire message. The part about the Flare's being manmade not only
haunted him, it tickled something in his brain, a memory he couldn't
quite latch on to. Even though the sign didn't say it outright, he knew

there was something else, and for the first time in a while he wished he could access the past for just a moment.

"It's right up here."

Red Shirt's voice pulled him back to the present. A small white car waited at the end of the block, just a few dozen feet down the street. Thomas desperately tried to think of a way out of this—if he got in that vehicle it might all be over. But could he really risk getting shot?

"You're going to slide nice and easy into the backseat," Red Shirt said. "I've got some cuffs in there, and I'm going to watch you put them on yourself. You think you can handle that without doing something stupid?"

Thomas didn't respond. He hoped desperately that Minho and the others were close, making a plan. He needed someone or something to distract his captor.

They reached the car and Red Shirt pulled out a key card and pressed it to the front passenger window. The locks clicked and he opened the back door, his gun trained on Thomas the whole time.

"Get in. Easy does it."

Thomas hesitated, searching the streets for anyone, anything. The area was deserted, but out of the corner of his eye he noticed movement. A hovering machine almost as large as a car. He spun to look and the cop machine swerved onto the street two blocks down and started heading their way. A humming sound grew louder as it approached.

"I said get in," Red Shirt repeated. "The cuffs are in the console in the middle."

"One of those cop machine things is coming," Thomas said.

"Yeah, so what? It's just patrolling, sees this stuff all the time. The people controlling it are on my side, not yours. Which is tough luck for you, big fella."

Thomas sighed—it had been worth a shot. Where were his friends?

He scanned the area one last time, then stepped up to the open door and slipped inside. Just as he looked up at Red Shirt the air filled with the sound of heavy gunfire. Then Red Shirt was stumbling backward, jerking and twitching. Bullets tore into his chest, sparks flying as they hit the metal mask. He dropped his gun, and his mask fell off as he slammed into the wall of the closest building. Thomas watched in stunned horror as the man slumped onto his side.

Then it stopped. Thomas was frozen, wondering if he'd be shot next. He heard the steady hum of the machine as it hovered just outside his open door, and he realized that it had been the source of the attack. The things were unmanned but heavily armed. A familiar voice rang out from a speaker on its roof.

"Get out of the car, Thomas."

Thomas shivered. He would know that voice anywhere.

It was Janson. The Rat Man.

CHAPTER 32

Thomas couldn't have been more surprised. He hesitated at first but quickly scooted out of the car. The cop machine hovered only a few feet away. A panel had opened on its side, revealing a screen from which Janson's face stared back at him.

Relief flooded him. It *was* Rat Man, but he wasn't in the cop machine—there was just a video feed of his image. Thomas could only assume that the man could see him as well. "What happened?" he asked, still stunned. He tried to avert his eyes from the man now lying on the ground. "How'd you find me?"

Janson was as grim-faced as ever. "It took a considerable amount of effort and luck, trust me. And you're welcome. I just saved you from this bounty hunter."

Thomas let out a laugh. "You're the ones paying them anyway. What do you want?"

"Thomas, I'm going to be frank with you. The only reason we haven't come to Denver to retrieve you is because the infection rate is astronomical. This was our safest means of contacting you. I'm urging you to bring yourself in and complete the testing."

Thomas wanted to scream at the man. Why would he return to WICKED? But the Red Shirt's attack—his body only feet away—was too clear in his mind. He had to play this right. "Why would I come back?"

Janson's expression was blank. "We've been using our data to select a Final Candidate, and you're the one. We need you, Thomas. It all rests on your shoulders."

Not in a million years, Thomas thought. But saying that wouldn't get rid of the Rat Man. Instead he cocked his head and pretended to consider, then said, "I'll think about it."

"I trust you will." The Rat Man paused. "There's something I feel obligated to tell you. Mainly because I think it will influence your decision. Make you realize that you have to do what we're asking."

Thomas had leaned back against the rounded hood of the car—the whole ordeal had exhausted him emotionally and physically. "What?"

The Rat Man's face screwed up to look even rattier, as if he reveled in telling bad news. "It's about your friend, Newt. I'm afraid he's in a tremendous amount of trouble."

"What kind of trouble?" Thomas asked, his stomach dropping.

"I know you're well aware that he has the Flare, and that you've already seen some of its effects taking place."

Thomas nodded, suddenly remembering the note in his pocket. "Yeah."

"Well, he seems to be succumbing to it rapidly. The fact that you were already seeing symptoms of anger and loss of concentration before you left means he'll be spiraling into madness very soon."

Thomas felt a fist clutch his heart. He'd accepted that Newt wasn't immune, but he'd thought it would take weeks, or months even, before it got really bad. Yet Janson had made sense—that the stress of everything seemed to be making Newt fall fast. And they'd left him all alone outside the city.

"You could very well save him," Janson said quietly.

"You enjoying this?" Thomas asked. "Because sometimes it seems like you enjoy it a lot."

Janson shook his head. "I'm just doing my job, Thomas. I want this cure more than anyone else. Except for you, maybe, before we took away your memories."

"Just go," Thomas said.

"I hope you'll come," Janson replied. "You have a chance to do great things. I'm sorry for our differences. But Thomas, you need to hurry. Time is running out."

"I'll think about it." Thomas forced himself to say it again. It made him sick to pacify the Rat Man, but it was the only thing he could think to say to buy himself time. And there was the possibility that if he didn't stall Janson, he could end up like Red Shirt—shot down by this cop machine hovering a few feet in front of him.

Janson smiled. "That's all I can ask for. I hope to see you here."

The screen blacked out and the panel closed; then the cop machine rose into the air and flew away, its hum slowly fading. Thomas watched until it disappeared around a corner. When it was gone, his eyes fell upon the dead man. He quickly looked away—that was the last thing he wanted to see.

"There he is!"

He whipped his head around to see Minho running down the sidewalk toward him, Brenda and Jorge close behind. Thomas had never been so happy to see anyone.

Minho pulled up short when he saw Red Shirt in a heap on the ground. "Holy . . . What happened to *him*?" He turned his attention to Thomas. "And you? You okay? Did you do that?"

Absurdly, Thomas felt like laughing. "Yeah, I pulled out my machine gun and blasted him to tiny bits."

Minho's face showed that he didn't appreciate the sarcasm, but Brenda spoke before he could come up with a retort.

"Who killed him?"

Thomas pointed at the sky. "One of those cop machines. Flew in here, shot him to death, then next thing I know the Rat Man appears on a screen. He tried to convince me that I need to go back to WICKED."

"Dude," Minho said, "you can't even—"

"Give me some credit!" Thomas yelled. "There's no way I'd go back, but maybe them needing me so much could help us at some point. What we should worry about is Newt. Janson thinks that Newt's succumbing to the Flare a lot faster than average. We have to go check on him."

"He really said that?"

"Yeah." Thomas felt bad for blowing up at his friend. "And I believe him on this. You saw how Newt's been acting."

Minho stared at Thomas, his eyes filled with pain. It hit Thomas that Minho had known Newt for two years longer than he had. So much more time to grow close.

"We better check on him somehow," Thomas repeated. "Do something for him."

Minho just nodded and looked away. Thomas was tempted to pull Newt's note out of his pocket and read it right then and there, but he'd promised he'd wait until he knew for sure the time was right.

"It's getting late," Brenda said. "And they don't let people in and out of the city at night—it's hard enough to keep things under control during the day."

Thomas noticed for the first time that the light was beginning to fade, the sky above the buildings taking on an orange hue.

Jorge, who'd been quiet until then, spoke up. "That's the least of our problems. Something weird's going on around this place, *muchachos.*"

"What do you mean?" Thomas asked.

"All the people seem to have vanished in the last half hour, and the few I've seen don't look right."

"That scene at the coffee shop *did* send everyone scattering," Brenda pointed out.

Jorge shrugged. "I don't know. This city is just giving me the creeps, *hermana*. Like it's alive and waiting to unleash something really nasty."

A strange unease crawled up Thomas's spine and he turned his focus back to Newt. "Can we get out there if we hurry? Or can we break out?"

"We can try," Brenda said. "Better hope we can find a cab, though— we're on the other side of the city from where we came in."

"Let's try it," Thomas offered.

They took off down the street, but the look on Minho's face wasn't good. Thomas sure hoped it wasn't a sign of bad things to come.

CHAPTER 33

They walked for an hour and didn't see a single car, much less a cab. They ran into only a few scattered people, and cop machines let out their eerie hum as they flew by at random. Every few minutes they'd hear a sound in the distance that brought memories of the Scorch back to Thomas—someone talking too loudly, a scream, an odd laugh. As the light faded to darkness, he began to feel more and more spooked.

Finally Brenda stopped and faced the rest of them. "We'll have to wait till tomorrow," she announced. "We're not going to find transportation tonight and we're too far to walk. We need to sleep so we'll be fresh in the morning."

Thomas hated to admit it, but she was right.

"There's gotta be a way to get out there," Minho countered.

Jorge squeezed his shoulder. "It's useless, *hermano*. The airport's at least ten miles from here. And by the looks of this town we'd get mugged or shot or beaten to death on the way. Brenda's right—better to rest up and go help him tomorrow."

Thomas could tell Minho wanted to be his usual defiant self, but he gave in without arguing. Jorge made too much sense. They were in a huge city, at night, completely out of their element.

"Are we close to our motel?" Thomas asked. He told himself that Newt could make it through one more night alone.

Jorge pointed to his left. "Just a few blocks."

They headed in that direction.

★ ★ ★

They were a block away when Jorge pulled up short, holding one hand in the air and putting a finger to his lips with the other. Thomas stopped dead in his tracks, alarm suddenly tingling through his nerves.

"What?" Minho whispered.

Jorge turned in a slow circle, scanning the area around them, and Thomas did the same, wondering what had suddenly made the older man so apprehensive. Darkness had completely fallen, and the few streetlights they passed barely put a dent in it. The world Thomas could see seemed made of shadows, and he imagined horrible things hiding behind every one of them.

"What?" Minho whispered again.

"I keep thinking I hear something right behind us," Jorge replied. "Whispering. Anyone else—"

"There!" Brenda shouted, her voice like a crack of thunder in the silence. "Did you see that?" She was pointing off to her left.

Thomas strained to look but saw nothing. The streets were empty as far as he could tell.

"Someone was just coming out from behind that building, then jumped back. I swear I saw it."

"Hey!" Minho yelled. "Who's over there?"

"Are you crazy?" Thomas whispered. "Let's get inside the motel!"

"Slim it, dude. If they wanted to shoot us or something, don't you think they would've done it by now?"

Thomas just sighed in exasperation. He didn't like the feel of this at all.

"I should've said something when I first heard it," Jorge said.

"Maybe it's nothing," Brenda responded. "And if it is, standing around won't help. Let's just get out of here."

160

"Hey!" Minho yelled again, making Thomas jump. "Hey, you! Who's over there?"

Thomas smacked him on the shoulder. "Seriously, would you stop that?"

His friend ignored him. "Come out and show yourself!"

Whoever it was didn't respond. Minho moved like he was going to walk across the street and take a look, but Thomas grabbed him by the arm.

"No way. Worst idea in history. It's dark, it could be a trap, it could be a lot of terrible things. Let's just get some sleep and keep a better eye out tomorrow."

Minho didn't put up much of an argument. "Fine. Be a wuss. But I get one of the beds tonight."

And with that they went up to their room. It took forever for Thomas to fall asleep, his mind spinning with the possibilities of who might be following them. But no matter where his thoughts wandered, they always came back to Teresa and the others. Where were they? Could that have been Teresa out on the street, spying on them? Or had it been Gally and the Right Arm?

And Thomas hated that they'd had no choice but to wait a night before checking on Newt. What if something had happened to him?

Finally his mind slowed, the questions faded away, and he fell asleep.

CHAPTER 34

The next morning, Thomas was surprised at how rested he felt. He'd tossed and turned all night, it seemed, but at some point he must have gotten some deep and recharging sleep. After a long, hot shower and breakfast out of a vending machine, he was ready to face the day.

He and the others left the motel around eight o'clock in the morning, wondering what they'd find in the city on their way to check on Newt. They saw some people here and there, but far fewer than they'd seen during the busy hours of the day before. And Thomas didn't notice any strange noises like the ones they'd heard the previous night during their long walk.

"Something's up, I'm tellin' ya," Jorge said as they made their way down the street in search of a cab. "There should be more folks out and about."

Thomas observed the few pedestrians around him. None of them would look him in the eye—everyone kept their head down, often with one hand holding their surgical mask to their face as if afraid that a sudden wind might blow it off. And they walked with a hurried, frantic gait, almost jumping out of the way when another person got too close. He noticed a woman studying a poster about the Flare just like the one he'd read the day before while being escorted by Red Shirt. It brought to mind that memory he hadn't been able to grasp—it was going to drive him crazy.

"Let's hurry and get to the shuck airport," Minho muttered. "This place is giving me the creeps."

"We should probably go up that way," Brenda said, pointing. "There have to be cabs around those business offices."

They crossed the street and headed down a narrower one that passed what looked like an empty lot on one side and an old, dilapidated building on the other.

Minho leaned into Thomas and half whispered, "Dude, I'm a little shucked in the head right now. I'm scared of what we're gonna find with Newt."

Thomas was scared, too, but didn't admit it. "Don't worry. I'm sure he's fine for now."

"Good that. And the cure for the Flare's gonna fly out of your butt any second."

"Who knows, maybe it will. Might smell funny, though." His friend didn't seem to think that was very humorous. "Look, we can't do anything until we get there and see him." Thomas hated sounding so insensitive, but things were hard enough—they couldn't assume the worst.

"Thanks for the pep talk."

The empty lot to their right contained the scattered remains of an old brick building, weeds filling every square inch. A large section of wall stood right in the middle, and as they passed, Thomas noticed movement on the far side of it. He stopped, and instinctively put a hand out to halt Minho as well. He shushed him before he could ask what was going on.

Brenda and Jorge noticed and froze in place. Thomas pointed at what he'd seen, then tried to get a better look.

A shirtless man had his back to them, and he was hunched over something, digging with his hands like he'd lost something in the mud and was trying to find it. Oddly shaped scratches covered his shoulders, and there was a long scab crossing the middle of his spine. His movements were jerky and . . . desperate, Thomas thought. His elbows kept popping back like he'd torn something loose from the ground. The tall weeds prevented Thomas from seeing the focus of the man's frantic attention.

Brenda whispered from behind. "Let's keep moving."

"That guy's sick," Minho whispered back. "How's he loose like this?"

Thomas had no idea. "Let's just go."

The group started walking again, but Thomas couldn't tear his eyes away from the disturbing scene. What was that guy *doing*?

When they reached the end of the block, Thomas stopped, as did the others. It was clearly bothering everyone as much as it was him—they all wanted to get one last look.

Without warning, the man sprang up and turned toward them; blood covered his mouth and nose. Thomas flinched and stumbled back into Minho. The man bared his teeth in a nasty grin, then held up bloody hands as if to show them off. Thomas was just about to yell at him when the guy bent back over and returned to his business. Thankfully they couldn't see exactly what that business was.

"This would be a good time to go," Brenda said.

Icy fingers crawled along Thomas's back and shoulders—he couldn't have agreed more. They all turned and ran, and they'd gone two blocks before they slowed to a walk again.

It took another half hour before they found a cab, but they were finally on their way. Thomas wanted to talk about what they'd seen in the empty lot, but he couldn't put it into words. It had sickened him through and through.

Minho was the first to speak about it. "That guy was eating a person. I just know it."

"Maybe . . . ," Brenda began. "Maybe it was just a stray dog." Her tone made Thomas think she didn't believe it for one second. "Not like that'd be okay, either."

Minho scoffed. "I'm pretty sure that's not something you're supposed to see during a nice leisurely stroll through a quarantined city in the middle of the day. I believe Gally. I think this place is crawling with Cranks, and soon the whole city's gonna start killing each other."

No one responded. They stayed silent the rest of the way to the airport.

It didn't take long to get through security and back outside the massive walls surrounding the city. If anything, the staff they encountered seemed thrilled that they were leaving.

The Berg was right where they'd left it, waiting like the abandoned shell of a giant insect on the hot and steamy concrete. Nothing stirred around it.

"Hurry up and open it," Minho said.

Jorge didn't seem fazed by the curt command; he pulled his small control pad out of his pocket and pressed some buttons. The ramp of the cargo door slowly pivoted down, hinges squealing, until its edge landed on the ground with a grating scrape. Thomas had hoped to see Newt come running down that ramp, a big smile on his face, glad to see them.

But nothing moved inside or out, and his heart sank.

Minho obviously felt the same way. "Something's wrong." He sprinted to the door and ran up the ramp before Thomas had a chance to react.

"We better get in there," Brenda said. "What if Newt's turned dangerous?"

Thomas hated the sound of the question but knew she was right. Without responding, he ran after Minho, entering the dark and stifling Berg. All the systems had been shut down at some point: no air-conditioning, no lights, nothing.

Jorge followed right at Thomas's heels. "Let me power her up or we'll all sweat till we're nothing but a pile of bones and skin." He moved off in the direction of the cockpit.

Brenda stood next to Thomas, both of them peering into the gloom of the ship, the only light coming from the few scattered portholes. They could hear Minho calling Newt's name somewhere deep in the ship, but the infected boy wasn't responding. A cavity seemed to open within Thomas, widening and sucking the hope out of him.

"I'll go to the left," he said, pointing toward the small hallway to the common area. "Why don't you follow Jorge and search up there. This isn't good—he would've been here to welcome us if everything was okay."

"Not to mention the lights and air would be on." She gave Thomas a grim look, then headed off.

Thomas went down the hallway to the main room. Minho sat on one of the couches, looking at a piece of paper, his face as stony as Thomas had ever seen it. The hollowness inside him grew even more, and his last ounce of hope faded.

"Hey," he said. "What is it?"

Minho didn't answer. He just kept staring at the paper.

"What's wrong?"

Minho glanced up at him. "Come see for yourself." He held up the paper in one hand while he slouched back on the couch, seeming on the verge of tears. "He's gone."

Thomas walked over and took the paper from him, then flipped it over. Scribbled in black marker, it said:

They got inside somehow. They're taking me to live with the other Cranks.
It's for the best. Thanks for being my friends.
Goodbye.

"Newt," Thomas whispered. His friend's name hung in the air like a pronouncement of death.

CHAPTER 35

Soon they were all sitting together. The goal was to talk over what should come next, but the reality was they had nothing to say. The group of four just stared at the floor and said nothing. For some reason, Thomas couldn't get Janson out of his head. Could going back really be a way to save Newt? Every part of him rebelled against the idea of returning to WICKED, but if he *did* go back, and was able to complete the testing . . .

Minho broke the sullen silence.

"I want you three to listen to me." He took a moment to look at each one of them, then continued. "Ever since we broke out of WICKED, I've basically gone along with whatever you slintheads ended up saying we should do. And I haven't complained. Much." He gave Thomas a wry grin. "But right here, right now, I'm making a decision and you're going to do what I say. And if anyone pushes back, to hell with you."

Thomas knew what his friend wanted, and he was glad for it.

"I know we have bigger goals in mind," Minho continued. "We need to connect with the Right Arm, figure out what to do about WICKED—all that save-the-world klunk. But first we're going to find Newt. This isn't open for discussion. The four of us—all of us—are flying to wherever we need to go, and we're getting Newt out of there."

"They call it the Crank Palace," Brenda said. Thomas turned to her and she was staring off into space. "It has to be what he was talking about. Some of those Red Shirts probably broke into the Berg, found

Newt and saw that he was infected. Let him leave us a note. I don't have any doubt that's what happened."

"Sounds fancy," Minho said. "You've been there?"

"No. Every major city has a Crank Palace—a place where they send the infected and try to make it bearable for them until they reach the Gone. I don't know what they do to them then, but it's not a pretty place to be, no matter who you are, so I can only imagine. Immunes run things there, and get paid a lot for it because a non-Immune would never risk catching the Flare. If you want to go, we should think long and hard about it first. We're completely out of ammunition, so we'll be unarmed."

Despite the ominous description, Minho had a glimmer of hope in his eyes. "Long and hard thinking done. You know where the closest one is?"

"Yeah," Jorge answered. "We passed over it on the way here. It's just on the far side of this valley, right up against the mountains to the west."

Minho clapped his hands once. "Then that's where we're going. Jorge, get this piece of klunk up in the sky."

Thomas expected at least a little argument or resistance. But none came.

"I'll be glad for a little adventure, *muchacho,*" Jorge said, standing up. "We'll be there in twenty minutes."

Jorge was true to his word on the timing. He landed the Berg in a clearing along the beginnings of a forest that stretched up the surprisingly green mountainside. About half of the trees were dead, but the other half looked as if they'd just begun to recover from years of massive heat spells. It made Thomas sad to think that the world would probably recover from the sun flares just fine someday, only to find itself uninhabited.

He stepped off the cargo ramp and took a good look at the wall surrounding what had to be the Crank Palace just a few hundred feet away. It was made of thick planks of wood. The closest gate was just beginning to open, and two people appeared, both of them holding huge Launchers. They looked exhausted, but wearily they took a defensive stance and aimed their weapons—they'd obviously heard or seen the Berg's approach.

"Not a good start," Jorge said.

One of the guards shouted something, but Thomas couldn't hear what he'd said. "Let's just go over there, talk to them. They must be immune if they have those Launchers."

"Unless the Cranks took over," offered Minho, but then he looked at Thomas with an odd grin. "Either way, we're going in, and we're not leaving without Newt."

The group held their heads up high and slowly walked to the gate, making sure not to do anything that would cause alarm. The last thing Thomas wanted was to be shot by a Launcher grenade again. As they got closer, he saw that the two guards looked worse up close. They were filthy, sweaty and covered in bruises and scratches.

They stopped at the gate and one of the guards stepped forward.

"Who the hell are you people?" he asked. He had black hair and a mustache and was taller than his partner by a few good inches. "You don't look much like the science goons that come in sometimes."

Jorge did the talking, just as he had at the airport when they'd arrived in Denver. "You wouldn't have known we were coming, *muchacho*. We're from WICKED, and one of our guys got captured and taken here by mistake. We'll be picking him up."

Thomas was surprised. What Jorge had said was technically the truth, when he thought about it.

The guard didn't seem too impressed. "You think I give a crap about you and your fancy WICKED jobs? You're not the first uppity-up to drop in here and act like you own the place. You wanna come hang out with Cranks? Be my guest. Especially after what's been going on lately." He stepped to the side and made an exaggerated sweeping gesture of welcome. "Enjoy your stay at the Crank Palace. No refunds or exchanges if you lose an arm or eyeball."

Thomas could almost smell the tension in the air, and he worried that Minho would add some smart remark and send these guys over the edge, so he spoke up quickly.

"What do you mean 'what's been going on lately'? What's happening?"

The guy shrugged. "It's just not a very happy place, and that's all you need to know." He didn't offer anything more.

Thomas already disliked the way things were going. "Well . . . do you know if any new"—saying *Cranks* didn't feel right to Thomas—"*people* were brought here in the last day or two? Do you have a register?"

The other guard—short and stocky, his head shaved—cleared his throat, then spit. "Who you lookin' for? A he or a she?"

"A he," Thomas answered. "His name is Newt. A little taller than me, blond hair, kinda long. Has a limp."

The guy spit again. "I might know somethin'. But knowin' and tellin' are two different things. You kids look like you got plenty of money. Wanna share?"

Thomas, daring to let himself hope, looked back at Jorge, whose face had tightened in anger.

Minho spoke before Jorge could. "We've got money, shuck-face. Now tell us where our friend is."

The guard jabbed the Launcher toward them a little more fiercely.

"Show me your cash cards or this conversation is over. I want at least a thousand."

"He's got it all," Minho said, jabbing a thumb at Jorge as his eyes lasered in on the guard. "Greedy slinthead."

Jorge pulled his card out and waved it in the air. "You'll have to shoot me dead to take this, and you know it won't do any good without my prints. You'll get your money, *hermano*. Now show us the way."

"All right, then," the man said. "Follow me. And remember, if any of your body parts become detached due to an unfortunate encounter with a Crank, I highly advise you to leave said body part behind and run like hell. Unless it's a leg, of course."

He turned on his heels and walked through the opened gate.

CHAPTER 36

The Crank Palace was a horrible, filthy place. The short guard proved to be very talkative, and as they made their way through the chaos of the frightening domain, he provided more information than Thomas ever would've asked for.

He described the village for the infected as a huge set of rings within rings, with all the communal areas—cafeteria, infirmary, recreation facilities—located in the middle and then row upon row of poorly built housing encircling them. The Palaces had been conceived as humane options—refuges for the infected until they reached a point where the madness took over. After that they were shipped to remote locations that had been abandoned during the worst of the sun flares. Those who had built the palaces had wanted to give the infected one last shot at a decent life before the end. Projects had sprung up near most remaining cities in the world.

But the well-intended idea had gone very bad. Filling a place with people who had no hope and knew they were about to descend into a rotten, horrific spiral of insanity ended up creating some of the most wretched anarchic zones ever known to man. With the residents well aware that there could be no real punishment or consequences worse than what they already faced, crime rates grew astronomically. And so the developments became havens of debauchery.

As the group walked past home after home—nothing more than shacks that had fallen into disrepair—Thomas imagined how truly awful it must be to live in such a place. Most windows in the buildings they passed were broken, and their guard explained how it had been a huge mistake to allow glass in the towns at all. It had become the number one source of weaponry. Trash littered the streets, and though he hadn't spotted any people yet, Thomas felt like he and his friends were being watched from the shadows. In the distance he heard someone yell a few obscenities; then a scream came from another direction, putting Thomas even more on edge.

"Why don't they just close the place down?" he asked, the first of his group to speak. "I mean—if it's gotten so bad."

"Gotten so bad?" the guard asked. "Kid, bad's a relative term. This is just how it is. What else are you gonna do with these people? You can't leave 'em hanging out with the healthy folks in the fortressed cities. You can't just dump 'em in a place full of Cranks way past the Gone and let 'em get eaten alive. And no government's gotten desperate enough yet to start killing people as soon as they catch the Flare. This is it. And it's a way for us Immunes to make some good money, since no one else would ever work here."

His statements left Thomas with a heavy dose of gloom. The world was in pitiful shape. Maybe he *was* being selfish by not helping WICKED complete the tests.

Brenda spoke up—her face had been creased into a look of disgust since they'd entered the town. "Why don't you just tell it like it is—you let the infected run around this godforsaken place until they're so bad that your conscience is clean enough to get rid of them."

"That about wraps 'er up," the guard responded matter-of-factly. Thomas had a hard time disliking the guy—he mostly just felt sorry for him.

They kept walking, passing row after row of houses, all of them broken, run-down and dirty.

"Where is everybody?" Thomas asked. "I thought this place would be packed wall to wall. And what did you mean earlier about something happening?"

This time the guy with the mustache answered, and it was good to hear another voice for a change. "Some—the lucky ones—are vegging on the Bliss in their homes. But most of them are in the Central Zone, eating or playing or up to no good. They're sending us too many—and faster than we can ship them out. Add to that the fact that we're losing Immunes left and right to who-knows-where, decreasing our ratio each and every day, and things were bound to reach a boiling point eventually. Let's just say this morning the water finally got hot enough."

"Losing Immunes left and right?" Thomas repeated. It looked like WICKED was tapping every resource they could for more Trials. Even if their doing so had dangerous consequences.

"Yeah, almost half our workers have disappeared over the last couple months. No sign of 'em, no explanations. Which only makes my job a thousand times harder."

Thomas groaned. "Just keep us away from the crowds and put us somewhere safe until you find Newt."

"That's more like it," Minho added.

The guard merely shrugged. "Okay. As long as I get my money."

The guards finally stopped two rings away from the Central Zone and told the group to wait. Thomas and the others huddled in some shade behind one of the shacks. The cacophony had grown louder by the minute, and now, so close to most of the Palace's population, it sounded as if a massive brawl was taking place just around the corner. Thomas hated every second he sat there, waiting, listening to those awful noises, wondering the whole time whether the guard would come back at all, much less with Newt in tow.

174

About ten minutes after he'd left, two people came out of a little hut across the narrow pathway from them. Thomas's pulse quickened, and he almost got up and ran before he realized they didn't look threatening in the least. They were a couple, holding hands, and other than being a little dirty and wearing wrinkled and worn clothes, they seemed sane enough.

The two approached the little group and stopped in front of them. "When did you get here?" the woman asked.

Thomas fumbled for words, but Brenda spoke up.

"We came in with the last group. We're actually looking for our friend who was with us. His name is Newt—blond hair, has a limp. Have you seen him?"

The man answered as if he'd just heard the dumbest question of his life. "Lots of people with blond hair around here—how're we supposed to tell who's who? What kind of name is Newt anyway?"

Minho opened his mouth to respond, but the noise coming from the center of town picked up and everyone turned to look. The couple gave each other concerned looks. Then, without a word, they scurried back inside their home. They closed the door and Thomas heard the click of a lock engaging. A few seconds later a wooden board appeared in their window, covering it up; a small shard of glass fell to the ground outside.

"They look about as happy to be here as we are," Thomas said.

Jorge grunted. "Real friendly. I think I'll come back to visit."

"They obviously haven't been here long," Brenda said. "I can't imagine what that must feel like. Finding out you're infected, being sent to live with Cranks, seeing what you're about to become right in front of you."

Thomas just shook his head slowly. It'd be misery in its purest form.

"Where are those *guards*?" Minho asked, impatience clear in his tone. "How long does it take to find someone and tell 'em their friends are here?"

Ten minutes later, the two guards reappeared around a corner. Thomas and his friends jumped to their feet.

"What'd you find out?" Minho asked in a rush.

The short one seemed fidgety, his eyes darting, as if he'd lost his brazenness from before, and Thomas wondered if a trip to what they'd called the Central Zone always did that to a person.

His partner answered. "Took some asking around, but I think we found your guy. Looks just like you described, and he turned toward us when we called his name. But . . ." The guards exchanged an uncomfortable glance.

"But what?" Minho pushed.

"He said—very pointedly, I might add—to tell you guys to get lost."

CHAPTER 37

The words stabbed Thomas, and he could only imagine how Minho felt.

"Show us where he is," his friend ordered curtly.

The guard held up his hands. "Did you not hear what I just said?"

"Your job's not done," Thomas insisted. He was with Minho one hundred percent. It didn't matter what Newt had said—if they were this close, they were going to talk to him.

The shorter guard shook his head adamantly. "No way. You asked us to find your friend and we did. Give us our money."

"Does it look like we're with him yet?" Jorge asked. "No one makes a dollar until you get us all together."

Brenda didn't say anything, but she stood next to Jorge and nodded to show her support. Thomas was relieved that everyone was on board to go to Newt despite the message he'd sent.

The two guards didn't look happy at all, and they whispered back and forth, arguing.

"Hey!" Minho barked. "If you want that money, let's go!"

"Fine," the guard with the mustache finally said. His partner gave him an exasperated glare. "Follow us."

They turned and headed back in the direction they'd come. Minho was right on their heels, and then everyone else.

As they made their way deeper into the compound, Thomas kept thinking things couldn't get worse, but they did. The buildings were shabbier, the streets dirtier. He saw several people lying on the sidewalks, their heads resting on filthy bags or wadded-up pieces of clothing. Each one of them stared at the sky with a glazed expression, a look of oblivious glee. The Bliss was aptly named, Thomas thought.

The guards marched ahead, sweeping their Launchers left and right at anyone who got within a dozen feet of them. At one point they passed a ravaged-looking man—his clothes torn, his hair matted with some kind of black goo, skin covered in rashes—as he fell on a drugged-out teenager and started beating him.

Thomas stopped, wondering if they should help.

"Don't even think about it," the short guard said before Thomas could get a word out. "Keep moving."

"But isn't it your job to—"

The other guard cut him off. "Shut up and let us handle things. If we meddled in every squabble and catfight we saw, we'd never be done. We'd probably be dead. Those two can sort out their own problems."

"Just get us to Newt," Minho said evenly.

They continued, and Thomas tried to ignore the gargled scream that suddenly rose behind them.

Finally, they reached a high wall with a big archway that led to an open area full of people. A sign at the top of the arch proclaimed in bright letters that this was the Central Zone. Thomas couldn't quite make out what was going on inside, but everyone seemed busy.

The guards stopped, and the one with the mustache addressed the group. "I'm only going to ask once. Are you sure you want to go in there?"

"Yes," Minho answered quickly.

"Okay, then. Your friend is at the bowling alley. As soon as we point him out, I want our money."

"Let's just get moving," Jorge growled.

They followed the guards through the arch and entered the Central Zone. Then they stopped to take it all in.

The first word that popped into Thomas's mind was *madhouse,* and he realized that it was almost literally true.

Cranks were everywhere.

They milled about in a circular area several hundred feet across that was bordered by what had apparently once been shops and restaurants and entertainment venues. Most of them were run-down and closed. The majority of the infected didn't seem quite as gone as the matted-hair fellow they'd seen out in the streets, but there was a frenzied air about the groups of people. To Thomas, everyone's actions and mannerisms seemed . . . exaggerated. Some people were laughing hysterically, a wildness in their eyes, as they slapped each other's backs roughly. Others cried uncontrollably, sobbing all alone on the ground or walking in circles, faces in their hands. Small fights had broken out everywhere, and here and there you'd find a man or woman standing still and screaming at the top of their lungs, faces red and necks corded.

There were also those who huddled in groups, arms folded and heads snapping left and right as if they expected to be attacked at any second. And just as Thomas had seen in the outer rings, some of the Cranks were lost in the haze of the Bliss, smiling as they sat or lay on the ground and ignored the chaos. A few guards walked around, weapons held at the ready, but they were vastly outnumbered.

"Remind me not to buy any real estate here," Minho quipped.

Thomas couldn't bring himself to laugh. He was filled with anxiety, and he desperately wanted to get this over with.

"Where's the bowling alley?" he asked.

"Over this way," the shorter guard said.

He headed to the left, sticking close to the wall as Thomas and the others followed. Brenda walked beside Thomas, their arms brushing with every step. He wanted to take her hand, but he didn't want to make any move that would call attention to himself. Everything about this place was so unpredictable he didn't want to do anything he didn't absolutely have to.

Most of the Cranks stopped their feverish activities and stared at the small group of newcomers as they approached and walked past. Thomas kept his gaze lowered, scared that if he made eye contact with anyone, they might get hostile or try to talk to him. There were catcalls and whistles, lots of crude jokes or insults thrown their way as they kept moving. They passed a dilapidated convenience store, and Thomas could see through the open windows—the glass was long gone—that almost all the shelves were empty. There was a doctor's office and a sandwich shop, but no lights shone in either one.

Someone grabbed Thomas's shirt at the shoulder. He spun to see who it was as he swatted the hand away. A woman stood there, her dark hair messy and a scratch on her chin, but otherwise she seemed some-what normal. Her face was drooping in a frown, and she stared at him for a moment before opening her mouth as wide as it would go, reveal-ing teeth that were in good shape other than looking as if they hadn't been brushed in a while, and a tongue that was swollen and discolored. Then she closed her mouth again.

"I want to kiss you," the woman said. "What do you say, Munie?" She laughed, a manic cackle that was full of snorts, and ran her hand lightly down Thomas's chest.

Thomas jerked away and continued walking—he noticed that the guards hadn't even stopped to make sure nothing bad happened.

Brenda leaned closer and whispered to him. "That might've been the creepiest thing yet."

Thomas just nodded and kept going.

CHAPTER 38

The bowling alley didn't have any doors—based on the thick rust that covered the exposed hinges, they'd been taken off and disposed of a long time ago. A large wooden sign hung above the entrance, but any words it had once displayed were gone, leaving only faded scratches of color.

"He's in there," the guard with the mustache said. "Now pay up."

Minho stepped past him to the empty doorway and leaned through the opening, craning his neck to see inside. Then he turned around and looked at Thomas.

"I can see him in the back," Minho said, his face pinched with worry. "It's dark in there, but it's definitely him."

Thomas had been so worried about finding their old friend, he realized he didn't have any clue what they'd actually say to him. Why had he told them to get lost?

"We want our money," the guard repeated.

Jorge appeared completely unfazed. "You'll get double if you make sure we get back to our Berg safely."

The two guards consulted; then the shorter one took a turn speaking. "Triple. And we want half of it now to make sure you're not blowing smoke out your butts."

"That's a deal, *muchacho.*"

As Jorge pulled out his card and touched it to the guard's, transferring the money, Thomas felt a grim satisfaction that they were stealing money from WICKED.

"We'll wait right here," the guard said when they were done.

"Come on," Minho said. He went inside the building without waiting for a response.

Thomas looked at Brenda, who was frowning.

"What's wrong?" he asked. As if there were just one thing.

"I don't know," she responded. "I just have a bad feeling."

"Yeah, you and me both."

She gave him a half smile and took his hand, which now he gladly accepted; then they went into the bowling alley with Jorge right behind them.

As with many things since his memory had been wiped, Thomas had images in his mind of what a bowling alley should have looked like and how it functioned, but he couldn't recall having ever bowled. The room they stepped into was far from what he'd expected.

The lanes where people had once bowled were now completely torn up, most of the wood panels ripped out or broken. Sleeping bags and blankets filled the spaces now, with people either napping or lying in a daze as they stared at the ceiling. Brenda had told Thomas that only the rich could afford the Bliss, so he wondered how people would dare reveal to others that they were using it in a place like this. He imagined it wouldn't be long before someone decided to do whatever it took to get the drug from them.

In the niches where the bowling pins used to stand, several fires burned, which couldn't have been very safe. But at least one person sat at each fire, tending it. The smell of burning wood wafted through the air, and a smoky haze choked the darkness.

Minho pointed to the far left lane, about a hundred feet away. Not many people were over there—most seemed to congregate in the middle lanes—but Thomas spotted Newt immediately despite the poor lighting. It was the flash of his long blond hair in the firelight and the familiar shape of his slumping body. His back was to them.

"Here goes nothing," Thomas whispered to Brenda.

No one bothered them as they carefully made their way to Newt, picking through the maze of people dozing in blankets until they reached the far lane. Thomas watched where he walked—the last thing he wanted was to step on some Crank and get bitten in the leg.

They were about ten feet away from Newt when he suddenly spoke in a loud voice that echoed off the dark walls of the bowling alley. "I told you bloody shanks to get lost!"

Minho stopped and Thomas almost ran into him. Brenda squeezed Thomas's hand, then let go, which was when he realized how much he'd been sweating. Hearing those words come out of Newt somehow let him know that it was over and done. Their friend would never be the same—he had only dark days ahead.

"We need to talk to you," Minho said, moving a couple of feet closer to Newt. He had to step over a skinny woman lying on her side.

"Don't come any closer," Newt answered. His voice was soft, but it was full of menace. "Those thugs brought me here for a reason. They thought I was a bloody Immune holed up in that shuck Berg. Imagine their surprise when they could tell I had the Flare eating my brain. Said they were doing their civic duty when they dumped me in this rat hole."

When Minho didn't say anything, Thomas spoke up, trying not to let Newt's words overcome him. "Why do you think we're here, Newt? I'm sorry you had to stay back and got caught. I'm sorry they brought you here. But we can break you out—it doesn't look like anyone gives a klunk who comes or goes."

Newt slowly twisted around to face them. Thomas's stomach dropped when he saw that the boy had a Launcher clutched in his hands. And he looked ragged, like he'd been running and fighting and falling down cliffs for three days straight. But despite the anger that had pooled in his eyes, he hadn't been taken by madness quite yet.

"Whoa, there," Minho said, taking a half a step back—he barely missed stepping on the lady at his heels. "Slim it nice and calm. There's no need to point a shuck Launcher at my face while we talk. Where'd you get that thing, anyway?"

"I stole it," Newt answered. "Took it from a guard who made me . . . unhappy."

Newt's hands were shaking slightly, which made Thomas nervous—the boy's finger hovered over the trigger of the weapon.

"I'm . . . not well," Newt said. "Honestly, I appreciate you buggin' shanks coming for me. I mean it. But this is where it bloody ends. This is when you turn around and walk back out that door and head for your Berg and fly away. Do you understand me?"

"No, Newt, I don't understand," Minho said, the frustration in his voice escalating. "We risked our necks to come to this place and you're our friend and we're taking you home. You wanna whine and cry while you go crazy, that's fine. But you're gonna do it with us, not with these shuck Cranks."

Newt suddenly jumped to his feet, so quickly that Thomas almost stumbled backward. Newt lofted the Launcher and pointed it at Minho. "I *am* a Crank, Minho! I *am* a Crank! Why can't you get that through your bloody head? If you had the Flare and knew what you were about to go through, would you want your friends to stand around and watch? Huh? Would you want that?" He was shouting by the time he finished, and was shaking more with each passing moment.

Minho didn't say anything, and Thomas knew why. He himself was trying to find words and coming up empty. Newt's glare shifted to him.

"And *you*, Tommy," the boy said, lowering his voice. "You've got a lot of nerve coming here and asking me to leave with you. A lot of bloody nerve. The sight of you makes me sick."

Thomas was stunned silent. Nothing anyone had ever said had hurt so much. Nothing.

CHAPTER 39

Thomas couldn't think of any possible explanation for the statement. "What are you talking about?" he asked.

Newt didn't respond, just kept staring at him with hardened eyes, his arms shaking, his Launcher pointed at Thomas's chest. But then he stilled and his face softened. He lowered the weapon and looked at the floor.

"Newt, I don't get it," Thomas persisted quietly. "Why are you saying all this?"

Newt looked up again, and there was none of the bitterness that had been there just seconds earlier. "I'm sorry, guys. I'm sorry. But I need you to listen to me. I'm getting worse by the hour and I don't have many sane ones left. Please leave."

When Thomas opened his mouth to argue, Newt held up his hands. "No! No more talking from you. Just . . . please. Please leave. I'm begging you. I'm begging you to do this one thing for me. As sincerely as I've ever asked for anything in my life, I want you to do this for me. There's a group I've met that are a lot like me and they're planning to break out and head for Denver later today. I'm going with them."

He paused, and it took every bit of Thomas's resolve to keep quiet. Why would they want to break out and go to Denver?

"I don't expect you to understand, but I can't be with you guys anymore. It's gonna be hard enough for me now, and it'll make it worse if I know you have to witness it. Or worst of all, if I hurt you. So let's say our bloody goodbyes and then you can promise to remember me from the good old days."

"I can't do that," Minho said.

"Shuck it!" Newt yelled. "Do you have any clue how hard it is to be calm right now? I said my piece and I'm done. Now get out of here! Do you understand me? Get *out* of here!"

Someone poked Thomas's shoulder and he spun to see that several Cranks had gathered behind them. The person who'd jabbed Thomas was a tall, broad-chested man with long, greasy hair. He reached out again and pushed the tip of his finger into Thomas's chest.

"I believe our new friend asked you people to leave him alone," the guy said. His tongue snaked out to lick his lips as he spoke.

"This is none of your business," Thomas replied. He could sense the danger, but for some reason he didn't care. There was only room enough inside him to be sick about Newt. "He was our friend way before he came here."

The man slicked his hand over his oily hair. "That boy's a Crank now, and so are we. That makes him our business. Now *leave* him . . . *alone.*"

Minho spoke before Thomas could respond. "Hey, psycho, maybe your ears are clogged with the Flare. This is between us and Newt. *You* leave."

The man scowled, then brought up a hand to show a long shard of glass gripped in his fist. Blood dripped from where he held it.

"I was hoping you would resist," he snarled. "I've been bored."

His arm flashed out, the glass slicing toward Thomas's face. Thomas ducked toward the floor and reached up with his hands to deflect the blow. But before the weapon hit him, Brenda stepped in and swatted the guy's hand away, which sent the glass shard flying. Then Minho was on him, tackling the Crank to the ground. They landed on the woman he'd

187

stepped over earlier to get to Newt, and she screamed bloody murder, started flailing and kicking. Soon the three of them were entangled in a wrestling match.

"Stop it!" Newt yelled. "Stop it now!"

Thomas had been frozen in place, crouching as he waited for an opportunity to jump in and help Minho. But he twisted around to see that Newt was holding his Launcher in shooting position, his eyes wild with fury.

"Stop or I'll start shooting and not give a buggin' piece of klunk who gets hit."

The man with the greasy hair pushed his way out of the melee and stood up, kicking the woman in the ribs as he did so. She wailed as Minho got to his feet, scratches covering his face.

The electric sound of the Launcher's charge filled the air just as Thomas got a whiff of burnt ozone. Then Newt squeezed the trigger. A grenade smashed into Greasy Hair's chest and lightning tendrils enveloped his body as he fell screaming to the ground, writhing, legs rigid, drool foaming out of his mouth.

Thomas couldn't believe the sudden turn of events. He looked at Newt with wide eyes, glad he'd done what he had, and happy he hadn't aimed the Launcher at him or Minho.

"I told him to stop," Newt half whispered. Then he aimed the weapon at Minho, but it was shaking because his arms were. "Now you guys leave. No more discussion. I'm sorry."

Minho held up his hands. "You're going to shoot me? Old pal?"

"Go," Newt said. "I asked nicely. Now I'm telling. This is hard enough. Go."

"Newt, let's go outside. . . ."

"Go!" Newt stepped closer and aimed more fiercely. "Get out of here!"

Thomas hated what he was seeing—the complete wildness that had taken over Newt. His whole body trembled and his eyes had lost any hint of sanity. He was losing it, completely.

"Let's go," Thomas said, one of the saddest things he'd ever heard himself say. "Come on."

Minho's gaze snapped to Thomas, and he looked like his heart had been shattered. "You can't be serious."

Thomas could only nod.

Minho's shoulders slumped, and his eyes fell to the floor. "How did the world get so shucked?" The words barely came out, low and full of pain.

"I'm sorry," Newt said, and there were tears streaming down his face. "I'm . . . I'm going to shoot if you don't go. Now."

Thomas couldn't take it for one more second. He grabbed Brenda by the hand, then Minho by the upper arm, started pulling them along toward the exit, stepping over bodies and winding his way through the blankets. Minho didn't resist, and Thomas didn't dare look at him, and could only hope that Jorge was following along. He just kept going, across the lobby, to the doors and through, outside into the Central Zone, into the chaotic crowds of Cranks.

Away from Newt. Away from his friend and his friend's diseased brain.

CHAPTER 40

There was no sign of the guards who'd escorted them there, but there were even more Cranks than when they'd entered the bowling alley. And most of them seemed to be waiting for the newcomers. They'd probably heard the sounds of the Launcher firing and the screams of the guy who'd been hit. Or maybe someone had come out to tell them. Whatever the case, Thomas felt as if every person looking at him were past the Gone and hungry for human lunch.

"Look at these jokers," someone called out.

"Yeah, ain't they pretty!" another answered. "Come to play with the Cranks. Or are you on your way to joining us?"

Thomas kept moving, making his way toward the arched entrance to the Central Zone. He'd let go of Minho's arm but still held Brenda's hand. They marched through the crowd, and Thomas finally had to stop meeting peoples' gazes. All he saw was madness and bloodlust and jealousy carved onto countless bleeding and mangled faces. He wanted to run but had the sense that if he did the whole crowd would attack like a pack of wolves.

They reached the arch, went through it without hesitating. Thomas led them down the main street, crossing through the rings of dilapidated houses. The ruckus of the Zone seemed to have started up again now that they were gone, and eerie sounds of crazed laughter and wild screaming followed the group on their trek. The farther they got from the noise, the less tense Thomas felt. He didn't dare speak to ask Minho how he was. Plus, he knew the answer.

They were just passing another set of broken homes when he heard a couple of shouts ring out, and then the sound of footsteps.

"Run!" someone yelled. "Run!"

Thomas came to a stop just as the two guards who'd abandoned them came careering around the corner. They didn't slow but ran toward the farthest ring of the town and the Berg. Neither of them had their Launchers anymore.

"Hey!" Minho shouted. "Get back here!"

The guard with the mustache looked back. "I said run, you idiots! Come on!"

Thomas didn't take time to think. He sprinted after them, knowing it was the only choice. Minho, Jorge, and Brenda followed close on his heels. He looked back to see a cluster of Cranks chasing them, at least a dozen. And they seemed frantic, as if a switch had been flipped and every one of them had reached the Gone at once.

"What happened?" Minho asked through heavy breaths.

"They dragged us away from the Zone!" the shorter man yelled. "I swear to God they were gonna eat us. We barely escaped."

"Don't stop running!" the other guard added. The two of them suddenly peeled off in another direction, down a hidden alley.

Thomas and his friends continued toward the exit leading to their Berg. Catcalls and whistles rose from behind them, and Thomas risked another glimpse back for a better look at their pursuers. Torn clothes, matted hair, muddied faces. But they'd gained no ground.

"They can't catch us!" he yelled, just as the exterior gate came into view ahead of them. "Keep going, we're almost there!"

Even so, Thomas ran faster than he'd ever run in his life—pushed harder even than he ever had in the Maze. The thought of getting caught by those Cranks filled him with horror. The group made it to the gate and passed through it without pausing. They didn't bother to close it, just ran straight for the Berg, its hatch opening as Jorge pushed the buttons on his pad.

They reached the ramp and Thomas ran up it and hurled himself inside. He turned to see his friends sliding to the floor around him, the ramp squealing as it started moving upward to close. The pack of Cranks chasing them would never make it in time, but they kept running, screaming and shouting nonsense. One of them reached down and picked up a rock, hurled it. The thing fell twenty feet short.

The Berg rose into the air just as the door sealed shut.

Jorge hovered the ship just a few dozen feet in the air while they gathered their wits. The Cranks were no threat from the ground—none of them had weapons. Not the ones who'd followed them outside the wall, at any rate.

Thomas stood with Minho and Brenda at one of the viewing ports and watched the deliriously angry crowd below. It was hard to believe that what he was seeing was real.

"Look at them down there," Thomas said. "Who knows what they were doing a few months ago. Living in a high-rise, maybe, working at some office. Now they're chasing people like wild animals."

"I'll tell you what they were doing a few months ago," Brenda answered. "They were miserable, scared to death of catching the Flare, knowing it's inevitable."

Minho threw his hands up. "How can you worry about *them*? Was I alone just now? With my *friend*? His name is Newt."

"Nothing we could've done," Jorge called from the cockpit. Thomas winced at the lack of compassion.

Minho turned to face him. "Just shut up and fly, shuck-face."

"I'll do my best," Jorge said with a sigh. He fiddled with some instruments and got the Berg moving.

Minho slumped to the floor, almost like he'd melted. "What happens when he runs out of Launcher grenades?" he asked no one in particular, looking at an empty spot on the wall.

Thomas had no idea how to respond, no way to express the sorrow that filled his chest. He sank down next to Minho on the ground and sat there without saying a word as the Berg rose higher and flew away from the Crank Palace.

Newt was gone.

CHAPTER 41

Eventually, Thomas and Minho got themselves up and went to sit on a couch in the common area while Brenda helped Jorge in the cockpit.

With time to think, the full reality of what had happened hit Thomas like a falling boulder. Ever since Thomas had entered the Maze, Newt had been there for him. Thomas hadn't realized just how much of a friend he'd become until now. His heart hurt.

He tried to remind himself that Newt wasn't dead. But in some ways this was worse. In most ways. He'd fallen down the slope of insanity, and he was surrounded by bloodthirsty Cranks. And the prospect of never seeing him again was almost unbearable.

Minho finally spoke in a lifeless voice. "Why did he do that? Why wouldn't he come back with us? Why would he point that weapon at my face?"

"He never would've pulled the trigger," Thomas offered, though he doubted it was the truth.

Minho shook his head. "You saw his eyes when they changed. Complete lunacy. I'd be fried if I'd kept pushing. He's crazy, man. He's gone wacker from top to bottom."

"Maybe it's a good thing."

"Come again?" Minho asked as he turned to Thomas.

"Maybe when their minds go, they're not themselves anymore. Maybe the Newt we know is gone and he's not aware of what's happening to him. So really, he's not suffering."

Minho almost looked offended by the notion. "Nice try, slinthead, but I don't believe it. I think he'll always be there just enough to be screaming on the inside, deranged and suffering every shuck second of it. Tormented like a dude buried alive."

That image made Thomas not want to talk anymore, and they fell silent again. Thomas stared at the same spot on the floor, feeling the full dread of Newt's fate, until the Berg landed with a thump back at the Denver airport.

Thomas rubbed his face with both hands. "I guess we're here."

"I think I understand WICKED a little more now," Minho said absently. "After seeing those eyes up close. Seeing the madness. It's not the same when it's someone you've known for so long. I've watched plenty of friends die, but I can't imagine anything worse. The Flare, man. If we could find a cure for that . . ."

He didn't finish the sentence, but Thomas knew what he was thinking. Thomas closed his eyes for a second—nothing about this was black-and-white. It never would be.

Jorge and Brenda joined them after they'd sat awhile in silence.

"I'm sorry," Brenda murmured.

Minho grunted something; Thomas nodded and gave her a long look, trying to let her know with his eyes how terrible he felt. Jorge just sat there, staring at the floor.

Brenda cleared her throat. "I know it's hard, but we need to think about what we're going to do next."

Minho flew to his feet and pointed at her. "You can think all you want about whatever shuck thing you want, Ms. Brenda. We just left our friend with a bunch of psychos." He stormed out of the room.

Brenda's eyes fell on Thomas. "Sorry."

He shrugged. "It's okay. He was with Newt for two years before I showed up in the Maze. It'll take him some time."

"We're really spent, *muchachos*," Jorge said. "Maybe we should take a couple of days and rest. Think it all through."

"Yeah," Thomas murmured.

Brenda leaned toward him and squeezed his hand. "We'll figure something out."

"There's only one place to start," Thomas replied. "Gally's."

"Maybe you're right." She squeezed his hand once more, then let go and stood up. "Come on, Jorge. Let's make something to eat."

The two of them let Thomas be alone with his sorrow.

After a dreadful meal during which no one spoke more than a couple of meaningless words at a time, the four of them went their separate ways. Thomas couldn't stop thinking about Newt as he wandered the Berg aimlessly. His heart sank when he thought about what their lost friend's life was going to become, what little left of it he had.

The note.

Thomas stood dazed for a moment, then ran to the bathroom and locked the door. The note! In all the chaos of the Crank Palace, he'd completely forgotten about it. Newt had said Thomas would know when the time came to read it. And he should've done it before they'd left him in that rancid place. If the time hadn't been right then, when would it have ever been?

He pulled the envelope out of his pocket and ripped it open, then took out the slip of paper. The soft lights that ringed the mirror lit up the message in a warm glow. It was two short sentences:

Kill me. If you've ever been my friend, kill me.

Thomas read it over and over, wishing the words would change. To think that his friend had been so scared that he'd had the foresight to

196

write those words made him sick to his stomach. And he remembered how angry Newt had been at Thomas specifically when they'd found him in the bowling alley. He'd just wanted to avoid the inevitable fate of becoming a Crank.

And Thomas had failed him.

CHAPTER 42

Thomas decided not to tell the others about the message from Newt. He didn't see what possible purpose it could serve. It was time to move on, and he did so with a coldness that he didn't know he had.

They spent two nights in the Berg, resting up and talking plans. None of them knew much about the city or had any solid connections. Their conversations always returned to Gally and the Right Arm. The Right Arm wanted to stop WICKED. And if it was true that WICKED might begin the Trials all over again with new Immunes, then Thomas and his friends had the same goals as the Right Arm.

Gally. They had to go back to Gally.

On the morning of the third day after their run-in with Newt, Thomas showered, then joined the others for a quick meal. It was obvious how anxious everyone was to get moving after two days of sitting around. The plan was to go to Gally's apartment and start from there. There'd been a little worry about what Newt had told them—that some Cranks were planning to break out of the Palace and go to Denver—but there'd been no sign of them from the air.

Once they were ready, Thomas and the others gathered at the hatch door.

"Let me do the talking again," Jorge said.

Brenda nodded. "And when we get in, we'll find a cab."

"Fine," Minho muttered. "Let's quit this shuck yapping and go."

Thomas couldn't have said it better himself. Movement was the only thing that would deaden the despair he felt about Newt and his dreadful note.

Jorge pressed a button and the huge ramp of the cargo door started to pivot downward. The door had only opened halfway when they saw three people standing just outside the Berg. By the time the bottom edge thumped the ground, Thomas had realized that they weren't there with a welcome banner.

Two men. One woman. Wearing the same metallic protective masks as Red Shirt back in the coffee shop. The men held pistols and the lady had a Launcher. Their faces were dirt-smeared and sweaty, and some of their clothes had been torn, as if they'd had to fight their way through an army to get there. Thomas could only hope it was security being extra cautious.

"What *is* this?" Jorge asked.

"Shut your mouth, Munie," one of the guys said, his mechanized voice making his words all the more sinister. "Now step down here nice and easy, or you won't like what happens. Don't. Try. Anything."

Thomas looked past their assailants and was shocked to see that both gates leading into Denver were standing wide open and two people lay lifeless in the narrow alley leading to the city.

Jorge was the first to respond. "You start firing that thing, *hermano*, and we'll be on top of you like stink on dookie. You may get one of us, but we'll get all three of you punks."

Thomas knew it was an empty threat.

"We've got nothing to lose," the man replied. "Give it your best shot. I'm pretty confident I'll nail two of you before anybody takes a single step." He lifted his gun a couple of inches and aimed at Jorge's face.

"Fair enough," Jorge muttered, and put his hands in the air. "You win for now."

Minho groaned. "You are one tough slinthead." But he raised his hands, too. "You guys better not drop your guard. That's all I'm saying."

Thomas knew they had no choice but to go along. He put up his hands and was the first to walk down the ramp. The others followed right behind, and they were led around to the back of the Berg, where an old beat-up van waited, the engine rumbling. A lady in a protective mask sat at the steering wheel, and two others holding Launchers sat on the bench seat behind her.

One of the men opened the side door, then gestured inside with a nod of the head. "In you go. One wrong move and bullets start flying. Like I said, we've got nothing to lose. And I can think of a lot worse things than the world with one or two less Munies in it."

Thomas climbed into the back of the van, all the time working at their odds. Six versus six, he thought. But they had weapons.

"Who's paying you to steal Immunes?" he asked as his friends clambered in to sit beside him. He wanted someone to confirm what Teresa had told Gally, that Munies were being rounded up and sold.

Nobody responded.

The three people who'd greeted them at the Berg got into the van and closed the doors. Then they aimed their weapons toward the back.

"There's a pile of black hoods in the corner," the lead guy said. "Put them on. And it won't sit well with me if I catch you peeking during the ride. We like to keep our secrets nice and safe."

Thomas sighed—arguing would be pointless. He grabbed one of the hoods and slipped it over his head. All he saw was darkness as the van lurched into motion with a roar of the engine.

CHAPTER 43

It was a smooth ride, but it seemed to last forever. And so much time to think about things wasn't exactly what Thomas needed—especially without being able to see. He was nauseated by the time they finally stopped.

When the side door of the van opened, Thomas instinctively reached up to take off his hood.

"Don't do it," the lead guy snapped. "Don't you dare take those off until we tell you to. Now get out, nice and slow. Do us a favor and keep yourselves alive."

"You sure are a tough shank," Thomas heard Minho say. "Easy to do when you've got six people with guns. Why don't you—"

He was cut off by the thump of a hard punch, followed by a loud grunt.

Hands grabbed Thomas and pulled him out of the van so roughly that he almost fell down. Once he got his balance, the person yanked again and started leading him away; Thomas was barely able to keep his feet under himself.

He kept quiet as he was led down a set of stairs and then down a long hallway. They stopped, and he heard the swipe of a key card, the click of a lock, then the creak of a door opening. As it did, the murmurs of hushed voices filled the air, as if dozens of people were waiting inside.

The woman gave him a push and he stumbled a few steps forward.

He immediately reached up and yanked the hood off his head, just as the door closed behind him.

He and the others stood in a huge room filled with people, most of them sitting on the floor. Dull lights in the ceiling illuminated the few dozen faces that stared back at them, some of them dirty, most of them scratched or bruised.

A woman came forward, her face twisted by fear and anxiety. "What's it like out there?" she asked. "We've been in here for a few hours, and things were falling apart. Has it gotten worse?"

More people started to approach their group as Thomas answered. "We were outside the city—they got us at the gates. What do you mean things were falling apart? What happened?"

She looked at the floor. "The government declared a state of emergency, without any kind of warning. Then the police, the cop machines, the Flare testers—they all disappeared. All at once, it seemed. We got snagged by these people trying to get work at the city building. There wasn't even time to figure out what was happening or why."

"We were guards over at the Crank Palace," another man said. "Others like us had been disappearing left and right, so we finally gave up and came to Denver a few days ago. We got nabbed at the airport, too."

"How'd everything get so bad, so suddenly?" Brenda asked. "We were here three days ago."

The man let out a sharp, bitter laugh. "The whole city is full of idiots thinking they've been containing the virus. It's been a long and slow rumble, but it's all finally exploded in our faces. The world has no chance—the virus is too strong. Some of us have seen this coming for a long time."

Thomas's gaze wandered back to the group of people approaching. He froze when he saw Aris.

"Minho, look," he said, elbowing him and pointing.

The boy from Group B had already broken into a grin and was jogging over. Behind him, Thomas could see a couple of girls who had been in Aris's Maze group. Whoever these people were who had taken them, they were good at their job.

Aris reached Thomas and stood in front of him as if he were about to give him a hug, then held out a hand instead. Thomas shook it.

"Glad you guys are okay," the boy said.

"You too." Seeing Aris's familiar face made Thomas realize that any bitterness he'd felt about what had happened between them in the Scorch was gone. "Where is everyone?"

Aris's face darkened. "Most of them aren't with us anymore. They got taken by another group."

Before Thomas could process what he'd said, Teresa appeared. Thomas had to clear his throat to get rid of the lump that had suddenly formed there. "Teresa?" He felt such a flurry of conflicted emotions he could barely get the word out.

"Hey, Tom." She stepped close to him, her eyes sad. "I'm so glad you're okay." Her eyes moistened with tears.

"Yeah, you too." Part of him hated her; part of him had missed her. He wanted to scream at her for leaving them behind at WICKED.

"Where did you guys go?" she asked. "How did you get all the way to Denver?"

Thomas was confused. "What do you mean, where did we go?"

She stared at him for a few seconds. "We've got a lot to talk about."

Thomas squinted. "What're you up to now?"

"I'm not up to . . ." Defiance gripped her voice. "There's obviously been some miscommunication. Look, most of our group was captured by different bounty hunters yesterday—they've probably already been taken back and sold to WICKED. Including Frypan. I'm sorry."

An image of the cook popped into Thomas's head. He didn't know if he could handle losing yet another friend.

Minho leaned in to speak. "I can see you're as cheerful as always. So glad to be back in your sunshiny presence."

Teresa completely ignored him. "Tom, they'll be moving us soon. Please come talk to me. In private. Now."

Thomas hated the fact that he *wanted* to, and he tried to hide his eagerness. "The Rat Man already gave me his big speech. Please tell me you don't agree with him and think I should go back to WICKED."

"I don't even know what you're talking about." She paused, as if battling her pride. "Please."

Thomas stared at her for a long moment, not sure how he felt. Brenda was just a few feet away, and it was clear she wasn't happy to see Teresa.

"Well?" Teresa asked. She motioned to their surroundings. "Not a lot to do in here but wait around. Are you too busy to talk to me?"

Thomas had to stop himself from rolling his eyes. He pointed to a couple of empty chairs in the corner of the large room. "Let's go, but make it quick."

CHAPTER 44

Thomas sat with his head against the wall, arms folded. Teresa had her legs pulled up under her, sitting so that she faced him. Minho had warned him not to listen to a word she said as they'd walked away.

"So," Teresa said.

"So."

"Where do we start?"

"This was your idea. You tell me. We can be done if you don't have anything to say."

Teresa sighed. "Maybe you could start by giving me the benefit of the doubt and quit acting like a jerk. Yes, I know I did things in the Scorch, but you also know why I did them—to save you in the long run. I didn't know it was all about Variables and patterns then. How about giving me a little credit? Talk to me like a regular person."

Thomas let silence fill the air for a few moments before he answered. "Okay, fine. But you left me behind at WICKED, which shows you—"

"Tom!" she yelled, looking as if she'd been slapped. "We did *not* leave you behind! What are you talking about?"

"What are *you* talking about?" Thomas was thoroughly confused now.

"We didn't leave you behind! We came after *you. You* left *us* behind!"

Thomas could only stare at her. "Do you really think I'm that stupid?"

"All anyone talked about at the complex was that you, Newt, and Minho had broken out and were in the surrounding forest somewhere. We looked but didn't see any sign of you. I've been hoping ever since that somehow you made it back to civilization. Why do you think I was so thrilled to see you alive!"

Thomas felt a stirring of familiar anger. "How can you possibly expect me to believe that? You probably knew exactly what Rat Man tried to tell me—that they needed me, that I'm the so-called Final Candidate."

Teresa slouched. "You think I'm the most evil person to ever walk the earth, don't you?" She didn't wait for him to answer her, though. "If you had just gotten your memories back like you were supposed to, you'd see that I'm the same Teresa I've always been. I did what I did in the Scorch to save you, and I've been trying to make up for it ever since."

Thomas was having a hard time staying angry—she didn't seem to be acting. "How can I believe you, Teresa? How?"

She looked up at him, and her eyes were glassy. "I swear to you, I don't know everything about the Final Candidate—that stuff was developed after we went to the Maze, so I have no memories of that. But what I *did* learn was that WICKED doesn't intend to stop the Trials until they get their blueprint. They're preparing to start another round, Thomas. WICKED is gathering more Immunes to begin testing if the Trials didn't work. And I can't do it again. I left to find you. That's it."

Thomas didn't respond. A part of him wanted to believe. Desperately.

"I'm so sorry," Teresa said through a sigh. She looked away and ran her hand through her hair. She waited several seconds before she looked at him again. "All I can tell you is that I'm torn up inside. Ripped apart. I did believe that a cure could happen, and I knew they needed you to do it. It's different now. Even with my memories back I can't think the same way I did before. I can see now that things will never end."

She stopped talking, but Thomas had nothing to say. He searched Teresa's face and saw a pain unlike any he'd ever seen before. She was telling the truth.

She didn't wait for him to speak before she continued. "So I made a deal with myself. I'd do whatever it took to make up for my mistakes. I wanted to save my friends first, and then other Immunes, if possible. And look what a great job I did."

Thomas searched for words. "Well, we haven't done much better, have we?"

Her eyebrows rose. "Were you hoping to stop them?"

"We're about to be sold back to WICKED, so what does it matter?"

She didn't answer right away. Thomas would've given anything to be inside her head—and not in the old way. For a brief moment he felt sad, knowing they'd shared countless hours together that he no longer had any memory of. They'd been best friends once.

She finally said, "If somehow we *could* do something, I hope that you'd find a way to trust me again. And I know we can convince Aris and the others to help us. They feel the same way I do."

Thomas knew he had to be careful. It was strange that she only agreed with him about WICKED now that she'd gotten her memories back.

"We'll see what happens," he finally said

She frowned deeply. "You really don't trust me, do you?"

"We'll see what happens," he repeated. Then he stood up and walked away, hating the look of hurt on her face. And hating himself for caring after everything she'd done to him.

CHAPTER 45

Thomas found Minho sitting with Brenda and Jorge when he returned, and Minho didn't seem happy to see him. He gave Thomas a nasty look. "So what did that shuck traitor have to say?"

Thomas sat down beside him. Several strangers had gathered closer, and he could tell they were listening in.

"Well?" Minho pushed.

"She said that the reason they escaped was because they found out WICKED plans to start all over again if they have to. That they were rounding up Immunes—just like Gally told us. She swears that somehow they were led to believe that we'd already broken out—and that they looked for us." Thomas paused—he knew Minho wouldn't like the next part. "And she'd help us if she can."

Minho just shook his head. "You're a slinthead. You shouldn't have talked to her."

"Thanks." Thomas rubbed his face. Minho was right.

"Hate to barge in here, *muchachos,*" Jorge said. "You can talk all day about this crap, but it means diddly unless we can get ourselves out of this nice little place. No matter who's on whose side."

Just then the door to the room opened and three of their captors walked in with big sacks stuffed full of something. A fourth followed, armed with a Launcher and a pistol. He swept the room, looking for trouble, and the others started passing out what was inside the bags— bread and bottles of water.

"How do we always get into these messes?" Minho asked. "At least we used to be able to blame everything on WICKED."

"Yeah, well, we still can," Thomas murmured.

Minho grinned. "Good. Those shuck-faces."

An uneasy silence settled on the room as the kidnappers moved around. People began to eat. Thomas realized that they'd have to whisper if they wanted to keep talking.

Minho nudged Thomas. "Only one of them has a weapon," he whispered. "And he doesn't look so bad. I bet I could take him."

"Maybe," Thomas answered under his breath. "But don't do anything stupid—he's got a gun as well as a Launcher. And trust me, you don't want to get shot by either."

"Yeah, well, you trust *me* this time." Minho gave Thomas a wink, to which Thomas could only sigh. The odds were not good that what was about to happen would go unnoticed.

The kidnappers approached Thomas and Minho and stopped at their little group. Thomas took a roll and a bottle of water, but when the man tried to hand some bread to Minho, he swatted it away.

"Why would I take anything from you? It's probably poisoned."

"You wanna go hungry, fine by me," the guy replied, moving on.

He had nearly passed them when Minho suddenly leaped to his feet and tackled the man holding the Launcher. Thomas flinched as it slipped out of the guy's grip and discharged, sending a grenade up toward the ceiling, where it crashed in a display of lightning. The kidnapper was still on the ground when Minho started punching him, struggling to grab the man's pistol with his free hand.

For a moment, everyone froze. But then movement exploded all at once before Thomas could react. The three other guards dropped their bags to go after Minho, but before they could take a step they had six people on them, throwing them to the ground. Jorge helped Minho drag the guard to the floor and was stomping the man's arm until he finally let go of the pistol he'd pulled from his belt; Minho kicked it across the floor, and a woman picked it up. Thomas saw that Brenda had grabbed the Launcher.

"Stop!" she shouted, aiming the weapon at the kidnappers.

Minho stood up, and as he stepped away from the man on the ground, Thomas could see that the guy's face was covered in blood. People were already dragging the other three guards over to lie next to their partner, lining them up so that all four were on their backs in a row.

It had all happened so fast, Thomas hadn't moved from his spot on the floor, but he immediately got to work.

"We have to get them to talk," he said. "We have to hurry before backup comes."

"We should just shoot them in the head!" a man called out. "Shoot them and get out of here." A few others shouted their agreement.

Thomas realized that the group had turned into a mob. If he wanted information he had to work fast—before things fell apart. He stood and made his way over to the woman with the gun and convinced her to hand it to him; then he turned and knelt beside the man who'd given him the bread.

Thomas put the gun to the guy's temple. "I'm going to count to three. You either start telling what WICKED plans to do with us and where you were going to meet them or I'll pull the trigger. One."

The man didn't hesitate. "WICKED? We got nothing to do with WICKED."

"You're lying. Two."

"No, I swear! This has nothing to do with them! At least as far as I know."

"Oh really? Then you want to explain why you're out kidnapping a bunch of immune people?"

The man's eyes flickered to his friends, but then he answered, looking straight at Thomas. "We work for the Right Arm."

CHAPTER 46

"What do you mean you work for the Right Arm?" Thomas asked. It made no sense.

"What do you mean what do I mean?" the man said, despite the gun at his head. "I work for the freaking Right Arm. Why's that so hard to understand?"

Thomas pulled the gun away and sat back, confused. "Then why would you be out capturing Immunes?"

"Because we want to," he said, eyeing the lowered weapon. "You ain't got no business knowin' nothing else."

"Shoot him and move on to the next one," someone in the crowd called out.

Thomas leaned back in, pressed the gun against the man's temple again. "You're awfully brave considering I'm the one with the gun. I'll count to three one more time. Tell me why the Right Arm would want Immunes or I'll just have to assume you're lying. One."

"You know I ain't lying, kid."

"Two."

"You ain't gonna kill me. I can see it in your eyes."

The man had called his bluff. There was no way Thomas could just shoot some stranger in the head. He sighed, pulled the gun away. "If you work for the Right Arm, then we're supposed to be on the same side. Just tell us what's going on."

The guy sat up, slowly, and so did his three friends, the bloody-faced man groaning with the effort.

"If you want answers," one said, "then you'll have to ask the boss. We seriously don't know anything."

"Yeah," added the man next to Thomas. "We're nobodies."

Brenda stepped closer with her Launcher. "And how do we get to this boss of yours?"

The man shrugged. "I have no idea."

Minho groaned and snatched the gun from Thomas's hands. "I've had enough of this klunk." He pointed the weapon at the man's foot. "Fine, we won't kill you, but your toe's gonna be smarting something real awful in three seconds if you don't start talking. One."

"I'm telling you, we don't know nothin'." The guy's face was pinched in anger.

"Fine," Minho replied. He fired the gun.

Thomas watched in shock as the man grabbed his foot, wailing in agony. Minho had shot him right in the pinkie toe—that part of the shoe and the toe itself were completely gone, replaced by a bleeding wound.

"How could you do that?" the guard next to him on the ground yelled as she moved to help her friend. She pulled a wad of napkins from her pants and pressed them against his foot.

Thomas was shocked that Minho had actually done it, but he had to respect the guy. Thomas couldn't have pulled the trigger, and if they didn't get answers now, they never would. He looked over at Brenda, and her shrug showed that she agreed. Teresa was watching from a distance, her face unreadable.

Minho kept at it. "Okay, while she's working on that poor foot of his, someone better start talking. Tell us what's going on or we're going to lose another toe." He waved the pistol at the lady, then the other two guys. "Why are you kidnapping people for the Right Arm?"

"We told you, we don't know anything," the woman answered. "They pay us and we do what they ask."

"And you?" Minho asked, pointing the gun at one of the men. "You wanna say something—save a toe or two?"

He held up his hands. "I swear on the life of my mom I don't know anything. But . . ."

He seemed to regret that last part immediately. His gaze shot to his friends and his face paled.

"But what? Spill it—I know you're hiding something."

"Nothing."

"Do we really need to keep playing this game?" Minho moved the gun directly up against the man's foot. "I'm done counting."

"Stop!" the guard yelled. "Okay, listen. We could take a couple of you back with us to ask them yourselves. I don't know if they'll let you talk to the one in charge, but they might. I'm not getting my toe shot off for no good reason."

"All right, then," Minho said, taking a step back and gesturing for the guy to stand up. "See, that wasn't so bad. Let's go visit this boss of yours. Me, you, and my friends."

The room burst into a rush of voices. No one wanted to be left behind and no one was going to be quiet about it.

The woman who'd brought in the water stood up and started yelling. The crowd went silent. "You people are a lot safer here! Just trust me on that one. If all of us tried to make it to where we'd need to go, I can guarantee half wouldn't get there. If these guys want to see the boss, then let them risk their necks. A gun and a Launcher aren't going to do a bit of good out there. But in here we have a locked door and no windows."

When she finished, another chorus of complaints filled the room. The woman turned to Minho and Thomas and spoke over the noise. "Listen, it's dangerous out there. I wouldn't take more than a couple of people. The more you have, the more likely you'll be seen." She paused and scanned the room. "And I'd go soon if I were you. From the looks of it, these people are only going to get antsier. Pretty soon there'll be no way to hold them off. And out there . . ."

She pursed her lips together tightly, then continued. "There are Cranks everywhere. They're killing anything that moves."

CHAPTER 47

Minho pointed his gun at the ceiling and fired, making Thomas jump. The noise of the crowd collapsed into complete silence.

Minho didn't need to say a word. He gestured to the woman to speak.

"It's crazy out there. It's all happened really quickly. Like they've been hiding and waiting for a signal or something. This morning the police were overpowered and the gates were opened. Some Cranks from the Palace joined them. They're everywhere now."

She paused and took the time to meet a few gazes. "I promise you don't want to go out there. And I promise that *we're* the good guys. I don't know what the Right Arm has planned, but I do know that part of it includes getting all of us out of Denver."

"Then why are you treating us like prisoners?" someone yelled.

"I'm just doing what I was hired to do." She turned her attention back to Thomas and continued. "I think it's a stupid idea to leave this place, but like I said, if you're going to, you can't take more than a couple of people. Those Cranks spot a big group of fresh meat walking around and it's all over. Weapons or no weapons. And the boss might not like it if a crowd shows up—our guards see a van full of strangers and they might start shooting."

"Brenda and I will go," Thomas said. He didn't even know he was going to say it until it popped out of his mouth.

"No way," Minho shook his head. "Me and you."

Minho was a liability. His temper was too short. Brenda thought before she acted, and that was what they needed to get out of this alive. And Thomas didn't want to let her out of his sight—plain and simple. "Me and her. We did pretty well for ourselves back in the Scorch. We can do it."

"No way, man!" Thomas could swear his friend almost looked hurt. "We shouldn't split up. All four of us should go—it'll be safer."

"Minho, we need someone back here to watch over things," Thomas said, and he meant it. This was a whole roomful of people who might be able to help them take WICKED down. "Plus, I hate to say it, but what if something *does* happen to us? Stay behind and make sure our plans don't die. They've got Frypan, Minho. Who knows who else. You said once that I should be the Keeper of the Runners. Well, let me do it today. Trust me. Like the lady said, the fewer we are, the better our chance of going unnoticed."

Thomas looked his friend in the eye and waited for a response. Minho didn't answer for a long time.

"Fine," he finally said. "But if you die I will *not* be happy."

Thomas nodded. "Good that." He hadn't realized how important it was that Minho still believe in him. It went halfway to giving him the courage he needed to do what he had to do.

The man who'd said they could take Thomas and his friends to the boss ended up being the one to guide them. His name was Lawrence, and regardless of what was outside, he seemed eager to get out of the room full of angry people. He unlocked the big door and gestured for Thomas and Brenda to follow him—Thomas with the pistol and Brenda with the Launcher.

The group made their way back down the long hallway and Lawrence stopped at the door leading out of the building. The dull light from the ceiling shone on the man's face, and Thomas could see that he was worried.

"Okay, we have to make a decision. If we go on foot, it'll take a couple of hours, but we have a lot better chance of getting through the streets. We can hide on foot easier than if we take the van. The van would get us there faster, but we'd be spotted for sure."

"Speed versus stealth," Thomas said. He looked at Brenda. "What do you think?"

"The van," she said.

"Yeah," Thomas agreed. The image of the bloody-faced Crank from the day before haunted him. "The thought of being out there on foot scares me to death. The van, definitely."

Lawrence nodded. "Okay, then, the van it is. Now keep your mouths shut and those weapons ready. First thing we gotta do is get in the vehicle and lock the doors. It's right outside this door. Ready?"

Thomas raised his eyebrows at Brenda and they both nodded. As ready as they'd ever be.

Lawrence pulled a stack of key cards out of his pocket and unlocked the many latches lined up on the wall. He clenched the cards in his fist and pushed his body up against the door, then slowly cracked it open. It was dark outside, a lone streetlamp providing the only light. Thomas wondered how long the electricity would hold up before it stopped, like everything else eventually would. Denver could be dead in days.

He could see the van parked in a narrow alley about twenty feet away. Lawrence peeked his head outside, looked left and right, then pulled it back in.

"Seems clear. Let's go."

The three slipped out, and Thomas and Brenda sprinted to the van as Lawrence secured the door behind them. Thomas felt like a live wire. Anxiety had him glancing up and down the street, sure he'd see a Crank jump out at any second. But though he could hear the far-off sound of crazed laughter, the place was deserted.

The van's locks disengaged and Brenda opened the door and slid inside just as Lawrence did. Thomas joined them in the front seat and slammed the door shut. Lawrence immediately engaged the locks and started the engine. He was just about to gun it when a loud pop came from right above their heads and the van shook with a couple of thumps. Then silence. Then the muted sound of a cough.

Someone had jumped onto the roof of the van.

CHAPTER 48

The van shot forward, Lawrence's hands gripped tightly on the wheel. Thomas turned and looked out the back windows—but there was nothing. Somehow, the person on top of the van was hanging on.

Just as Thomas spun back around, a face started creeping down the front windshield, staring at them upside down. It was a woman, her hair whipping in the wind as Lawrence sent the van tearing down the alleyway at breakneck speed. The woman's eyes met Thomas's, and then she smiled, showing a set of surprisingly perfect teeth.

"What's she holding on to?" Thomas yelled.

Lawrence answered, his voice strained. "Who knows. But she can't last long."

The woman's eyes stayed locked on Thomas, but she had freed one of her hands and balled it into a fist, then started pounding the window. *Thump, thump, thump.* Her smile stayed wide, her teeth almost glistening in the lamplight.

"Would you *please* get rid of her?" Brenda shouted.

"Fine." Lawrence slammed on the brakes.

The woman flew into the air, shooting forward like a launched grenade, her arms windmilling and her legs splayed, until she crashed to the ground. Thomas winced and squeezed his eyes shut, then strained to get a look at her. Shockingly, she was already moving, shakily getting to her feet. She regained her balance, then turned slowly toward them, the headlights from the van brightly illuminating every inch of her.

219

She was no longer smiling, not at all. Instead her lips had curled into a fierce snarl; a big welt reddened the side of her face. Her eyes bore into Thomas once more, and he shivered.

Lawrence gunned the engine, and the Crank looked like she was going to hurl herself in front of the vehicle, as if she could somehow stop it, but at the last second she pulled back and watched them pass. Thomas couldn't take his eyes off her, and in his last glimpse, her face melted into a frown and her eyes cleared, as if she'd just realized what she'd done. As if there was something left of the person she used to be.

And seeing that made it worse for Thomas. "She was like a mix of sane and not sane."

"Just be glad she was the only one," Lawrence muttered.

Brenda squeezed Thomas's arm. "It's hard to look at. I know how it felt for you and Minho to see what'd happened to Newt."

Thomas didn't answer, but he put his hand on top of hers.

They reached the end of the alley, and Lawrence swerved to the right onto a bigger street. Small groups of people dotted the area up ahead. A few were struggling as if they were fighting, but most were digging through trash or eating things Thomas couldn't quite make out. Several haunted, ghostly faces just stood and stared at them with dead eyes as they drove by.

No one in the van said anything, as if they were afraid that speaking would somehow alert the Cranks outside.

"I can't believe it happened so fast," Brenda finally said. "You think they were somehow planning to take over Denver? Could they really *organize* something like that?"

"Hard to know," Lawrence replied. "There were signs. Locals disappearing, reps from the government disappearing, more and more infecteds being discovered. But it looks like a huge number of them suckers hid out, waiting for the right time to make their move."

"Yeah," Brenda said. "It seems like it was a matter of Cranks finally outnumbering healthy people. Once the balance tipped, it tipped all the way over."

"Who cares how it happened," Lawrence said. "The only thing that matters is how it *is*. Look around us. The place is a nightmare now." He slowed down to make a tight turn into a long alley. "Almost there. We need to be more careful now." He turned off the headlights, then picked up speed again.

As they drove, it became darker and darker, until Thomas couldn't see anything more than large, formless shadows that he kept imagining would suddenly leap out in front of them. "Maybe you shouldn't drive so fast."

"We'll be fine," the man replied. "I've driven this route a thousand times. I know it like the back of my—"

Thomas flew forward and was snapped back by the seat belt. They'd run over something, and it was caught beneath the van—metal, from the sound of it. The van bounced a couple of times, then came to a stop.

"What was that?" Brenda whispered.

"I don't know," Lawrence responded in an even quieter voice. "Probably a trash can or something. Scared the crap out of me."

He inched forward and a loud, scraping screech filled the air. Then came a thump and another crash and everything fell silent.

"Got her loose," Lawrence murmured, not bothering to hide his relief. He continued, but slowed to a fraction of his earlier speed.

"Maybe you should turn the lights back on?" Thomas suggested, amazed at how fast his heart was beating. "I can't see a thing out there."

"Yeah," Brenda added. "I'm pretty sure anyone out there heard that racket anyway."

"I guess so." Lawrence turned them on.

The headlights illuminated the entire alley in a spray of bluish-white light that, compared to the previous darkness, seemed brighter than the sun. Thomas squinted at the glare, then opened his eyes fully and a bloom of horror rose up in him. About twenty feet in front of them, at least thirty people had emerged and now stood packed together, completely blocking the road.

Their faces were pale and haggard, scratched and bruised. Ripped, filthy clothes hung from their bodies. They stood there, every one of them looking into the bright lights as if they weren't fazed in the least. They were like standing corpses, raised from the dead.

Thomas shivered from the chill that iced his body.

The crowd started to part. They moved in sync, and a large space cleared in the middle as they backed to the sides of the alley. Then one of them waved an arm, gesturing that the van should go ahead and drive past.

"These are some awfully polite Cranks," Lawrence whispered.

CHAPTER 49

"Maybe they're not past the Gone yet?" Thomas answered, even though the statement sounded stupid even to him. "Or not in the mood to get run over by a big van?"

"Well, gun it," Brenda said. "Before they change their mind."

To Thomas's relief, Lawrence did just that; the van shot forward and he didn't slow down. The Cranks lining the walls stared at them as they sailed past. Seeing them close up—the scratches and blood and bruises, those maddened eyes—made Thomas shiver again.

They were just approaching the end of the group when several loud pops sounded and the van jolted and swerved to the right. Its front end slammed into the wall of the alley, pinning two Cranks against it. Thomas stared in horror through the windshield as they screamed in agony and beat bloody fists against the front of the vehicle.

"What the hell?" Lawrence bellowed as he put the van in reverse.

They screeched backward several feet, the vehicle shaking horribly. The two Cranks fell to the ground and were immediately attacked by the ones closest to the front of the van. Thomas quickly looked away, filled with a nauseating terror. On all sides, Cranks started thumping the van with their fists. At the same time, the tires were spinning and squealing, unable to gain traction. The combination of noises was like something from a nightmare.

"What's wrong?" Brenda yelled.

"They did something to the tires! Or the axels. Something!"

Lawrence kept switching the van from reverse to drive, but each time it only went a few feet. A lady with wild hair approached the window to Thomas's right. She was holding a huge shovel in both hands, and he watched as she raised it over her head, then swung it down against the window. The glass didn't give.

"We really need to get out of here!" Thomas shouted. Helpless, he didn't know what else to say. They'd been stupid to let themselves fall into such an obvious trap.

Lawrence kept shifting and gassing the van, but they merely jerked back and forth. A series of familiar thumps sounded from the roof. Someone was up there. Cranks were attacking all the windows now, with everything from wooden sticks to their own heads. The lady outside Thomas's window didn't give up, smacking her shovel into the glass over and over again. Finally, the fifth or sixth time she did it, a hairline crack shot across the window.

The growing panic made Thomas's throat constrict. "She's going to smash it!"

"Get us out of here!" Brenda said at the same time.

The van moved a few inches, just enough to make the woman miss with her next swing. But someone slammed a sledgehammer into the windshield from above and a huge spiderweb blossomed like a white flower in the glass.

Again the van jolted backward. The man holding the sledgehammer tumbled onto the front hood before he could slam the glass again and landed in the street. A Crank with a long gash on top of his bald head yanked the tool from the man's grip and got two more whacks in before a group of other people started fighting him for his weapon. The cracks in the windshield almost completely obscured the view from inside the van. The sound of breaking glass came from the rear; Thomas spun around to see an arm wriggling through a gash in the window, the jagged edges tearing its skin.

Thomas unbuckled his seat belt and squirmed into the back of the van. He grabbed the first thing he found, a long plastic tool with a brush on one end and a sharp edge on the other—a snow pick—and crawled over the middle row of seats; he slammed the thing into the Crank's arm, then again, then a third time. Screaming, whoever it was pulled their arm out, knocking pieces of glass onto the cement outside.

"You want the Launcher?" Brenda called back to him.

"No!" Thomas shouted. "It's too big inside the van. Grab the gun!"

The van lurched forward, then stopped again; Thomas smacked his face on the back of the middle bench, and pain shot through his cheek and jaw. He turned to see a man and woman tearing away at the remaining glass in the broken window. Blood from their hands oozed down both sides of the hole as it got bigger.

"Here!" Brenda yelled from behind him.

He turned and took the gun from her, then aimed and fired, once, then twice, and the Cranks fell to the ground, any screams of agony drowned out by the awful noise of the squealing tires and overworked engine, the pounding of the Cranks' attack.

"I think we're almost loose!" Lawrence shouted. "I don't know what the hell they did!"

Thomas turned to look at him; he was covered in sweat. A hole had appeared at the middle of the spiderweb on the windshield. Cracks completely lined the other windows—almost nothing outside was visible anymore. Brenda held her Launcher, ready to use it if things got completely hopeless.

The van went backward, then forward, then backward again. It seemed to be under a little more control, was shaking less than it had been. Two sets of arms came through the big hole in the back, and

Thomas let off two more shots. They heard screams, and a woman's face—twisted into a hideous scowl, her every tooth edged with grime—appeared at the window.

"Just let us in, boy," she said, her words barely audible. "All we want is food. Just give us some food. *Let me in!*"

She screamed the last few words and pushed her head through the opening as if she actually thought she could fit. Thomas didn't want to shoot her but held the gun up, readied himself in case she somehow managed to get inside. But when the van bolted forward again, she fell out, leaving the edges of the broken window covered in blood.

Thomas braced himself for the van to go backward again. But after a short, jolting stop, it went forward several more feet, turning in the right direction. Then a few more.

"I think I've got it!" Lawrence yelled.

Again forward, this time maybe ten feet. The Cranks followed as best they could—the short moment of silence as they were left behind didn't last, though. Soon the screams and thumps and bangs began all over again. A man reached through the hole in the back with a long knife, started slashing left and right at anything and nothing. Thomas lifted his gun and fired. How many had he killed? Three? Four? *Had* he killed them?

With one last long, terrible squeal, the van shot forward and then didn't stop. It bounced a couple of times as it ran over the Cranks who'd been in their path; then it smoothed out and picked up speed. Thomas looked out the back, saw bodies falling off the roof and onto the street. The remaining Cranks gave chase, but soon they were all left behind.

Thomas collapsed onto the seat, lying on his back, staring up at the dented roof. He sucked in huge, heavy breaths, tried to regain control of his emotions. He was barely aware of Lawrence turning off the one headlight that hadn't been smashed, making two more turns, then slipping through an open garage door that closed as soon as they cleared it.

CHAPTER 50

When the van pulled to a stop and Lawrence shut off the engine, silence enveloped Thomas's world. The only thing he heard was the rush of pumping blood inside his head. He closed his eyes and tried to slow his breathing. Neither of the other two said anything for a couple of minutes, until Lawrence broke the silence.

"They're out there, surrounding us, waiting for us to get out."

Thomas forced himself to sit up and face the front again. Outside the broken windows, it was totally dark.

"Who?" Brenda asked.

"The boss's guards. They know this is one of their vans, but they won't approach us until we get out and show ourselves. They need to confirm who we are—I'd guess we have about twenty weapons aimed at us right now."

"So what do we do?" Thomas asked, not ready for another confrontation.

"We get out, nice and slow. They'll recognize me soon enough."

Thomas crawled over the seats. "Do we get out at the same time, or should just one of us go first?"

"I'll get out first, tell them it's okay. Wait until I knock on the window to get out," Lawrence answered. "Ready?"

"I guess," Thomas sighed.

"It would really suck," Brenda said, "if we went through all that just to have them shoot us. I'm sure I look like a Crank right about now."

Lawrence opened his door and Thomas waited, anxious for his cue. The loud rap on the frame of the van startled Thomas, but he was ready.

Brenda eased her door open slowly and stepped out. Thomas followed her, straining to see in the darkness, but the room was pitch-black.

A loud click sounded and the place was instantly flooded with bright white light. Thomas threw his hands up and squeezed his eyes shut, then, shielding himself, squinted to see what was going on. A huge spotlight mounted on a tripod was pointed directly at them. He could just make out the silhouettes of two figures on either side of it. Scanning the rest of the room, he saw that there were at least a dozen other people, all holding various types of weapons, just as Lawrence had said there would be.

"Lawrence, is that you?" a man called out, his voice echoing against concrete walls. It was impossible to tell which person had spoken.

"Yeah, it's me."

"What happened to our van, and who are these people? Tell me you didn't bring infecteds in here."

"We got jumped by a huge group of Cranks down the alley a ways. And these guys are Munies—they forced me to bring them to you. They want to see the boss."

"Why?" the man asked.

"They said—"

The man cut Lawrence off. "No, I want to hear it from them. State your names, why you forced our man to come here and destroy one of the few vehicles we have left. And it better be a good reason."

Thomas and Brenda exchanged a look to see who should talk and Brenda nodded to him.

He returned his gaze to the spotlight, focusing on the person to the right of it. That was his best guess at who'd been doing the talking. "My name is Thomas. This is Brenda. We know Gally—we were with him

228

at WICKED and he told us about the Right Arm and what you guys are doing a few days ago. We were on board to help, but not like this. We just want to know what you're planning, why you're kidnapping immune people and locking them up. I thought that was WICKED kind of stuff."

Thomas didn't know what he'd expected, but the guy started to chuckle. "I think I'll let you see the boss just so you get the damn idea out of your head that we'd *ever* do anything like WICKED."

Thomas shrugged. "Fine. Let us see your boss." The man seemed sincere in his disgust with WICKED. But it still didn't make sense why they'd taken all those people.

"You better not be blowing things out your butt, kid," the guy said. "Lawrence, bring them in. Somebody else check the van for weapons."

Thomas kept silent as he and Brenda were led up two flights of dingy metal stairs. Then through a weathered wooden door, down a dirty hallway with one lightbulb and wallpaper peeling from the walls, then finally to a large space that might've been a nice conference room fifty years earlier. Now all it held was a big, scarred table with plastic chairs scattered haphazardly around the room.

Two people sat at the far side of the table. Thomas noticed Gally first, on the right. He looked tired and disheveled, but he managed a slight nod and a small smile—nothing more than an unfortunate wrinkle in the mess that was his face. A huge man was next to him, more fat than muscle, his girth barely contained between the arms of the white plastic chair he sat in.

"This is the headquarters of the Right Arm?" Brenda asked. "Consider me a little discouraged."

Gally answered, his smile gone. "We've moved around more times than we can count. But thank you for the compliment."

"So which one of you is the boss?" Thomas asked.

Gally nodded at his companion. "Don't be a slinthead—Vince is in charge. And show some respect. He's risked his life just because he believes that things should be made right in the world."

Thomas held his hands up in a conciliatory gesture. "I didn't mean anything. The way you acted in your apartment, I thought you might be the guy in charge."

"Well, I'm not. Vince is."

"Does Vince know how to talk?" Brenda asked.

"Enough!" the large man yelled in a deep, booming voice. "Our whole city is overrun with Cranks—I don't have time to sit here and listen to childish spats. What do you people want?"

Thomas tried to hide the anger that had lit up inside him. "Just one thing. We want to know why you captured us. Why you're kidnapping people for WICKED. Gally gave us a lot of hope—we thought we were on the same side. Imagine our surprise when we found out the Right Arm was just as bad as the people they're supposedly fighting against. How much money were you going to make selling humans?"

"Gally," the man said in response, as if he hadn't heard a single word Thomas had said.

"Yeah?"

"You trust these two?"

Gally refused to meet Thomas's gaze. "Yeah." He nodded. "We can."

Vince leaned forward, resting his massive arms on the table. "Then we can't waste any time. Boy, this is a look-alike operation and we didn't plan on making a single dime off of anybody. We're collecting Immunes to mimic WICKED."

The response surprised Thomas. "Why in the world would you do something like that?"

"We're going to use them to get inside their headquarters."

CHAPTER 51

Thomas stared at the man for a few seconds. If WICKED really was responsible for the disappearance of the other Immunes, it was so simple he could almost laugh. "That just might work."

"I'm glad you approve." The man's face remained unreadable and Thomas couldn't tell if he was being sarcastic or not. "We have a contact, and the deal is already arranged to sell them. It's our way in. We have to stop those people. Prevent them from wasting even more resources on a pointless experiment. If the world is going to survive, they need to use what they have to help the people left alive. Keep the human race going in a way that makes sense."

"Do you think there's any chance they could ever find a cure?" Thomas asked.

Vince let out a long, low chuckle that rumbled in his chest. "If you believed that for even a second, you wouldn't be standing here in front of me, would you? You wouldn't have escaped, wouldn't be seeking revenge. Which is what I'm assuming you *are* doing. I know what you've been through—Gally told me everything." He paused. "No, we gave up on their . . . *cure* a long time ago."

"We're not here about revenge," Thomas said. "It's not about us. That's why I like it that you talk about using their resources for something different. How much do you know about what WICKED is doing?"

Vince leaned back in his chair again, the whole thing squeaking as he shifted. "I just told you something, a secret that we've guarded with loss of life. It's your turn to repay the trust. If Lawrence and his people had known who you were, they would've brought you here first thing. I apologize for the rough treatment."

"I don't need apologies," Thomas answered. Though it did bother him that the Right Arm would have treated him differently than anyone else if they'd known who he was. "I just want to know what you have planned."

"We go no further until you share what *you* know. What can *you* offer *us*?"

"Tell him," Brenda whispered, nudging Thomas with an elbow. "This is what we came for."

She was right. His gut had told him to trust Gally from the very moment he'd gotten the note from him, and it was time to commit. Without help, they'd never make it back to their Berg, much less accomplish anything else.

"Okay," he said. "WICKED thinks they can complete the cure, that they're almost there. The only missing piece is me. They swear it's the truth, but they've manipulated and lied so much, it's become impossible to know what's real and what's not real. Who knows what their motives are now. Or how desperate they've gotten, or what they might be willing to do."

"How many of you are there?" Vince asked.

Thomas thought about it. "Fewer than four more—waiting back where we were taken by Lawrence. We don't have numbers, but we have a lot of inside knowledge. How many in your group?"

"Well, Thomas, that's a hard question to answer. If you're asking how many people have joined the Right Arm since we started meeting and gathering forces a few years back, then there are well over a thousand. But as for how many are still around, still safe, still willing to see it all through to the end . . . Well. Then we're only talking a few hundred, unfortunately."

"Are any of you immune?" Brenda asked.

"Almost none. I myself am not, and—after what's come to light in Denver—I'm pretty sure I've got the Flare by now. Hopefully the majority of us do *not* have the virus yet, but it's inevitable in this crumbling world. And we want to make sure that something is done to salvage what's left of this beautiful race called humans."

Thomas pointed to a couple of chairs close by. "Can we sit down?"

"Of course."

Almost as soon as Thomas took a seat he began with the many questions that had built up. "So what exactly are you planning to do?"

Vince let out that rumbling chuckle of his again. "Calm down, son. Tell me what you have to offer in all this, and then I'll tell you my plans."

Thomas realized he was almost out of his seat, leaning across the table. He relaxed and sat back. "Look, we know a lot of things about WICKED's headquarters and how things work there. And we have some in our group who've had their memories returned. But the most important thing is that WICKED *wants* me to come back. And I think we can use that to our advantage somehow."

"That's it?" Vince asked. "That's all you have?"

"I never said we could do much without help. Or without weapons."

At this last comment, Vince and Gally exchanged a knowing look.

Thomas knew he'd struck a chord. "What?"

Vince turned his attention first to Brenda, then Thomas. "We've got something that's infinitely better than weapons."

Thomas leaned forward again. "And what could that possibly be?"

"We have a way to make sure no one can *use* any weapons."

CHAPTER 52

"How?" Brenda asked, before Thomas could speak.

"I'll let Gally explain that."Vince gestured to the boy.

"Okay, think about the Right Arm," Gally said. He stood up. "These people aren't soldiers. They're accountants, janitors, plumbers, teachers. WICKED basically has their own little army. Trained in the finest and most expensive weaponry. Even if we could find the largest stash in the world of Launchers and everything else they use, we'd still be at a huge disadvantage."

Thomas couldn't imagine where this was going. "So what's the plan, then?"

"The only way to even the playing field is to make sure they don't have any weapons. Then we might stand a chance."

"So you're going to steal them somehow?" Brenda asked. "Stop a shipment? What?"

"No, nothing like that," Gally responded, shaking his head. Then a look of childlike excitement came over his face. "It's not about *how many* you can recruit to your cause, but *who* you can recruit. Of everyone the Right Arm has gathered, one woman is the key."

"Who?" Thomas asked.

"Her name is Charlotte Chiswell. She was a lead engineer for the biggest arms manufacturer in the world. At least for the advanced weaponry that uses second-generation technology. Every pistol, Launcher, grenade—you name it—used by WICKED comes from there, and they all rely on advanced electronics and computer systems to function. And Charlotte's figured out a way to render their weapons useless."

"Really?" Brenda asked, her tone full of doubt. Thomas found the idea hard to believe also, but he listened intently as Gally explained.

"There's a common chip in every weapon they use, and she's spent the last several months trying to figure out a way to reprogram the things remotely—to jam them. She finally did it. It'll take a few hours once she starts, and a small device needs to be planted inside the building for it to work, so our people who plan to hand over the Immunes will do the job. If it works, we won't have weapons, either, but at least we'll have a level playing field."

"If not an advantage," Vince added. "Their guards and security detail are so trained in using those weapons that it's second nature by now, I'm sure. But I bet they've grown lax in hand-to-hand combat. Real fighting. Sparring with knives and bats and shovels, sticks and rocks and fists." He grinned mischievously. "It'll be an old-fashioned brawl. And I think we can take them. If we didn't do it that way, if their weapons were still working, we'd get destroyed before it even got going."

Thomas thought back to the battle they'd had with the Grievers inside the Maze. It had been like what Vince just described. He shuddered at the memory, but it sure beat going against full-blown weapons.

And if it worked it would mean they had a chance. A rush of excitement hit Thomas. "So how do you do it?"

Vince paused. "We have three Bergs. We're going in with about eighty people—the strongest we could find in our group. We'll hand over the Immunes to our contact inside WICKED, plant the device— though that's going to be our hardest task—and when it does the job, we'll blow out a hole in the wall and let everyone else in. Once we've gained control of their facility, Charlotte will help us get enough of the weapons running again to *stay* in control. We'll do this, or every last one of us will die trying. We'll blow up the place if we have to."

Thomas took it all in. His group could be invaluable in an assault like this. Especially those with their memories intact. They knew the layout of the WICKED complex.

Vince continued, and it was as if he'd read Thomas's mind. "If what Gally says is true, you and your friends will be a huge help to our planning team, since some of you know the facility inside and out. And every extra body counts—I don't care how old or young you are."

"We have a Berg also," Brenda offered. "Unless Cranks have ripped the thing to shreds. It's just outside the Denver walls on the northwest side. The pilot is back with our other friends."

"Where are your Bergs?" Thomas asked.

Vince waved his hand toward the back of the room. "Thataway. Safe and sound enough. Everything's close. We'd love to have another week or two to prepare, but don't have much choice. Charlotte's device is ready. Our first eighty people are ready. We can spend the next day or so letting you and the others share what you know, make final preparations, and then we move. No reason to make it sound any more glamorous. We'll just go in and do it."

Hearing him say it like that made it more real for Thomas. "How confident are you?"

"Boy, listen to me," Vince said, his expression grave. "For years and years all we've heard about is the mission of WICKED. How every penny, every man, every woman, every resource—how it all had to be devoted to the cause of finding a cure to the Flare. They told us they'd found Immunes, and if we could just figure out why their brains don't succumb to the virus, why then the whole world would be saved! While in the meantime, cities crumble; education, security, medicine for every other malady known to man, charity, humanitarian aid—the whole world goes to pot so WICKED can do whatever they want to do."

"I know," Thomas said. "I know all too well."

Vince couldn't stop talking, spilling thoughts that had obviously churned inside him for years. "We could've stopped the *spread* of the disease a lot better than we've been able to *cure* the disease. But WICKED sucked up all the money and all the best people. Not only that, they gave us false hope, and nobody took the care they should've. Thought the magical cure would save them in the end. But if we wait any longer we'll run out of people to save."

Vince looked tired now. The room fell silent as he sat and stared at Thomas, waiting for a response. And Thomas couldn't argue with what the man had said.

Vince finally spoke again. "Our people selling the Immunes could certainly plant the device once they're inside, but it would be a lot easier if it was in place when we arrive. Having the Immunes will get us into the airspace and permission to land, but . . ." He raised his eyebrows at Thomas as if he wanted him to state the obvious himself.

Thomas nodded. "That's where I come in."

"Yes," Vince said, smiling. "I believe that's where you come in."

CHAPTER 53

A surprising calm settled over Thomas. "You can drop me off a few miles away and let me hike in. I'll pretend I've come back to finish the Trials. Based on what I've seen and heard, they'll welcome me with open arms. Just show me what I need to do to plant the device."

Another genuine smile crossed Vince's face. "I'll have Charlotte do it herself."

"You can get information and help from my friends—Teresa, Aris, others. Brenda here knows a lot, too." Thomas's decision was quick and absolute, but he'd accepted the dangerous task. It was the best chance they had.

"All right, Gally," Vince said. "What's next? How are we going to do this?"

Thomas's old enemy stood up and looked at him. "I'll get Charlotte to train you on the device. Then we'll take you to our Berg hangar, fly you close to the WICKED headquarters and drop you off while the rest of us are getting ready with the main assault team. You better be up for some good acting out there—we should wait a couple of hours before we come in with the Immunes or it'll look suspicious."

"I'll be fine." Thomas made an effort to pull in deep breaths, to calm himself.

"Good. We'll move Teresa and the others over here when you leave. I hope you don't mind another little jaunt through the city."

* * *

Charlotte was a quiet, petite woman and she was all business. She explained the disabling device's functions to Thomas in a curt, efficient manner. It was small enough to fit in the backpack they provided him along with some food and extra clothing for the cold hike he'd have to take. Once the device was planted and activated, it would search for and connect with the signals from each weapon, then scramble its system. It would take about an hour to render all of WICKED's weapons useless.

Simple enough, Thomas thought. The hard part would be planting the thing when he got in without arousing suspicion.

Gally decided that Lawrence would be the one to take Thomas and the pilot to the abandoned hangar where they kept the Bergs. They'd fly to WICKED's headquarters straight from there. It meant another van trip through the Crank-infested streets of Denver, but they'd take the most direct route, which was down a major highway, and dawn had arrived. For some reason that made Thomas feel a little better.

Thomas was busying himself helping to gather last-minute supplies for the trip when Brenda appeared. He nodded at her and gave her a small smile.

"You gonna miss me?" Thomas asked. He made it sound like a joke, but he really wanted her to say yes.

She rolled her eyes. "Don't even say that. You sound like you're giving up already. We'll all be back together, laughing about the good ol' days before you know it."

"I've only known you a few weeks." He smiled again.

"Whatever." She put her arms around him and spoke into his ear.

"I know I was sent into that Scorch city to find you and pretend to be your friend. But I want you to know that you *are* my friend. You ..."

He pulled away so he could see her face again, which was unreadable. "What?"

"Just ... don't let yourself get killed."

Thomas swallowed, not sure what to say.

"Well?" she said.

"You be careful, too" was all he could get out.

Brenda reached up and kissed him on the cheek. "That's the sweetest thing I've ever heard you say." She rolled her eyes again but smiled.

And her smile made everything seem a little brighter to Thomas. "Make sure they don't screw things up," he said. "Make sure all the plans make sense."

"I will. We'll see you in a day or so."

"Okay."

"And I won't get killed if you won't. I promise."

Thomas pulled her into one last hug. "Deal."

CHAPTER 54

The Right Arm gave them a newer van. Lawrence drove and the pilot sat in the passenger seat next to him. She was silent and not very friendly, keeping mostly to herself. Lawrence wasn't in the greatest of moods, either, probably because he'd gone from being a food distributor in a locked-down facility to serving as designated driver through a city of Cranks. Twice.

The sun had risen, glinting off the buildings of what seemed like an entirely different city from the night before. For some reason the light made the world feel a little safer.

Thomas had been given his pistol back, fully loaded, and he had it stuck in the waist of his jeans. He knew a round of twelve bullets wouldn't do a whole lot if they got ambushed again, but it went far for his peace of mind.

"Okay, remember the plan," Lawrence said, finally breaking the silence.

"And what was the plan?" Thomas asked.

"Make it to the hangar without dying."

It sounded good to Thomas.

They lapsed back into quiet, the only sounds those of the engine and the bumps of the road. Such a moment couldn't help but force Thomas to think about all the horrible things that could go wrong in the next day or two. He tried hard to shut his mind off, focus on the fallen city passing by outside.

So far he'd only seen a few people here and there, most of them at a distance. He wondered if the majority had stayed up late, scared of what might jump out of the darkness—or whether they had been doing the jumping themselves.

The sun gleamed on the high windows of the skyscrapers—the massively tall buildings seemed to stretch in every direction for eternity. The van drove right through the heart of the city, down a wide road scattered with abandoned cars. Thomas saw a few Cranks hiding in vehicles, peeking out the windows as if they were waiting to spring a trap.

Lawrence turned off after a mile or two, then headed down a long, straight highway that led to one of the gates of the walled city. Barricades edged both sides of the road—probably built in better times to keep the noise of countless cars from disturbing the city residents whose homes were set close to the thoroughfare. It seemed impossible that such a world had ever existed. A world where you weren't scared for your life every day.

"This'll take us all the way," Lawrence said. "The hangar is probably our most protected facility, so all we have to do is make it there. An hour from now we'll be up in the air, happy and safe."

"Good that," Thomas said, though after the night before it sounded far too easy. The pilot remained quiet.

They'd gone about three miles when Lawrence started to slow the vehicle. "What in the world?" he murmured.

Thomas turned his attention back to the road ahead to see what the man was talking about and saw several cars driving in circles.

"I guess I'll just try to get past them," Lawrence said, almost talking to himself.

Thomas didn't respond, knowing that every person in the vehicle understood very well that whatever was going on could only mean trouble.

Lawrence picked up his speed again. "It'll take us forever to back-track and try a different way. I'm just going to try to get through."

"Just don't do anything stupid," the pilot snapped. "We certainly won't get there if we have to walk."

As they approached, Thomas leaned forward in his seat and strained to see what was going on. A crowd of about twenty people were fighting over a big pile of something he couldn't quite make out, tossing debris and pushing and shoving, throwing punches. Maybe a hundred feet past them were the cars—swerving and spinning out and crashing into each other. It was a miracle no one on the road had been hit yet.

"What are you planning?" Thomas asked. Lawrence hadn't slowed one bit, and they were almost there.

"You need to stop!" the pilot shouted.

Lawrence ignored the command. "No. I'm going through."

"You'll get us killed!"

"We'll be fine. Just shut up for a second!"

They neared the group of people, still going at each other and whatever was in that huge pile. Thomas slid over to the side of the van, tried to get a better look. The Cranks were ripping apart huge sacks of garbage—pulling out old packages of food and half-rotten meat and scraps of leftovers—but no one was able to hold one thing in their hand before someone tried to steal it. Punches flew and fingers clawed and scratched. One man had a huge gash under his eye, a smear of blood dripping down his face like red tears.

The van swerved with a screech and Thomas turned his attention ahead. The drivers of the cars—old models, their shells dented, most of the paint gone—had stopped, and three of them were lined up facing the oncoming van. Lawrence didn't slow down. Instead he turned, heading for the larger gap between the car to the right and the one in the middle. Then in a flash the car on the left bolted forward, turning sharply to try to catch the van before it got by.

"Hold on!" Lawrence screamed, then gunned it even faster.

Thomas gripped the seat below him as they shot toward the gap. The two cars lining the gap didn't move, but the third car was banking and heading straight for them. Thomas saw that they had no chance, almost had time to shout it out, but it was too late.

The front hood of the van had just crossed the threshold of the gap when the third car slammed into the back of its left side. Thomas flew to his left and hit the bar between the two side windows, which shattered with a horrible crunch. Glass flew in all directions and the van spun in circles, its tail end like a whip. Thomas bounced all over, trying to get a grip on anything. The sounds of squealing tires and metal scraping against metal filled the air.

The noise stopped when the van finally hit the cement wall.

Thomas, battered and bruised, was on the floor, on his knees. He pulled himself up in time to see all three vehicles driving off, the sounds of their engines fading as they disappeared down the long, straight road, back the way Thomas and the others had come. He glanced over at Lawrence and the pilot, both of whom were fine.

Then the strangest thing happened. Thomas looked out the window and saw a banged-up Crank staring at him from twenty feet away. It took him a second to register that the Crank was his friend.

Newt.

CHAPTER 55

Newt looked horrible. His hair had been torn out in patches, leaving bald spots that were nothing more than red welts. Scratches and bruises covered his face; his shirt was ripped, barely hanging on to his thin frame, and his pants were filthy with grime and blood. It was like he'd finally given in to the Cranks, joined their ranks fully.

But he stared at Thomas, as if he recognized that he'd stumbled upon a friend.

Lawrence had been talking, but Thomas only now processed his words.

"We're okay. She's shot to hell, but hopefully she'll get us another couple of miles to the hangar."

Lawrence shifted into reverse and the van wobbled away from the cement wall, the crunch of broken plastic and metal and the squeal of tires erupting in the complete silence that had fallen. Then he started to drive off, and it was like a switch clicked in Thomas's head.

"Stop!" he yelled. "Stop the van! Now!"

"What?" Lawrence replied. "What're you talking about?"

"Just stop the freaking van!"

Lawrence slammed on the brakes as Thomas scrambled to his feet and went for the door. He started to open it when Lawrence grabbed his shirt from behind and yanked him backward.

"What the hell do you think you're doing?" the man yelled at him.

Thomas wouldn't let anything stop him now. He yanked the gun out of his pants and pointed it at Lawrence. "Let go of me. Let go of me!"

Lawrence did, throwing his hands up in the air. "Whoa, kid. Calm down! What is *wrong* with you?"

Thomas backed away from him. "I saw my friend out there—I want to see if he's okay. If any trouble starts, I'll run back to the van. Just be ready to get us out of here when I do."

"You think that thing out there is still your friend?" the pilot asked coldly. "Those Cranks are way past the Gone. Can't you see that? Your friend is nothing but an animal now. Worse than an animal."

"Then it'll be a short goodbye, won't it," Thomas answered. He opened the door, then backed out onto the street. "Cover me if I need it. I have to do this."

"I'm gonna kick your butt before we get on that Berg, I can promise you that," Lawrence growled. "Hurry. If those Cranks by the garbage heap head this way, we start firing. I don't care if your mommy and uncle Frank are out there."

"Good that." Thomas turned away from them, slipping the pistol back into his jeans. He walked slowly toward his friend, who stood alone, far away from the pack of Cranks still working on their pile of refuse. For the moment they seemed satisfied with that—they didn't seem interested in him.

Thomas walked half the distance to Newt, then stopped. The worst part about his friend was the wildness in his eyes. Madness lurked behind them, two festering pools of sickness. How had it happened so quickly?

"Hey. Newt. It's me, Thomas. You still remember me, right?"

A sudden clarity filled Newt's eyes then, almost making Thomas step back in surprise.

"I bloody remember you, Tommy. You just came to see me at the Palace, rubbed it in that you ignored my note. I can't go completely crazy in a few days."

Those words hurt Thomas's heart even more than the pitiful sight of his friend. "Then why are you here? Why are you with . . . them?"

Newt looked at the Cranks, then back at Thomas. "It comes and goes, man. I can't explain it. Sometimes I can't control myself, barely know what I'm doing. But usually it's just like an itch in my brain, throwing everything off-kilter just enough to bother me—make me angry."

"You seem fine right now."

"Yeah, well. The only reason I'm with these wackers from the Palace is because I don't know what else to do. They're fighting, but they're also a group. You find yourself alone, you don't have a bloody chance."

"Newt, come with me this time, right now. We can take you somewhere safer, somewhere better to . . ."

Newt laughed, and when he did his head twitched strangely a couple of times. "Get out of here, Tommy. Get away."

"Just come with me," Thomas begged. "I'll tie you up if it makes you feel better."

Newt's face suddenly hardened into anger and his words shot out in a rage. "Just shut up, you shuck traitor! Didn't you read my note? You can't do one last, lousy thing for me? Gotta be the hero, like always? I hate you! I always hated you!"

He doesn't mean it, Thomas told himself firmly. But they were just words. "Newt . . ."

"It was all your fault! You could've stopped them when the first Creators died. You could've figured out a way. But no! You had to keep it going, try to save the world, be the hero. And you came to the Maze and never stopped. All you care about is yourself! Admit it! Gotta be the one people remember, the one people worship! We should've thrown you down the Box hole!"

Newt's face had colored to a deep red, and spit flew from his mouth as he yelled. He started taking lumbering steps forward, his hands balled into fists.

"I'm gonna blast him!" Lawrence yelled from the van. "Get out of the way!"

Thomas turned. "Don't! It's just me and him! Don't do anything!" He faced Newt again. "Newt, stop. Just listen to me. I know you're okay in there. Enough to hear me out."

"I hate you, Tommy!" He was only a few feet away and Thomas took a step backward, his hurt over Newt turning to fear. "I hate you I hate you I hate you! After all I did for you, after all the freaking klunk I went through in the bloody Maze, you can't do the one and only thing I've ever asked you to do! I can't even look at your ugly shuck face!"

Thomas took two more steps back. "Newt, you need to stop. They're going to shoot you. Just stop and listen to me! Get in the van, let me tie you up. Give me a chance!" He couldn't kill his friend. He just couldn't.

Newt screamed and rushed forward. An arc of Launcher lightning shot from the van, skidding and crackling across the pavement, but it missed him. Thomas had frozen in place, and Newt tackled him to the ground, knocking the breath out of him. He struggled to fill his lungs as his old friend climbed on top of him and pinned him down.

"I should rip your eyes out," Newt said, spraying Thomas with spit. "Teach you a lesson in stupidity. Why'd you come over here? You expected a bloody hug? Huh? A nice sit-down to talk about the good times in the Glade?"

Thomas shook his head, gripped by terror, very slowly reaching for his gun with his free hand.

"You wanna know why I have this limp, Tommy? Did I ever tell you? No, I don't think I did."

"What happened?" Thomas asked, stalling for time. He slipped his fingers around the weapon.

"I tried to kill myself in the Maze. Climbed halfway up one of those bloody walls and jumped right off. Alby found me and dragged me back to the Glade right before the Doors closed. I hated the place, Tommy. I hated every second of every day. And it was all . . . your . . . *fault!*"

Newt suddenly twisted around and grabbed Thomas by the hand holding the gun. He yanked it toward himself, forcing it up until the end of the pistol was pressed against his own forehead. "Now make amends! Kill me before I become one of those cannibal monsters! Kill me! I trusted *you* with the note! No one else. Now do it!"

Thomas tried to pull his hand away, but Newt was too strong. "I can't, Newt, I can't."

"Make amends! Repent for what you did!" The words tore out of him, his whole body trembling. Then his voice dropped to an urgent, harsh whisper. "Kill me, you shuck coward. Prove you can do the right thing. Put me out of my misery."

The words horrified Thomas. "Newt, maybe we can—"

"Shut up! Just shut up! I trusted you! Now do it!"

"I can't."

"Do it!"

"I can't!" How could Newt ask him to do something like this? How could he possibly kill one of his best friends?

"Kill me or I'll kill you. Kill me! Do it!"

"Newt . . ."

"Do it before I become one of them!"

"I . . ."

"KILL ME!" And then Newt's eyes cleared, as if he'd gained one last trembling gasp of sanity, and his voice softened. "Please, Tommy. Please."

With his heart falling into a black abyss, Thomas pulled the trigger.

CHAPTER 56

Thomas had closed his eyes when he did it. He heard the impact of bullet on flesh and bone, felt Newt's body jerk, then fall onto the street. Thomas twisted onto his stomach, then pushed himself to his feet, and he didn't open his eyes until he started running. He couldn't allow himself to see what he'd done to his friend. The horror of it, the sorrow and guilt and sickness of it all, threatened to consume him, filled his eyes with tears as he ran toward the white van.

"Get in!" Lawrence yelled at him.

The door was still open. Thomas jumped through it and pulled it shut. Then the van was moving.

No one spoke. Thomas stared out the front window in a daze. He'd shot his best friend in the head. Never mind that it was what he'd been asked to do, what Newt had wanted, what he'd pleaded for. Thomas had still pulled the trigger. He looked down, saw that his hands and legs were shaking, and he suddenly felt freezing cold.

"What have I done?" he mumbled, but the others didn't say a word.

The rest of the trip was a blur to Thomas. They passed more Cranks, even had to shoot some Launcher grenades out the window a couple of times. Then they were through the outer wall of the city, through the fence to the small airport, through the enormous door of the hangar, which was heavily guarded by more members of the Right Arm.

Not much was said, and Thomas just did as he was told, went where he was supposed to go. They boarded the Berg, and he followed as they walked through it and did an inspection. But he never said a word. The pilot went to fire up the big ship, Lawrence disappeared somewhere, and Thomas found a couch in the common room. He lay down and stared at the metal grid of the ceiling.

Since he'd killed Newt, he hadn't thought once about what he had set out to do. Free of WICKED, finally, and here he was voluntarily going back.

He didn't care anymore. Whatever happened, happened. He knew that for the rest of his life he'd be haunted by what he'd seen. Chuck gasping for air while he bled to death, and now Newt screaming at him with raw, terrifying madness. And that last moment of sanity, eyes begging for mercy.

Thomas closed his own, and the images were still there. It took a long time for him to fall asleep.

Lawrence woke him up. "Hey, rise and shine, boy. We'll be there in a few minutes. We're dropping your butt, then getting the hell out of there. No offense."

"None taken." Thomas groaned and swung his legs off the couch. "How far will I have to walk to get there?"

"A few miles. Don't worry, I don't think you'll have too many Cranks to deal with—it's gotten cold in the wilderness. Might see a few angry moose, though. Wolves might try to eat your legs off. Nothing much."

Thomas looked at the man, expecting a big grin, but he was busy in the corner, putting things in order.

"A coat and your backpack are waiting for you at the cargo door," Lawrence said as he moved a small piece of equipment onto a shelf.

"You've got food and water. We want to make sure you have a nice, enjoyable hike—relish the joys of nature and all that." Still no smile.

"Thanks," Thomas muttered. He was trying so hard not to slide back into the dark pit of sadness in which he'd fallen asleep. He still couldn't get Chuck and Newt off his mind.

Lawrence stopped what he was doing and turned to him. "I'm only going to ask you this once."

"What?"

"You sure about this? Everything I know about these people is rotten. They kidnap, torture, murder—do anything to get what they want. Seems crazy to let you waltz in there all by yourself."

For some reason Thomas wasn't scared anymore. "I'll be fine. Just make sure you come back."

Lawrence shook his head. "You're either the bravest kid I ever met or plain crazy. Anyway, go get yourself a shower and fresh clothes—gotta be some in the lockers."

Thomas didn't know how he looked at that moment, but he imagined something like a pale and lifeless zombie with dead eyes. "Okay," he said, and headed off to try to wash some of the horror away.

The Berg pitched and Thomas held on to a bar in the wall as the ship lowered to the ground. The ramp door started cranking open with the squeal of hinges while they were still a hundred feet up, and cool air blasted inside. The sound of the thrusters burning roared louder. Thomas could see that they were above a small clearing in a large forest of snow-dusted pine trees—so many that the Berg wouldn't be able to land. Thomas would have to jump.

The ship descended and Thomas steadied himself.

"Good luck, boy," Lawrence said, nodding toward the ground when they got close. "I'd tell you to be careful, but you're not an idiot, so I won't."

Thomas gave him a smile, hoping for one in return. He felt like he needed it, but got nothing. "Okay, then. I'll get the device planted as soon as I get in. I'm sure everything will go down with no problems. Right?"

"I'll have little lizards flying out my nostrils if we have no problems," Lawrence replied, but there was kindness in his voice. "Now get. Once you're out there, go that way." He pointed to the left, toward the edge of the forest.

Thomas pulled on a coat, slipped his arms through the straps of the backpack, then carefully walked down the big metal slab of the cargo door and crouched on its edge. It was only about four feet to the snow-covered ground, but he'd still have to be careful. He jumped and landed in a soft spot—a fresh snowdrift. All the while, his insides were numb.

He'd killed Newt.

He'd shot his own friend in the head.

CHAPTER 57

The clearing was scattered with trunks of trees felled long ago. The tall, thick pines of the forest surrounded Thomas, reaching up to the sky like a wall of majestic towers. He shielded his eyes from the fierce wind as the Berg boosted its thrusters and rose into the air, and he watched as it vanished into the southwestern sky.

The air was crisp and cool and the forest felt fresh, like he was standing in a brand-new world—a place untouched by disease. He was sure that not many people got to see anything like this today, and he felt lucky.

He tightened up his backpack and set out in the direction Lawrence had indicated, determined to make it there as quickly as possible. The less time he had to dwell on what he'd done to Newt, the better. And he knew that being alone out there in the wild would only give him too much time. He took the last few steps out of the snowy clearing and entered the darkness of the thick pines. He allowed their pleasantly overwhelming scent to wash over him and he did his best to shut down his mind again and stop thinking altogether.

He did pretty well, concentrating on his path, the sights and sounds of birds and squirrels and insects, the wonderful smells. His senses weren't used to such things, since he'd spent most of the life he remembered inside. Not to mention the Maze and the Scorch. As he hiked through the woods, he found it hard to believe that such a different place—the

Scorch—could exist on the same planet. His mind wandered. He wondered what life would be like for all these animals if humans really did go away for good.

He'd walked for over an hour when he finally reached the edge of the woods and a wide swatch of barren, rocky earth. Islands of dark brown dirt, devoid of vegetation, dappled the treeless expanse where the snow had been blown away by the wind. Craggy stones of all sizes dotted the land, which sloped toward a sudden drop-off—a huge cliff. Beyond that lay the ocean, its deep blue ending on the horizon, where in a sharp line it changed to the light blue of the brilliant sky. And resting on the edge of the cliff, about a mile ahead of him, was WICKED's headquarters.

The complex was enormous, made up of wide, unadorned interconnected buildings; the walls were peppered with narrow slits in the white cement, allowing for an occasional window. One rounded building rose up amid the others like a tower. The fierce weather of the region, mixed with the moisture from the sea, had taken its toll on the facades of the buildings—cracks spiderwebbed the exteriors of the complex—but they looked like structures that would exist there forever, unyielding to whatever man or weather threw at it. It called to mind a barely held memory of something from storybooks—some sort of haunted asylum. It was the perfect place to house the organization trying to prevent the world from becoming just such a madhouse. A long, narrow road led away from the complex, disappearing into the forest.

Thomas set out across the rock-strewn section of earth. An almost disturbing quiet settled over the land. The only thing he could hear besides the thump of his footsteps and his own breathing was the sound of distant waves breaking on the bottom of the cliff, and even that was faint. He was certain that the people at WICKED had spotted him by now—the security was surely thorough and tight.

A scuttling sound, like clicks of metal against stone, made him stop and look to his right. As if summoned by the thought of security, a beetle blade stood perched on a boulder, its red eye gleaming in Thomas's direction.

He remembered how it had felt the first time he'd seen one of them inside the Glade, just before it scurried away and into the small woods there. It seemed like a lifetime ago.

He waved at the beetle blade, and then he kept walking. In ten minutes he'd be knocking on the door of WICKED, asking, for the first time, to be let in. Not out.

He made his way down the last section of the slope and stepped onto an icy sidewalk that encircled the campus. It looked like there'd once been an effort to make the grounds a little prettier than the barren land around it, but the bushes and flowers and trees had long succumbed to winter, and the patches of gray dirt he could see amid the snow bore only weeds. Thomas walked along the paved lane, wondering why no one had come to greet him yet. Maybe the Rat Man was inside, watching, guessing that Thomas had finally come over to their side.

Two more beetle blades captured his attention, both roaming the snow-covered weeds of the flower beds, scanning left and right with their red beams as they scuttled along. Thomas looked up at the closest set of windows but saw only darkness—the glass was heavily tinted. A rumble coming from behind made him turn to look. A storm was moving in, its clouds dark and heavy, but it was still a few miles distant. As he watched, several bolts of lightning zigzagged across the grayness, and it took him back to the Scorch, to that awful rain of lightning that had met them as they approached the city. He could only hope the weather wasn't so bad this far north.

He resumed his path along the sidewalk and slowed as he approached the front entrance. A large set of glass doors awaited him, and a sudden, almost painful surge of memory pounded inside his skull. The escape from the Maze, the flight through the corridors of WICKED, coming out these doors into the pouring rain. He looked to his right into a small parking lot, where an old bus squatted next to a row of cars. It had to be the same one that had run over that poor Flare-infested woman, then whisked them away to those dorms, where their minds were played with and a Flat Trans eventually took them to the Scorch.

And now, after all he'd been through, he stood at WICKED's threshold, there by his own choice. He reached out and knocked on the cold, dark glass in front of him. He could see nothing on the other side.

Almost immediately, a series of locks disengaged, one after the other; then one of the doors swung out. Janson—who'd always be the Rat Man to Thomas—extended a hand.

"Welcome back, Thomas," he said. "No one believed me, but I've been saying all along that you'd return. I'm glad you made the right choice."

"Let's just get on with it," Thomas said. He'd do this—he'd play the part—but he didn't have to be nice about it.

"Sounds like an excellent idea." Janson stepped back and bowed slightly. "After you."

With a chill along his spine to match the frosty weather outside, Thomas walked past the Rat Man and entered WICKED's headquarters.

CHAPTER 58

Thomas stepped into a wide lobby with a few couches and chairs, fronted by a large, empty desk. It was different from the ones he'd seen the last time he was there. The furniture was colorful and bright, but it did nothing to perk up the dreary feel of the place.

"I thought we'd spend a few minutes in my office," Janson said, and pointed down the hallway that branched off to the right off the lobby. They started walking that way. "We're terribly sorry about what happened in Denver. A shame to lose a city with such potential. All the more reason we need to get this done and get it done quickly."

"What is it you have to do?" he forced himself to ask.

"We'll discuss everything in my office. Our lead team is there."

The device hidden in his backpack weighed heavily on Thomas's thoughts. Somehow he had to get it planted as soon as possible and get the clock ticking.

"That's fine," he said, "but I really need to use the bathroom first." It was the simplest idea he could come up with. And the only sure way to get a minute alone.

"There's one just up ahead," the Rat Man replied.

They turned a corner and continued down an even duller corridor that led to the men's room.

"I'll wait out here," Janson said with a nod toward the door.

Thomas went inside without saying a word. He pulled the device from his backpack and looked around. There was a wooden cabinet for storing toiletries above the sink, and the top of it had a lip just tall enough that Thomas could slip the gadget in and it would be concealed. He flushed the toilet and then turned on the water at the sink. He activated the device as he'd been taught, wincing at the slight beep that sounded, then reached up and deposited it on top of the cabinet. After shutting off the water, he calmed himself while the hand blower ran its course.

Then he stepped back into the hallway.

"All finished?" Janson asked, annoyingly polite.

"All finished," Thomas replied.

They continued walking, passing a few crookedly hung portraits of Chancellor Paige just like the ones on the posters in Denver.

"Am I ever going to meet the chancellor?" Thomas finally asked, curious about the woman.

"Chancellor Paige is very busy," Jansen answered. "You have to remember, Thomas—completing the blueprint and finalizing the cure are only the beginning. We're still organizing the logistics of getting it out to the masses—most of the team is working hard at it as we speak."

"What makes you so sure this will work? Why just me?"

Janson glanced at him, flashed his rodentlike smile. "I know, Thomas. I believe it with every ounce of my being. And I promise you'll get the credit you deserve."

For some reason Thomas thought of Newt just then. "I don't want any credit."

"Here we are," the man replied, ignoring Thomas.

They'd reached an unmarked door and the Rat Man let him inside. Two people—a man and a woman—sat facing a desk. Thomas didn't recognize them.

The woman wore a dark pants suit and had long red hair, and thin-framed glasses were perched on her nose. The man was bald, angular and skinny, dressed in green scrubs.

"These are my associates," Janson said, already moving to sit behind the desk. He motioned for Thomas to take the third seat between his two visitors, which he did. "Dr. Wright"—he pointed at the woman— "is our lead Psych, and Dr. Christensen our lead physician. We have a lot to discuss, so you'll pardon me if I'm short on introductions."

"Why am I the Final Candidate?" Thomas asked, cutting to the chase.

Janson gathered himself, needlessly moving things around on his desk before sitting back and folding his hands on his lap. "Excellent question. We had a handful of—pardon the term—subjects slated in the beginning to . . . compete for this honor. Recently it was narrowed to you and Teresa. But she has a way of following orders that you don't. Your tendency toward freethinking is what ultimately determined that you are the Final Candidate."

Played to the end, Thomas thought bitterly. His own attempts to rebel had turned out to be exactly what they wanted. Every ounce of his anger was directed at the man sitting in front of him. At the Rat Man. To Thomas, Janson had come to represent WICKED from top to bottom.

"Let's just get this over with," he said. He did his best to hide it, but he could hear the fury in his own voice.

Janson seemed unfazed. "Some patience, please. This won't take long. Keep in mind that collecting the killzone patterns is a delicate operation. We're dealing with your mind, and the slightest mishap in what you're thinking or interpreting or perceiving can render the resultant findings worthless."

"Yes," Dr. Wright added, tucking her hair behind her ear. "I know A.D. Janson told you about the importance of coming back, and we're glad you made the decision." Her voice was soft and pleasant and somehow exuded intelligence.

Dr. Christensen cleared his throat, then spoke, his voice thin and reedy. Thomas immediately disliked him. "I don't know how you could've made any other decision. The whole world's on the verge of collapse, and you can help save it."

"So you say," Thomas responded.

"Exactly," Janson said. "So we say. Everything is ready. But there's still a little more to tell you so you can understand this decision you've made."

"A little more to tell me?" Thomas repeated. "Isn't the whole point of the Variables that I don't know everything? Aren't you going to throw me in a cage with gorillas or something? Maybe make me walk through a field of land mines? Dump me in the ocean, see if I can swim back to shore?"

"Just tell him the rest," Dr. Christensen answered.

"The rest?" Thomas asked.

"Yes, Thomas," Janson said through a sigh. "The rest. After all the Trials, after all the studies, after all the patterns that have been collected and scrutinized, after all the Variables we've put you and your friends through, it comes down to this."

Thomas didn't say anything. He was barely able to breathe because of a strange anticipation, the simultaneous desires to know and *not* know.

Janson leaned forward, elbows on desk, a grave look shadowing his face. "One final thing."

"And what's that?"

"Thomas, we need your brain."

CHAPTER 59

Thomas's heartbeat sped up to rattling thumps in his chest. He knew that the man wasn't testing him. They'd gone as far as they could in analyzing reactions and brain patterns. Now they'd chosen the person best suited to . . . take apart in their effort to build the cure.

Suddenly, the Right Arm couldn't get there fast enough.

"My brain?" he forced himself to repeat.

"Yes," Dr. Christensen answered. "The Final Candidate holds the missing piece to complete the data for the blueprint. But we had no way to tell until we monitored the patterns against the Variables. Vivisection will give us our final data, your systems functioning properly while we do it. Not that you'll feel any pain—we'll heavily sedate you until . . ."

He didn't need to finish. His words drifted off into silence and the three WICKED scientists awaited Thomas's response. But he couldn't speak. He'd faced death countless times over what he could remember of his life, yet he'd always done so in the desperate hope to survive, doing anything in his power to last one more day. But this was different. He didn't just have to last through some trial until his rescuers came. This was something he wouldn't come back from. This was the end if they didn't come.

He had a random, horrible thought: did Teresa know about this?

It surprised him how deeply the idea hurt.

"Thomas?" Janson asked, breaking Thomas's train of thought. "I know this must come as quite a shock to you. I need you to understand that this is not a test. This is not a Variable and I'm not lying to you. We think we can complete the blueprint for the cure by analyzing your brain tissue and how, combined with the patterns we've collected, its physical makeup allows it to resist the Flare virus's power. The Trials were all created so we wouldn't have to just cut everyone open. Our whole aim was to save lives, not waste them."

"We've been collecting and analyzing the patterns for years, and you've been the strongest by far in your reactions to the Variables," Dr. Wright continued. "We've known for a long time—and it was the highest priority to keep this from the subjects—that in the end we'd have to choose the best candidate for this last procedure."

Dr. Christensen went on to outline the process while Thomas listened in numb silence. "You have to be alive but not awake. We'll sedate you and numb the area of the incision, but there aren't any nerves in the brain so it's a relatively painless process. Unfortunately, you won't recover from our neural explorations—the procedure is fatal. But the results will be invaluable."

"And if it doesn't work?" Thomas asked. All he could see was Newt's final moments. What if Thomas *could* prevent that horrible death for countless others?

The Psych's eyes flickered with discomfort. "Then we'll keep . . . working at it. But we have every confidence—"

Thomas cut her off, unable to help himself. "But you don't, do you? You've been paying people to steal more immune . . . *subjects*"—he said the word with vicious spite—"so you can start all over again."

No one answered at first. Then Janson said, "We will do whatever it takes to find a cure. With as little loss of life as possible. Nothing else needs to be said on the matter."

"Why are we even talking?" Thomas asked. "Why not just grab me and tie me down, rip my brain out?"

Dr. Christensen answered. "Because you're our Final Candidate. You were part of the bridge between our founders and the current staff. We're trying to show you the respect you deserve. It's our hope that you'll make the choice yourself."

"Thomas, do you need a minute?" Dr. Wright asked. "I know this is difficult, and I assure you we don't take it lightly. What we're asking for is a huge sacrifice. Will you donate your brain to science? Will you allow us to put the final pieces of the puzzle together? Take another step toward a cure for the good of the human race?"

Thomas didn't know what to say. He couldn't believe the turn of events. After everything, could it be true that they only needed one more death?

The Right Arm was coming. Newt's image seared across his mind.

"I need to be alone," he finally got out. "Please." For the first time, a part of him actually wanted to give in, let them do this. Even if there was only a small chance that it would work.

"You'll be doing the right thing," Dr. Christensen said. "And don't worry. You're not going to feel an ounce of pain."

Thomas didn't want to hear another word. "I just need some time alone before all this begins."

"Fair enough," Janson said, standing up. "We'll accompany you to the medical facilities and get you in a private room for a while. Though we need to get things started soon."

Thomas leaned forward and put his head in his hands, staring at the floor. The plan he'd concocted with the Right Arm suddenly seemed foolish beyond measure. Even if he could escape this group—even if he *wanted* to now—how would he survive until his friends arrived?

"Thomas?" Dr. Wright asked, reaching out to put a hand on his back. "Are you okay? Do you have any more questions?"

Thomas sat up, brushed her hand away. "Just . . . let's go where you said."

The air suddenly seemed to go out of Janson's office and Thomas's chest tightened. He stood and walked to the door, opened it and stepped out into the hallway. It was all too much.

CHAPTER 60

Thomas followed the doctors, but his mind was racing. He didn't know what to do. There was no way to communicate with the Right Arm, and he'd lost his ability to speak inside Teresa's—or Aris's—mind.

They turned a couple of corners, and the zigzagging made Thomas think of the Maze. He almost wished he were back there—things were so much simpler then.

"There's a room right up here on the left," Janson explained. "I already put a typing pad in there if you'd like to leave any messages for your friends. I'll figure out a way to deliver them."

"I'll make sure you get something to eat, also," Dr. Wright called from behind.

Their politeness annoyed Thomas. He remembered stories of killers being put to death in the old days. They always got a last meal, too. As fancy as they wanted it.

"I want steak," he said, stopping to look at her. "And shrimp. And lobster. And pancakes. And a candy bar."

"I'm sorry—you'll have to settle for a couple of sandwiches."

Thomas sighed. "Figures."

Thomas sat in a soft chair, staring at the typing pad on the small table in front of him. He had no intention of writing a note to anyone, but he didn't know what else to do. The situation had proven to be way more complicated than he could've imagined. He didn't know what he'd expected, but the notion that they'd dissect him alive had never crossed his mind. He'd figured whatever they did, he could just play along until the Right Arm showed up.

But there wouldn't be any coming back from playing along now.

He finally typed goodbye messages to Minho and Brenda just in case he ended up dead; then he rested his head in his arms until the food arrived. He ate slowly, then rested again. He could only hope his friends showed up in time. Either way, he certainly wouldn't leave this room until he absolutely had to.

He dozed as he waited, the minutes stretching on.

A knock at the door startled him awake.

"Thomas?" came the muffled voice of Janson. "We really need to get things started."

The words lit a fire of panic in Thomas. "I'm . . . not ready yet." He knew he sounded ridiculous.

After a long pause, Janson said, "I'm afraid we don't have much of a choice."

"But . . . ," Thomas began, but before he could pull his thoughts together, the door opened and Janson stepped inside.

"Thomas—waiting will only make it worse. We need to go."

Thomas didn't know what to do. He was surprised that they'd been so calm with him so far. He realized he'd pushed it to the limit and he'd run out of time. He took a deep breath.

"Let's get it over with."

The Rat Man smiled. "Follow me."

Janson led Thomas to a prep room with a wheeled bed surrounded by all kinds of monitors and several nurses. Dr. Christensen was there, dressed from head to toe in scrubs, a surgical mask already in place on his face. Thomas could only see his eyes, but he looked eager to get started.

"So that's it?" Thomas asked. A surge of panic raced through his gut, and it felt as if something were trying to chew through his chest. "Time to cut me open?"

"I'm sorry," the doctor answered. "But we need to begin."

The Rat Man was just about to speak again when a blaring alarm erupted throughout the building.

Thomas's heart lurched and relief flooded his system. It had to be the Right Arm.

The door swung open and Thomas turned just in time to see a frantic-looking woman announce, "A Berg arrived with a delivery, but it was a trick to get people inside—they're trying to take over the main building this very second."

Janson's response almost stopped Thomas's heart.

"Looks like we need to hurry and get this procedure started. Christensen, put him under."

CHAPTER 61

Thomas's chest constricted and his throat seemed to swell. Everything was on the line, but he was frozen.

Janson barked orders. "Dr. Christensen, quickly. Who knows what these people are up to, but we can't waste a second now. I'll go tell operating personnel to stand their ground, no matter what."

"Wait," Thomas finally croaked. "I don't know if I can do this." The words felt empty—he knew they wouldn't stop at this point.

Janson's face burned red. Instead of answering Thomas, he turned to the doctor. "Do whatever it takes to open this kid up."

Just as Thomas opened his mouth to speak, something sharp pricked his arm, sending jolts of heat through his body, and he went limp, collapsing onto the gurney. From his neck down he was numb, and terror flared inside him. Dr. Christensen leaned over him and passed a spent syringe to a nurse.

"I'm really sorry, Thomas. We have to do this."

The doctor and a nurse pushed him farther onto the bed, hoisting his legs up so that he lay flat on his back. Thomas could move his head slightly from side to side, but that was all. The sudden turn of events overwhelmed him as he realized the implications. He was about to die. Unless somehow the Right Arm got to him immediately, he was going to die.

Janson stepped into his view. Nodding approvingly, the Rat Man patted the doctor on the shoulder. "Get it done." Then he turned and disappeared; Thomas could hear someone shouting in the hallway before the door closed.

"I just need to run a few tests," Dr. Christensen explained. "Then we'll get you into the operating room." He turned to fiddle with some instruments behind him.

It felt like the man spoke to him from a hundred miles away. Thomas lay helpless, his mind spinning as the doctor took blood, measured his skull. The man worked in silence, barely blinking. But the beads of sweat on his forehead showed that he was racing against who-knew-what. Did he have an hour to get this done? Several hours?

Thomas closed his eyes. He wondered if the weapons-disabling device had done its job. Wondered if anyone would find him. Then he realized, did he even want them to? Was it really possible that WICKED almost had a cure? He forced himself to breathe evenly, focus on trying to move his limbs. But nothing happened.

The doctor suddenly straightened and grinned at Thomas. "I believe we're ready. We'll wheel you to the operating room now."

The man walked through the door and Thomas's gurney was pushed into the hallway. Unable to move, he lay staring up at the lights in the ceiling flashing by as he rolled down the corridor. He finally had to close his eyes.

They'd put him to sleep. The world would fade. And he'd be dead.

He snapped his eyes open again. Closed them. His heart pounded; his hands grew sweaty and he realized he was gripping the sheets on the gurney in two balled fists. Movement was coming back, slowly. Eyes open again. The lights zooming by. Another turn, then another. Despair threatened to squeeze the life out of Thomas before the doctors could do it.

"I . . . ," he started to say, but nothing else came out.

"What?" Christensen asked, peering down at him.

Thomas struggled to speak, but before he could force any words out a thunderous boom rattled the hallway and the doctor tripped, his weight pushing the gurney forward as he scrambled to stop himself from falling. The bed shot to the right and crashed into the wall, then rebounded and spun until it hit the other side. Thomas tried to move, but he was still paralyzed, helpless. He thought of Chuck and Newt, and a sadness like none he'd ever known seized his heart.

Someone screamed from the direction of the explosion. Shouts followed; then everything grew silent again, and the doctor was up on his feet, hurrying to the gurney, straightening it out, pushing it again, banging through a set of swinging doors. A host of people dressed in scrubs awaited them in a white operating room.

Christensen started barking orders. "We have to hurry! Everyone, get to your places. Lisa, get him fully sedated. Now!"

A short lady responded. "We haven't done all the prep—"

"It doesn't matter! As far as we know the whole building's gonna burn down."

He placed the gurney next to an operating table; several sets of hands were lifting Thomas and moving him over before the gurney even came to a complete stop. He settled on his back, strained to take in the beehive buzz of doctors and nurses, at least nine or ten of them. He felt a prick in his arm, glanced down to see the short lady inserting an IV into his vein. All the while the only movement he could manage was in his hands.

Lights were placed in position just above him. Other things were stuck into his body in various places; monitors started beeping; there was the hum of a machine; people talking over other people; the room was filled with the scurry of movement, like an orchestrated dance.

And the lights, so bright. The room spinning, though he lay per-fectly still. The rising terror of what they were doing to him. Knowing it was ending, right here, right now.

"I hope it works," he finally managed to get out.

A few seconds later, the drugs finally took him and it all went away.

CHAPTER 62

For a long time, Thomas knew only darkness. The break in the void of his thoughts was just a hairline crack—only wide enough to let him know about the void itself. Somewhere on the edge of it all, he knew that he was supposed to be asleep, kept alive only so they could inspect his brain. Take it apart, probably slice by slice.

So he wasn't dead yet.

At some point as he floated in this confusing mass of blackness, he heard a voice. Calling his name.

After hearing *Thomas* several times, he finally decided to go after it, find it. He made himself move toward the voice.

Toward his name.

CHAPTER 63

"Thomas, I have faith in you," a woman said to him as he fought to regain consciousness. He didn't recognize the voice, but it was somehow soft and authoritative at the same time. He continued struggling, heard himself moan, felt himself shifting in his bed.

Finally, he opened his eyes. Blinking against the brightness of the overhead lights, he noticed a door closing behind whoever had been there to wake him.

"Wait," he said, but it came out as nothing more than a gravelly whisper.

By force of will he got his elbows under him and pushed himself up. He was alone in the room, the only sounds distant shouts and an occasional rumble like thunder. His mind began to clear, and he realized that other than a little grogginess, he felt fine. Which meant that, unless the miracles of science had really taken a leap, he also still had his brain.

A manila folder on the table beside his bed caught his attention. In big red letters, *Thomas* had been written across the front of it. He swung his legs around to sit up on the edge of the mattress and grabbed the folder.

There were two pieces of paper inside. The first was a map of the WICKED complex, with black marker tracing several routes through the building. He quickly scanned the second: it was a letter, addressed to him and signed by Chancellor Paige. He put the map down and started to read the letter from the beginning.

Dear Thomas,

It's my belief that the Trials are over. We have more than enough data to create a blueprint. My associates disagree with me on this matter, but I was able to stop this procedure and save your life. It's now our task to work with the data we already have and build a cure for the Flare. Your participation, and that of the other subjects, is no longer necessary.

You now have a great task ahead of you. When I became chancellor I realized the importance of creating a back door of sorts to this building. I placed this back door in an unused maintenance room. I'm asking you to remove yourself, your friends, and the considerable number of Immunes we've gathered. Time is of the essence, as I'm sure you're aware.

There are three paths marked on the map I've enclosed. The first shows you how to leave this building through a tunnel— once outside, you'll be able to find where the Right Arm has made their own entrance to another building. There, you can join them. The second route will show you how to get to the Immunes. The third shows you how to find the back door. It's a Flat Trans that will transport you to what I hope will be a new life. Take them all and leave.

Ava Paige, Chancellor

Thomas stared at the paper, his mind in a spin. Another rumble sounded far away and jarred him back to reality. He trusted Brenda, and she trusted the chancellor. All he could do now was move.

He folded the letter and the map and stuffed them in his back pocket, then slowly stood up. Surprised at how quickly his strength had returned, he ran to the door. A peek out into the hallway showed that it was empty. He slipped out, and just as he did, two people came running by from behind. They didn't so much as glance at him, and Thomas realized that the chaos brought about by the Right Arm's attack might be the thing that ended up saving him.

He pulled out the map and studied it carefully, following the black line that led to the tunnel. It wouldn't take long at all to get to it. He memorized the path and started jogging down the hall, scanning the two other paths Chancellor Paige had marked on the map as he went.

He had only gone a few yards when he stopped, stunned by what he was seeing. He pulled the map closer to make sure—maybe he wasn't reading it right. But there was no mistaking what it showed.

WICKED had hidden the Immunes in the Maze.

CHAPTER 64

There were two mazes on the map, of course—the one for Group A and the one for Group B. Both must've been built deep into the bedrock that lay under the main buildings of WICKED's headquarters. Thomas couldn't tell which one he'd been directed to go to, but either way he was going back to the Maze. With a sickening dread, he started running toward Chancellor Paige's tunnel.

He followed the map and ran down hallway after hallway until he got to a long set of stairs that descended into a basement. The path took him through empty rooms and then, finally, to a small door that opened to a tunnel. The tunnel was dark but, Thomas was relieved to see, not completely black. Several uncovered lightbulbs hung from the ceiling as he ran along the narrow corridor. After about two hundred feet he came to a ladder that had been marked on the map. Up he went, and at the top there was a round metal door with a wheel handle that reminded him of the entrance to the Map Room in the Glade.

He spun the handle and pushed with all his strength. A dim light came in as Thomas forced the door up, and as it flipped open on its hinges, a great gust of cold air blew over him. He heaved himself out and onto the ground, next to a big rock in the barren, snow-covered land between the forest and WICKED headquarters.

He carefully hefted the lid to the tunnel up and over to close it again, then crouched behind the stone. He didn't notice any movement, but the night was too dark to see very well. He looked up into the sky, and when he saw the same heavy gray clouds he'd noticed when he'd reached the complex, he realized that he had no idea how much time had passed since then. Had he been in the building for only a few hours, or had a full night and day come and gone?

Chancellor Paige's note said that the Right Arm had made their own entrance into the buildings, probably with the explosions Thomas had heard earlier, and that was where he needed to go first. He saw the wisdom of connecting with the group—there was safety in numbers—and he had to let them know where the Immunes were hidden. Judging from the map, the best option Thomas had was to run to the cluster of buildings farthest from where he'd come out and search the area.

He went for it, edging around the boulder and sprinting for the closest building. He crouched as he ran, trying to stay as low as possible. Lightning streaked through the sky; it illuminated the cement of the complex and flashed off the white snow. Thunder followed quickly, rumbling across the land and rattling deep in his chest.

He reached the first building and pushed through the line of ragged bushes up against the wall. He edged along the side of the structure but found nothing. He stopped when he came to the first corner and peered around it—in the space between buildings were a series of courtyards. But he still saw no way inside.

He skirted the next two buildings, but as he approached the fourth one, he heard voices and immediately dropped to the ground. As quietly as he could, he scooted along the frozen dirt toward an overgrown bush, then peeked around it to search for the source of the noise.

There it was. Rubble lay strewn across the yard in huge heaps, and behind them a massive hole had been blasted in the side of the building. Which meant that the explosion had originated from the inside. A faint light shone from the opening, casting broken shadows on the ground. Sitting on the edge of one of those shadows were two people wearing civilian clothes. The Right Arm.

Thomas had started to stand up when an icy hand gripped his mouth tightly and he was jerked backward. Another arm wrapped around his chest and pulled him, dragging him along the ground; his feet burrowed through the snow. Thomas kicked out, struggling to free himself, but the person was too strong.

They turned the corner of the building into another small court-yard, and Thomas was thrown to the ground on his stomach. His captor flopped him onto his back and clamped a hand again over Thomas's mouth. It was a man he didn't recognize. Another figure crouched over him as well.

Janson.

"I'm very disappointed," the Rat Man said. "Looks like not everyone in my organization is on the same team after all."

Thomas could do nothing but struggle against the person pinning him to the ground.

Janson sighed. "I guess we're going to have to do this the hard way."

CHAPTER 65

Janson pulled out a long, slender knife, held it up and inspected it with narrowed eyes. "Let me tell you something, kid. I've never thought of myself as a violent man, but you and your friends sure have driven me to the brink. My patience is stretched to a minimum, but I'm going to show restraint. Unlike you, I think about more than myself. I'm working to save people, and I *will* finish this project."

Thomas forced his every inch to relax, to be still. Struggling hadn't accomplished a thing, and he needed to save his energy for when the right opportunity presented itself. It was clear that the Rat Man had lost it, and judging from that blade, he was determined to get Thomas back in the operating room at any cost.

"That's a good boy. No need to fight this. You should be proud. It will be you and your mind that save the world, Thomas."

The man holding Thomas down—a squat guy with black hair—spoke then. "I'm going to let go of your mouth now, boy. Let out one peep and A.D. Janson's gonna give you a nice poke with that blade of his. Understand? We want you alive, but that doesn't mean you can't have a few war wounds."

Thomas nodded as calmly as he could and the man let go of him and sat back. "Smart boy."

It was Thomas's cue to go for it. He swung his leg violently to his right and kicked Janson in the face. The man's head jerked backward and his body crashed to the ground. The dark-haired man moved to tackle Thomas, but Thomas squirmed out from under him and went after Janson again, this time kicking the hand that held the knife. It flew out of his grasp, skipping across the ground until it smacked into the side of the building.

Thomas turned his attention to the blade, and that was all the squat man needed. He lunged at Thomas, who landed on his back on top of Janson. Janson squirmed beneath them as they wrestled, and Thomas felt a desperation seize him, adrenaline exploding through his body. He screamed and pushed, kicked, fought his way out from between the two men. Scrabbling and clawing with his hands and feet, he got loose and dove toward the building for the knife. He landed next to it, grabbed it and spun around, expecting an immediate attack. Both men were just getting to their feet, obviously stunned by his sudden burst of strength.

Thomas stood up as well, holding the knife out in front of him. "Just let me go. Just walk away and let me go. I swear if you come after me I'm gonna go crazy with this thing and won't stop stabbing till you're both dead. I swear it."

"It's two against one, kid," Janson said. "I don't care if you have a knife."

"You've seen what I can do," Thomas replied, trying to sound as dangerous as he felt. "You've watched me in the Maze and the Scorch." He almost wanted to laugh at the irony. They had made him into a killer . . . to save people?

The short guy scoffed. "If you think we're—"

Thomas reared back and threw the knife as he'd seen Gally do, handle over blade. It cartwheeled through the space between them and slammed into the man's neck. There was no blood at first, but he reached up, shock transforming his face, and clawed at the knife stuck in him. That was when the blood came, spurting in jets in time with his heartbeat. He opened his mouth, but before he could speak he collapsed to his knees.

"You little . . . ," Janson whispered, his eyes wide with horror as he stared at his colleague.

Thomas was shocked by what he'd done, and froze to the spot, but the moment broke as Janson turned his head to look back at him. Thomas burst into a sprint out of the courtyard, around the corner of the building. He had to get back to the hole in the building, had to get back inside.

"Thomas!" Janson shouted; Thomas heard his footsteps in pursuit. "Get back here! You have no idea what you're doing!"

Thomas didn't even pause. He passed the bush he'd hidden behind and ran full-bore toward the gaping hole in the side of the building. A man and a woman still sat nearby, crouched on the ground so that their backs touched. Upon seeing Thomas, they both clambered to their feet.

"I'm Thomas!" he yelled at them just as they opened their mouths to ask questions. "I'm on your side!"

They exchanged a look, then returned their attention to Thomas just as he skidded to a stop in front of them. Heaving for breath, he turned to look back, saw the shadowed figure of Janson running toward them, maybe fifty feet away.

"They've been looking all over for you," the male guard said. "But you're supposed to be in there." He jabbed a finger at the hole.

"Where is everybody? Where's Vince?" Thomas panted.

And as he spoke he knew Janson was still tearing after him. Thomas turned to face the Rat Man, whose face was screwed up in unnatural rage. It was a look Thomas had seen before. It was the same insane anger he'd seen in Newt. The Rat Man had the Flare.

Janson spoke between heavy breaths. "That boy . . . is property . . . of WICKED. Hand him over."

The lady didn't flinch. "WICKED doesn't mean a pile of goose crap to me, old man. If I were you, I'd get lost, and I wouldn't go back inside, either. Bad things are about to happen to your friends in there."

The Rat Man didn't respond, just kept panting, his eyes darting between Thomas and the others. Finally, he started to back away, slowly. "You people don't get it. Your self-righteous arrogance will be the end of everything. I hope you can live with that while you rot in hell."

Then he turned and ran away, disappearing into the gloom.

"What'd you do to piss *him* off?" the lady asked.

Thomas tried to catch his breath. "Long story. I need to find Vince, or whoever's in charge. I need to find my friends."

"Calm down there, kid," the man responded. "Things are kind of quiet right now. People getting in position, planting, that sort of thing."

"Planting?" Thomas asked.

"Planting."

"What does that mean?"

"Explosives, you idiot. We're about to bring this whole building down. Show old WICKED that we mean serious business."

CHAPTER 66

Everything came into focus at that moment for Thomas. There'd been a fanaticism about Vince that hadn't fully hit him until now. And there was the way the Right Arm had treated Thomas and his friends in the van after taking them hostage at the Berg. Also, why did they have all these explosives but no real conventional weapons? It didn't make sense unless their goal was to destroy, not take over. The Right Arm wasn't exactly on the same page as he was. Maybe they thought their motives were pure, but Thomas was beginning to realize that the organization had a darker purpose.

He needed to step carefully. All that mattered at that moment was saving his friends and finding and releasing the others who'd been captured.

The lady's voice interrupted Thomas's thoughts. "You're doing a lot of heavy thinking in that noggin of yours."

"Yeah ... sorry. When do you think they're going to set off the explosives?"

"Pretty soon, I suppose. They've been planting for hours. They want them all to detonate at the same time, but I'm guessing we aren't quite that skilled."

"What about all the people inside? What about the ones we came to rescue?"

The two of them looked at each other, then shrugged. "Vince hopes to get everyone out."

"He hopes? What does that mean?"

"He hopes."

"I need to talk to him." What Thomas really wanted was to find Minho and Brenda. Right Arm or no Right Arm, he knew what they had to do: get to the Maze and lead everyone out of there to the Flat Trans.

The lady pointed to the hole in the side of the building. "Just through there a ways is an area they've pretty much taken over. You'll probably find Vince there. Careful, though. WICKED's got guards hiding all over the place. And they're vicious little buggers."

"Thanks for the warning." Thomas turned, eager to get inside. The hole loomed over him, dusty darkness waiting within. There were no more alarms or flashing red lights. He stepped through.

At first Thomas didn't see or hear anything. He walked on in silence, careful of what might be around each turn. The lights got brighter the farther he walked, and he finally spotted a door at the end of the hallway that had been propped open. He jogged to it and peered in to see a large room with tables scattered across the floor set on their sides like shields. Several people crouched behind them.

The people were watching a large set of double doors on the other side of the room, and no one noticed him as he squeezed against the doorframe, hiding most of his body from the inside. He leaned his head in to get a better look. He spotted Vince and Gally behind one of the tables, but didn't recognize anyone else. On the far left side of the room, there was a small office, and he could tell that at least nine or ten people were huddled inside. He strained to see, but he couldn't make out any faces.

"Hey!" he whispered as loudly as he dared. "Hey! Gally!"

The boy turned immediately, but had to glance around a few seconds before he spotted Thomas. Gally squinted, as though he thought his eyes might be tricking him.

Thomas waved to make sure he saw him and Gally motioned for him to come over.

Thomas looked around again to make sure it was safe; then he crouched down, ran over to the table and collapsed on the ground next to his old nemesis. He had so many questions he didn't know where to begin.

"What happened?" Gally asked him. "What did they do to you?"

Vince shot him a glare but didn't say anything.

Thomas didn't know how to answer. "They . . . ran a few tests. Look, I found out where they're keeping the Immunes. You can't blow the place up until we get them out."

"Then go get ' em," Vince said. "We've got a one-shot deal here, and I'm not going to waste it."

"You *brought* some of those people here!" Thomas looked to Gally for support, but he only got a shrug in response.

Thomas was on his own.

"Where's Brenda, Minho, everyone else?" he asked.

Gally nodded toward the side room. "Those guys are all in there, said they wouldn't do anything until you came back."

Thomas suddenly felt sorry for the scarred boy beside him. "Come with me, Gally. Let these guys do whatever they want, but come help us. Don't you wish someone had done the same for us when we were in the Maze?"

Vince spun on them. "Don't even think about it," he barked. "Thomas, you knew coming in here what our goals were. If you abandon us now I'll consider you a turncoat. You'll be a target."

287

Thomas kept his focus on Gally. He saw a sadness in the boy's eyes that made his heart break. And he also saw something he'd never seen there before: trust. Genuine trust.

"Come with us," Thomas said.

A smile formed on his old enemy's face and he responded in a way Thomas never would have expected.

"Okay."

Thomas didn't wait for Vince to react. He grabbed Gally's arm and they scooted away from the table together, then ran to the office and slipped inside.

Minho was the first to him, pulling him into a bear hug as Gally watched awkwardly from the side. Then the others were there, Minho. Brenda. Jorge. Teresa. Even Aris. Thomas almost got dizzy from the quick exchange of hugs and words of relief and welcome. He was especially thrilled to see Brenda, and he held on to her longer than anyone else. But as good as it felt, he knew they didn't have time for it.

He pulled away. "I can't explain everything right now. We have to go find the Immunes WICKED took, then find this back-door Flat Trans I learned about—and we need to hurry before the Right Arm blows this place up."

"Where are the Immunes?" Brenda asked.

"Yeah, what did you learn?" Minho added.

Thomas never thought he'd say what he had to say next. "We need to go back to the Maze."

CHAPTER 67

Thomas showed them the letter he'd discovered next to him in the recovery room, and it only took a few moments for them all to agree— even Teresa and Gally—to abandon the Right Arm and set off on their own. Set off for the Maze.

Brenda looked at Thomas's map and said she knew exactly how to get there. She gave him a knife and he gripped it tightly in his right hand, wondering if his survival would come down to one thin blade. They slipped out of the side room and made for the double doors while Vince and the others yelled at them, called them crazy, told them they'd get killed within minutes. Thomas ignored every word.

The door was still cracked, and Thomas was the first one through. He crouched, ready for an attack, but the hall was empty. The others fell in behind him, and he decided to trade stealth for speed, sprinting down that first long hallway. The gloomy light made the place feel haunted, as if the spirits of all the people WICKED had let die were there waiting in the corners and alcoves. But to Thomas, it felt like they were on his side.

With Brenda pointing the way, they turned a corner, went down a flight of stairs. Took a shortcut through an old storage room, down another long hallway. Down more stairs. A right and then a left. Thomas kept a fast pace, constantly scanning for danger. He never paused, never stopped to catch his breath, never doubted Brenda's directions. He was a Runner again, and despite everything, it felt good.

They approached the end of one hallway and turned to the right. Thomas had only gone three more steps when out of nowhere someone was on top of him, gripping his shoulders and throwing him to the ground.

Thomas fell and rolled, pushing to get the person off of him. He heard shouts and the sounds of others struggling. It was dark and Thomas could barely see who he was fighting, but he punched and kicked, slashed with his knife, felt it connect and rip something. A woman screamed. A fist smacked into his right cheek, something hard nailed him in the upper thigh.

Thomas paused to brace himself, then pushed with all his strength. His attacker slammed into the wall, then jumped back on top of him again. They rolled, bumped into another pair of people fighting. It took every bit of his concentration to hold on to the knife, and he kept slashing, but it was hard being so close to his assailant. He jabbed with his left fist, hit under his attacker's chin, then used the moment of reprieve to slam his knife into the person's stomach. Another scream—again a woman, and definitely the person who was attacking him. He pushed her off for good.

Thomas stood, looked around to see who he could help. In the bare light, he saw Minho straddling a man, whaling on him, the guy showing no resistance. Brenda and Jorge had teamed up on another guard, and just as Thomas looked the man scrambled to his feet and fled. Teresa, Harriet, and Aris were leaning against a wall, catching their breath. They'd all survived. They needed to run.

"Come on!" he yelled. "Minho, leave him!"

His friend threw another couple of punches for good measure, then stood up, giving his guy one last kick. "I'm done. We can go."

And the group turned and kept running.

They ran down another long flight of stairs and stumbled one by one into the room at the bottom. Thomas froze in shock when he realized where he was. It was the chamber that housed the Griever pods, the room they'd found themselves in after they escaped from the Maze. The observation room windows were still shattered—the glass lay in shards all over the floor. The forty or so oblong pods where the Grievers rested and charged looked like they'd been sealed closed since the Gladers had come through weeks earlier. A layer of dust dulled what had been a shiny white surface the last time Thomas had seen them.

He knew that as a member of WICKED he'd spent countless hours and days in this place as they'd worked on creating the Maze, and he felt the shame of it all over again.

Brenda pointed out the ladder that led up to where they needed to go. Thomas shuddered at the memory of going down the slimy Griever chute during their escape—they could've just climbed down a ladder.

"Why isn't anybody here?" Minho asked. He turned in a circle, searching the place. "If they're holding people in there, why no guards?"

Thomas thought about it. "Who needs soldiers to keep them in when you have the Maze doing the job for you? It took us long enough to figure a way out."

"I don't know," Minho said. "Something's fishy about it."

Thomas shrugged. "Well, sitting here isn't gonna help. Unless you've got something useful, let's get up there and start bringing them out."

"Useful?" Minho repeated. "I got nothin'."

"Then up we go."

Thomas climbed the ladder and pulled himself out into another familiar room—the one with the input stations where he had typed the code words to shut down the Grievers. Chuck had been there, and he'd been terrified but brave. And not even an hour after that he was dead. The pain of losing his friend filled Thomas's chest once again.

"Home, sweet home," Minho muttered. He was pointing at a round hole above them. It was the hole that exited to the Cliff. Back when the Maze was fully operational, holotech had been used to conceal it, to make it look like part of the fake, endless sky beyond the stone edge of the drop-off. It was all turned off now, of course, and Thomas could see the walls of the Maze through the opening. A stepladder had been placed directly under it.

"I can't believe we're back here," Teresa said, moving to stand beside Thomas. Her voice sounded haunted, and it echoed how he felt inside.

And for some reason, with that simple statement, Thomas realized that standing there, the two of them were finally on equal ground. Trying to save lives, trying to make up for what they'd done to help start it all. He wanted to believe that with every ounce of his being.

He turned to look at her. "Crazy, huh?"

She smiled for the first time since . . . he couldn't remember. "Crazy."

There was so much Thomas still didn't remember—about himself, about her—but she was here, helping, and that was all he could ask for.

"Don't you think we better get up there?" Brenda asked.

"Yeah." Thomas nodded. "We better."

He went last. After the others climbed through, he scaled the ladder, pushed himself up onto the ledge, then walked over two boards that had been placed across the gap to the Maze's stone floor at the Cliff edge. Below him was just a black-walled work area that had always looked like an endless drop before. He looked back up at the Maze and had to pause to take it all in.

Where the sky had once shone blue and bright, there was now only the dull gray ceiling. The holotech off the side of the Cliff had been completely shut down, and the once-vertigo-inducing view had been transformed into simple black stucco. But seeing the massive ivy-covered walls leading away from the Cliff took his breath away. Those had been towering even without the help of illusion, and now they rose above him like ancient monoliths, green and gray and cracked. As if they'd stand there for a thousand years, enormous tombstones marking the death of so many.

He was back.

CHAPTER 68

Minho led the way this time, his shoulders squared as he ran, every inch of him showing the pride he'd felt for those two years when he'd ruled the corridors of the Maze. Thomas was right behind him, craning his neck to see the walls of ivy majestically rising toward the gray ceiling. It was a strange feeling, being back in there after everything they'd been through since their escape.

No one said much as they ran toward the Glade. Thomas wondered what Brenda and Jorge must think of the Maze—he knew it had to seem enormous. A beetle blade could never translate size like this back to the observation rooms. And he could only imagine all the bad memories crashing back into Gally's brain.

They turned the final corner that led to the wide corridor outside the East Door of the Glade. When Thomas came to the section of wall where he'd tied Alby up in the ivy, he looked at the spot, could see the mangled mess of the vines. All that effort to save the former leader of the Gladers, only to see him die a few days later, his mind never fully recovered from the Changing.

A surge of anger burned like liquid heat in Thomas's veins.

They reached the huge gap in the walls that made up the East Door, and Thomas caught his breath and slowed. There were hundreds of people milling about the Glade. He was horrified that there were even a few babies and small children scattered among the crowd. It took a moment for the murmurs to spread across the sea of Immunes, but within seconds every eye was trained on the new arrivals and utter silence fell upon the Glade.

"Did you know there were this many?" Minho asked Thomas.

There were people everywhere—certainly more than the Gladers had ever numbered. But what stole Thomas's words was seeing the Glade itself again. The crooked building they called the Homestead; the pathetic copse of trees; the Bloodhouse barn; the fields, now only hardened weeds. The charred Map Room, its metal door blackened and still hanging ajar. He could even see the Slammer from where he stood. A bubble of emotion threatened to burst inside him.

"Hey, daydreamer," Minho said, snapping his fingers. "I asked you a question."

"Huh? Oh . . . There's so many—they make the place look smaller than it ever did when we were here."

It didn't take long before their friends spotted them. Frypan. Clint, the Med-jack. Sonya and some other girls from Group B. They all came running, and there was a short burst of reunions and hugs.

Frypan swatted Thomas on the arm. "Can you believe they put me back in this place? They wouldn't even let me cook, just sent us a bunch of packaged food in the Box three times a day. Kitchen doesn't even work—no electricity, nothing."

Thomas laughed, the anger easing. "You think you were a lousy cook for fifty guys? Try feeding this army."

"Funny man, Thomas. You are a funny man. I'm glad to see you." Then his eyes got big. "Gally? Gally's here? Gally's *alive*?"

"Nice to see you, too," the boy responded dryly.

Thomas patted Frypan on the back. "Long story. He's a good guy now."

Gally scoffed but didn't respond.

Minho stepped up to them. "All right, happy time is over. How in the world are we going to do this, dude?"

"Shouldn't be too bad," Thomas said. He actually hated the idea of trying to funnel all these people not only through the Maze itself, but then all the way through the WICKED complex to the Flat Trans. Still, it had to be done.

"Don't feed me that klunk," Minho said. "Your eyes don't lie."

Thomas smiled. "Well, we've certainly got a lot of people to fight with us."

"Have you *looked* at these poor saps?" Minho asked, sounding disgusted. "Half of 'em are younger than us, and the other half look like they haven't so much as arm wrestled before, much less had a fistfight."

"Sometimes numbers are all that matters," Thomas responded.

He spotted Teresa and called her over, then found Brenda.

"What's the plan?" Teresa asked.

If Teresa was really with them, this was when Thomas needed her—and all the memories she'd had returned.

"Okay, let's split them into groups," he said to everyone. "There's gotta be four or five hundred people, so . . . groups of fifty. Then have one Glader or Group B person be in charge of them. Teresa, do you know how to get to this maintenance room?"

He showed her the map and she nodded after examining it.

Thomas continued. "Then I'll help move people along as you and Brenda lead the way. Everyone else guide one of the groups. Except Minho, Jorge, and Gally. I think you guys should cover the rear."

"Sounds good to me," Minho said, shrugging. Impossibly, he looked bored.

"Whatever you say, *muchacho*," Jorge added. Gally just nodded.

They spent the next twenty minutes dividing everyone into groups and getting them into long lines. They paid special attention to keeping the groups even in terms of age and strength. The Immunes had no problem following orders once they realized the new arrivals had come to help rescue them.

Once they were organized into groups, Thomas and his friends lined up in front of the East Door. Thomas waved his hands to get everyone's attention.

"Listen up!" Thomas began. "WICKED is planning to use you for science. Your bodies—your brains. They've been studying people for years, collecting data to develop a cure for the Flare. Now they want to use you as well, but you deserve more than a life as lab rats. You are—we all are—the future, and the future isn't going to happen the way WICKED wants it to. That's why we're here. To get you out of this place. We'll be going through a bunch of buildings to find a Flat Trans that'll take us somewhere safe. If we're attacked, we're going to have to fight. Stick with your groups, and the strongest need to do whatever it takes to protect the—"

Thomas's last words were cut off by a violent crack—like the sound of stone splintering. And then, nothing. Only an echo bouncing off the enormous walls.

"What was *that*?" Minho yelled, searching the sky for the source.

Thomas inspected the Glade, the walls of the Maze rising up behind him, but nothing was out of place. He was just about to speak when another crack sounded, then another. A thunderous din of rumbling crossed the Glade, beginning low and increasing in depth and volume. The ground started to tremble, and it seemed as if the world was going to fall apart.

People turned in circles, looking for the source of the noise, and Thomas could tell panic was spreading. He'd lose control soon. The ground shook more violently; the sounds amplified—thunder and grinding rock—and now screams erupted from the mass of people standing in front of him.

Suddenly it dawned on Thomas. "The explosives."

"What?" Minho shouted at him.

Thomas looked at his friend. "The Right Arm!"

A deafening roar shook the Glade, and Thomas spun around to look up. A large portion of the wall to the left of the East Door had broken loose, great chunks of stone flying everywhere. A huge section seemed to hover at an impossible angle, and then it fell, toppling toward the ground.

Thomas didn't have time to shout a warning before the massive piece of rock landed on a group of people, crushing them as it broke in half. He stood for a moment, speechless as blood oozed out from the edges and pooled on the stone floor.

CHAPTER 69

The wounded screamed. Rumbles of thunder and the sound of rock fracturing combined to make a horrible chorus as the ground beneath Thomas continued to shake. The Maze was falling apart around them— they had to get out.

"Run!" he yelled at Sonya.

She didn't hesitate—she turned and disappeared into the corridors of the Maze. The people who'd been standing in her line didn't need to be told to follow.

Thomas stumbled, regained his balance, ran over to Minho. "Bring up the rear! Teresa, Brenda and I need to get to the head of the pack!"

Minho nodded and gave him a push to get him going. Thomas glanced back in time to see the Homestead split down the middle like a cracked acorn, half of its slipshod structure collapsing to the ground in a cloud of splintered wood and dust. His gaze swept to the Map Room, its concrete walls already crumbling to pieces.

There was no time to spare. He searched the chaos until he found Teresa. He grabbed his old friend and she followed him to the gap into the Maze. Brenda was there, trying her best with Jorge to facilitate who would go next, to prevent everyone from going at once in a stampede that would surely kill half of them.

Another splintering crack sounded from above; Thomas looked up to see a section of wall falling toward the ground by the fields. It exploded when it hit, luckily with no one underneath. With a sudden jerk of horror he realized that the roof itself would eventually collapse.

"Go!" Brenda yelled at him. "I'm right behind you!"

Teresa grabbed his arm, yanked him forward, and the three of them ran past the jagged left edge of the Door and into the Maze, weaving their way around the crowd of people heading in the same direction. Thomas had to sprint to catch up with Sonya—he had no idea whether she'd been a Runner in Group B's Maze or whether she'd remember the layout as well as he did, if it was even the same.

The ground continued to tremble, and lurched with every distant explosion. People stumbled left and right, fell, got back up, kept running. Thomas dodged and ducked as he ran, jumping over a fallen man at one point. Rocks tumbled from the walls. He watched one hit a man in the head, knocking him to the ground. People bent over his lifeless body, tried to lift him, but there was so much blood that Thomas could tell it was already too late.

Thomas reached Sonya and ran past her, leading everyone turn after turn.

He knew they were getting close. He could only hope that the Maze had been the first place to get hit and the rest of the compound was intact—that they'd still have time if they could just get out. The ground suddenly jumped underneath him and an earsplitting crack pierced the air. He fell face-first, scrambled to get up. A hundred feet or so in front of him, a section of the stone floor had shifted upward. As he watched, half of it exploded, sending a rain of rocks and dust in all directions.

He didn't stop. There was a narrow space between the protruding ground and the wall, and he ran through it, Teresa and Brenda on his heels. But he knew the bottleneck would slow things down.

"Hurry!" he yelled over his shoulder. He slowed to watch and could see the desperation in everyone's eyes.

Sonya exited the gap, then paused to help funnel the others through, grabbing hands, pulling and pushing. It went faster than Thomas could've hoped, and he continued toward the Cliff at full speed.

Through the Maze he went, the world shaking, stone crumbling and falling all around them, people screaming and crying. There was nothing he could do but lead the survivors onward. A left and then a right. Another right. Then they were into the long corridor that ended at the Cliff. Beyond its edge, he could see the gray ceiling end at the black walls, the round hole of the exit—and a large crack shooting up and across the once-false sky.

He turned to Sonya and the others. "Hurry! Move!"

As they approached, Thomas got a full view of the terror. Faces white and twisted in fear, people falling to the ground, getting back up. He saw a boy who couldn't have been more than ten, half dragging a lady until she finally got her feet underneath her. A boulder the size of a small car toppled from high off the wall and struck an older man, throwing him several yards before he hit the ground and collapsed in a heap. Thomas was horror-struck but kept running, all the while yelling encouragement to everyone around him.

Finally he reached the Cliff. The two boards were firmly in place, and Sonya gestured to Teresa to cross the makeshift bridge and go through the old Griever hole. Then Brenda crossed with a line of people trailing her.

Thomas waited on the edge of the Cliff, waving people on. It was agonizing work, almost unbearable, to see the people so slowly making their way out of the Maze when the whole place seemed ready to collapse on itself at any second. One by one they ran across the boards and dropped into the hole. Thomas wondered if Teresa was sending them down the chute instead of the ladder to make it go more quickly.

"You go!" Sonya yelled to Thomas. "They need to know what to do once they're down there."

Thomas nodded, though he felt horrible for leaving—he'd done the same thing the first time he'd escaped, abandoning the Gladers to fight while he'd punched in the code. But he knew she was right. He took one last look at the quaking Maze—chunks of the ceiling torn loose and stone jutting from the ground where it had once been smooth. He didn't know how they'd all make it, and his heart ached for Minho, Frypan, the others.

He squeezed into the flow of people and crossed the boards to the hole, then swerved away from the crowd at the chute and ran to the ladder. He picked his way down the rungs as quickly as he could and was relieved to see at the bottom that the damage hadn't reached that section yet. Teresa was there, helping people get up after they landed and telling them which direction to head.

"I'll do this!" he yelled to her. "Get to the front of the pack!" He pointed through the double doors.

She was about to answer when she caught sight of something behind him. Her eyes widened in fear, and Thomas spun around.

Several of the dusty Griever pods were opening, their top halves lifting upward on hinges like the lids of coffins.

CHAPTER 70

"Listen to me!" Teresa screamed. She grabbed him by the shoulders and turned him around to look him in the face. "On the tail end of the Grievers"—she pointed at the closest pod—"what the Creators called the barrel—inside the blubber, there's a switch, like a handle. You have to reach through the skin and pull it out. If you can do it, the things will die."

Thomas nodded. "Okay. You keep people going!"

The tops of the pods continued to open as Thomas sprinted to the closest one. The lid was halfway up when he reached it, and he strained to look inside. The Griever's huge, sluglike body was trembling and twisting, sucking up moisture and fuel from tubes connected to its sides.

Thomas ran to its far end and pulled himself up on the lip of the container, then stretched over and leaned down to the Griever inside. He slammed his hand through the moist skin to find what Teresa had described. He grunted with the effort, pushed until he found a hard handle, then yanked on it with all his strength. The whole thing tore loose and the Griever fell into a limp mass of jelly at the bottom of the pod.

He threw the handle to the floor and ran to the next pod, where the lid was lowering to the ground. It took him only a few seconds to pull himself up and over the side, bury his hand in the fatty flesh and yank out the handle.

As he ran to the next pod, Thomas risked a quick glance up at

Teresa. She was still helping people from the floor after they slid down the chute and sending them through the doors. They were coming fast, landing on top of each other. Sonya was there, then Frypan, then Gally. Minho came flying through even as he watched. Thomas reached the pod, the lid now completely open, the tubes connecting the Griever to the container detaching themselves one by one. He pulled himself up and over, slammed his hand into the thing's skin and ripped out the handle.

Thomas dropped to the ground and turned to the fourth pod, but the Griever was moving, its front end slipping up and over the edge of the open pod, appendages bursting out of the skin to help it maneuver. Thomas barely reached it in time, jumped up and heaved himself over the side of the pod. He pushed his hand inside the blubbery skin, grabbed the handle. A pair of scissoring blades swiped at his head; he ducked as he wrenched the piece out of the creature's body and it died, its mass pulling it back into the coffinlike container.

Thomas knew it was too late to stop the last Griever before it exited its pod. He turned to assess the situation and watched as its full body sloshed out onto the ground. It was already scanning the area with a small observer socket that extended from its front; then, as he'd seen them do so many times before, the thing curled up into a ball and spikes burst from the skin. The creature spun forward with a great whirring of the machines within its belly. Concrete kicked up in the air, the Griever's spikes tearing through the flooring, and Thomas watched, helpless, as it crashed into a small group of people who'd come through the chute. Blades extended, it sliced through several people before they even knew what was happening.

Thomas looked around, searching for anything he could use as a weapon. A piece of pipe about the length of his arm had broken off from something in the ceiling—he ran to it and picked it up. When he turned back toward the Griever, he saw that Minho had already made it to the creature. He was kicking at it with a fierceness that was almost frightening.

Thomas charged the monster, yelling at the others to get away. The Griever spun toward him as if he'd heard the command, and it reared up on its bulbous back end. Two appendages emerged from the creature's sides and Thomas skidded to a halt—a new metal arm buzzed with a spinning saw, the other with a nasty-looking claw, its four tips ending in blades.

"Minho, just let me distract it!" he yelled. "Get everyone out of here and have Brenda start leading them to the maintenance room!"

Even as he said it, he watched a man trying to crawl out of the Griever's way. Before the man could get a few feet from it, a rod shot out of the creature and stabbed him in the chest, and he collapsed to the floor, spitting blood.

Thomas ran in, raising his pipe, ready to beat his way past the appendages, find his way to the handle. He'd almost made it when Teresa suddenly flashed in from his right, throwing her body onto the Griever. It immediately collapsed into a ball, all its metal arms retracting to press her to its skin.

"Teresa!" Thomas screamed, pulling up short, not sure what to do.

She twisted around to look at him. "Just go! Get them out!" She started kicking and clawing, her hands disappearing in the fatty flesh. So far she appeared to have escaped major injury.

Thomas inched in closer, gripping the pipe tighter, looking for an opening to attack without hitting her instead.

Teresa's eyes found him again. "Get out of—"

But her words were lost. The Griever had sucked her face into its blubbery skin and was pulling her farther and farther in, suffocating her.

Thomas stared, frozen. Too many people had died. Too many. And he wasn't going to stand there and let her sacrifice herself to save him and the others. He couldn't let that happen.

He screamed, and with all of the force he had, he ran and leaped into the air, smashing into the Griever. The spinning saw flew toward his chest and he dodged to the left, swinging the pipe around as he did. It connected, hard, and the saw broke off, flew through the air. Thomas heard it hit the ground and clatter across the room. He used his balance to swing back, driving the pipe into the creature's body, just to the side of Teresa's head. He strained with all he had to pull it back out, then drove it in again, then again.

An appendage with a claw clamped down on him, lifted him into the air and threw him. He slammed onto the hard cement floor and rolled, jumped back to his feet. Teresa had gained some leverage on the creature's body, had gotten to her knees, was swatting at the Griever's metal arms. Thomas charged in again, jumped and clung to its fatty flesh. He used the pipe to whack at anything that came near him. Teresa fought and struggled from below and the creature lurched to the side, then spun in a circle, flinging her at least ten feet through the air before she landed.

Thomas grabbed hold of a metal arm, kicking away the claw as it swiped at him again. He planted his feet against the blubber, pushed himself down the creature's side and stretched. He plunged his arm into the flabby flesh, felt for the handle. Something sliced his back, and pain ripped through his body. He kept digging, searching for the handle— the deeper he went, the more the creature's flesh felt like thick mud.

Finally his fingertips brushed hard plastic and he forced his hand forward another inch, grabbed the handle, pulled with all his strength and spun his body off of the Griever. He looked up to see Teresa batting back a pair of blades just inches from her face. And then a sudden silence filled the room as the creature's machine core sputtered and died. It collapsed into a flat, oblong pile of fat and gears, its protruding appendages falling to the ground, limp.

Thomas rested his head on the floor and sucked in huge lungfuls of air. And then Teresa was by his side, helping him roll over onto his back. He saw the pain on her face, the scratches, the flushed, sweaty skin. But then somehow she smiled.

"Thanks, Tom," she said.

"You're welcome." The respite from the battle felt too good to be true.

She helped pull him to his feet. "Let's get out of here."

Thomas noticed that no one was coming through the chute anymore, and Minho had just ushered the last few people through the double doors. Then he turned and faced Thomas and Teresa.

He bent over, hands on knees to catch his breath. "That's all of them." He stood straight with a groan. "All that made it, anyway. Guess we know now why they let us in so easy—they planned to slice us to bits with shuck Grievers if we came back out. Anyway, you guys need to push up to the front and help Brenda lead the way."

"She's okay, then?" Thomas asked. The relief he felt was overwhelming.

"Yeah. She's up there already."

Thomas crawled to his feet, but didn't take two steps before he stopped again. A deep rumble came from somewhere, from everywhere. The room shook for a few seconds then stilled.

"We better hurry," he said, and broke into a sprint, following the others.

CHAPTER 71

At least two hundred people had made it out of the Maze, but for some reason they'd stopped moving. Thomas dodged people in the crowded hallway, struggling to get to the front.

He weaved around men, women and children until finally he spotted Brenda. She pushed her way toward him and pulled him into a hug and kissed his cheek. With every bit of his heart, he wished it could all be over right then—that they could be safe, not have to go any farther.

"Minho made me leave," she said. "He forced me to go, promised to help if you needed it. He told me that getting everyone out was too important and you guys could handle the Griever. I should've stayed. I'm sorry."

"I told him to," Thomas responded. "You did the right thing. The only thing. We'll be out of here soon."

She gave him a little push. "Then let's hurry and make it happen."

"Okay." He squeezed her hand and they joined Teresa, moving toward the front of the group again.

The hallway was even darker than before—the lights that worked at all were dim, and flickered off and on. The people they passed huddled in silence, waiting anxiously. Thomas saw Frypan, who said nothing but did his best to give an encouraging smile, which, as usual, looked more like a smirk. In the distance, the occasional boom thundered through the air and the building trembled. The explosions still felt far enough away, but Thomas knew it wouldn't last.

When he and Brenda reached the front of the line, they found that the group had stopped at a stairwell, unsure whether to go up or down.

"We need to go up," Brenda said.

Thomas didn't hesitate. He motioned for the group to follow and started climbing, Brenda at his side.

He refused to succumb to the fatigue. Four flights, five, six. He stopped on the landing, catching his breath, and looked down, saw that the others were coming. Brenda guided him through a doorway, down another long hallway, left and then right, up another flight of stairs. One more hall and then *down* some stairs. One foot in front of the other. Thomas just hoped that the chancellor had been honest about the Flat Trans.

An explosion sounded somewhere above him, jolting the entire building and throwing him to the floor. Dust choked the air, and small pieces of the ceiling tiles landed on his back. Sounds of things creaking and breaking filled the air. Finally, after several seconds of shaking, everything grew quiet and still again.

He reached out for Brenda, made sure she wasn't hurt.

"Everybody okay?" he shouted down the hallway.

"Yeah!" someone called back.

"Keep moving! We're almost there!" He helped Brenda to her feet and they continued, Thomas praying the building would stay in one piece just a little while longer.

Thomas, Brenda, and those following them finally made it to the section of the building the chancellor had circled on the map—the maintenance room. Several more bombs had detonated, each one closer than the one before it. But nothing strong enough to stop them, and now they were practically there.

The maintenance room was situated behind a huge warehouse area.

Neat rows of metal racks full of boxes lined the right wall, and Thomas crossed to that side of the room, then began waving everybody in. He wanted everyone together before they went through the Flat Trans. There was one door at the back of the space—it had to lead to the room they'd been looking for.

"Keep them coming and get them ready," he told Brenda; then he sprinted for the door. If Chancellor Paige had lied about the Flat Trans, or if someone from WICKED or the Right Arm figured out what they were doing, they were finished.

The door led to a small room filled with tables that were littered with tools and scraps of metal and machine parts. On the far side, a large piece of canvas had been hung against the wall. Thomas ran to it and ripped it down. Behind it he found a dully shimmering wall of gray framed by a rectangle of shiny silver, and next to it, a control box.

It was the Flat Trans.

The chancellor had told the truth.

Thomas let out a laugh at the thought. WICKED—the *leader* of WICKED—had helped him.

Unless . . . He realized he needed to know one last thing. He had to test it to see where it led before he sent everyone through. Thomas sucked in a deep breath. This was it.

He forced himself to step through the icy Flat Trans surface. And he came out into a simple wooden shed, its door wide open in front of him. Beyond that he saw . . . green. Lots and lots of green. Grass, trees, flowers, bushes. It was good enough for him.

He stepped back through to the maintenance room, exhilarated. They'd done it—they were almost safe. He ran out to the storage area.

"Come on!" he yelled. "Get everyone in here—it works! Hurry!"

An explosion rattled the walls and the metal racks. Dust and debris rained down from the ceiling.

"Hurry!" he repeated.

Teresa already had people running, shepherding them Thomas's way. He stood just inside the door of the maintenance room, and when the first person crossed the threshold he took the woman by the arm and led her to the gray wall of the Flat Trans.

"You know what this is, right?" he asked her.

She nodded, bravely trying to hide her eagerness to get through the thing and out of there. "I've been around the block a few times, kid."

"Can I trust you to stand here and make sure everyone goes through?"

She blanched at first, but then she nodded.

"Don't worry," Thomas assured her. "Just stay here as long as you can."

As soon as she agreed he ran back to the door.

Others had packed the small room, and Thomas stepped back. "It's right through there. Make space on the other side!"

He squeezed his way past the knot of people and back into the warehouse. Everyone had lined up and was filing into the maintenance room. And standing at the back of the crowd were Minho, Brenda, Jorge, Teresa, Aris, Frypan and a few members of Group B. Gally was there, too. Thomas weaved his way to his friends.

"They better be quick about it up there," Minho said. "The explosions are getting closer and closer."

"The whole place is gonna fall down," Gally added.

Thomas scanned the ceiling as if he expected it to happen right that second. "I know. I told them to hurry. We'll all be out of here in a—"

"Well, what do we have *here*?" a voice shouted from the back of the room.

A few gasps sounded around Thomas as he turned to see who'd spoken. The Rat Man had just come through the door from the outside hallway, and he wasn't alone. He was surrounded by WICKED security guards. Thomas counted seven total, which meant that he and his friends still had the advantage.

Janson stopped and cupped his hands to shout over the rumble of another explosion. "Strange place to hide out when everything's about to come down!" Pieces of metal fell from the ceiling, clattering to the ground.

"You know what's here!" Thomas shouted back. "It's too late— we're already going!"

Janson pulled out the same long knife he had outside and flashed it. And as if on cue, the others revealed similar weapons.

"But we can salvage a few," Janson said. "And it looks like we have the strongest and brightest right here in front of us. Even our Final Candidate, no less! The one we need most, yet who refuses to cooperate."

Thomas and his friends had spread out in a line between the dwindling crowd of prisoners and the guards. The others in Thomas's group were searching the floor for anything they could find to use as a weapon—pipes, long screws, the jagged edge of a metal grid. Thomas spotted a warped piece of thick cabling that ended in a spike of rigid wires, as deadly-looking as a spear. He grabbed it just as another explosion rocked the room, sending a huge section of the metal shelving crashing to the floor

"I've never seen such a menacing bunch of thugs!" the Rat Man yelled, but his face was crazed, his mouth contorted into a wild sneer. "I have to admit I'm terrified!"

"Just shut your shuck mouth and let's get this over with!" Minho shouted back at him.

Janson focused his cold, mad gaze on the teenagers facing him.

"Gladly," he said.

Thomas ached to lash out for all the fear and pain and suffering that had defined his life for so long. "Go!" he shouted.

The two groups charged each other, their yells of battle drowned out by the sudden concussion of detonating explosives that shook the building around them.

CHAPTER 72

Somehow Thomas kept his balance, despite the entire room quaking from the closest series of explosions yet. Most of the racks collapsed, and objects were launched across the room. He dodged a jagged chunk of wood, then jumped over a round piece of machinery that spun past him.

Gally, who was at Thomas's side, tripped and fell; Thomas helped him up. They continued charging. Brenda slipped but caught her balance.

They crashed into the others like the first line of soldiers in an ancient foot battle. Thomas met the Rat Man himself, who was at least half a foot taller than him, wielding his blade; it came down in an arc toward Thomas's shoulder, but Thomas thrust upward with his stiff cable and connected with the man's armpit. Janson screamed and dropped his weapon as a stream of blood gushed from the wound; he clamped his other hand over it and backed away, glaring at Thomas with hate-filled eyes.

To his right and left, everyone was fighting. Thomas's head was full of the sounds of metal against metal, screams and shouts and grunts. Some had matched up two-on-one; Minho ended up fighting a woman who seemed twice as strong as any of the men. Brenda was on the ground, wrestling a skinny man, trying to knock a machete out of his hand. Thomas saw all this with a quick glance but then returned his attention to his own foe.

"I don't care if I bleed to death," Janson said with a grimace. "As long as I die after I get you back up there."

Another explosion jolted the floor beneath him and Thomas stumbled forward, dropping his scavenged weapon and slamming into Janson's chest. They both crashed to the ground, and Thomas struggled to push off the man with one hand while swinging as hard as he could with the other. He smashed Janson's left cheek with his balled fist and watched as the Rat Man's head snapped to the side, blood spraying from his mouth. Thomas reached back to swing again, but the man arched his body violently, throwing him off; he landed on his back.

Before he could move Janson had jumped on top of him and gotten his legs wrapped around his torso, pinning Thomas's arms with his knees. Thomas squirmed to get loose as the man rained down blows with his fists, punching Thomas's unprotected face over and over. Pain flooded him. Then adrenaline surged through his body. He wouldn't die here. He pushed his feet against the floor and thrust his stomach toward the ceiling.

He only rose a few inches off the ground, but it was enough to free his arms from the man's knees. He blocked the next punch with both of his forearms, then threw both fists up and at Janson's face, connected. The Rat Man lost his balance; Thomas pushed him off, then kicked him by coiling both legs and slamming the bottoms of his feet into Janson's side, then again, and again, and again. The man's body inched away with each kick. But when Thomas next pulled back with his legs, Janson suddenly flipped around and came at him, grabbing Thomas's feet and throwing them to the side. Then he jumped on top of Thomas yet again.

Thomas went nuts; kicking and punching and squirming to get out from under the man. They rolled, each gaining the advantage for only a split second before toppling over again. Fists flew and feet kicked—

bullets of pain riddled Thomas's body; Janson clawed and bit. They continued to roll, beating each other nearly senseless.

Thomas finally got a good angle to slam his elbow into Janson's nose; it stunned the man, and both of his hands flew to his face. A burst of energy shot through Thomas; he jumped on top of Janson and put his fingers around the man's neck, began to squeeze. Janson kicked out, flailed his arms, but Thomas held on with feral rage, clutching, leaning forward with all his weight to crush as he constricted his hands tighter and tighter. He felt things snapping and pulling and breaking. Janson's eyes bulged; his tongue jutted from his mouth.

Someone swatted him on the head with an open palm; he could tell words were being spoken to him but he didn't hear them. Minho's face appeared in front of his. He was yelling something. A bloodlust had completely taken Thomas over. He wiped his eyes on his sleeve, focused again on Janson's face. The man was long gone, still and pale and battered. Thomas looked back at Minho.

"He's dead!" his friend was yelling. "He's dead!"

Thomas forced himself to let go, stumbled off of the man, felt Minho lifting him to his feet.

"We put them all out of commission!" Minho shouted in his ear. "We need to go!"

Two explosions rocked both sides of the storage room at the same time and the walls themselves collapsed inward, throwing chunks of brick and cement in all directions. Debris rained down on Thomas and Minho. Dust clouded the air and shadowy figures surrounded Thomas, swaying and falling and getting back up again. Thomas was on his feet, moving, heading in the direction of the maintenance room.

Pieces of the ceiling fell, crashing and exploding. The sounds were awful, deafening. The ground shook violently; bombs continued to detonate over and over, seemingly everywhere at once. Thomas fell;

Minho jerked him to his feet. A few seconds later Minho fell; Thomas yanked and dragged until they were both running again. Brenda suddenly appeared in front of Thomas, terror in her eyes. He thought he saw Teresa nearby as well, all of them struggling to keep their balance as they moved forward.

A splintering, shattering noise split the air so loudly that Thomas looked back. His eyes drifted upward, where a massive section of the ceiling had torn loose. He watched, hypnotized, as it fell toward him. Teresa appeared in the corner of his vision, her image barely discernible through the clogged air. Her body slammed into his, shoving him toward the maintenance room. His mind emptied as he stumbled backward and fell, just as the huge piece of the building landed on top of Teresa, pinning her body; only her head and an arm jutted out from under its girth.

"Teresa!" Thomas screamed, an unearthly sound that somehow rose above everything else. He scrambled toward her. Blood streaked her face, and her arm looked crushed.

He shouted her name again, and in his mind he saw Chuck, falling to the ground, covered in blood, and Newt's bulging eyes. Three of the closest friends he'd ever had. And WICKED had taken them all away from him.

"I'm so sorry," he whispered to her, knowing she couldn't hear. "I'm so sorry."

Her mouth moved, working to speak, and he leaned in to make out what she was trying to say.

"Me . . . too," she whispered. "I only ever . . . cared for . . ."

And then Thomas was being dragged to his feet, yanked away from her. He didn't have the energy or will to fight it. She was gone. His body ached with pain; his heart stung. Brenda and Minho pulled him up, got his feet under him. The three of them lurched forward, pushed ahead. A

317

fire had started burning in a gaping hole left by an explosion—smoke billowed and churned with the thick dust. Thomas coughed but only heard roaring in his ears.

Another resounding boom shattered the air; Thomas turned his head as he ran to see the back wall of the storage room exploding, falling to the ground in pieces, flames licking through the open spaces. The remainder of the ceiling above it began to collapse, any support now gone. Every last inch of the building was coming down once and for all.

They reached the door to the maintenance room, squeezed inside just in time to see Gally disappear through the Flat Trans. Everyone else was already gone. Thomas stumbled with his friends across the short aisle between the tables. In seconds they'd be dead. The sounds of things crashing and crumbling behind Thomas grew impossibly louder, cracks and creaks and squeals of metal and the hollow roar of flames. All of it rose to an unimaginable pitch; Thomas refused to look, though he sensed it all coming down, as if it were just feet away, its leading edge breathing against his neck. He pushed Brenda through the Trans. The world was collapsing around him and Minho.

Together, they jumped into the icy gray wall.

CHAPTER 73

Thomas could barely breathe. He was coughing, spitting. His heart raced, refused to slow down. He'd landed on the wooden floor of the shed, and now he crawled forward, wanting to get away from the Flat Trans in case any nasty debris came flying through. But he noticed Brenda out of the corner of his eye. She pushed some buttons on a control panel, and then the gray plane winked out of existence, revealing the cedar planks of the shed wall behind it. *How did she know how to do that?* Thomas wondered.

"You and Minho get out," she said, an urgency in her voice that Thomas didn't understand. They were safe now. Weren't they? "I have to do one last thing."

Minho had gotten to his feet, and he came over to help Thomas stand. "My shuck brain can't spend one more second thinking. Just let her do whatever she wants. Come on."

"Good that," Thomas said. The two of them then looked at each other for a long moment, catching their breath, somehow reliving in those few seconds all the things they'd gone through, all the death, all the pain. And mixed in there was relief, that maybe—just maybe—it was all over.

But mostly Thomas felt the pain of loss. Watching Teresa die—to save his life—had been almost too much to bear. Now, staring at the person who'd become his true best friend, he had to fight back the tears. In that moment, he swore to never tell Minho about what he'd done to Newt.

"Good that for sure, shuck-face," Minho finally replied. But his trademark smirk was missing. Instead was a look that said to Thomas he understood. And that they'd both carry the sorrow of their loss for the rest of their lives. Then he turned and walked away.

After a long moment, Thomas followed him.

When he set foot outside, he had to stop and stare. They'd come to a place he'd been told didn't exist anymore. Lush and green and full of vibrant life. He stood at the top of a hill above a field of tall grass and wildflowers. The two hundred or so people they'd rescued wandered the area, some of them actually running and jumping. To his right the hill descended into a valley of towering trees that seemed to stretched for miles, ending in a wall of rocky mountains that jutted toward the cloudless blue sky. To his left, the grassy field slowly became scrub brush and then sand. And then the ocean, its waves big and dark and white-tipped as they crashed onto a beach.

Paradise. They'd come to paradise. He could only hope that one day his heart would feel the joy of the place.

He heard the door of the shed close then the whoosh of fire behind him. He turned to see Brenda; she gently pushed him a few steps farther away from the structure, which was already engulfed in flames.

"Just making sure?" he asked.

"Just making sure," she repeated, and gave him a smile so sincere that he relaxed a little, feeling the tiniest bit comforted. "I'm . . . sorry about Teresa."

"Thanks." It was the only word he could find.

She didn't say anything else, and Thomas figured there wasn't much she needed to. They walked over and joined the group of people who'd fought the last battle with Janson and the others, everyone scraped and bruised from top to bottom. He met Frypan's eyes just like he had

Minho's. Then they all faced the shed and watched as it burned to the ground.

A few hours later, Thomas sat atop a cliff overlooking the ocean, his feet dangling over the edge. The sun had almost dipped below the horizon, which appeared to be glowing with flames. It was one of the most amazing sights he'd ever witnessed.

Minho had already started taking charge down below in the forest where they'd decided to live—organizing food search parties, a building committee, a security detail. Thomas was glad of it, not wanting another ounce of responsibility to ever rest on his shoulders again. He was tired, body and soul. He hoped that wherever they were, they'd be isolated and safe while the rest of the world figured out how to deal with the Flare, cure or no cure. He knew the process would be long and hard and ugly, and he was one hundred percent positive that he wanted no part of it.

He was done.

"Hey, there."

Thomas turned to see Brenda. "Hey, there, back. Wanna sit?"

"Why, yes, thank you." She plopped down next to him. "Reminds me of the sunsets at WICKED, though they never seemed quite so bright."

"You could say that about a lot of things." He felt another tremor of emotion as he saw the faces of Chuck and Newt and Teresa in his mind's eye.

A few minutes went by in silence as they stared at the vanishing light of day, the sky and water going from orange to pink to purple, then dark blue.

"What're you thinking in that head of yours?" Brenda asked.

"Absolutely nothing. I'm done thinking for a while." And he meant it. For the first time in his life, he was both free and safe, as costly as the accomplishment had been.

Then Thomas did the only thing he could think of. He reached out and took Brenda's hand.

She squeezed his in response. "There are over two hundred of us and we're all immune. It'll be a good start."

Thomas looked over at her, suspicious at how sure she sounded— like she knew something he didn't. "What's *that* supposed to mean?"

She leaned forward and kissed him on the cheek, then the lips. "Nothing. Nothing at all."

Thomas put it all out of his mind and pulled her closer as the last wink of the sun's light vanished below the horizon.

EPILOGUE

Final WICKED Memorandum, Date 232.4.10, Time 12:45
TO: My Associates
FROM: Ava Paige, Chancellor
RE: A new beginning

And so, we have failed.

But we have also succeeded.

Our original vision didn't come to fruition; the blueprint never came together. We were unable to discover either a vaccine or a treatment for the Flare. But I anticipated this outcome and put into place an alternate solution, to save at least a portion of our race. With the help of my partners, two wisely placed Immunes, I was able to plan and implement a solution that will result in the best outcome we could've hoped for.

I know the majority of WICKED thought that we needed to get tougher, dig deeper, be more ruthless with our subjects, keep searching for an answer. Begin new rounds of Trials. But what we neglected to see was right before our eyes. The Immune are the only resource left to this world.

And if all has gone according to plan, we have sent the brightest, the strongest, the toughest of our subjects to a safe place, where they can begin civilization anew while the rest of the world is driven to extinction.

It is my hope that over the years our organization has in some part paid the price for the unspeakable act committed against humanity by our predecessors in government. Though I am fully aware that it was an act of desperation after the sun flares, releasing the Flare virus as a means of population control was an abhorrent and irreversible crime. And the disastrous results could never have been predicted. WICKED has worked ever since that act was committed to right that wrong, to find a cure. And though we have failed in that effort, we can at least say we've planted the seed for mankind's future.

I don't know how history will judge the actions of WICKED, but I state here for the record that the organization only ever had one goal, and that was to preserve the human race. And in this last act, we have done just that.

As we tried to instill in each of our subjects over and over, WICKED is good.

ACKNOWLEDGMENTS

What a ride this trilogy has been. In so many ways it's been a collaborative effort between me; my editor, Krista Marino; and my agent, Michael Bourret. I can't possibly thank these two people enough. But I'll keep trying.

Many thanks go to all the good people at Random House, especially to Beverly Horowitz and my publicists, Emily Pourciau and Noreen Herits. Also to all the incredible team members of sales, marketing, design, copyediting, and all the other vital parts of making a book come to life. Thank you for making this series a success.

Thank you, Lauren Abramo and Dystel & Goderich, for making sure these books are available around the world. And thank you to all my publishers abroad for giving them a chance.

Thank you, Lynette and J. Scott Savage, for reading early drafts and giving feedback. I promise it's gotten a lot better!

Thank you to all the book bloggers and Facebook friends and the Twitter #dashnerarmy for hanging out with me and pushing my stories to others. To you and to all my readers, thank you. This world became real to me, and I hope you've enjoyed living in it.

ABOUT THE AUTHOR

James Dashner was born and raised in Georgia but now lives and writes in the Rocky Mountains. He is the author of the Maze Runner trilogy, as well as the 13th Reality series. To learn more about him and his books, visit jamesdashner.com.

To whom it may concern:

We were able to recover the following material from the hard drives of several computers found in the remains of a building. We believe this building was the headquarters for AMRIID—the Army Medical Research Institute for Infectious Diseases.

This information is alarming. Please proceed with caution.

TO ALL SURVIVORS OF THE SUN FLARES

The Flares Information Recovery Endeavor, henceforth known as FIRE, hereby calls upon municipal units, police agencies, social services and any surviving governmental entities for help. Because most means of communication have been rendered useless, this flyer is being disseminated to the four corners of the world by any available means, including Netblock, Berg, plane, boat, car, and horse.

So far FIRE comprises representatives from the North American Alliance, Russia, the European Union, the United States of Africa, and Mexico, all countries that have suffered catastrophic damage from the sun flares. We hope to gather more representatives from around the world as quickly as possible.

The globe has been ravaged by this disaster. But now is the time to pull together to do what we have always done: survive. FIRE's first task is to assemble world leaders and collect information. We will then organize governing units, police forces, and food and shelter coordination plans.

If you read this message, please find a way to send word back to the FIRE headquarters in Anchorage, Alaska.

Post-Flares Coalition Memorandum, Date 217.11.28, Time 21:46
TO: All board members
FROM: Chancellor John Michael
RE: Population concerns

The report presented to us today, copies of which were sent to all members of the coalition, certainly left no room for doubt as to the problems that face this already crippled world. I am certain that all of you, like me, went to your shelters in stunned silence. It is my hope that the harsh reality described in this report is now clear enough that we can begin talking about solutions.

The problem is simple: the world has too many people and not enough resources.

We have scheduled our next meeting for a week from tomorrow. I expect all members to come prepared to present a solution, no matter how extraordinary it seems. You may be familiar with an old business saying, "think outside the box." I believe it is time we do just that.

I look forward to hearing your ideas.

To: John Michael
From: Katie McVoy
Subject: Potential

John,

I looked into the matter we discussed over dinner last night.
AMRIID barely survived the flares, but they're confident that
the underground containment system for the most dangerous
viruses, bacteria, and biological weapons didn't fail.

It took some wrangling, but I got the information we need. I've
looked through it and come up with a recommendation. All the
potential solutions are far too unpredictable to be usable.
Except one.

It's a virus. It attacks the brain and shuts it down, painlessly.
It acts quickly and decisively. The virus was designed to
slowly weaken in infection rate as it spreads from host to host.
It will be perfect for our needs, especially considering how
severely limited travel has become. It could work, John. And as
awful as it seems, I believe it could work efficiently.

I'll send over the details. Let me know your thoughts.
—Katie

To: Katie McVoy
From: John Michael
Subject: RE: Potential

Katie,

I need your help preparing my full proposal for the virus
release presentation. We need to focus on how a controlled kill
is the only way to save lives. Though it will make survival
possible for only a select portion of our population, unless we
take extreme measures, we face the eventual extinction of the
human race.

You and I both know how hypothetical this solution is. But
we've run the simulations a thousand times and I just can't see
any alternative. If we don't do this, the world will run out of
resources. I firmly believe it is the most ethical decision—the
risk of race extinction justifies the elimination of a few. My
mind is made up. Now it's a matter of convincing the others on
the board.

Let's meet at my quarters, 1700. Everything has to be worded
perfectly, so prepare yourself for a long night.

Until then,
John

To: Randall Spilker
From: Ladena Lichliter
Subject:

I'm still sick from the meeting today. I just can't believe it. I can't accept that the PCC actually looked us in the eyes and presented that proposal. Seriously. I was stunned.

And then more than half the room AGREED WITH THEM! They supported it! What the hell is going on? Randall, tell me what the HELL is going on? How can we even THINK about doing something like that? How?

I've spent the afternoon trying to make sense of it all. I can't take it. I can't.

How did we get here?

Come see me tonight. Please.

—LL

Post-Flares Coalition Memorandum, Date 219.02.12, Time 19:32
TO: All board members
FROM: Chancellor John Michael
RE: EO draft

Please give me your thoughts on the following draft. The final
order will go out tomorrow.

Executive Order #13 of the Post-Flares Coalition, by
recommendation of the Population Control Committee, to be
considered TOP-SECRET, of the highest priority, on penalty of
capital punishment.

We the Coalition hereby grant the PCC express permission to
fully implement their PC Initiative #1 as presented in full
and attached below. We the Coalition take full responsibility
for this action and will monitor developments and offer
assistance to the fullest extent of our resources. The virus
will be released in the locations recommended by the PCC and
agreed upon by the Coalition. Armed forces will be stationed
to ensure that the process unfolds in as orderly a manner as
possible.

EO #13, PCI #1, is hereby ratified. Begin immediately.

To: John Michael
From: Katie McVoy
Subject: Potential

John,

We received the following radio message from soldiers at
Ground Zero EU: an exchange between a Lieutenant Larsson
and a private named Kibucho that began during a helicopter
flyover. I have to warn you, it's a little disturbing.

Begin transmission

Larsson: What the *expletive* is that down there? Through that gash in
    the roof. What's all that movement?
Kibucho: They're supposed to be *expletive* dead by now. It has to be
    animals or something.
Larsson: No way. But it's too dark. We need to get down there and have
    a look.
Kibucho: I'll tell them.

Three-minute break in transmission

Larsson: Open the door.
Kibucho: Are you sure?
Larsson: Open the *expletive* door, Private!
Kibucho: Going in.

Two-minute break in transmission

Kibucho: He chopped off my leg! He chopped off my *expletive* leg!

Larsson: What? What the *expletive* are you talking about?

Kibucho: [Garbled response.]

Larsson: Private! What's going on?

Kibucho: Half of them are alive! Get me out!

Larsson: Backup, backup, backup! We need backup in Sector Seventeen of Ground Zero EU immediately!

Kibucho: [Garbled screams.]

Larsson: Holy *expletive*! Holy *expletive*! They're eating him! My God, they're eating him!

Kibucho: [Garbled screams that cut off abruptly.]

Larsson: They have me cornered! Oh, *expletive*, they have me cornered!

End transmission

We need to gather the board.

—Katie

To: Randall Spilker
From: Ladena Lichliter
Subject: Unbelievable

I know you've been sick, but the reports are flying in now. Have
you seen any of them? These aren't rumors anymore, Randall.
They have at least 27 confirmed sightings of infected groups.
The virus didn't kill them! None of the doctors or scientists
can nail down what's gone wrong. But most of the people living
at Ground Zero locations are completely insane, like animals.
They're monsters!

But that's not even the worst part. What has the Coalition
terrified is that victims even had time to escape from the
remote camps. The Coalition thought the incubation period and
onset of death would be much faster. And there are reports of
symptoms in citizens outside the hot zones. Everywhere.

Randall, we have a major, major crisis on our hands. They
should've listened to us. They should've listened!

God help us.
—LL

To: John Michael
From: Katie McVoy
Subject: Some last words

John,

There's no way we can stop this. You're right. I hate to admit it,
but it's true. Every effort we made to prevent the spread was
pointless. The virus is jumping bodies every second. We can only
hope that the rumors of the presence of Immunes are true. They
might be the only chance we've got for survival.

A cure. I can't think of any other possible solution. Somehow, we
have to find a cure.

Did you hear what the media has taken to calling it? The Flare.
I'm sure it'll stick.

I have it. I know I do. I'm leaving. I don't want to infect anyone.

You were a true friend in this madness.

Goodbye, John.
—Katie

Post-Flares Coalition Memorandum, Date 220.05.01, Time 11:23
TO: All board members
FROM: Chancellor John Michael
RE: Another solution

The killzone. That's their word for the brain now. Where the
Flare does its damage and slowly kills you with lunacy. And
they already have a nickname for the Immunes, too. The Munies.
What utter ridiculousness.

But jargon matters not. What matters is how it all connects.
The killzone. The Flare. The Immunes. A world that's in complete
catastrophe. We need to find a cure. There is no other way to go
forward.

We will meet tomorrow, 0800.
I have an idea.

BUS-ING

Thomas J. Cottle

BEACON PRESS / BOSTON

Library of Congress Cataloging in Publication Data

Cottle, Thomas J
    Busing
    1. School children — United States — Transportation.
2. School integration — United States. I. Title.
LC214.52.C67   370.19′342   76–7740
ISBN 0–8070–0494–4

For Claudia and Jason Cottle

ACKNOWLEDGMENTS

Let me thank first the people whose words appear in this book; without them there is no work. Next, I wish to thank the men and women of The Children's Defense Fund of the Washington Research Project and its director Marian Wright Edelman, as well as the Guggenheim Foundation, Gordon N. Ray, President, for untold support and encouragement.

Many friends and colleagues have helped me in the preparation and writing of this book. They are Lincoln Caplan, Kathy Dalton, Oliver W. Holmes, Michael Kessler, Jennifer King, Orlando B. and Sara Lawrence Lightfoot, Sally Makacynas, Gary T. Marx, Gerald M. Platt, Martin and Anne Peretz, Richard and Ruth Rogers, Harvey Shapiro, Fred Stern, and Paul M. Strudler.

A thank you to my friends and editors at Beacon Press: Ray Bentley, David Ford, Marie Goldstein, Lois Randall, and Pat Harrison.

Finally, for myriad reasons, a special thank you to Kay M. Cottle.

CONTENTS

INTRODUCTION

THERE IS NO ENEMY

Chico Dowling is one of the tallest men I know. When he walks his eleven-year-old son Bobby to where the school bus picks up the children each morning, he towers over everybody, a giant among little people. "Be good," he tells his son. "Don't get into no trouble. Do what they tell you and for God's sake don't miss the bus coming home. You hear me? Don't miss the coming home bus!"

Then he tells me as we walk back to his home, "Well, they're still busing. Been weeks now and they're still busing. City's shaking. You can feel it shake, can't you? Like even the sidewalks don't hold you firm like they used to. Black folks and white folks making this city shake. Hell man, with the bad news everybody's trying to stir up around here, you'd think it was Selma or Montgomery or Little Rock. They are sure enough busing in Boston."

Indeed, they are busing school children in Boston and in many cities throughout America. It has made for bitter autumns, bitter winters. The newspapers are filled with stories of desegregation, busing rulings, the transfer of students, and the scramble to assign a few more black teachers here and there. Radio and television news teams seem parked near every school. I watched a student approach one of the local TV cameramen.

"You here again?" the student asked. "You been here more days than I've been here."

"I like it here," the cameraman replied.

"Hell you do. You're waiting for the riot to start. You come down here with all that equipment and it ain't worth your effort till something big happens. You ain't here to cover no story. You're here to see if you can't start one. You and the cops. You're incitin' action. If you all would just stay away things might be all right. Why don't you go cover a fire or somebody getting murdered for a change!"

It has been a painful, frightening time for many in American cities. There isn't a story, a ruling, a law that all people embrace. The slightest sound, the barest whisper splits factions even wider apart and makes the heartache, confusion, and anger more intense.

"You think it's good to have policemen on horseback so close to your school?" I ask.

Teacher: "That man rides off, I'll ride off with him. He's my only protection."

Student: "All these cops do is make trouble and all these horses do is make a mess. Get 'em out of here!"

Student: "I wouldn't go in that building without that policeman there. I stood behind that tree yesterday morning waiting for them to come. If they didn't come, I wasn't going to school. I'm not taking any political side, but I'll be damned if I want to get killed."

Teacher: "What's the difference if they're here or they're not here. This school will never be the same. This city will never be the same. It's the racists versus the black folks, and the police have never helped the black folks. Ever. Nowhere!"

Policeman: "I came here because they say to come here. I've never shot anyone or at anyone for the nine years that I'm on this police force. You think I want to start now? You think I'm looking forward to some afternoon when I may have to draw my gun on some *kid*? Some thirteen-, fourteen-year-old *kid*? You actually think policemen are like the way they paint us in the media?"

Inevitably, it comes down to the question, are you for or against busing? That's the basis of the division, and the proper answer to the question is your passport into the communities

that have the most to gain and the most to lose from school desegregation.

"Don't mess around with the liberal man," a woman in her fifties shouted at me. "You with them or with us? Just say yes or no. It's a black-white issue, you know what I mean? There's no place for nobody to be in between. It's like America against Germany. You fought on one side or the other. Nobody fights on both sides. How'd you stand when Israel went to war?"

"I suppose I was for Israel."

"There you are. This is the same thing. Arabs or Israel? Blacks or whites."

Another woman in another neighborhood said much the same thing. "There's only one place to stand. You say you're for desegregation, then you can't be compassionate towards those folks who are fighting against us. It's a war, and it may just be a bloody one. This city hasn't done a thing for black folks from the time it began. It's a white city with a white mayor and a white government. The best they can do is let us get our kids into some of the few decent schools. So you better believe we'll grab this chance. Knowing this country, there won't be a chance coming again for another 150 years!"

From a young black man: "I'm not going near any school where I might get hurt. I'm going to school for one reason: I want college and a profession. There's no way people are going to ruin that for me by breaking a bottle over my head or breaking my back with a club. When it's cool I'll go."

From a young white man: "The world has soldiers and pacifists. I don't go to school to wage war. I go to school to get educated. This is only the beginning for me. I have a long way I'm supposed to go in school. I can't afford all the trouble. I have nothing against anyone, I just want to learn. If my folks had money I'd go to a private school and forget *all* these people, their kind *and* my kind."

"Times haven't changed all that much." A woman shook her head. "What's been in the south comes to the north. May come slowly but it gets here. Same as folks like us got here. Slowly, but we made it. There's always been rich folks making the laws—like where you can send your children to school—and

poor folks obeying those laws. Busing's the same thing. Hypocritical rich folks pushing people around, saying, do like I say
but not like I do. No surprises to this busing business. All you
have to do is read your history, you'll find the same thing in
every country where they got rich folks who make the laws and
poor folks who obey them. Sometimes it works for us, sometimes it works against us. If the law were the same for all
people, I'm not sure all these government people would be
pushing so hard for desegregating the schools. If it were *their*
children riding these buses every morning, they'd play it different."

So the password question in many of America's special
communities is: Are you for or against busing? Attendance
figures in certain high schools are watched as closely as some
people watch the Dow Jones average. Anti-busing boycotts
build. Stories of violence fill the newspapers. And people
everywhere look to these special communities and wonder how
they are going to fare. The people in these special communities
are feeling again the squeeze they have always felt, and some
pressures they have never known before. At issue are racism,
economic inequality, neighborhood autonomy, learning, and
jobs, the past, present, and future—people.

Busing children into communities for the purpose of desegregating schools has become one of the most controversial,
incendiary issues America has faced in recent years. There is
perhaps no more complex and emotionally charged problem in
American education than desegregation of schools through
involuntary busing. Some claim busing is the quintessential
American dilemma, for it raises the question of whether America can absorb two races. They claim that busing is a ghost
issue, for it is not busing that evokes bitterness, but the demand
that certain human beings integrate their lives with other
certain human beings.

Other people have alleged that busing has little to do with
racial matters. It is an unjust demand that poor and working
class people lead their lives according to the dictates of those in
power, even when their rulers find ways of skirting these

dictates. It is strictly a class issue, these critics contend; racial prejudice has nothing to do with it.

There are people who view busing in terms of money, millions of dollars wasted on court rulings that should never have been made. There are people who see busing in terms of children, hundreds of thousands of young people whose lives are being psychologically and intellectually assaulted, even permanently damaged by busing programs. These critics have collected social scientific studies to support their claims. There are people who see busing in terms of the hundreds of thousands of children whose psychological and intellectual development can only be enhanced and uplifted by busing. These people, too, have accumulated social scientific studies to support their claims. Some people perceive busing in terms of educational issues, some as a political and economic advance or retreat for black people and white people; some in terms of a social psychological, even symbolic, sexual confrontation; and some in terms of bus safety and American road conditions. On the question of the morality of busing or not busing there is always someone to argue, and vociferously, any side of the issue one could possibly imagine.

Importantly, and a matter rarely discussed in the popular press, disagreements over questions relating to busing exist not only among citizens of a particular neighborhood or school district, but among members of the same family. The matter of busing has ignited the impulse to engage in racial warfare. No one needs to be told that human beings are being physically attacked because of their attitudes and the color of their skin. But men and women of the same name, the same blood and heritage, are also feeling impelled to do battle with one another over busing. The reality of busing consumes people, gives to some a sense of hope they have never known, to others a feeling of hopelessness they never believed could be so overwhelming.

It is not being melodramatic to say that the matter of busing, irrespective of what it means to a particular person, necessarily arouses in that person the most fundamental emotions and questions of self-regard. One's position on busing is a statement about one's identity, an assessment of one's prior and present

position in the world, a statement of one's dreams for a desirable society.

Anyone who listens to the people whose lives are directly affected by busing, or indeed people who feel implicated in busing decisions, knows well that what he or she is hearing is not the expression of a simple attitude or opinion. One hears powerful recitations that evoke theological and sociological imagery, historical accounts and personal episodes, experiences that have resounded so intensely in the lives of these people, their bodies respond in the telling of their stories. One knows too, that upon hearing these recitations, one is automatically drawn into the life of the person one is listening to; for these few moments one is an ally, a friend. When a simple attitude is being expressed, one feels that disagreement, indeed argument, is a legitimate response. When, however, this same person's belief emerges within the body of a life story, within the context of an entire developmental history, then one no longer feels so free to disagree or to question each image of the other person's perspective. Like it or not, one becomes implicated in the lives of people with wholly different backgrounds, circumstances, and attitudes on busing. And in this mysterious process of becoming implicated, one ceases to indulge in typical arguments, typical forms of reasoning and rebuttal, typical styles of conversation.

It is for these reasons, I think, that so few accounts of busing focus on the lives of people, but focus instead on strict reporting of attitudes and opinions. People are portrayed as one-dimensional men and women with only busing on their minds. How busing fits into their daily lives or emerging histories is something we rarely read about. In response, we are able to agree with the attitudes of some, disagree with others, and not experience feelings. We can hold the matter of busing at a safe and comfortable distance; we need not become implicated.

As a personal note, I felt a strong desire to turn away from the accounts of busing I was hearing in the homes I visit regularly. Although for ten years my research has consisted of nothing more than speaking with people—most of them in poor communities—about how their lives are being led, the busing

question almost caused me to turn away from those who for a long time had shared so much of themselves with me. The conversations were becoming too intense, unmanageable, filled with an animus I had never known. Always there had been a warming-up period, several minutes of renewing our friendship, a chat about the little things in life that help people to reconvene. Now, however, these same people were meeting me on their doorsteps, leaning out their windows and beginning their arguments, their harangues, their demonstrations of rage —what some people call their riffs—even before I had greeted them.

I resolved, therefore, never to write about my encounters when busing was at the heart of the conversation. It couldn't be done. One could not capture the spirit, the intensity, the sense of feeling overwhelmed that these people were communicating. One could barely describe, moreover, the life story in which busing played such a vital role. Ironically, like so many others, I had for years complained that no one wants to hear about the world in which poor people survive. No one wants to hear about bad housing, bad schooling, hunger, health problems, unemployment, gang wars. Life is bad enough without having to learn about other people's problems. This, of course, is not entirely true, for hundreds of books deal with such themes and facts. More accurately perhaps, my complaint was based on the notion that nothing the so-called common man or common woman, the ordinary person that is, ever does, is found newsworthy. Like everyone else, it is said, they have their attitudes, their outlooks, their lives. Leave it to the sociologists, psychologists, and journalists to record these attitudes. Even if the rest of us aren't particularly interested in their thoughts, they belong somewhere in the human book.

Then suddenly, the attitudes about busing held by the very people I was speaking with every day had not only become newsworthy, they hit the top of the news. The whole world, it seemed, was looking at Boston, Detroit, Denver, Louisville. Still, it was attitudes, at best a few anecdotes, that were sought, not life studies. The people I had been speaking with well before we ever discussed busing encouraged me to write, and gave full

approval to having their words published. Indeed, they felt it
important that even bits of their stories be told. "It's a dangerous project," I told one woman whose words appear in this
book. "No matter what I say, no matter how much I allow
people merely to speak for themselves, I'll be accused of biased
interviewing, of advocating one side of the busing debate." The
woman merely shook her head slowly from side to side. Her
expression could only be read one way: My, my, such a tough
life, such a tough problem: how to steer clear of people's lives,
political controversies, human issues.

This book is based on conversations I have had with a group
of people over the last several years. Some have been friends for
almost a decade; others I have known for only three years. I
have tried to capture their words, their language, as accurately
as possible. All have read what I have written about them to
check for errors in fact and tone. Fictitious names have been
used in order to preserve anonymity, although no one requested
it. In planning the book, my editor and I sought a balance of
attitudes about busing, as well as a sampling of people from
various age groups. We believed that there should be parents,
students, teachers, and other school personnel represented, as
well as residents of cities and suburbs. With each person I spoke
to, I stressed that my interest lay only in what *they* had to say; I
was not about to view anyone as a representative of some
greater category of people. Inevitably, those I spoke to knew of
my own reactions to busing, reactions which could never
coincide completely with their own. Nonetheless, each was able
to quiet me, to look beyond my own viewpoints long enough to
recount their stories, founded always on the most personal and,
for them, delicate historical moments.

It may be true, as many allege, that people love to talk about
themselves. Yet, if we can rely on the psychiatric and particularly psychoanalytic literature, it is equally true that people
resist speaking about a great many personal issues. To express
one's attitudes about busing may not require one to surmount
this resistance. But to trace one's racial attitudes, even implic-
itly, through the daily experiences of one's life, and the textured
layers of one's mind, is an extraordinary task, even a coura-

geous one. It is not what we normally expect or desire in conversation. It may be easier to speak about some personal matters with an acquaintance one may never see again. To speak personally and on a regular basis, however, with someone whose lifestyle, whose station in life is so different from one's own, is not an easy matter. And when, as was true in the following conversations, a matter of such magnitude as busing scorched every word and twisted conversations and friendships into irreconcilable ends and unbelievable spaces, one can only feel privileged to have been allowed the opportunity to become implicated in these others' lives. It seems that in the introductory remarks of all my work, I am thanking people for this chance to hear a few of the personal moments of their lives. I do so again here.

Some people are raised with the dictum, Never run away from a good fight. I, apparently, was raised on a softer plot of earth. I often feel rage, I often do battle with words, but I have never thrived, really, on argument and toe to toe confrontation. I confess to referring to those holding values and attitudes in conflict with my own as enemies, but inside I want so much to agree with one of the people in this book who told me: "Everybody's arguing over busing. You'll hear every opinion that has ever been said. You'll see people lined up on this issue like soldiers on a battlefield waiting for the signal to begin the war. Nobody can be neutral, nobody can be objective. Everybody has their attitudes, born in their hearts as much as in their minds. The best thing to do then, if you really want to hear what they're saying, is to be quiet and listen to them until they've finished. Whether you speak or not, they'll know how you stand. But disagreeing with them won't make them be quiet. The only thing that will quiet them is them thinking that you treat them as the enemy. If you want to keep your conversations alive, then keep telling yourself, 'There is no enemy.' "

1

I'M GOING TO PLAY

WITH THE SOULS OF YOUR CHILDREN

Raymond Herman hitched up his belt and spread his legs slightly as he stood on the gymnasium floor looking out at the boys running about in front of him. The noise in the gymnasium was deafening, hundreds of games and battles, it seemed, were taking place simultaneously. Yet Ray Herman seemed not to hear a whisper. After staring at the children, his eyes would move in space as if what he was about to say were written somewhere, written in the smells and sounds of the gymnasium where only he could read them.

Searching for the proper starting point, he smiled modestly, a schoolboy in that instant hunting desperately as time ran out for an answer to a complicated mathematics problem. Perhaps he wasn't alone in the gymnasium. Perhaps there were others watching him.

In the Porter Elementary school where Ray Herman has worked for the last six years as an administrator and part-time physical education instructor, they say that there are as many Ray Hermans as there are people willing to talk to him. Some report he is one of the kindest gentlemen they have ever known. Others claim he is the meanest, quick-tempered, and ill-mannered middle-aged ruffian they have ever had the displeasure of meeting. Some see him as tough and contentious, others

as generous, giving, and a loyal friend. Ray Herman himself
loves the myriad labels thrown at him. He will say straight out
that the way to be a successful school administrator is not to let
anybody know who you really are. Treat each person and each
situation as the moment warrants, but let no one get close
enough to sabotage your work.

"School's a high-powered intelligence game," he once told a
group of people. "You got to keep an eye open for everything
that happens. Teachers don't have to think this way, but there's
not an administrator I know doesn't have to figure out ways to
learn what's going on in his school. You set up your spies, you
find out. That means you do a little strong-arming with some
people and a little soft-talking with others."

"And does that mean," someone asked him, "that you
yourself are so many different people you don't even know who
you really are?"

"I know me, baby," Ray shot back quickly. "I know me all I
need to know. Don't you worry about that!"

The boys in the gymnasium were running laps before retiring
to the locker room. Ray Herman barely saw them. He was
scratching his head, careful not to mess his neatly combed
pitch-black hair.

"All right, here it goes. I think man has made all sorts of
fabulous inventions to help him. You know what I mean?
Someone had to understand what fire could do for man, and the
wheel, and all the rest. Busing's got to stack up as the number
one error ever made, maybe in the history of mankind. Whoever
designed the concept is a lunatic. Either that, or he's somebody
very, very rich who never once put his kid on a bus. You take
World War Two. Why'd we fight in World War Two? Because a
madman was getting set to take over the world. The man had
destroyed Poland, devastated it. Moved into Holland, sent
millions of innocent people into prisons you wouldn't put a dog
into, killed 'em. Killed women, killed babies. I mean, this was a
mad man. Either you got him or he'd eat you alive. Nobody
could disagree with that. Jesus Christ, the people in France and
England would have cut off their arms for us the day we won

that war. Should we have been there? You bet your sweet you know what we should have been there.

"Vietnam war? Korean war? You can argue it any way you like, up one side, down the other. But you can't look back at these things. You look at them, both these wars, as they looked when they began, when we first got into them. And I say we should have been in both of 'em. Certainly we had a place, a commitment in Korea. You make promises to these countries, and you have to keep to them. More madmen trying to take over something that isn't theirs. That's what all these wars are about. Look at it this way. You got two kids, not children, grown-up kids. We'll make 'em fourteen, fifteen. Here they are, right in the middle of the gym, going at each other. They'd kill each other if someone didn't stop them. All right? Now, you think another kid that age is going to interfere? Not a chance. Doesn't have the strength, but more important, he doesn't have the smarts. He's too excited with the fight. He's pulling for one of the guys maybe, or maybe he's hoping someone will get hurt. He doesn't even know the kids who are fighting but he wants someone hurt. It happens. So now you're me or some teacher, an adult. You interfere? Fast as you can. That's Korea and Vietnam as I see it."

Ray Herman had begun walking through the large double door. The boys, save for a few stragglers, had disappeared into the locker room at the other end of the gymnasium. He fixed his tie and buttoned the middle button of his brown tweed suit jacket. No matter what anyone said about Ray Herman's personality, everyone agreed he looked at least ten years younger than his age. No one questioned his manners, moreover. He rose from his chair in the presence of a woman, he never passed through a door without holding it for anyone with whom he happened to be chatting. It was the same with those who worked for him as with those he did not know. His manners were impeccable; his colleagues appreciated this quality in him.

"All those wars," Ray Herman was saying as he headed towards his second floor office," were caused by people bullying people. People who hadn't the singlest right in the world to force other people to do things against their will. That's busing in a

nutshell. It's got nothing to do with racial prejudice. Believe me, I know. I couldn't care less what Negroes do with their children. They want to send them to their schools, ship them off to our schools, I couldn't care less. But *telling* people, *ordering* them, you gotta go here or there, seems to me that's exactly what the whole damn set of wars we've been fighting for fifty years is all about. Nobody can make such a policy. They may *think* they can, but no one has that kind of power.

"Are there prejudiced people in this school? I'd have to say yes, there are. I could name them if I had to. I know people in this school who can't stand the fact they have to teach Negro children. You can hate these people if you want, but I prefer to feel sorry for them. All they're doing is living with the feelings and attitudes their parents gave them. They're not bad people, they just haven't grown up. In many ways, I'll admit it, they really aren't a helluva lot more mature than the children they teach. It's a fact. We had an assistant principal in this school for twenty years before I came. Actually we overlapped the first year I was hired. You want to talk about mean, here was a guy who just told the Negro kids, 'I don't care a damn how much you guys want to play on a basketball team. Long as I'm here there won't be a Negro on any team.' He told 'em this right out. I heard him one time. I thought I'd fall over. Kids came to me to help them. Jesus, I had parents screaming in my office. 'It's against the law, it's against the law,' they were yelling. It was a goddam zoo here then. Third week in this new job and I'll bet I had every parent of every Negro kid in the whole school pushing and shoving in my office. There was nothing I could do. That guy Kierney, Harry Kierney was his name, the late, great Harry Kierney, he couldn't be budged. He had the power. I'd have spoken up against him, I'd have been not only out of this school, I'd have been out of the *system*. So I told these parents, I'll do what I can, but I knew there wasn't a thing I could do. And that old weasel was good to his word too. There wasn't a Negro boy on a single school team. Not one. You talk about outbursts, I thought those kids would burn down the school. I'll tell you something else. I wouldn't have blamed them. They were being deprived. No doubt about it. They were being screwed to the

wall. If it had happened to me, I'd have been tempted to do away with that weasel. I might have done anything to stop him."

Ray Herman lowered himself into his huge leather-backed desk chair that seemed to moan under the weight of his body. The walls of the old office were lined with diplomas, charts, tables depicting costs, students' grades, and attendance records. Of his many obligations, his prime concern was daily attendance. He had made a pledge when he began the job that at any minute of any day he would know exactly how many children were out of school and why. It had become a mission, a passion really, this interest in absent children. A child's tardiness might upset him slightly, but to know that children were missing from school for long periods of time deeply annoyed him. He often said that one of his great quarrels with busing was that students were kept out of school and refused to go. The numbers on his attendance chart soared, and rather than muster the strength it took to account for all the absences, he would fall into a state of sadness. Some people in the school claimed that Ray Herman actually grew depressed when large numbers of students were absent. It was strange, almost frightening to see him during these times. They wondered about him, sensing a rage behind the sadness, an anger directed at someone that only he knew.

The man many students called "Tiger Boy" because he would prowl quietly about the rooms of the enormous school checking up on people and stalking missing children, was well aware of his attitudes about attendance and the feelings evoked in him by low attendance figures.

"No, you don't want to blame this anti-busing attitude on people being prejudiced. Harry Kierney was a prejudiced man. There was no way else you could see that man. He hated them. Show him black skin and he'd damn near go into some kind of fit. But that's not what gets most people about the busing. It isn't the mixing of the kids, it's the pushing people around. Telling a man, I don't care that you've spent your life working to make the money to live in this one small block of one small community in the middle of this city. I don't care that you want to live near the people you grew up with and your parents and maybe grandparents grew up with. I don't care that you want to

keep your children with their own kind so they can see how
important it is for them to learn about their own kind, the
history of their people *and* their neighborhood. I'm going to bus
your kids God only knows where. Don't worry, I got tests here
that say it won't hurt them any. I don't care that you Irish got
feelings about your neighborhood, or you Italians or you
Germans or you Portuguese. That don't mean nothing to me. I'm
going to move your children all over hell and gone just so I can
mix up the schools a little bit. That's what it's all about. That's
the objection people raise to busing. It isn't constitutional,
hasn't been from the day these people, whoever the hell they
are, put it in.

"What you're doing with busing is saying to people, I'm
breaking up your family. You got all these connections with the
people you live with, your ancestors, people who made you
what you are? Well, I'm going to do something that will break
your backs. Play with your pocket book? Nope, I ain't going to
touch your money. Mess with your job? Nope, I couldn't care
less what you're doing. Mess with your stores, your churches? I
ain't going to touch a building anywhere. You know what I'm
going to do? I'm going to play with the souls of your children.
I'm going to take the most important people to you and I'm
going to mess with their minds. I'm going to bus 'em all over this
goddam city so they won't even know where they're going half
the time, or who their new friends are, or their old friends for
that matter. That's what these boys who practice busing are
saying to these white families. They are telling these families, all
right, you can do all the protesting and bellyaching you want,
but we'll take your kid out of your house and truck 'em all over
hell, even if we have to do it over your dead bodies. And they
would too.

"These people get an idea in their mind that innocent kids
have to be bused, there isn't a soul in the world going to stop
them. Not even the President. I honestly can't blame these
families for keeping their children out of school. They should
never let themselves be pushed around like this. Makes my job
harder, of course, having to count the missing ones and go
looking for them, but I can't blame these parents. I'll tell you

something, in general principle now, I think it's more important for these families to keep their children *out* of school than it is to let them come right now. You have to make a start on principles. You have to say to people, I won't do it! You can't shove me around any more. I won't have it. It's better for these classrooms to go empty, really, all of them, than have these people beaten down by people who couldn't give a damn about them. Believe me, I know the feeling. I know the feeling of having someone push you down until you're practically owned by them, and watching them drive off in their rich man's cars, telling you they care about your life when all they're worried about is getting what they want. They don't care about you or me, those people. Believe me, I know all about them."

Ray Herman turns his head slowly from side to side as though watching the path of a ball being tossed back and forth. There is pain in his body that shows on his face. He is a man eager for retaliation, revenge, but the movement of his head and the surprising calmness in his body says that there will never be revenge for the scene he now imagines.

The coal mining towns in Pennsylvania have struggled in the same ways and survived the same circumstances as the mining towns in West Virginia, only the ones in Pennsylvania rarely receive national attention. When catastrophe hits them, the newspaper people come running and the usual cries are heard about the lack of mine safety. But the rest of the time—and the years are long in these towns—no one visits, no one comes to hear about or witness the everyday world of the families who have been here, it seems, forever.

As a small boy, Ray Herman, who the neighbor children always called Ray-Ray, used to wait anxiously for school to be over so he could run to the entrance to the mines and watch the men, dirty, grimy, coughing, come out of the giant tunnels and elevators. The rule of the mine was that no one as young as Ray-Ray was allowed anywhere near the mine entrances. Still, the ritual of running from school to the entrance and seeing his father and his father's three brothers ascend from the pits each day gave him almost as much pleasure as actually descending

into the underground world with the men. "When I get big like Daddy and Uncle Teddy and Uncle Billy and Uncle Monty," he would tell his mother, "I'm going to work down there too."

Lorraine Herman would shrug. If she had to, she would blow up the mine before permitting her son to work down there. Her grandfather had started mining when he was eleven years old, her father when he was fifteen. Her husband, John Herman, known to everyone as Jock, was sent away from home in order to finish high school. He lived with relatives near Pittsburgh who urged him to think hard about going to college. As he laughingly told everyone years later, that's exactly what he did. He thought hard about college. The day after graduating from high school, where his grades had been good and where he had performed marvelously as a football player and trackman, he returned to the place of his birth and entered the same mining company that employed his father. One week after graduating he was working side by side with his father, a man approaching fifty-five.

Jock Herman saw his father die on the old green flowered sofa in the small row house on Ligonier Road. The man was coughing up blood for five weeks before his wife could get a doctor to examine him. A representative of the mine had stopped in several times to check on him, but it was five weeks before a doctor came. When he did, there was nothing he could do but suggest to Mrs. Herman and Jock that they bring the old man into the hospital. "I'd rather have him die in his own home," Mrs. Herman had responded. "The man grew up in this town, lived his entire adult life in this house, that's where he wants to be now."

"You're making a mistake," the doctor had said respectfully. But young Jock could hear in the man's voice that he understood. His father was a proud man, proud of his physical strength, proud of the way he had maintained himself over the last thirty-five years. He enjoyed flexing his large forearms and gripping things tightly with his giant hands. Jock could never think about his father without imagining the strong hands, the long well-shaped fingers, and the rich color of the fingernails.

"You're making a mistake," the doctor had repeated as he opened the front door to the Herman's home.

"Hell she is." It was John Herman himself, standing weakly, then heaving his thin body against the wooden door jamb. His cheeks were sunken in, and his hair, always so finely black, looked damp. The signs of his former strength were there, but his son could see the man was dying. Please don't let him die standing there with the doctor here, young John said to himself. "Hell she is," his father was saying over and over again, barely able to get the words out before being stricken by a paroxysm of coughing, his body lurching as if the final remains of his shredded lungs had just been expelled.

The doctor merely nodded and left, but he, like Jock, had seen death in John Herman's eyes. There was no need to take the old man to the hospital. The Mrs. had been right. Jock helped his father to his bed in the small alcove adjoining the front room, but the man signaled that he preferred to lie down on the couch just as his wife had said. Jock held his father around the chest, frightened by his thinness. John Herman lay on the couch perfectly still, except for the fits of coughing which always caused a small amount of blood to come from his mouth. For two days he remained there. The room smelled of his feces and urine. "It's the stink of death," Jock's mother whispered, apologizing to friends who came to her door. "You live your life with the stink of the mines. Every day the same sights, the same smells, the stink of the mines. They give you life all right, if you call that measly sum of money life. Then the stink of death comes and it's all over for your man." The neighbors and friends since childhood nodded. How deeply they felt her words, and how much they honored her clear-eyed resignation and her understanding of what it was all about.

Jock Herman was asleep in a chair when his father died. His mother woke him to say that the Lord had taken the man they loved away. "I don't want you to cry now," she told her son, the only one of her four children still living in the house on Ligonier Road. "There'll be plenty of time for crying. That's the minister's business. I want only one thing for you now, right in

this moment when your father's body is still warm from the bits of life he had while he was with us. You promise me that your children will never once in their lives see the insides of those mine pits. Never once. This must end. No one dies in this country at such ages. Men beaten at the age of thirty and thirty-five from work conditions not fit for cattle and dogs. And all these men running around here at election time telling us this and that and making promises not one of them intends keeping. They haven't fooled me for forty years. Their type only knows one way of talking, and that's lying."

Jock Herman promised his mother that he would be the last in the family to work the mines. Years later, the promise proved especially difficult for his children, particularly Ray-Ray and James, because as the only boys, it was frustrating to tell their friends that their father refused to hear of their desire to work in the mines with him, as he had worked with Big John, their grandfather whom they had never known. Ray-Ray told himself that maybe if he ran to meet his father and his uncles every day after school, it might change his father's mind. The technique had worked in the past. Jock would refuse his sons something, but they would beg and nag him until he broke down and gave in to them. Lorraine disliked seeing Jock so easy with the boys. She said that a child had to understand the meaning of the word "no," but Jock would argue that if parents had something, why not give it to their children. "The girls are better-mannered," Lorraine would say. "Girls are supposed to be," Jock would come back, running his large hands through James's or Ray-Ray's long straight hair. Then the boys would run off, happy that of all the fathers in the world, even the rich ones, they had Jock as their dad.

Occasionally Ray-Ray waited around outside the kitchen to hear what his mother might say after he and James had left. But it wasn't his mother who spoke when the boys, presumably, were out of hearing distance; it was his father.

"I'm not going to live that long anyway," Jock would say. "How long you think it's going to be before the whole business kills me off? If it isn't the lungs, it will be a disaster. It's got to be

something. All these strong bodies, like my father's, they can't hold up more than a few years against it. Nothing's going to change. Nothing's changed and nothing will. They come in their cars, make their foolish inspections, and leave. The senators, the big men, all of them. My mother was right about them. You see any changes that will make any of it better for us? There's not a hope. Tomorrow, forty or sixty-eight could come down, and don't think for a minute the timber they got down there is worth a nickel. Or the gases may leak, or a fire or a mechanical failure. We'd all go. Like that." Ray-Ray would hear his father's broad hand smack down on the wiggly rough-top table where the six of them ate breakfast.

"Mine's no stronger than this table. Any minute it goes. It will go too, 'cause the big men of this country make rules and set down laws and tell little people like us what to do, where to go to work every morning, how to raise our children. They wouldn't have this sort of living for nothing. There isn't one of those people who owns anything that would trade places with us. Not one of them. I know. I know them now the same way my mother knew them. Same way my father and your father knew them, only *they* knew they had to keep their mouths shut. When those gates open in the morning and close in the afternoon, you better be there. When they call your name, you better just be standing there. That's what those bosses talk about with us. Safety, health, a little bit of money, as though it would kill them, not a word of honesty comes from them. Just be there when they call your name, and for God's sake, don't get sick too soon or the insurance benefits won't even pay your woman enough to eat for a year. So you tell me what it's worth."

"We've talked about this before," Ray-Ray would hear his mother say, knowing she couldn't appease her husband. "We both know it. Why carry on with the same words?" Ray-Ray could hear them moving about in the kitchen which always seemed cold, even in the autumn before the weather changed. It seemed dusty too, no matter how often his mother cleaned, which was once a day. There was no way to keep anything clean. The air was filled with the dust, the evil sprinkle as his

grandmother called it, the devil's dirt. The children said it never
bothered them, they never knew it was there. But their parents
said when you got older you never got used to it.

"It was like being blind," Lorraine had told Ray-Ray and his
sister Judith. "You know you can't see. You may not think
about it, but when you go to see, you can't. It's the same with
the dirt. When you go to breathe deeply, you can't do it. It's
killing us off slowly."

"Even the children?" Judith had asked.

"Even the children," Lorraine had nodded. "The bosses and
owners could make it better for all of us, but they never will."
The children had looked at each other, not fully understanding
their mother, but certainly aware of what her phrase "even the
children" meant.

No matter how the discussions started, Ray-Ray, either
standing in the kitchen with his parents or overhearing them,
they invariably ended the same way, with his father's speech:

"No one's telling my children how to live their lives. If they're
other children around here who want to do what their fathers
do, that's fine, but not these boys. They're not going to work
with me, they're not going to have their souls owned by people
who'd sell them out cheap. Don't let anyone fool you, Lorraine,
the ones I watch the closest are the ones who used to work in
there with us. Going about saying how they'll protect us when
they get the chance. They'd sell their mothers off too, like all
those other ones. Just give them the chance. Everybody wants
to be out of here. Any chance that comes along they'll grab on to
it. There aren't those chances for us, so I'm telling you when the
time is right, you're taking those kids out of here. With me or
without. You cannot keep doing the things your grandparents
and great grandparents set up for you to do. Someone has to
say, 'Stop.' My sons won't follow me."

Jock Herman died at the age of thirty-eight, when Ray-Ray
was eleven years old. A gas leak in the mine, an explosion, a
mistake, the reason for his death was never determined. The
family went to the main office of the mine where Jock Herman
and the other miners, one of whom looked at first to be his
brother but wasn't, were brought up. Lorraine Herman barely

cried. It seemed as though she knew this day was coming. For months prior to the accident, Jock Herman had been depressed. He had talked about ending his life, and not caring if he got caught some night a million feet deep in the earth.

The bodies of the men lay on the floor, on their backs, their faces and hands filthy with coal dust. Ray-Ray went with his mother and his oldest sister Helen. The children looked at their father who appeared to be sleeping. A man went to Ray-Ray shaking his head slowly. He was well-dressed and his face and hands were clean. He whispered, "The niggers of the earth. Rotten mine niggers." Later that evening, as he lay in bed crying, Ray-Ray heard his mother moving busily about the house. She was already packing. The day after the funeral, she moved the children to her sister's home in Wheeling, West Virginia.

Ray Herman did not return to the town of his birth until he was twenty-eight years old. Married and the father of three children, his oldest boy having been named John after his father and grandfather, he had taken his family on a vacation to eastern Pennsylvania. They had toured Pennsylvania Dutch country for several days when suddenly he was overcome with a desire to visit his father's grave. He hunted in the town on a Saturday morning for people he thought he remembered, but while store owners knew the names, no one could be located. Ray visited with his Uncle Ben, one of the men who had worked with his father, now in his early sixties and in surprisingly good health. Then he went to the small cemetery on the knoll just west of town. From the top of the knoll he could see the hills and mountains, and the road leading to the main entrance of the mine where his father had died. He watched cars pass on the road and found himself trembling with fright and rage. He feared that he might faint at the sight of the grave, or break down and cry. He recalled the faces of the owners who attended his father's funeral and searched his memory trying to remember how his mother had received them. They were enemies of his family, yet it seemed his mother was willing to be comforted by them. Perhaps they had given her money.

The grave was smaller than he had remembered, a low stone with his father's name and the dates of his birth and death, overrun with wild flowers and a greenish moss on which slugs attached themselves. Ray could only look down at the bit of land, so undistinguished and plain, and wonder why he had come. He was unaware of the tears until he saw them falling on the ground near his feet.

For two hours, Ray Herman, his sleeves rolled up and his shoes muddy with the brown dirt, ripped away the weeds and moss that grew on his father's and grandparents' graves. Then he went to the village, bought small flowering plants and vegetable seeds, and returned to the grave sites. There, until the light was so poor he could barely see, he planted the flowers and the seeds, telling himself that it would now be lovely, and in the Spring there would be food for his father to eat. The greens near the graves, he whispered, would purify the air. He was amused by his childlike reasoning, but pleased that he had made the trip. As he walked away from the graves for the last time, his hands and arms dirty from the planting, he heard the words of the well-dressed man with the clean fingernails who had whispered to him the afternoon the workers had brought his father's body up from the mine: "Rotten mine niggers." They did look like niggers too, he thought, the filth of their skin matching the filth of their clothes. He asked himself, how could the owners let it come to this?

"There's a lot of my childhood tied up in this busing thing, I'll tell you," Ray Herman was saying as he glanced at the papers covering his large metal desk. "I can't help but think of all the people in the world being bullied, pushed around. I'll tell you now the same words I heard my father tell my mother. Fact, I can't even think about busing without hearing his voice, though I barely remember the sound of it. I only have one photograph of him. Can you imagine after all these years that people would live like they did and not have more than one photograph of themselves? I don't know that the man ever had an identification card with his picture on it other than the one he carried for the mine. But he said it all. Some people are born to work in the

mines, do the rotten jobs, die young. Other people are born to make sure that those people keep doing those rotten jobs and die young.

"Everybody's up in arms about busing. They got a right to be. But then you read how these other people, the so-called intelligent members of the city, are so surprised or outraged by the protest. The rich Irish look down at the poor Irish, the rich Italians look down at the poor Italians. It's always the same. These well-to-do people, living out there in their comfortable suburban homes, what they're really saying is they're surprised that all these working-class types are putting up such a protest. They're angry with the protestors, they see these people as standing in their way.

"It's exactly like the miners union types taking on the owners. Oh, the owners will act polite in front of the public and make these nice statements how it's important to sit down at the negotiating table and talk out the differences. But deep down they're thinking, what's come over you people that you think you have the right to argue with us on these matters. Our business is to make the decisions, your business is to accept whatever the hell we decide. I can see these rich people, some of them who grew up in the same areas where the families now are being asked to bus their children, saying, 'What in the name of the Lord are these people causing all this trouble about. In the first place, they aren't smart enough to come up with any good arguments to busing, and in the second place, it's their obligation in society to keep their tiny little mouths shut and follow orders.'

"I see school buses rolling in, I see these kids, black and white coming into this school, any school really, doesn't make a difference, I tell myself, here come the little miners. Here come the little miners thinking life's really going to be different for them now. The only mistake my father made was not to let me and Jimmy hear those conversations he had with my mother. I was only five or six, but they should have let us listen. What he said was more important than anything I ever learned in college or graduate school. That man knew wisdom because he lived it. He lived those experiences on the earth and so far beneath it, it would scare those judges out of their minds to go down there

where he went every day to earn his living. He knew damn well what slavery was all about because he was a slave himself. You know in the south a lot of the slaves got paid? Did you know that? A lot of them got money for the work they did. Miners got paid. Some of them don't do all that badly, actually, if they can survive long enough where they've accumulated enough years. Lots of people working in this country who get paid are still slaves. Don't you make a mistake about it. But don't you think they like what they do or that they don't go home at night and tell their wives the same things my father told my mother. It's amazing that she was willing to listen to the same speech as often as she did.

"Well, busing's now a part of that speech. He didn't know a thing about it, of course, but the speech fits. Absent owners pushing hard working people around, people who never complained. I grew up knowing that. My parents used to tell us how we had to act if we met these rich people. 'Got to be polite, make them think we're grateful,' my mother used to say. I'm sure he said the same thing, but I honestly can't remember my father telling us we had to act nice in front of them. Jesus, he must have hated them. The same way these parents who are causing all the fuss hate the people who are telling them how to live their lives now.

"When my father looked around him he saw the same thing, the same world, his father saw. He saw the same houses, the same roads, same stores, same people, same jobs. Day after day, year after year, nothing changed. There wasn't anything that *could* change. It had to be the same. But nobody was telling him what to do with anyone in his family, directly that is. It was understood how he'd lead his life, of course, but no one legislated about his children. If he had a way of getting out, he got out. Goodbye. But this busing thing, it says this is what you *have* to do with your *children*. Now I mean, that has to take the cake as being the most unfair, illegitimate law that ever came over the mountain. It's like these owners saying, not only do the men go down, they *have* to, don't you see. And they would have passed that kind of legislation too if they thought it was in their best interest to do it. I know them. They'd have crushed anyone

who got in their way. You know what they would have done if
people had protested their rulings, they'd have taken them out
and beaten them to a half-living pulp. Don't kid yourself. You're
supposed to have a right to assembly in this country? You're
supposed to be protected when you protest? They never would
have allowed it. Those miner families were imprisoned. Go and
look at their houses. See how they lived, how they're living
today. Go see them. They're nothing but prisoners. And the
people being bused are even in worse shape for one important
reason. They're being led to believe they're free. But the
government has taken a bunch of hostages: their children. The
children, all of them, they're just hostages. The parents are told
they're free, free to live where they want and work where they
want and think what they want and worship where they want.
But the children are hostages. You tell me where you're going to
find a man or woman thinking they're free and happy when
someone in the government or in a law court has their children
tied up! Tied up. I mean it.

"Busing's a sham, my friend, one of the biggest swindles this
country's ever seen. I'll tell you something else. These Negro
families who think they're benefiting from it, I feel sorry for
them. I swear to God, I feel just as sorry for them as I do for the
white families. They're being lied to and tricked. The country's
not doing a damn thing for them. You see the way they live, half
of them. You believe the government would allow people to live
in half those projects the government paid for itself? Someone
got it in his mind that segregated schools were bad. So they
integrate them and now nobody can find any way to prove that
black children or white children are doing any better, or any
worse for that matter, from all this disruption and confusion and
nonsense. You go talk to the black families, really get in there
and talk to them like I do, they'll tell you the same thing. You
know what busing does? It takes a whole lot of people for a ride.
It's a tease, a pretty expensive one, but it's a tease, that's all it is.
It's doing no good at all and one helluva lot of harm. To both
sides too. Believe me.

"I had a mother in here not three days ago. 'Mr. Herman,' she
says, and she's practically crying as she's talking to me, 'You

got to help us switch schools.' That's what she's coming to me
for. Three days ago. Right in the middle of the term. Her life's
too disrupted. That kid of hers has to go God only knows how
long in a bus, fifty minutes maybe, for no good reason, and she's
sitting home all day worrying about what's happening to him.
She doesn't even think about whether he's learning anything
coming all the way over here. You know what I told her?
'There's not a thing in the world I can do.' Officially, I follow the
rules. Rules say if your child is supposed to be bused, then he
gets bused. If I had anything to say about all this, I'd have put an
end to this idiocy a long time ago, certainly before it got this far.
But I told her, if she can get the rules changed so there's no more
busing, I'd be the happiest man in the world to obey those laws.
And she'd be a helluva lot happier too. Believe me. Everybody
would be happier, except the big people, of course. They're only
happy when the money rolls in and their cute little ideas that
help no one but themselves get put into action and everyone
obeys them."

Ray Herman was standing up near the door to his office where
the large attendance charts were taped to the wall. His weight
shifted from one side to the other and he pushed his hands
against the papers to hold them flat. He screwed up his face,
making calculations of some sort, trying to conjure up, it
seemed, the faces of the absent ones. Today's list appeared
particularly long. He rubbed his cheek against the grain of his
whiskers making a gentle crackling sound. He didn't seem
particularly perturbed by the large number of students he would
attempt to contact, but it did seem that he might have been
looking beyond the list to others no longer counted in the
attendance rolls.

Without turning away from his work, and speaking to the
large paper charts, he said: "Funny, everybody called me
Ray-Ray when I was a kid except my father. He had nicknames
for me, of course. All fathers do that. Tiger, Buster, Big Fellow.
But usually he just called me Ray, or son. I could never
remember what the hell I called him until that time I visited the
grave. It came to me when I was working there, trying to clean
the place up a little. I kind of heard myself say 'Daddy.' Sounds

weird, doesn't it, a grown man calling his father 'daddy.' But I
never spoke to him much as a little boy. Hell, he died before he
ever reached the age of a grown man. I mean, he was young
when he died."

Ray Herman turned finally and rubbed his hands together as
though warming them. He shook his head in that way that says
what follows is sarcasm. "My father, young when he died. You
could just as well say young when they killed him, along with
those other two men. That's what people with power do. They
don't just make decisions that affect your life, or the lives of
your children. They kill when they see fit, even if they do it so
indirectly nobody recognizes what they're doing and when
they're doing it. The real leaders in a country lead you into life.
The powerful owners, they lead you into death. Believe me, I
know. They lead you to the brink, in a mine shaft, maybe even
on a school bus. If you don't die from what they do, you can
count yourself as one of the lucky ones. But don't go celebrating
the fact that you're still alive 'cause there's always your mother
and father to wonder about, and there's always your children.
There's always the children."

2

FOLKS UP HERE WORRIED ABOUT

WHAT A LITTLE BUSING CAN DO

Often in the middle of a winter's night when the Boston weather is at its coldest, Annie London swears she can hear the whining motors in the old tire factory where her father worked. It is hard to believe that she has not actually heard those motors in twenty-five years. Could it really be, she asks herself, huddled in bed, that a quarter of a century has passed since those hot dry afternoons when her father showed her and her oldest brother Justy where he worked—when there was work.

"Helena, Arkansas, doesn't exist," Annie London whispers to herself, as if wiping away memories. "There isn't a place in the world called Helena, Arkansas. If my parents were really there, if my father really showed me around that ugly factory, then I've never been there. I've only heard about it, or made it up from the pictures I saw almost every day of my life." She smiles, and shakes her head as if to say, folks up here think they got to fight the changes of a few black children coming into their schools, that's what all those folks call change?

"All those scientific types going around trying to test the ill-effects of taking a child from out of his neighborhood and putting him in a school a few miles away. That's what they're worried about? Worried about it to where they'll go and kill someone to stop it? Well, those folks don't know what change

really is, or what busing really is. Busing isn't taking a kid out of his neighborhood and sending him off to a school a few miles away. Busing is taking a little girl from Helena, Arkansas, and sending her all the way to Philadelphia. *That's* busing. Oh my word, *that's* busing. All the way across the country, now *that's* what you call busing for desegregation. Talk about people being moved around in this country, thinking black children and white children going to hurt themselves, or mess up their minds just 'cause they're going to have to bounce a little on some old bus. Folks should have studied *me* coming up on the bus from Shreveport that one time with Justy. Oh my God was that some trip. Everybody so worried about people hurting people's minds by putting 'em in class with some black children. Only thing that hurts your mind is not having a job, not having food, not having the slightest chance under God of finding neither. *That* hurts your mind. *That's* going to cripple you, cripple you when you don't even know you're being crippled.

"Busing children a little ways to school causes all this racket and commotion. Folks ought to be ashamed of themselves. Nobody said nothing when they bused me and Justy nine miles to school every morning. Nobody said nothing about how we couldn't go to the school five miles away 'cause they didn't want no *coloreds*. No one said nothing about *that* hurting anybody's mind. No one said nothing to my mother when my father died, broken, beaten, pitiful sight of a man. Where were all the demonstrations then? Forty-three years old and dying of a heart condition a doctor said he had all his life and no one ever examined the man? And there's my mother standing at that bus station in Shreveport, waving at us, smiling and crying and wondering what was ever going to happen to us and whether she was making the right decision to send us up north. Wondering, 'cause you could see it on her face plain as day, why no one in the whole world, white or black, ever knew about that medical condition in my father's heart. Was it because my father was poor all his life, or because he was black. Oh mamma, I can still see you. I'll always see you standing there, looking at us and waving. I remember Justy was crying and I was crying and nobody in that whole bus station even noticed

us. Nobody even saw our family dividing up for the last time. All they saw was a mother putting her children on a bus and sending them away. And somewhere, God only knows how many miles from there, my father was lying in what has to be the world's ugliest cemetery. Folks up here worried about what a little busing can do. I'm not sure anyone can understand what busing can do, 'cause you have to take the buses away and see these people before you know what busing can do. You have to see the people, even the people you can't see anymore because they were so poor all their lives no one bothered to examine them to find out they were going to die at the age of forty-three."

Annie London hears the whirring sounds of the factory again. She sees her father walking slowly for a man his age, although still too quickly for the two little children to keep up with him. Her small apartment is quiet. Winter brings a peculiar night quiet, the quiet of a body wholly at peace.

When Annie London was seven years old, she left Helena, Arkansas, and traveled to a small town just outside Harrisburg, Pennsylvania, where she lived in the home of Hattie and Fred Simpson. Everyone in the London family called Hattie an aunt although in truth she was merely a close friend of Annie's mother from childhood days. Hattie Simpson's own daughter Billie died in infancy from an illness no one ever spoke of, so that Hattie was only too happy to have children in her home. Justy and Annie were God-sent, she said.

Hattie's husband, known to everyone as Big Freddy, wasn't so sure taking in other people's children was such a good idea. "There's no replacing your own," he argued with Hattie. "When a child dies it leaves a hole in your heart. You can take in all the children in the world and not ever once begin to fill in that hole. There's no sense trying. These kids lost their daddy, we lost a daughter, and everybody's sending people all over the country, one thousand miles, thinking nobody's going to be missing their kin no more. But it don't work out that way. Everybody's lying to themselves if they think those holes folks carry in their hearts going to disappear when strangers come and live with you. Who's going to take care of Mrs. London, living back there in a

rotten town where black folks would get shot 'fore they'd have a chance even to vote for the mayor?"

Annie rarely heard Big Freddy argue with Aunt Hattie. She sensed his feelings, but she could see that Big Freddy, who acted a little stiffly with the children when they first arrived in late August of Annie's seventh year, was beginning to soften. Mainly it was Justy who was getting to him. Big Freddy had never really been a father, his daughter having died so soon.

Perhaps Annie substituted somewhat for the dead girl. But Justy was a real bonus, a boy at the perfect age for doing things with his father, or substitute father. Annie could see everything happening just as Hattie could. Justy was melting Big Freddy to the point where the older man was enjoying having both children around.

The Simpsons didn't have much money, but Big Freddy found a few dollars somewhere to buy Justy a baseball glove. And without the slightest prodding from his wife, he brought home a doll for his new daughter, for Justy's sister.

Annie London received that doll when she was seven years old. She is now thirty-two. The years that have passed haven't dulled her memory of the gift in the slightest. It was a pink-skinned doll with red cheeks, blue eyes, and golden hair, made of a ropelike material that irritated her fingers when she touched it. The doll came in a red, white, and blue box with cellophane pulled tight across the top, and was called Baby Bo. It was dressed in a little gingham dress, white socks, and shiny black shoes Annie called party shoes.

"Looked just like me," Annie recalls, grinning. But the doll meant something special; Big Freddy was willing to accept her. It might have been Justy's presence that softened his attitude toward the London children, but whatever it was, Annie felt wanted.

She remembers, or believes she remembers, that for one whole week following the arrival of the doll, she didn't think once about her mother. Until that rainy afternoon Big Freddy had arrived with the two large boxes under his arm, Annie had thought about nothing but her mother. Every night she lay in bed alongside Justy, with whom she slept for three years in the

tiny room off the kitchen, remembering the scene at the Shreveport bus station. All she could see was her mother standing on the roadside, looking up at the tall bus and her children, waving to them gently, and crying. Annie would begin to cry, softly so Justy wouldn't hear her, but he always did. Sometimes she even began to shake and Justy would have to hold her arms tightly, or else he'd get mad and tell her if she didn't stop making so much noise, he'd call Big Freddy. Justy's anger and threat to call Big Freddy were enough to quiet Annie, although she never felt calm lying in the dark in the small gray room. The children had learned early that Big Freddy was a man with a quick temper. One didn't push him the wrong way, especially when one was a child, and not his own.

The years with the Simpsons were not unhappy ones, although their mother's absence and father's death continued to disturb the children. Justy seemed to be faring worse than his sister. When he first came north he was a quiet child, very much unlike the boy he had been at home. As he began to feel more comfortable in the Simpson house, he opened up, slowly at first, then more and more. School helped him. He received encouragement from his first teacher, a black woman who understood the consequences not only of being apart from one's parents, but of migrating from one part of the country to another. Big Freddy grew more impatient with Justy. He understood the reasons for the boy's diffidence and shyness, but his level of tolerance was low. Peculiarly, as Justy began to assume his old ways, Big Freddy complained to his wife and the school about Justy's excessive desire to please people. "You can't be a real man," Big Freddy told anyone who would listen, "going around trying to be nice to everyone. He's acting like a nurse or an old grandmother." But even his men friends admonished him for this outlook.

"What the hell's with you, Fred?" Annie heard one of Big Freddy's friends say to him one evening. "Nobody sees his father die and then get put on a bus and have to say goodbye to his mother and go one thousand miles away to strangers and not

come away hurt. Especially not a ten-year-old boy or seven-year-old girl.''

The men were talking just outside the window of the children's bedroom. "Your own daughter died nine years ago and you ain't never got over it. Ain't that what you said? So why the hell you so damn impatient with those children in there, 'specially that boy? They're trying. They're trying damn hard. And you can bet they want to please you and Hattie, 'cause whether they know it or not, they must be wondering in their minds what they did to make it all come out this way. They're wondering same as you are. What did they do that they got to be living in Pennsylvania with their mamma way back there where you and I ought to be most probably. And you're wondering too what you might have did that made that little baby of yours die a hundred years before she was supposed to.''

Annie never heard Big Freddy say anything to the other man. She was afraid to peek out the window. Years later she would be glad she had overheard that conversation. At seven, she was sorry she had heard the man speaking, sorry that she wasn't home with her mother, sorry that her father wasn't around to take her to the old, decrepit tire factory even though she was always frightened by the sounds of the giant motors running night and day.

All of this was part of her childhood, the years that went by in such a way as to make her think history was forgetting her. As all children do, she viewed some months as though time hadn't passed at all and aging as something that happened only to other people. But there were moments too, when she felt her body drinking in time faster than any child in the world. Big Freddy's temper made her age. It came on unexpectedly, an explosion seemingly touched off by nothing at all. He would come home from work, sit down on the old canvas chair he loved so well, and begin to drink from a can of beer. Annie would go to another part of the house, or if the weather allowed, to the bit of land behind what used to be a garage. Big Freddy didn't want anyone around in these times. He might have allowed Justy to sit in the room with him, but no girl would

stand a chance with him. Then the explosion would be heard—
Big Freddy swearing, breaking things, the beer can thrown
against the wall, cataracts of the golden fluid staining the soiled
wallpaper.

Annie would hide in the yard, terrified but fascinated. Often
she would see Big Freddy staring out the window, his shirt
pulled open, his hand pushing back his hair, causing his
forehead to stretch and his eyes to appear enormous as the lids
were yanked up. He looked like a monster, a monster gone blind
with rage, and no one, surely not Annie, would go inside and ask
him what had happened and what could she do to help.

Yet strangely, as separated from him as she would feel in his
moments of fury, she felt, even as a child, that she could
understand his rage. As inexplicable as the onset of the tan-
trums were, Big Freddy's behavior never seemed wholly incomprehensible. Perhaps the power generated by his frustrations
erupted as its own special form of communication. Perhaps,
although the thought sounded peculiar, the eruption was part of
his everyday conversation, but a part he saved for the times he
was alone. Maybe Big Freddy was on intimate terms with his
anger in a way Annie believed she never could be. She certainly
never envied him his capacity to display intense anger, but she
did feel in touch with him, somehow, when she saw him through
the window, foaming with outrage and frustration.

Freddy was either a supreme spokesman of freedom, or a
sickening prisoner, Annie would say about him many years
later, after she had become a teacher in Boston. The years in
Pennsylvania were by then merely part of a complicated store of
memory. "The man had spirit like no one could ever know. The
way the country has it set up, black folks aren't supposed to
have pride. Slaves aren't supposed to know the feeling of pride.
They're meant to do their work and be so tired at the end of the
day that there's no emotion left in them. Work's supposed to
drain their minds and bodies and souls. If they're properly
enslaved, they ought to about make it home each night and not
even think about the fact no one should be forced to live in
homes like theirs, or eat the little bit of food they're supposed to
eat. You just clump on home, nod to anybody you happen to see,

which usually turns out to be nobody important, just your family, and lie down on whatever you use as a bed. Then the next day you stagger off to work again.

"The country has it beautifully planned. They keep their slaves in the constant state of being spent. Everybody talks about black folks being oversexed. What a laugh. Nobody that tired all the time could be oversexed. It's amazing, now that I think about it, that Big Freddy ever had the energy to bellow like he did. Maybe that's why I never felt I could hate him for his vile displays. He had a rotten temper, there was no doubt about that. But while Justy and I were definitely afraid of him when he got so angry—even though we didn't always understand *what* was bothering him—at least he showed us that he was full of feelings. We didn't know this side of people from our own folks, our real folks, I mean. They were part of the slave pattern, always hungry and tired. They had tempers, only they didn't have much time for showing them, and none of the energy Big Freddy had.

"It's strange to say, but Big Freddy gave me a sense of hope. I grew up in Arkansas learning that the way things were was the way they were supposed to be. Nobody thought about changing things. I don't remember anybody talking about it, although I was very small. The bus came and took us to school. If it went fifty feet, that was fine. If it went fifty miles, that was all right too. Everybody knew the school wasn't any good, but you went there. Even when you were sick you went in the bus to that dreadful school because your parents worked and you couldn't stay home.

"First time I heard Big Freddy scream, I ran off as fast as I could. Never heard temper like that in my life. But later I listened to what he was saying, what he was yelling really. That man wasn't screaming for personal hurt alone, or self-pity. He was screaming for all of us. He was screaming because the way he and Hattie and all of us were leading our lives was unbearable. It had always been unbearable and always would be unless people got furious about their conditions and accepted nothing but equality with everyone else. I see that man standing at the kitchen window, pulling back at his hair, and I hear him, I

hear him yelling at the world, at us, at white folks. It didn't matter what he said. Didn't even matter what made him so angry on a particular day. Point was that he was letting us know you could hear fury and be fury and scream fury. It could be part of the way you sing about the world, change the world. I owe a debt to Big Freddy. I don't know what he thought or felt about what he was doing; doesn't matter really. But I like to think the man was making art, or at least finding the force and energy from which a person begins to make his art.

"I remember something else about those old scenes with Big Freddy. That canvas chair he used to sit on when he'd come from work and Hattie wasn't there yet. When she was home he'd go into the kitchen with her and they'd talk. Used to amaze me that with both of them having such rotten jobs, him in a warehouse doing nothing and her as a chamber maid—if that doesn't glorify it, 'cause knowing the way they treat black folks they probably only let her clean toilets in that hotel—they always had something to talk about from what happened each day. Anyway, that canvas chair had these two big holes in the arm. Big Freddy, he'd sit there with his beer or a paper or nothing, most likely, and I'd watch him stick his fingers into those cuts. I used to do it too when he wasn't around. I figured maybe he stuck coins in there for safekeeping. 'Course there was nothing in those slash cuts but ripped up canvas and cotton. But I remember the cuts, the look and feel of them.

"I found them again too, not in that chair but in the seats in the school buses. First in the buses I used to go to school in and now in the buses that bring the children to my school. There isn't a bus in this country that doesn't have cut-up seats. I can't ride on them or talk to one of the children without having my eyes wander about the backs of those seats, hunting for the slash cuts. They're always there too, like Big Freddy got to every bus in America and put them there himself.

"I imagine anger in those cuts. I imagine black families standing in their kitchens yelling at the world that they've had it up to here with being told the junk of the country belongs to them; the lousy schools, the rotten fruits, the burned-out land, the useless homes, the tenth-class hospitals, even the tenth-

class dope! I see those cuts and I hear Big Freddy bellowing his song, his great big manly song, 'Don't let nobody do nothing to you 'less you want it that way.' That's what he always cried. 'Don't let 'em do it to you. They'll kill you. Give 'em the chance and they'll kill you, put you on a filthy platter and eat you, your goddam shoes and socks and all if you ain't the child of a slave and got shoes and socks. Otherwise they'll fry your toe nails along with your black, black skin. You watch 'em God,' he'd yell, pulling at his hair the way he always did. 'You watch 'em God. Either you don't want to know it's happening or you give up on all of us. But it's happening. You've let it happen, Lord. Guess I can't talk to you no more 'cause you were invented by *them,* not us. We'd have invented you, Lord, it'd all be mighty different now. Mighty different. That's why I hate it all. You hear? That's why I hate it. 'Cause there's nobody to make it better and I'm being killed off every day and all they're doing is laughing. I see 'em laughing, I hear 'em laughing. And you, Lord, not talking back to me when I talk to you means you must be laughing too. So go on and kill me. Go on. GO ON!'

"I can remember that man so clearly. His intense desire, that need of his growing in his body from a million years ago to fight it out, find something he could really attack and fasten himself to it. That's what it was all about, to fight back. Because no matter what our lives were all about, the idea grew in everybody, whether we felt it in there or not, that we were being pushed down. Always pushed down and nobody was around to push back. That's what Big Freddy despised so much. There was nobody to push back. There was no way even to push. You just took it. You took it all the time, so much you didn't even know what it was that you were taking.

"When no one was around, Big Freddy screamed. This was his politics. It was also his frustration, the bitter, bitter disappointment about his life. He knew full well that if anybody had been around he'd have kept his mouth shut. Fact is, I never even saw him get that upset when Hattie was there. Oh, he'd get angry and they'd fight about things. Like all those times he'd tell her how he didn't think it was a good idea to have us around after my father died, but he knew he couldn't let that fury of his

out in public. I knew he wasn't trying to show me or other children that he was some sort of tough guy. Big Freddy didn't do anything in his life to impress people, make them think he was something he wasn't. In that way he was like both my mother and father. They never did nothing to impress a living soul.

"Rich folks don't think much about poor folks trying to impress one another, but they do. Hattie, as much as I loved her, she was always trying to impress people. Not us, I don't think, but just about everyone else I ever saw her with. She'd go into a store, you know, and buy a loaf of bread. Maybe it'd cost twenty cents. I'd watch her dip into her purse, you know, hunting for coins. Now, she had dimes and quarters in her purse, I could see them. All she had to do was pull out a quarter, but no, she'd empty the whole purse on the counter and make some comments about all this loose change she had. All she was doing was letting people think she had more than she had. Everybody knew no one had nothing. Everybody knew that everybody was stealing food as often as they were buying it. With the money folks made they couldn't get half of what they needed. But old Hattie, bless her, she'd have to show anybody that would pay her the slightest bit of attention that she had money to burn, or melt anyway, 'cause no one had much beyond a mess of coins. But don't think folks didn't pay attention to her when she'd throw all those coins down on the counter. And what was running through their minds was for sure easy to tell.

"When you live like we did in those days, in the same community, in the same twenty blocks, or whatever it was, everybody knows what everybody's doing. It's not that people gossip or that all the children go to the same school even, and pass on at home everything they heard that day. It's just that a network exists, everyone seems to know what's happening, not through what they say only, but through kinship. Everyone knows that everyone is struggling. They know when someone gets into special trouble, or does something that gives them an edge. Hattie, like, she always wanted people to think she had an edge on them. Being poor always bothered her. Big Freddy used to tell her all the time, 'Why'd you think it's any different for you than for all the other niggers?' But she'd just smile at him. She

knew what he was saying was that he wanted it different for himself, or if not for him then for Justy and me. Everybody wants to be special. Most of the time it makes you feel good enough that you're living and working among your own people, but sometimes you have to feel that among them, you stand out for one reason or another. Fact is, sometimes the urge to stand out is so strong you can't hold yourself back anymore. Maybe that's another reason Big Freddy had to bellow."

Annie London sat on a wooden bench on a wide street near the school where she teaches. She wore a simple blue dress and a wide-brimmed hat which the wind kept threatening to blow away. The traffic was noisy, the air filled with the smells of oil and burning rubber. Occasionally she looked down at her shoes, as if debating whether she should tell more.

"So let us talk about busing," she said suddenly, sitting up straight and setting her feet firmly on the pavement. "Let us ask ourselves about what it means, to me. Just to me." The street was filled with shoppers, a group of boys playing, a couple walking with their arms around each other.

"I was bused to school all my life, so it's not anything new. When I say I went to school in buses, I mean in the worst buses you ever saw. The question of the day was always whether the bus was going to make it. Lots of them didn't. They were breaking down all the time. Every month you heard about an accident because some bus failed to work properly. Folks like us got used to it. We just assumed the buses would break down. New buses were used to take the white children to school. When the new buses got old, they used them to haul black children. When the old buses broke down, they practically left them where they fell. Americans had ways of recycling things, you see, even before the ecology movement. They just gave all the garbage to poor folks and black folks. When we got through with them, they weren't good for anyone. I love the way these people fighting busing worry about whether it's dangerous riding the buses. Loved to have heard those voices twenty years ago. I'll bet Big Freddy would have too.

"I remember once, a bus broke down carrying Justy and me

and a bunch of other kids. We were going to a segregated school in Harrisburg, although nobody there ever said anything about it being segregated. The few of us black kids who went there came on a bus, but no one said too much about it. We would have gone to a school that was practically all black except they said they had no room for us. Big Freddy always told Hattie, just go to the office and *tell* them you want them in that school, they won't turn you away. She kept saying she did and the school kept saying no, there wasn't any room. Everyone said no, all the time. I think he may have been right but she probably felt the school we went to was better. She couldn't work out our going there another way. So she had us bused.

"Justy hated the school. I don't think he was beaten up more than three hundred times. School didn't mind so much black girls being a little intelligent, but they hated the idea that Justy was smart. They also never believed he was really shy. They thought his being quiet meant he was thinking of ways to make trouble. Once they even called the police and had him arrested because they saw him playing around in the boys toilet. Somebody saw him go in there looking funny. That's what they told the police. Justy was in the bathroom trying to clean himself after being in one of his fights. He told Hattie he was ashamed to go back into class with blood on his shirt. He told Big Freddy it wasn't his blood and Big Freddy got so excited he squeezed Justy and almost choked him. But can you see it, my little brother standing at the wash basin washing his shirt in the middle of a school day. Can you imagine, and for that they arrested him. It was a wonderful school. But Hattie, I suppose, was right when she said it was lucky he was only arrested and not suspended. He only missed one afternoon of school. You certainly wouldn't want to miss a day in school with the chance of being beaten up by some gangster. And for that great privilege we got to ride in a bus fifty minutes one way.

"I'll tell you something else about that trip. Cloverland was the name of the street where they picked us up. I should say where they were *supposed* to pick us up. The only problem was that Cloverland was right in the middle of where all the colored people lived, right? It figures that if you want to take some black

children to school, it might be that you have to come into the little lovely, law-abiding community where they live. Okay? But the people who drove the buses, they didn't like the idea that you had to come down the streets where the colored lived. What they really wanted was that we should go to where *they* lived. So instead of picking us up on Cloverland, they decided on Dalyrimple Street, which is exactly four miles from where I lived, way on the other side of the district. So we had to get up at six in the morning to take a bus that went from where we lived to Dalyrimple Street so we could get the bus to school. The school bus left at exactly seven. If we missed the bus, we didn't get to school. They chose Dalyrimple Street because there was a police station right where the school bus stopped. Wasn't that convenient?

"If that wasn't bad enough, this bus driver we had, he not only hated us, he was always terrified that we'd do something to him. I never understood what he used to get so upset about. What did he think nine-, ten-, and eleven-year-olds would do to him, or the bus for that matter? *We* were totally dependent on *him*, and all he could think about was that we were going to either kill him or steal his bus. We were thinking how fortunate we were that the man was good enough to be in front of the police station every morning waiting for us. As it was, the one driver they had first with this bus refused to drive it even to Dalyrimple Street. So they had a black man drive it eight blocks, really, eight blocks to Kenzie Drive where this white man got in and drove us the rest of the way to school. For some reason he could get himself to drive us to Dalyrimple Street in the afternoons after school. I always used to wonder what the poor man who drove us the eight blocks in the morning did after he drove us. It probably was his only job. I also remember seeing this white man, the regular driver, park in front of the police station and practically run out the door before any of the children even stood up. He looked like a child himself running away from something, looking to the police for protection. He must have been running away from some very scary fears.

"Now, every morning I come to school and I see the buses drive in and the crowds that wait for them in September and

October and then again in the Spring. I see the children get off
and everybody pushing and screaming, people waiting for
something to happen. They're looking for a confrontation,
groping around, pushing, clawing, trying to get the best view of
the trouble. These people remind me of all those folks who used
to stare at the counter when Hattie would throw her coins out.
Everybody looking, like they shouldn't miss the action. Nobody
realizes how much they're teaching the children by observing
them that way. They don't understand. There's so much teaching going on in that minute or two it takes a child to get off the
bus in the morning and get back on at night. A person could get
a college degree from all that teaching.

"I see these buses coming in as though I were looking at them
driving through a fog. It's all fuzzy, like I was seeing them and a
movie of them at the same time. I see millions of years passing
in that fog. Every morning I see the children coming off those
buses, then I see my brother getting off them too. I see him
scrubbing the blood off his shirt, I see Big Freddy, I see my
mother waving. Nobody looks at those buses coming and going
every day and sees only them. Nobody black, at any rate. You
see your whole life rolling in and rolling out. All those buses
bringing in children, they're bringing memories in with them
too. Don't let nobody fool you, they bring in years of experiences, some of them fun and worth remembering, most of them
sad, memories you'd like to forget. I see my mother waving
goodbye. All right, that's a special experience, I don't expect
everybody to share that with me. But nobody black, *nobody*,
sees these buses coming and doesn't think about how their
kinfolks went to school, or didn't go to school, or weren't
allowed to go to school. I see buses coming and going and I see
children walking along some Mississippi or Louisiana road
somewhere, black, black feet walking to school, mile after mile,
day after day, and all of it leading to what? Hell, they told all
those folks they could vote if they could read, as unfair as that
law was. Then they educated them, if you can call it that, and
still they didn't let them vote, even after they proved they could
read. But those feet keep walking. Child after child. If it rained
so much you couldn't get cars through those back roads,

couldn't even get the toughest animals to pull those wagons and carts they used to have, it didn't make any difference. The few kids they let go to school, they just started that much earlier in the morning and got home that much later in the afternoon. Those children probably never saw the sun. Night children. All of them night children.

"This isn't poetry I'm telling you. I'm telling you what I see when those buses drive in. When I see the crowds of protestors, those mad people throwing rocks at the buses, I see the movie again, the buses in the fog. I see my cousin Tarby Hunratt from Savannah, Georgia, getting hit in the head with a rock while he was walking to school. Rock was so damn big it took two boys to pick it up out of the back of the car and push it out on top of him. Savannah, Georgia, 1951. This country, this century. A boy going to school. Then they shoved him into a ditch because they got scared, I suppose, when they saw how badly he was hurt. I don't know, what did they expect to happen to a little boy when an enormous boulder crashes down on him. They expect him to say, 'yessir, thank you, sir.' He lay there all day before anybody found him. Lost an eye, and his left leg and left arm were practically no good to him because of the damage done to his brain."

"Hello, Miss London." A little girl dressed in a yellow dress walking with her mother crossed in front of Annie.

"Well what are you doing out on a Saturday afternoon?" Annie asked, leaning forward and patting the child on her shoulder. The little girl was embarrassed and clutched her mother's hand.

"Sees you every day in class and here she is and can't say a word," the woman said, almost as an apology.

"You think it's fun being a little shy?" Annie asked the child, still touching the girl's shoulder, but holding on to her own hat as well so it wouldn't blow away.

The girl nodded. Her body revealed a peculiar blend of discomfort and excitement upon seeing her teacher.

"I think it's sort of fun to be shy too," Annie told her kindly. "Bet you make a lot of noise at home, though, don't you?"

The girl said nothing. She only fidgeted.

"Loudest child in the project," the mother announced with delight. "You can always hear her. Ten blocks away and you can hear her."

Annie gently pushed the child away, a woman launching a toy boat. "We'll be listening for you, Cleo. So yell good!"

The child never looked back. Annie London, without pausing to enjoy the sight of the child walking quickly away, resumed where she left off.

"Brain damage, blind in one eye, left to die in a ditch. I've never visited in Georgia or Mississippi, I never even saw that cousin of mine. But I see it all, the tar roads, the buses, the mud, those boys in some flashy convertible breaking their backs just to heave out a rock big enough to destroy a child's life. That's what I see in the mist that embraces these school buses. They must never stop. That's the lesson of all this, my childhood, Justy's, that cousin of mine in Georgia. Folks have never made it easy for us. They think, well, we gave you that, now why doesn't *that* satisfy you for a few decades. Or they bring out their measures and tests. This child has not benefited from busing because his I.Q. hasn't changed in ten years. How many times do I have to read that? Nobody's life changes in the ways that these little, insignificant tests measure. I'll show you fifty, a hundred children who've learned to read or do mathematics who'll show up on these tests like college professors, but they've learned nothing, or very little. You don't learn the most about someone by measuring something about him on a test. You learn *your* ways, maybe, but you haven't gotten to know the person. Where's the test for a father dying and children moving away from their parents? There's no guidance counselor going to test a child on what it was like to hear Big Freddy yell, standing alone, looking out his window.

"How do I feel about busing? I say it's the law, you obey it. White folks can't just *visit* the schools black children go to and say they're good or bad. You have to be black to know the feel of the schools black children attend in this country. You can lecture about it all you want, but no one can test you on the sight of that one bus driver's face when he pulled that bus up in front of the police station on Dalyrimple Street and ran out of

there like, Thank God, he was free of those gorilla children for
one more night. What do you suppose that does to a person's
self-image? Experiences like that probably affect a person's I.Q.
too. If the man can't wait to get away from you, he's even afraid
to come near your home to pick you up, then you must be plenty
terrible.

"Busing's not the answer to all problems, everybody knows
that. But black folks don't have a say in this country, we haven't
a shred of power. Lot of guys running about thinking they
control communities here and there, maybe they do. But in the
state and in the federal government, you can be mighty sure that
what black folks need is last on everyone's list. This little period
in history belongs to the buses. Next decade they'll have more
surprises for us, more ways a few of them will try to help a few
of us without upsetting *them* too much. That's the way it works.
Keep the niggers in their place. My word, if you bus these little
children around and they get a chance to see what they've been
missing, they might try to start some revolution, so keep them
right there where you can watch them very closely. That's what
I mean by the children learning just coming to school and going
home each day. This whole country is saying to these children,
start something, go ahead and start something. They're making
it so the child thinks that school is connected with violence or
some ridiculous form of revolution. Nobody wants to believe
that black families just like to have their children educated. You
never hear about that side of it. It's always, we want our
children bused because of this political action, or that desegregation model.

"Nobody knows how rotten the schools are in these poor
communities. Nobody knows. Black parents know. Hattie knew
damn well what she was doing when she fixed it for Justy and
me to go to that other school in Harrisburg. And my mother,
although she never talked about it, she knew our chances would
be a lot better in the north. They had to be. I suppose she was
right, too. I might have ended up cleaning toilets in Little Rock,
or Selma. But see, that was part of the nonsense we learned
during our childhoods, that it was always better in the north. Go
to Pennsylvania, New York, Illinois, Massachusetts, it was

better up there. I heard that all my life, sometimes even from black folks. Black folks, though, they knew nothing was safe anywhere, that it was a white society through and through. It's not better in the north. It's only better where people work hard to give somebody else's child a chance, or what they think is a chance."

Annie London was walking home. She went the long way around, making certain to pass the enormous housing project that occupied almost two city blocks. The gray bricks of the buildings and the dirt of the small playfields came together to produce a collage of shadows. The few trees that had been planted were not flourishing. Two boys, no more than ten, were climbing out of a first floor window, watched carefully by a group of smaller children.

The first boy jumped and landed heavily on a bank of gravel and dirt. "I broke my leg!" he screamed out. "I broke my leg." The children continued watching. Then the second boy jumped from the window, a distance of about eight feet. He landed practically on top of his friend. "I broke my leg," the second boy moaned, doing a poor imitation of his friend. The first boy punched him, then they ran off together, chasing each other behind the buildings.

"Runs pretty well for a boy with a broken leg," Annie commented, her eyes following the children. "You think nothing happens on these grounds," she said. "So much happens that nobody sees. Life, conversation, religion, happen in these projects. I think sometimes they ought to force everybody to live in them for some part of their lives. We'd all be a bit better for it. We'd all grow from jumping out those windows and believing we'd broken our legs. How my mother believed in giving us a chance to get out. She could have kept us in the south with her. She needed us, I'm sure of that, as much as we needed her. But she dreamed the big dream, didn't she? Send them north, give them the northern chance, find them new land. The rest of the world goes on thinking that women like my mother are good for only two things, having babies and shipping their children off to people who will give them more opportunities than they can. I can't talk about busing, what it does to children, what it might

do for this entire nation, without going back to those experiences in my own life.

"Busing is more than a political or legal decision, it's more than anything you read about in the papers. It's people's lives, and people's lives don't start and stop with busing. A child's day doesn't stop and start with school. Every day matters, every year matters. There's no drop in the ocean more important than any other drop. It's part of an enormous body, and nobody can see all of it. That's what I think about busing. It's my parents, my work, the children I teach, and don't teach, it's my feelings for this country. And it's always Big Freddy, Hattie, and Justy. Sweet Justy. He's a minister, little Justy. Where does time go? A little boy washing off the blood, now he's telling a congregation what they ought to be thinking about God. Busing, you could say, got him there, or got him part way there. I believe he'd tell you that. He keeps his feelings to himself, like my mother always did. But he'd say that being in the best schools available to us made a difference. It's got to. You can survive eating the worst food, but you won't grow from it. You only grow from eating the best foods. Busing's a way to get some of us closer to the best foods, you know what I mean?

"Now you listen good to my words—that was something Hattie used to say—you two, Justy and me, you listen good to my words. I say the bus makes it possible for a few children to eat steak once in a while instead of cold pork every day. That's all I said. I didn't say *all* children eating steak everytime they get hungry. When they make it possible for poor children, black children, Spanish-speaking children, *all* children to eat steak every time they get hungry, when they make it possible for poor children, black children, Spanish-speaking children, *all* children to eat steak every time they feel even the littlest bit of hunger in their insides, then I say you can take all the buses and shove 'em in the ocean, use 'em for scrap iron, do anything you want with 'em. For all I care you can double park 'em in front of that police station on Dalyrimple Street, right there for that man to drive away. He'd probably feel all right too, driving empty school buses around the state of Pennsylvania the rest of his life."

There was no self pity in Annie London's tone. It had been a day for reflection, a day devoted to letting some memories return. Walking when one has no particular destination often evokes memories. It is as though certain kinds of memories are attached, somehow, to physical movement. One doesn't neces- sarily feel lighter or cleaner merely for walking and remem- bering, but the moments of the past and present are enriched, as if two life schemes were playing themselves out simultaneously. Time, movement, feeling, become a conversational dance. Too often, however, we fail to see the dangers of education and politics as they rip at the dancer, distorting personal images, tampering with the running of a person's body and the way that person conceives of time and space. Then, too, listening to another person becomes such a physical effort, we can only manage it for small bits of time.

"I've said what I can say," Annie London announced on the steps leading to the apartment building where she has lived alone for three years. "I'm thinking about a man, a man whose name I'll never know. What did that man who wouldn't pick us up on Cloverland Street think about? Where did he learn what he learned? I wonder, did he die yet, and if he did, did he die thinking the same things he thought all his life? I'd love to find that man and go up to him and say, 'Look, can you look at me, Mr. Man? Can you see that I'm a woman, with pride, with a real job, helping people, not just my own kind? Can you really see me without running away to that police station you were so glad to get to every afternoon? Don't you see how you helped? Don't you see you did a good thing for us, no matter how badly you did your job? You must have done as much for me and Justy as a doctor does delivering a child. And all you were was a bus driver. Nothing more complicated than that. Just a bus driver, like I'm just a teacher. You know why you did what you did? Because the law and the money system and the government, the whole country, told you that's what you got to do five mornings a week. And lo and behold if you in your frightened way didn't do it!' "

Annie London was grinning like a child who had just leaped out of a kitchen window and teased a friend with complaints of

a broken leg. "The Lord said, 'Mr. Bus Driver, I've got a wonderful job for you. I want you to deliver those twelve black children to Harrisburg. That's right, Mr. Driver.' " Annie raised her hand to silence an imaginary person who evidently was about to register a holy complaint. " 'Deliver those children so that they shall be free.' 'But to Cloverland Avenue, Lord?' 'Well, Mr. Driver, since it's still early in the *movement* days, I'll let you start your delivery on Dalyrimple Street. But your son, mind you, your son when he gets old enough to do your job, will start his delivery from Cloverland. Fact, if we're still needing those buses, he'll go door to door and pick up those little girls and boys, one by one. One by one, with every single one of them being counted.' "

NOW IT'S THE SENATORS

SAYING BUSING IS FINE—

ONLY NOT FOR THEM

The morning after her first major public address, Marjorie Milliken awoke from a fitful sleep. There had been a great deal of anxiety and excitement connected with the address, but she thought it would be gone when the talk was over. Yet the next morning seemed as difficult psychologically as the days prior to the talk, and she had never lived through a more fitful month in her life.

For six months, Marjorie Milliken, ardently supported by her husband Peter, had been working in her neighborhood's most vocal and eventually most powerful anti-busing organization. At first it was just Marjorie and several friends, women who, like her, were incensed by the idea that their children were being bused to a school almost four miles from their home. They found the idea of busing preposterous, the practice totally unacceptable. Informal talks and animated phone conversations led to their forming a small organization which ultimately attracted so many people, Marjorie and her original group chose to merge with other organizations. Now there were more than five hundred people in the organization and it was growing every

day. Never one to be a leader, Marjorie nonetheless found herself assuming the important roles in all decisions and actions. That she became the organization's chairperson was no surprise to anyone, except perhaps her four children who had always seen her as merely a competent housewife. Still, given their attitudes toward busing, they could not have been more proud of their mother. At thirty-eight years of age, Marjorie had begun a new career.

The days working for the organization were not without headaches and seemingly insurmountable setbacks. Every week Marjorie was dashing downtown to protest city hall decisions, urge newspaper people to write more sympathetically about the city's anti-busing forces, or speak to someone important who might help her side. Where once she was able to go months without speaking about a single local or national political issue, she now was consumed with work, driven by a source of energy she never even knew she possessed. There was something more to the work too; a noticeable felt change in her personality. It was as though the opportunity to attack court-ordered busing was allowing a part of her personality to break through invisible barriers:

"I've got a hold of an anger—wow, I never knew this old lady ever had this kind of anger. What a great feeling to be able to take it out on all these ridiculous decisions, fight them. We've got a lot of people joining us who've lived with this anger all their lives. They knew they had it, they just didn't know what to do with it. It's the only *good* thing about the busing movement. It allowed me to find that anger, and brother, am I angry—every minute of the day.

"I used to be able to ride a bus in the middle of the worst traffic. We'd have minutes on that bus when we wouldn't go ten feet. People would be arguing and upset and old Marjorie would just be sitting there, you know, thinking, if I don't make it at four, I'll get there at five or six or seven. Who cares if dinner's a little late. But ever since I took over in this group, I can't stand to be stopped in traffic. Got to keep moving; too many things to do.

"I want action, I want to put the pressure on these people. I want to tell them as loud as I can that they can take this

desegregation stuff and shove it right up their you-know-whats. I don't give a good damn what the outcomes are supposed to be or all this crap about it being as good for my child as it is for the black child. For Christ sakes, that's a lot of TV commercialism. I've had it up to here with busing. The people, their goddam children, all this waste of money, *my* money. It's a crock, brother, and if you don't think that way, then let's not waste each other's time. I'm sure you got work to do and I sure as hell know *I* got work to do."

Marjorie Milliken was standing on the wooden stairs leading from the small back yard of the apartment building into her kitchen, the original headquarters of the neighborhood anti-busing group. Clotheslines were strung between the rear of the building and several large gray posts set into the ground at the rear of the yard. Behind the back fence was another small yard and an apartment building almost identical to the Milliken's. Both buildings are owned by a Mr. Alex O'Connell who has given a large amount of money to Marjorie's group.

The April day is overcast. A chill is in the air, the tops of the trees lining McHenry Boulevard two blocks away are moving rather ominously. Marjorie Milliken makes a move to ascend the stairs but there is more she wants to say.

"You want to know what busing is? It's breakfast cereal. Breakfast cereal, the junk you eat every rotten morning of your life. No, make it the junk we serve our *children* every morning of our lives even though we know it's terrible for them. There's not a damn thing in breakfast cereal that's any good for anybody. You ever read the sides of the boxes? All of them, every one of them, are the biggest food crime going. You know why they're halfway good for the kids, because you can't eat that stuff without milk. It's the *milk* that makes it halfway decent. Good old *white* milk, brother. The rest is a load of nothing. You ask anybody, they'll tell you, it's the biggest steal going in the whole damn food industry. I'm not even talking prices. That's a whole 'nother story. I'm just talking food value. There's none in cereal. That's busing too, brother boy. That's what your little busing business is all about. Busing's the cereal; there's nothing in it of

any value. When you mix the milk in, *then* you got something. The milk is *our* white kids.

"My child, my son. *He's* what's going to help them out. My money, my effort, my time, my kid. Everything set up to help *them*. Doesn't help me at all. Fact, just like the cereal, I got to make sure he has a fantastic dinner to make up for all the crap he eats at breakfast and lunch. That means my husband has to earn a good living which these days is no small thing, and I got to work my tail off to make sure that kid is going to grow up the way he's supposed to, *despite* the busing. Busing isn't going to help him. Get him to meet Negro kids? What's he need that for? Show me anyone important in the world, someone who's made a lot of money or gotten somewhere, who hangs around with Negroes. It's the biggest racket anyone's ever invented. Run around with Negro kids and that's supposed to make you a better person? That's supposed to make your kid smarter? That's supposed to make your school better or make it that your kid's going to have more money when he grows up than some rich white kid who's going to school in a suburb somewhere? They honestly expect us to believe that crap? Let me tell you why we eat cereal in the morning."

Marjorie has forgotten about the chill and the greyness of the day. She marches down the few stairs and holds tightly to the bag of laundry she has carried from the kitchen to the yard, then back to the kitchen and now again to the yard.

"We eat cereal for a very simple reason. It's the easy way out. It just so happens that the old lady likes resting in bed at night watching a little television. That means ten lousy minutes to herself when she doesn't have to worry about this one's dirty underwear and that one who needs a dress for a party and that one who wants a new shirt and this one who has to wear the same damn pants everyday and they always have to be clean. So I stay up a little late—for God sakes don't tell the police—and when morning comes I don't want to face the hot stove with pancakes and bacon and eggs. They're big kids, they want a big breakfast, let them shop for it and let them prepare it. I don't say this with meanness. I'll do dinner from top to bottom. The older

ones can help—that's their job—but I'll take responsibility, and with four kids and a husband, it's a little work, believe me. But for breakfast, it's every man for himself." Marjorie grins and looks toward the kitchen window feigning an expression of sheepishness. "Every *person* for himself or *herself*. Too goddam many political movements coming around here at one time, you know that." She runs her fingers through her hair. "Where was I? Cereal, yeah.

"All right, so cereal's the easy way out. Takes no intelligence, it just comes easiest. Doesn't upset anyone to open the box and pour it in a bowl. Doesn't do them any good but, so what. If you really want to do something good for children, brother, you make their schools better, you don't bus 'em around the city. Busing's the easy way out because it means the rich people and these two-bit politicians who change their minds every twenty seconds when the wind shifts direction would have to stand in front of the hot stove in the morning, the afternoon, *and* the evening and none of them wants to do that!

"They don't even want to get their precious little hands dirty, poor babies. All they want to do is send our children into God knows what kind of a neighborhood so that Negro children can have life a little better. That's right. That's exactly how I feel about them at this point, too. But these Negro people don't do a damn thing for themselves. All they do is complain about where they live, where they go to schools, their jobs, transportation. But you think they do anything about it? Sure, they do something about it. They find a bunch of softie liberals who cough up a little money to help them. It's no sweat off their backs, so what do they care.

"My husband drives a truck. As a kid he used to be a hooker in a foundry out near Worcester. Now he drives. All right? He complains about something at work and he's out. Bang! So long Peter my boy, you're fired! That man has worked every day of his life. He complains? You bet your rear he complains. You know a guy tryin' to hold down any job in this country's got nothing to complain about? Anybody sees these prices and what's happening to this great American economy, they're

either complaining or they're dead. But nine to five, he works. He hates it a lot of the time but he does it.

"But these Negro people, all right, they had it hard, maybe harder than anybody else in the country. They were slaves, okay? My people weren't slaves. We never had a lot of money but we weren't slaves. They were slaves, okay? But how long they got to keep telling us that? How many days of my short life do I have to get out of bed and look at the papers and read, we were slaves, give us food. My grandfather was a slave, make my school better. My grandmother was a slave, give me a car. Give me welfare. Give me *more* welfare. Get me a job. I love that one. First *you* go out and find me a job, right? And if I don't like the one you pick, then I expect you to find me another one. Then, if I like the job you find for me but it turns out 'cause I'm descended from all these slaves that I don't know how to do the job, then *you* train me, and *you* pay me while you're training me. I'd give those people a whole lot less than cereal for breakfast if I had any power in this city. One whole helluva lot less, believe me.

"So now you know exactly where I stand. Now I'm going to work. I got laundry which I've carried up these stairs twenty thousand times and three different meetings today. This is a busy woman now. Very busy, very busy. Brother, I'd love to see my father's face if he could see me doing this everyday. He'd be plenty surprised, wouldn't he."

It had been fourteen years since Albert Xavier O'Neill died, leaving his wife and six children. Marjorie was the fourth. She spoke little in public about her father. She thought of him when she saw the younger children in the neighborhood playing with elderly uncles and grandfathers. It was a shame that Albert hadn't even seen two of Marjorie's children. It might have changed some of his attitudes, perhaps even eased the tension between him and his daughter, although on the busing issue he would have seen eye to eye with Marjorie. A man who had never gone beyond the fourth grade and who, by the age of twelve, had worked ten jobs, Albert Xavier O'Neill was a quick-tempered, embittered man. To the day he died he complained about world

conditions, and especially the ugly treatment of the Irish. But it was himself that he pitied most and looked out for. He told his friends, the few he could keep, that he would do anything for his Katherine and the children, but everyone heard the emptiness in his words. It was Albert O'Neill, they said, that Albert O'Neill cared for. He might talk about high values and the sacredness of the family, but if given half a chance, he would have dropped them all, Katherine, the children, his brothers and sisters, and run off and forgotten them the second he passed the city limits.

When he wasn't complaining, Albert O'Neill brooded. For months at a time his family saw no other moods, just fury alternating with a moroseness that frightened and annoyed his wife. Katherine did her best to keep the children away from their father when he was in his "foul moods," but there was no way to conceal this powerful and oppressing personality from anybody. One minute he would complain about the noise of children playing in the five-room apartment, the next minute he would wonder about the silence. "Where are they?" he would call out. "Afraid of me or something? Is that what it is?"

Katherine O'Neill could tolerate the moods. It seemed that at times she thrived on them, conceiving her role as nurse, mother, wife, the only person in the world able to contain this mercurial man she continued to love. She kept her equanimity and stayed at the job of supporting him as much for him as the children. At least this is what she told her friends, and later, after Albert had died, she told her children as well. She loved him. She had made a decision to marry him, "and in those days people didn't just go taking a bunch of marital vows with the idea that when things get tough one can step out and demand a divorce." She had made her commitment and so a great deal more than Albert's exceptional moods and long-standing bitterness would drive her to the point of separating from him.

There were, however, two qualities about her husband, two excesses really, that Katherine O'Neill could not condone. Worse even than the infrequent drinking binges when he would come home vomiting, pale, and sick, and pass out on the doorstep, she despised the hypocritical manner in which he spoke about money and his intense hatred of black people. She

could understand the former but not the latter, but her efforts to change him in these two areas were weak and ineffectual. Everybody she had grown up with was poor, or nearly poor. No matter what they said about their financial circumstances, none could rid themselves fully of the shame poverty breeds. It wasn't that her own family and Albert's family never had enough. Katherine knew that no amount of money would ever satisfy Albert if there was one man anywhere with more money. Albert, after all, was making a good living at the chain store where he was a salesman. The family never would be rich, but then again, they would also never be poor. Still, Albert always had to have more, or at least present himself as someone with money. How many times he strutted around in public, to a bar, even to church, with a new shirt or new tie, while the children went without toys or clothes or special treats.

Then there was his undying hatred of Negroes, whom he invariably blamed for all the world's problems. Once a week at least, more often if he could find someone to listen to him, he railed against Negroes. They were ruining the building industry, he claimed, ruining neighborhoods and schools, making the country dirty, and worst of all, corrupting anyone who came within miles of them. They gave America a bad name in the world. How could it be he wondered that the government would let these people travel anywhere they wanted, in any city, when everyone knew how much trouble they caused and how dangerous they were. "They're an oversexed group of wild animals," he would proclaim. "A person would be wise to have a gun if they know of niggers living anywhere near them. I'd have a gun under my bed if I knew they were around here. To look at them is to hate them, if they didn't kill you first. They're a goddam plague. An evil plague!"

At first Katherine pitied him for holding such thoughtless attitudes, but eventually she grew to despise his unfounded rantings and was deeply afraid that his words would affect the way the children felt about Negroes. But there was nothing she could do to change him. No matter what he railed at—the government, the mayor, his boss, the church, prices, even the weather—his attack inevitably turned on Negroes. It was

Negroes who caused the problem that aggravated him so, and made life unbearable.

As a small child Marjorie O'Neill often heard her father's fury and his hatred of Negroes, although, as she remembers, his opinions never really sunk in, for they never made sense. All she knew was that a group of people had seriously hurt her father and it was best to stay away from them, not that she ever saw them in her school or neighborhood. But surely her father had good reason to hate them as he did.

Whenever Katherine reached a point where she believed she could go on no longer, Albert would reveal his streak of decency, if not piety. He believed intensely in family values and the significance of a good marriage and stable home life. One had to be strict, although not overbearing, with children and teach them the right ways and wrong ways. This task began and ended at home; it could not be left in the often irresponsible hands of teachers and clergy. In this fundamental principle Katherine wholeheartedly agreed. As long as parents were alive to raise children and provide direction for the children's lives, it was their duty to act as parents. On this point she backed her husband to the hilt.

The children, for the most, honored their parents' principles. According to Marjorie they were too afraid of what their father might do to them if they disobeyed. On many occasions Albert beat his sons for minor acts. When the girls misbehaved, they were given long lectures and weeks of stern, unyielding treatment. The price, then, of misbehaving in the O'Neill household was too dear. Marjorie O'Neill and her brothers and sisters knew this, but her actions in her eighteenth year, the summer marking her graduation from high school and settling in to a new secretarial job, might have made one think differently.

She was never in love with Chuck Kennedy although he might have been in love with her. It was merely an attraction for a young man with an easy style and a rare knack for finding fun things to do. Chuck never had much money. For a young man just starting out with the telephone company he couldn't be expected to be rich, but he could make a dollar go a long,

long way, especially when it was being spent on entertainment.

Chuck and Marjorie had a marvelous summer together, going places, laughing a lot, discovering fun spots in the city they had always heard about. They even rented a motor boat one Sunday and discovered a stretch of beach where no one else ever swam. All day they lay together in the sun, swimming, and taking rides in the boat. That evening on the beach they made love. It was Marjorie's first time, and while she knew her parents would be furious if they ever found out, there was no way they could. Chuck spoke of marriage but she couldn't think about anything except the events of that extraordinary Sunday.

As Autumn came, Marjorie's interests turned to other men, two in particular, and Chuck was slowly eased aside. While Marjorie felt uncomfortable about treating him coldly, she felt it the best thing to do, for there was no future with him and it was better to cut off the relationship at once. But Chuck Kennedy didn't see it that way. He was infuriated by the rejection. "What the hell was all the sex about?" he asked Marjorie bitterly. "What do you, just do it with anybody who comes along? You tell 'em all the same stories about your being a virgin and how your father would kill you if he found out what a bullshit artist you are."

After one confrontation, Marjorie, feeling ashamed but also riled up, slapped Chuck across the face, but the young man hit her right back. The blow gave Marjorie quite a bruise on her face which she had a hard time explaining to her family, but at least she believed she had rid herself of young Mr. Kennedy, the boy who always had to have things his own way. But he continued calling her and even wrote her a long letter filled with hurt and attempts to hold on to a shattered self-esteem. It was this letter filled with references to their sexual experiences that Albert O'Neill discovered. How she was careless enough to leave it lying around, she could not explain. Perhaps she wished for her father to find the letter so she could receive the cleansing punishment she deserved for violating one of his principles.

On finding the letter Albert O'Neill exploded with fury. He was humiliated, incensed, uncontrollable in his assault on his daughter. Katherine, too, was shocked. "How could you? How

could you?" she interrogated her daughter over and over again, as if trying to make Marjorie reveal some secret information or hidden motivation. But her father cared nothing at all about reasons and explanations. There were two facts, he said. She did it, and she didn't confess it. That left her with two choices. Either she lived at home as she had always done, promising not to have any relationships with men until she was married, or she could leave now and be disowned.

It was an obvious decision, Marjorie Milliken would say many years later. "No one wants to be sent away from their home and on top of it have their father say they're going to be disowned. I mean, who the hell wants to hear *that*? So I told him that I'd stay and behave myself. I knew I was lying; there were already other guys around I liked. We were brought up Catholic, naturally, and heard all the stuff about how you got to do this and not do that. But it always bothered me, how come the girls had to be virgins when they got married and the boys didn't. Who the hell were the boys finding to be with? You know what I mean? You think the fact that men make all the rulings in the family and at church has anything to do with it?

"Anyway, I told my father, 'Yes, I'll be a good girl, don't disown me, I'll make you proud you're my father.' The whole story, right? Oh my God, was I lying, lying, lying. But there was something funny too, going on with me then. I think I must have been beginning to hate him or something, because after a while I didn't really care what he said or did. I began to see him for what he was, not all bad, but certainly not all good either. Lots of things he said I didn't agree with at all, in fact I thought he was off his rocker about them. But a lot of things I did agree with, like his thing about the Negroes.

"I was starting to get out more, you know, and seeing what the world was like. My father was right. Negroes were complaining about everything just like he said. I mean, you met a few good ones now and then, but in the main he was absolutely right. All you had to do in those days was read the papers and you could see he was right in everything he said about them. They wanted the whole goddam world at their doorstep, and they wanted people like me and my husband *and* my father to

put it there for them. So I agreed with him about that, and he *was* my father, and that meant a lot to me, too. I still didn't get on so well with my brothers and sisters and I hardly was ready, at the ripe old age of eighteen, to leave home and let them have all the things that *all* the children were supposed to get. I mean, I wanted my share of whatever it was my parents were giving away, love, money, old clothes, anything.

"But then one day, this was maybe two months after he found the letter from Chuck, I went to him and told him I'd changed my mind, that I couldn't live like he wanted me to. 'I guess that means I have to leave then, right?' That's exactly what I said to him. I remember how I smiled like a little girl to myself. My father never even batted an eye. He just kept reading, or pretending to read his paper, then he said, 'Get out of here. I don't pay rent on this house to protect a goddam whore!' It was like someone threw a chunk of ice in my face. I couldn't believe him saying that. Actually, I hadn't been with a man, physically you know, since the time he found the letter. I couldn't believe that he saw me as a whore. I was even known in the neighborhood as the girl nobody could touch. I was the local icicle. There were guys that didn't even believe Chuck Kennedy had dated me. But to my old man I was the local whore. So, I left. And you know what he did? He did exactly what he said he'd do. My younger sister Laura told me. He burned all my old scrap books and pieces of junk I had left over in my room from grammar school and high school. He actually did it. He went in there the night I left and had Laurie show him all the things in the room that were mine, and he took them in the back yard, set a fire, on this hot night too in early November, and burned every single thing he could find. I suppose he would have burned me too if someone had given him the chance.

"You didn't cross my father when it came to his principles, and I sure had broken the major one. I guess you could say he was a madman or a bad guy, but he had his rules and he gave you all the warnings in the world. He treated you like an adult, and as long as you lived in his house, and it was *his* house, you had to toe the line. I committed what he thought was a crime, so I was out. He had the power to lay down the law. That's what he

spent his whole life at, making sure he had the power in his own house. No one was going to cross him on that, not the government, not the church, not his wife, not his kids. I was out of that house within three hours of telling him I was going to leave. One second after I was out that door I was out of his life. He never spoke to me again after that. We saw each other from time to time, and he saw my two oldest children, but never at my house or his house. If I was, like, at my sister's and he was there, that was all right, but never at either one of our houses. In a strange way, I admire that. Lot of people say they have principles, but when it comes to acting on them they back off. The test, you see, and all of this gets right to the heart of the busing matter, is how far will you let people push you around, and will you take stuff from people in your own family, your own children even, or will you say, well, my principles are only good under this condition or that condition.

"That's liberal talk, talking for the 'burbs is what they call it around here. A person says, my principle is that busing is good for all the kids involved. So you ask him, what about your kid? Will you voluntarily bus *your* kid a long way from your home just to desegregate some school somewhere? Of course the families in the suburbs are for busing, some of them. Why shouldn't they be? Their kids aren't involved and never are going to be involved. You go find out if any of these people who make the decisions and claim all these great principles would ever do what they're always asking *us* to do. Look at all the senators, standing up there in the congress arguing busing yes, busing no. It's a show. They're all a show. Which one of them has their kids bused to school? None of them, I bet. The truth is that most of them have their kids in private schools because the public schools in Washington, D.C., are so terrible. And you want to know *why* they're so terrible? Because that whole city is filled with colored people. You better believe they'd like to have a bunch of senators' and congressmen's children going to their schools. It'd be about the only thing that would save those schools and they know it. Those colored people there, Negroes, they're not stupid. They know exactly what they want and they've got it all worked out how to ask for it. Give 'em the old

'we're the sons and daughters of slaves' routine so we got it coming. Of course no senator is going to bus his child ten miles from one state to another to help colored people's schools. Why should they? They know there's nothing in it for them but trouble and violence and their kid not learning a damn thing that's worthwhile. But there they are, everyone of those big deal senators, standing up in front of the television cameras spouting off about how important busing is, and then—and when they do this I could really throw up—calling out the name of Martin Luther King. Now they know damn well what kind of a man King was. Why do they have to start making themselves sound like these little gods.

"A lot of people would say my father really did a bad thing when he threw me out. Of course I didn't like it. I'm probably still crying inside from what he did. He's dead more than ten years and those memories are fresh in my mind. They stick out more than any memories I could tell anyone about. But he lived by his principles and he treated his children like he treated all human beings. The exact same way. He didn't make a speech saying *your* children should do something but *his* children didn't have to. He said if you broke the rules you were out. I'll tell you something else. The colored man is just as guilty as anybody else. You have people saying that maybe some Negroes should stand up, you know, and say, what we need is better schools and not busing. There are some that do it. But most of them are just as afraid as all those famous liberals.

"They say they want a voice in their communities, they want a major hand in setting up their lives for themselves. Then two seconds later there they are saying they're in favor of busing. Now how can you have it both ways? Either you want to control your own lives and your neighborhoods, everything around you, or you want other people to sacrifice themselves, or rather their *children* so *your* children can have a better school and *you* don't have to lift a goddam finger. That's a set-up, brother, someone has to explain to me. You know what it really means! It means I want power and the right to lay down the law in my house but I don't want to work for it. I just want it 'cause I decided I'm *entitled* to it because the entire country made my great-great-

great-grandmother a slave. Well, I don't know about anybody
else, but this little girl is fed up with that line. You want to claim
you got something coming 'cause your great-great-grandparents
had it bad, that's fine, but you better the hell make sure that
everybody whose great-great-grandparents had it bad has it
good now. A lot of people who never even knew about slavery,
like *my* grandparents, had it plenty bad. How come you never
hear people talking about the potato famine? Don't they teach
that in school anymore, or are they too busy teaching about
Martin Luther King.

"That's number one. Number two is, when these colored
people talk about people having slaves, why the hell are they
always looking in my direction. Someone ought to tell them that
not every white person in this country had a slave just because
they're white. No, they go after us as though it was *us* who made
them slaves. They're always talking about schools having black
history, you'd think maybe they'd want to read a little of their
own black history and find out just exactly what families did
own slaves and what families didn't. Thomas Jefferson, he
owned slaves. Did you know that? Presidents of the United
States and they owned slaves. I'll bet they gave speeches on
how terrible it was for poor slaves, picking their miserable
cotton, while those people were picking that miserable stuff on
their land. *Their* land. You see how nothing ever changes? Now
it's the senators saying that busing is fine, only not for them.

"You got a lot of people living around here, people I know,
grew up with all my life, you know what they're saying? They're
coming here to the organization and saying, let's give up, move
out of the city, put the money together, send the kids to private
schools. Or they'll say, okay, we'll stick with it and hope the
years our kids are in school go fast. Honest to God. That's what
a lot of them say. I feel like they do plenty of time, believe me. I
tell my husband I'm guilty, come on, let's move to Randolph or
some place far out and let the colored people take over the
whole damn city. Let 'em have it all. That's how I feel. Let 'em
have the whole state, the whole country if they want to. You
want it, take it! Then I think, Milliken, you nuts? You going to
give up the little bit you worked for? You going to sacrifice your

whole family, your whole race? You going to let a great country—we got problems, I know, but it's still the greatest country anybody's seen yet—go right down the old air shaft because some colored people are screaming how bad they got it because of the color of their skin? The hell I'll give it up for that!

"If I learned anything from my father it was stick to your principles. Die for them if you have to. If you don't believe in what you're talking about, and your children don't believe in what you're talking about, then how in God's name can you expect anyone anywhere to believe it! If you have to throw your own daughter out of your house because in your eyes she's a whore, then that's exactly what you do. And maybe I was a whore, not only in his eyes, but for real. I don't know, maybe I was. Maybe I feel toward my own daughter a lot like he felt toward me. There's plenty of time for sex. Kids don't have to start so young. They can grow up. I don't know, maybe he was right about a lot more things than I ever thought about, although, I don't think I'll ever get to the point where I'll agree with him burning my few little possessions. I mean, a grammar school yearbook? Really? Well, I suppose if you go all the way, you go all the way."

The afternoon prior to her big speech to the combined anti-busing organizations of several neighborhoods, Marjorie Milliken trembled with fright. In the morning her children were sympathetic with what they decided was the worst "case of nerves" they had ever seen. Maybe she should consult a psychiatrist, they suggested. By the afternoon they were bored and irritated with her constant complaining. They even lost interest in trying to keep her from smoking and from drinking five cups of coffee an hour. Every few minutes she would march off to her bedroom, close the door and stand before the long mirror practicing lines from the speech and gesticulating to an invisible audience. "Must stay calm and collected," she kept repeating. "People believe you more when you're calm." Then she would reappear in the living room, affecting a casual pose. At one point, she threw her family and friends into gales of laughter by stating: "I look calm and collected, right? Everybody

can see I'm calm and collected. So please, will someone tell me
what the hell does collected mean? Like the men in the white
coats are coming to collect me?"

During the meeting, just before the speech, she seemed to find
some calming resource within herself. She sat quietly at the
dignitaries' table on the stage in the school gymnasium, listening to speeches and a list of proposals for protest tactics that
seemed endless. Her neighbors, too, while noisily supporting
what was being said, were growing anxious to hear Marjorie. At
last her time came. Jimmy D'Allesandro, a prominent anti-
busing leader from another part of the city, had made a special
trip to introduce her. He praised Marjorie for her steadfast
opposition to what must rate as the worst assault the working-
class man had ever felt. He spoke about a simple everyday
housewife who "opened her eyes one morning and said so loud
everybody in her neighborhood could hear, 'I'm going to fight
those people.' And she kept her word.

"Look and listen closely to this great lady," Jimmy D'Allesandro told them, straightening his tie and pulling at his suit jacket.
"After she leads us to a victory over this little busing matter, she
just may be the person some of you might like to send to that
little hill they got in Washington for senators and congressmen
and congresswomen."

Everybody cheered and applauded and Marjorie rose to
speak, the announcement of her name lost in the noise. But
everyone there knew exactly who Mr. D'Allesandro was intro-
ducing. This was their lady!

To say that Marjorie's speech, brief as it was, became the
biggest success of the century, is to convey very little of her
triumph that night. The crowd applauded her ten different times
during the address and gave her a standing ovation when she
concluded. Her daughters cried, she cried, Peter walked around
afterward as if his wife had actually been elected to Congress.
"Gorgeous," Jimmy D'Allesandro shouted over and over again.
"You were gorgeous." Everyone agreed with him. Everyone
congratulated Marjorie, everyone felt hopeful. It seemed as
though singlehandedly Marjorie Milliken had stopped the busing program for school desegregation in her city.

"We're going to win," she had told them in the speech. "It's going to take long hard work, but we're going to win. We want good schools for *all* children, white, black, rich, poor. But no one's using *our* kids for any cheap experiment." The audience had risen to their feet on hearing this. They practically exploded when she told them about eating cereal for breakfast and how "white children were the milk, the only valuable, nutritious part of the whole meal!" Their faces glowed with pride and a bit of surprise that Marjorie could be so articulate and clever. "We're not saying that one race is better than the other," she had finished her speech, "but I'm not about to lie down and let our race be trampled on. Our race, our income group, our neighborhoods. If I have to, I'll educate my children myself, in the house, in front of the TV even, rather than let them push those buses down our throats. We're going to win!"

Afterwards, Marjorie seemed particularly pleased that the many young people in the audience had appreciated her words. "It's the children we're doing this for," she told a group of adults. "It's much better for them to be here tonight than at school tomorrow, the way schools are going." Everyone laughed when she playfully scolded the children for being out so late.

Then finally, it was over, the long day, the anxiety, the speech, and Marjorie Milliken lay in her bed, listening to Peter sleeping, breathing deeply. The house on Marble Avenue was quiet. How lucky we were, she thought, that the weather had stayed nice. Everybody was able to come to the meeting. She was too excited to sleep. Eyes wide open, hands folded over her stomach, she let her mind wander about in a way that she had rarely experienced. She could actually visualize the bills she had to pay. She saw pages of the newspaper, whole columns she had read in the last few days, so clearly she could almost read from them.

Peter had begun to snore and Marjorie turned over to one side, her back to her husband, her eyes feeling heavy. The speech had gone so well. It would have been marvelous if someone had recorded it. There was a man in the back of the gymnasium taking pictures. Maybe he was a reporter. No one even thought to watch the news to see if the meeting had been mentioned.

The next morning Marjorie woke early, an hour before she had to get her children off to school. The light of the dawn was just beginning to appear. Her heart was beating fast as if she had been running, and she was breathless. Peter remained asleep. She had had a terrifying dream:

A young black man with a powerful body and handsome face confronts her on a street in a city that seems wholly unfamiliar. He quietly invites her to have sex with him, insisting that she knows in her heart she is eager to be with him. "You know you want it, you know you want it," he dares her. She refuses by shaking her head. The scene is taking place in broad daylight and a crowd has begun to gather. The young man keeps moving closer to her, taunting her and making gestures of invitation with his hands and body. The crowd looks first to him, then back to her, awaiting her response. Still she refuses, unable either to speak or retreat. "You really want to," he is saying. "You're dying for it. Everybody wants you to do it. Do it for me, for them, for all of us. For the city." He has almost reached her. She is terrified. She is afraid to look at the crowd for fear of what the young man might do if she takes her eyes off him. "You must do it, otherwise I'll be forced to burn you." Her body begins to tremble and still she cannot find the strength to speak or run away. "Last chance. You might as well. You want it so much." Terrified, she is barely able to shake her head.

From somewhere behind him the young man has taken hold of a can of gasoline. He looks inside it at the shiny black liquid. "Last and final offer," he says seductively. She stands perfectly still. He throws the gasoline at her, the cool fluid drenching and causing her to shiver. He lights several matches which he holds in his hand. The crowd watches silently. He brings his hand back, a soldier about to heave a grenade, and she awakens sharply.

Wiping her forehead and pressing back her hair with the sheet, Marjorie Milliken looked over at her husband. Trembling, she walked to the bathroom, washed her face, then dried it with a small hand towel. It was better to stay up and begin work, she thought, than attempt to sleep the extra minutes before morning.

4

DO YOU SEE ME AS A HUMAN BEING

OR JUST ANOTHER BLACK FACE?

His name is Henry George Macon, but there is not a person probably in any of the hundreds of cities he claims to have lived in who knows him by this name. If you visited the neighborhoods, the rooming houses, and small apartment buildings where he has resided and asked for Mr. Henry George Macon, the people there would say they had never heard of such a man.

"Henry George Who? You sure you got the right name?" asked the seventy-four-year-old woman who looks after his room and collects the twenty-five dollars a week he pays in rent. "I've known every person who has lived at this address for the last thirty-five years. I can tell you there has never been anybody by that name living here, or anywhere around here as far as I know."

But if you go to this same lady, this robust and feisty lady whose love for money and gossip hasn't diminished in all the years she's lived in this city, and ask, "Could you tell me please where Mr. Willie Christmas lives," then she'll have an answer.

"Willie Christmas? Do I know where Willie . . . ? Well, why in the name of the Lord didn't you ask for him straight out? What's all this jabbering about a Macon fellow? Mr. Henry . . . what was that name again?"

"Henry George Macon."

"Now lookit you," she'd say, staring you in the eyes so hard you feel as though some mysterious force were pulling you out the front door, "if you want Willie, then why'd you go asking for this other guy?"

"Because this other guy is really Willie Christmas," you answer. Willie has told you so himself, along with a warning that no one will know what you're talking about if you ask for Mr. Macon.

"You know what, boy," the old lady will say. "I don't know who you are. If you know Willie, then that clears it with me. 'Course, everyone seems to know that man so that don't mean too much. But you coming in here asking for a man no one knows, then for a man everybody knows, everybody decent is more like it, and telling me it's the same guy, I'd have to say something's a little bit wrong with one of us, and I know for sure it ain't me."

Born in January of 1905 in Charlottesville, Virginia, Henry George Macon hasn't used his real name in over sixty years. The seventh of nine children—two others died before they completed a year of life—Henry, according to his mother, was supposed to be born in December. In fact, she confided to a few of her friends in the black community of Charlottesville, there was a good chance that her baby might be born on Christmas day. A very good chance. She couldn't tell for sure of course, but something in her made her think that this child, her first one not born in the spring or fall, might be a Christmas child.

Before anyone knew it, the neighbors had not only accepted Cora Macon's hunch as the gospel truth, they began calling the child "Christmas boy, the little Christmas boy." "Seems to me," Cora would say to her well-wishers—and she and her husband McCall Macon had a great many in their neighborhood—"that you folks aren't only taking a little for granted about the day this child's coming into the world, but aren't you taking a little liberty making out that it's already a boy?" Everybody would laugh, but Cora's gentle attempts to dissuade them never met with much success. The Christmas boy was coming on the day his name foretold.

Everyone, naturally, took it as a personal insult that Cora Macon did not see fit to give birth to her baby until the end of the first week of January. That the child was a boy made up somewhat for the incorrect prediction of the birth date. Henry George missed by two weeks being the Christmas baby he was supposed to be. If Cora had had a hunch, it meant that God had whispered something to her. Something went wrong, the neighbors said. But no matter, the child was healthy, his brothers and sisters were already helping their mother take care of him, and the end of the first week in January was close enough to Christmas to allow everyone to call the child Henry George Christmas Macon. As for the Willie part of his name, that had a story of its own.

Young Christmas Macon never did too well in school. Not in Charlottesville, not in Baltimore where his parents moved when he was eight, not in Wilmington where his mother moved when he was twelve, his father having run off and left the family just before the move, not in Hartford, Connecticut, where his mother and three sisters and brother moved when he was fourteen.

He liked school, in fact he liked it a great deal. The teachers treated him well, and while there were always troublemakers among the students, most everybody liked the boy named Christmas. There were fights and the days of being suspended from school, especially around the time his father disappeared, but Cora Macon understood the new-found rage in her youngest boy. She knew that McCall's sudden departure would be hard on all the children, even the oldest ones who were able to carry on without their father, but hardest on young Christmas. She tolerated the boy's occasional outbursts and by the time the family, or what was left of it, had settled into the rundown house on Wentworth Boulevard, in the northeast corner of Hartford, Christmas seemed to be over the fits of anger which inevitably got him into trouble at school. His grades didn't improve in the all-black Hartford school, but for some reason he seemed a bit more calm, less edgy. The suspensions ceased, and for two years he attended classes dutifully and caused his mother no worry.

At sixteen, Christmas quit school. He promised his mother he would return, but never did. Still, he liked school, and kept

hoping that someday he would either resume his studies or find a job connected with a school. He promised his mother that something good would happen with him. She'd see.

Cora Macon's reaction to her son's leaving school alternated between crying and moments of fury. With the tears pouring down her cheeks she yelled at him: "You've ruined everything. There's nothing left. Why is it you can't see that? There's no money without school, no jobs, no meeting anybody but the ordinary criminals you're going to know now. There's nothing left for no one to give you. You've spoiled it, and I'll be damned if you're going to put the blame on me or your father for this. This is all your doing. Don't you dare come running back to this house in five days or five years or fifty years crying that the world didn't show you no way out, or give you no chance. There's no one saying you've been going to any perfect school. God only knows, the worst of their schools are better than the schools they leave over for us. But you had a chance while you stayed in them. If a black baby has the slightest chance in hell of making it in this country, and God knows that chance is small, school's going to give him that chance. Not me, and not the church either. One place going to give you opportunities. One place. And you tell me you're going to find a *job* in a school? That's a laugh. Why you think there's a school anywhere's going to give you a job. They ain't even going to give you a chance to get back in there if you go changing your mind. White child with some money in his pocket, school's going to let him back in. You can bet on that. But you, little nigger child without a dime, no way of finding a job, boy been tossed out of school more times than anyone can count, there's no way you're getting back in. You spoiled it. You go back there tomorrow or you're out for good. There's no second chance. There never is when you come from what we come from."

It is more than fifty years since Cora Macon spoke those words. Willie Christmas can still see her standing with her back to the window in the room with the faded wallpaper. He remembers everything she said and can see in his mind the faded greens and yellows and blues of the paper with its pattern of fruit which he always found so lovely. He can even recall the

way the edges of the individual rolls were peeling off the wall and how his mother always whacked his hand when she found him trying to tear the paper. "It's ugly as sin," she would mutter to him, half as admonishment, half as encouragement, "but you ain't pulling it off till you got something better to put up."

"I'll go back to school," he would tell his mother, knowing he was lying.

"I'll tell you about going back," she said to him, tears falling down her cheeks. "I'll tell you that you got a single choice to make and I don't care who says it ain't a fair one. You go back to that school, rotten as it is, filled with those people they got working so hard to walk all over us, or you leave this home and don't come back!"

"What about my belongings?" Willie had asked. But his mother heard the freshness in his tone.

"You ain't got belongings as of this minute. You ain't even got a mother starting right now if you ain't already making plans for getting yourself set up in that school, or some other school. You can leave this country and go to school in Paris, France, for all I care about this minute. But if you want to say to people that you got a mother back in Hartford, then you better have the school you pick send me a letter saying you're in school full-time and passing all your subjects."

"I'll do it."

"Well, you just make that decision before you leave this house. 'Cause either way there is nothing here that belongs to you. Nothing at all."

"What about my clothes?"

"You got enough brains to figure out that school isn't important enough for you, then you got enough brains to figure out a way to get yourself money to buy a suitcase. And when you get that suitcase, then you come by and I'll tell you which clothes I'll be letting you take with you, and which clothes I'll be keeping right here in this house."

"What are you going to do with my clothes?"

"None of your business."

"Is too. They're *my* clothes."

"You want them, you stay here and go to school. You got

better things to do, I'll give them to somebody's child intelligent enough to have a sense of judgment. 'Course, judgment's something they teach you in school, so I guess I can't expect you to be knowing how to make a judgment. You've already shown you can't make the right decision.''

"What do you know about decisions?" Willie began, realizing as he spoke that he was heading in a dangerous direction. "You'd had any judgment, you'd never married that man you did."

His mother's hand landed just above his left ear. The blow made a thumping noise and for an instant he couldn't hear anything. The left side of his head felt like it had swelled to ten times its normal size and the pain was excruciating. Still, he prided himself that he was able to hold back the tears until he was outside near the old tar-surfaced playfield that served as recreation facility for an entire neighborhood. In the shadows of the house he had lived in for less than two years and certain that no one could see him, he cried openly and thought about his mother and father and, strangely too, his grandmother whom he had never seen or heard about since the family left Baltimore. He envied the two children his mother had borne whom he had never known, and tried to figure out a way he could get back inside his house without his mother finding out. He hated her for what she had said. She was no better than all the white women teachers in his school. None of them cared in the slightest for the students, particularly the boys. All those teachers cared about was that nobody messed up their plans. It was his parents' fault and his teachers' fault that he had to leave school. He might not have been able to make decisions as his mother had said, but the decision about leaving school was made by the people who were supposed to be caring for him, and teaching him. But they let him down like they let all the boys in his school down, so he had to leave.

Christmas walked out from behind the building where he had been crying and began climbing the stairs to his house. But he couldn't make it even to the first landing. Consumed by nausea and dizziness, he vomited on the stairs and on his pants. Hearing him in distress, his mother opened the door on the

second floor, but the boy clamped his hand over his mouth and ran down the concrete stairs and out the door, across the field and beyond the empty lot in the direction of the pool hall. As he ran, he saw the face of his mother but he heard himself saying over and over again, "I'll show him. I'll show him."

That night and for the next several nights he slept at a friend's house, a boy whose mother was rarely home and therefore wouldn't wonder what the Macon boy was doing sleeping over. Christmas told his friend about the fight with his mother and how he was preparing to run away from home. He was going back to Baltimore to look for his old friends.

"What you going to do?" Nat Beele asked as the two boys lay on a mattress in the darkness.

"I'm going to go to school," Christmas answered. "I'm going to work in a school someday, too."

Nat was astonished. "Work in a school? You crazy? What you want to be doing spending the rest of your life in a school for?"

"Best place to be," Christmas said. "Don't know why exactly, just seems like the best place to be."

Nat Beele was bewildered as well as angered. "Your mother's right. You *got* to be crazy. All of us are counting the days to get out of that prison, and you're running away so you can go somewhere else so you can go to another school so you can end up your life *working* in a school. You musta lost your mind here one of these months. Maybe the school did that to you, Christmas. You know that? Maybe one day when you wasn't looking they came into your classroom and took your mind away. The sane part of it, anyway. What'd you say?"

"I say I'm going to Baltimore. I'm going to end up working in a school someday if I can, but I'll tell you one thing, I ain't going to end up in one of *our* schools. I'm going to work where the white kids go. No more this wasting time in places like we go. Either I work in a school where black kids go with white kids, or I'll think of something else."

"You was going to say," Nat interrupted, "go to school *just* with white kids, wasn't you."

"No, I wasn't."

"Hell, you wasn't. No place in white schools for you or me."

"No place in white schools?" Christmas let Nat hear his surprise. "I know kids been to white schools. In the south and in the north. They're the best schools."

"Everything they got is the best. But if you think that's where you're going, you better look in a mirror. I can just see you going to school, like at Pauley High. You wouldn't get near the gate. 'Hey, Mister Pauley High, they got a nigger trying to get into our school. Could you please send someone out there and tell that boy he's lost.' You're lost, Christmas, you know that? I don't want you sleeping here no more. You got to go home pretty soon. You don't have no plan that's going to work."

Christmas lay in the darkness telling himself that it was important for him to remember this night forever, because of his desire to find work in a school where white children go.

Almost sixty years have passed since that night with Nat Beele. Many jobs have passed too, in more cities than this elderly gentleman could ever list. He has worked, he claims, twenty-five different jobs in the train stations of Baltimore, Philadelphia, and New York alone. Baggage carrier, men's room attendant, newspaper hauler, janitor, floor cleaner, handyman to white people who ran the soda bars and pharmacies, and shoe shine boy.

"Shined more shoes in the 1930s than the Florsheim company made in all the time since. Got my name shining shoes, my other name. Two guys sitting up in the high chairs, being worked on by me and this other fellow. Benny something was his name. Cripple fellow, never could straighten up. Men waiting in the chair for him to finish never knew when he was done 'cause they was expecting him to stand up straight, but he couldn't do it. White man would look down at him, you know, asking him with his expression, you done, or you just taking a rest? I'd have to say, he's done. So these two guys are sitting up there one day having this argument, you know, about something. And Benny and me, we're rubbing and spitting like we do, and this one guy takes my shoulder and he say, 'You tell 'em who's right, Willie. Willie, that's your name, ain't it?' I didn't say nothing. Old Benny, he don't even look up. He pretend he don't even hear

nothing, you know what I mean. So this goes on for a while, then he do it again. He takes my shoulder, push me a little, you know, and he say like, 'Ain't that right, Willie?' or 'What do you think, Willie?' I just say yessir to him 'cause I don't want no trouble. Hell, they were firing shine boys every twenty minutes in those days. One customer tell the station master he has trouble with one of us, he was gone next day. Twenty guys waiting all the time to take our place.

"So later on, we're all finished, this guy Benny worked on, he say to my guy, 'Say, how come you say you never been to New York before and you know this guy's name is Willie?' And my guy, he says, 'They're all named Willie. Don't you know? They all got names like Willie.' Benny don't say nothing. He just keeps working, cleaning up 'fore the next guy comes along. 'Willie Christmas,' I say to myself. 'It's a name. Ain't *my* name, but it's a name.'

"Maybe ten years go by. Now I'm working up here in this school where I had a friend let me help him in the boiler room and kitchen. Fellow by the name of Loden, big tall guy but he was always sick. Think maybe he had cancer. He'd come into work one day, then he'd be so weak he couldn't come in maybe two, three days. So he took me in there with him 'cause he's afraid to lose his job. He wasn't making no more than twenty-five dollars a week back there. That's all. They didn't have no insurance or nothing like that, and this fellow Loden, he wasn't so old, but he didn't have no way to make a living. So he acted like he was fine. I helped him out, figured this was the job in the school I was supposed to be getting, though I never figured I'd get it that way. Never went back to school, see. My mother was right. She knew me better than I did. Folks like her always know better than children. But when you're a kid you got to go prove you're something. You know what I mean. I wasted the time. Maybe you get to learning about people from shining their shoes. Maybe even you get to know the most important thing about a white man from shining his shoes. Do he pay you respect? Do he listen to what *you* have to tell him? Do he see you as a human being or you just another black face? You can tell all that just from him settin' up in that easy chair a few minutes. He

don't have to say much, you can read him like you might be reading a book, see what I mean. Everyday I worked that job I thought about that, how I was always learning things about people. But I told myself, if shining shoes was such a good way to be learning about the world and all the people, how come they only gave the job to poor old black boys like us? How come no black man, or only rarely, ever got up in one of those easy chairs?

"So I was glad to take that job with Loden. Darnell Loden was his name. Tall fellow with big ears, but he was thin looking when I knew him. You could see he was getting sicker and sicker every day. Didn't need to be no doctor to know that. Told him I had a plan for working in a school. He asked me did I go to high school. I told him sure. Then later on I got scared, 'cause maybe if he found out I lied to him I couldn't work with him no more. But he didn't care. He must have knowed anyway I lied. He was lying to everybody about him working there himself. Every time people came down to the basement asking for him I'd say he was out somewhere, you know. Could I help them out. They didn't care none. Long as the place was warm in the winter and the wastebuckets in the rooms was clean when the teachers got there in the morning, what'd they care which one of us did the work. Fact is, I don't know to this day whether the man who was the principal ever did find out it was me and not Loden who was doing all the work.

"I didn't even know he died 'til maybe three, four months after it happened. Started seeming strange him not coming in at all. Used to come in at least once a week, then he disappeared for a long time, so I figured he must have died. But someone would have told me, I said, so the guy must be alive. But he wasn't. Died in his sleep, which is the best way. Never even went to the hospital. Cost too much, he said, and besides, he said he knew he was going to die. What'd he want to spend the last months of his life in a hospital for. He always said he'd live a helluva lot longer being *out* of a hospital than *in* one. I couldn't tell him different. He was my boss, kind of, and you don't go crossing your boss. Like the shoe-shining, boss gets rid of me, he puts another fellow in the minute I'm gone. Loden could have

done it any time too. Said once he had a nephew needed work. I figured, well sir, that's the end of me. Brought the kid around too, to look at the place. Now I *know* I'm on the way out again. Job 8,450, I say to myself, goodbye. But the kid, big kid too, could have done both our work in half the time, he say the job ain't for him. He wants something more important. I heard him say that, I knew the job was mine for good, or long as I wanted it." Willie Christmas laughed. "And here I am, thirty-five years later, almost, and I ain't left yet."

When he first arrived at the school, Henry George was confused about what to give as his name. It seemed as if everyone had a different name for him, and despite his anger at being called Willie that one time in Grand Central Station, he occasionally introduced himself to people as Willie Christmas. To some people he remained Henry George Christmas, to others plain Christmas, and to a few, like his nephew and nieces, Mr. Macon, or Uncle Henry George.

About a year after Loden had brought him into the school, Henry George walked into the large third-floor room where a group of fifth-grade boys were working in the wood shop. Two white boys were having a verbal battle over the right of ownership of a tool.

"I had it first," one was saying.

"But I need it now and it don't matter who had it first. It only matters who needs it. Ain't that right?" The second boy had turned to Henry George who was carrying out the shop waste barrels. While Henry George was interested in the dispute, he felt it was his place to remain inconspicuous. "It ain't right, is it, Willie?" the boy asked plaintively.

Henry George looked at the boy, surprised that once again he had been called "Willie." "Seems to me you two are old enough to get along together and share those fine tools you got there."

The second boy was delighted with the older man's words. "Thanks Willie," he said. He turned to the first boy. "See, I told you. You heard what Willie said."

"I don't see why Willie's word has to count," the first boy argued, hurt that the decision had gone against him. "Willie isn't the only one who makes decisions." Never once did the boys

question how the name Willie had been established. But from then on, Henry George Macon became Willie Christmas, although even now in the school he has served more than thirty-five years, very few know about the origin of Christmas and fewer still know his real name, the name given him by his father and mother.

Willie Christmas has seen a great deal of change in the years he has served his school. He is the first to say that his job is the only thing that hasn't changed in all this time. Whereas mornings used to be spent stoking furnaces, now Willie makes certain that oil pressures and fuel supplies are at the levels the large boilers demand. He will clean in the boiler room at least an hour every day, then spend an hour before lunch cleaning various rooms like the assembly room where he picks up the paper, gum and candy wrappers. He mops the floor of the gymnasium, for the perspiration and dust that collects on the old hardwood floor can make it slippery, and this may cause accidents. Ten years ago he missed work for three days with a cold. A friend checked on the boiler but never mopped the gym floor. A boy slipped on the floor one of the afternoons Willie was ill and damaged his knee. Several students told Willie about the accident when he returned. They never realized, they said, how important his job really was. They knew it was important that he shoveled snow in the winter and emptied waste paper baskets because the teachers had this thing about needing clean baskets and freshly wiped blackboards. But they had to admit, they told him, that they never had understood the reason for him always mopping the gym floor.

Willie Christmas knows almost every child in the school by name. He watches the children going to class and stops to talk with as many as he can. He prevents fights, helps children who cannot open their lockers, makes sure no one leaves books or clothes after school. "He's a fixture," everyone on the teaching and administrative staff will say.

"A fixture?" Willie laughs. "I thought a fixture meant, like a chandelier. I know I ain't no chandelier. Everybody around here's got their job. Even the smallest one. I got mine. Anybody

can see it ain't the most important one. Day I die they'll get someone else in here and forget all about Willie Christmas."

In years of service, no one has put in more time at this one urban school than Willie. Thirty-five years ago the school was all black, except for a number of the teachers and administrators. Then slowly, too slowly in the eyes of many, a few more black teachers were hired, and occasionally black administrators as well. The head principal, however, was always white. It had been the same when Willie himself was a student in Baltimore and Hartford. But in the last several years the school has seen changes. Because of busing, the school is now desegregated and the atmosphere, according to the one man who has witnessed it all, the history of and the resistance to busing, the new groups of students are different.

"I've watched them start all the changes." Willie Christmas seated himself on the end of an old couch that he once saved from going into the garbage and brought into the little room outside the boiler room. Here he has made a place for himself to rest. Occasionally he sleeps here too, as he feels the fatigue from his job more intensely. "I watched them fighting over how they were going to do it. Bring in white kids but keep the black kids they already got. Hold on to these kids, let those ones go. I watched 'em test 'em. They even asked my opinion one time. I told 'em, 'All black children want, seems to me, is going to the very best school they can. Everybody who follows the action knows the best school is where the rich folks go, and everybody knows that the rich folks are most usually the white folks.' They got some rich black folks. Some black folks gone out and did all right for theirselves. You see 'em around, driving their big cars and wearing nice clothes. But most of the folks you see around here, they're only pretending to be rich. You can see right through those folks. I had an uncle who was like that. Always drove a big car and wore those funny-looking suits, but he didn't have a dime. One day they came to repossess his car but they couldn't find him. He knowed they'd get him sooner or later. Guess maybe my own father was that way. Strutting down the street after church on Sunday making folks think he had lots of

money. Hell, everybody knew he didn't even have no job, so how could he have money.

"I used to say to people, way you can really tell how a person stacks up in the world, you know, is what kind of school he's got his children going to. If a man is black, everyone expects him to send his child to a black school. Same is true for the white man. From what I can see, the white man's going to find a better school than the black man, 'cause he's going to be living in a better neighborhood. Just 'cause a few black men send their children to a school mostly white don't mean that they theirselves is really a part of the white man's world. There's no black man alive really part of the white man's world. No way he's ever going to be neither, least while I'm on this earth.

"So now, you see, the black man looks around and he say, which is the best school for my child? Everybody answers him, you take and put that child right smack in a school where the white children go. So he say, what school they got open for me? And they say, beggar can't be choosy. Any school that'll open up for him, that's the school for your child to go to. You see where I'm getting to. That's the reason you got to have busing right now at this time. Don't make no difference how they set about it, you going to have white folks screaming their heads off about how blacks coming into their school going to ruin that school for the white children. Or you'll hear, like people will be saying, you bring those black children in, we going to pick up and get out of the city. Turn the city over to the black man, they'll be shouting. But see, from how I look at it, and I been looking at it a lot of years, white men did about as bad a job handling the city as anybody'd ever see. Can't do worse than improve it, no matter even if you are a black man. So maybe they ought to decide that a black man ought to take over the city, see what happens. Make it like an experiment. They got black men running cities in the country, important ones too, like Atlanta and Los Angeles. You don't see those cities falling into the ocean. But everybody thought they would when those black men got in."

Willie Christmas wiped his brow with a red and black handkerchief. He was smiling, shaking his head as if he had just told an amusing joke. But there was a tension in this man,

something that made its presence felt in the way he moved his arms and body. His eyes hunted for the next words, the best way to express the feelings and attitudes he had developed and discussed with his friends.

It is a long time since the days when he used to stand alongside his father watching the neighborhood boys in the Philadelphia schoolyard play ball, and wonder, would he ever grow tall enough and big enough to hit a ball like the older boys. His father had assured him he would be bigger than all the boys and be able to hit a ball farther than any of them. A few years later his father would disappear forever. And a few years after that he would argue with his mother about his decision to leave school. He would see her over the years, but they never would again achieve the closeness and confidence they once had. She would go to her grave unhappy, as she always said, about more things than even God could keep in His head at one time. Most of all, she was beaten by Henry George's desire to up and quit. She told him then he was throwing away the only chance he ever had. Nothing he could do would change her mind. Nothing he did dissuaded her from believing this.

Almost seventy years old, Willie Christmas had never lost the feeling that his life had been a waste. He had made his decision and it had gone against him, as his mother said it would. He could reflect on it with calmness and equanimity, but her words were alive inside him. All her predictions came true as if from the grave, even, she had shaped the years of his life.

Strangely, his aging and the distance in time from that crucial decision has never really taken hold in his mind and spirit. No one could accuse him of denying his age or the circumstances of his existence. More properly, it could be said that he never relinquished the feelings of those days when he was fifteen, and so it always has seemed as if some significant changes in his life might still occur. He himself might announce that his days are numbered, but to himself there remains the possibility of his making some final hour arrangements that might help him to achieve the goals his mother had wanted for him, and that he wanted as well.

Willie Christmas's eyes moistened with emotion, the ends of

his mouth lifted slowly, and the wrinkles in his forehead seemed deeper than before, as though they were now permanently set. His head tilted slightly and he scanned the tiny room as though he were following an arc of light.

"This busing's a winner and a loser. The black man, see, he got to say he stands for busing. If he say, I don't want busing, he got every white man in the country and a whole lot of 'em from outside the country too, coming into his home to shake his hand. That's what they would call an honest nigger. He knows the truth, they'd say, 'cause he knows his place. So the black man, he got to say he's for the busing, bring in all the buses they can. Now he knows too, they going to get a lot of good things coming from the busing. That's got to happen. Right off, his children going to be in a better school building. Probably be reading better books, having better teachers. And he's going to learn from those white kids. They're going to teach him. You see that every day if you look around this school like I do. I see things nobody else can see 'cause I'm here and I'm not here at the same time, if you get my meaning. I can look around, and I see those children black and white, going to teach each other a whole lot of things. Got to have busing for something like that happening in the school. Never saw a white child in all the years I went to school. When I did, I remember, I stared at them same way they stared at me probably. Couple of animals in the jungle trying to scare each other half to death, and inside everybody's feeling lonely and scared. You believe me when I tell you.

"But see, you got a growing problem when you have this busing. I don't mean all the people arguing the idea, I mean something more important that all those white folks, as angry as they get, don't understand. If you tell a black child, you see here, we going to send you to a real good school, but the way you going to get to school is go on a bus to where the white folks be living, then that child may be happy, because he knows he's going to a good school, better school maybe than all his friends go to, you see what I mean. He's going to be happy, this little child, 'cause he's hearing he's about to get the best deal in town. But what he don't know is that he's learning another lesson with the busing, which is that every time he needs or he wants the

best things, he's got to go where the white folks live. Now that means white folks not only has it better than black folks, it means that white folks *is* better than black folks. The child don't know he's learning this but that's what he's learning all right. Busing tells him, you got to be well-behaved and make a nice impression when you go to their school. Then you come home every night and be the bum everybody knows you really are. See my point? If they wanted to set up the busing to make it fair, then what they got to do is make all the white schools as good as they can and all the black schools as good as they can, then tell everybody, all the schools are real good, so pick the one you want to go to and we'll find you a bus that'll take you right where you want to go. All they got now is a bunch of cities where the white folks got a little or a lot and black folks got a little or nothing at all.

"Busing, see, it's not for the long run. It's for now. You got to have it now 'cause black folks, don't you see, they ain't got no power in the government. They ain't got no power anywhere. All they got is what people tell them they can have, but they don't have no buying power, or political power. They got no power at all in the schools. When I was a kid, we was all black, every student in every school I ever went to, and every one of 'em had a white principal or superintendent. Every one of 'em. Folks used to say they was pretty brave, white folks coming down to work in our schools. But there was nothing brave about them folks. They was just doing their job which was to keep us quiet and out of their own schools.

"So what's the answer to busing. I say this: Right now you got to have it, you got to get black children going to these other schools only 'cause they're better schools. You take this school. This school went way up when they started mixing the children. You could tell. Children were studying better things, they had better desks and books. Teachers were smarter, spending more time teaching the children 'stead of just making them behave. You could see from what I was pulling out of the baskets every night, the school was getting better. 'Course, you had some of the children did good, some did bad. Some liked being in what they call a desegregated school, some, you could tell, they didn't

like it at all. Black and white, some liked it, some didn't. You always have the troublemakers. They'd be there no matter what kind of school you have. You put a bunch of men in jail and you going to find troublemakers. You don't listen to them or anybody in their families. With the other children though, you got to watch them real careful. Some fit in fine. Don't make no difference to them who's in the class with them. Others, it takes a long time for them to catch on. It's like mathematics. Some folks seem to be born so's they can understand it first time. Other folks seem to be born so's they can never understand it. You always hear the children talking about their mathematics. So you got to work harder with those kids. Help them to learn their mathematics. Everybody's got to learn to read and write and do mathematics. Everybody's got to learn to live with people different from them. You may not like it but that's the way it is. Like, I'll talk with some of the boys and girls in the afternoon and they'll have to go to the dentist, and oh, they are scared. They'd practically be crying if they didn't have no one to talk to. Now, what do you say to a child so afraid, waiting before he has to go to the dentist? You say, it's going to hurt, son. I can tell you. I been there. Man don't want to hurt you, but he does anyway. You got to be strong.

"Same is true with desegregating all these schools. Going to be a little hard at first. Going to hurt, just like the dentist. No one wants it to hurt, but you can't put two animals, lonely, frightened, been raised not to like each other, in a little room and don't expect some smoke. Got to be some smoke. Got to be some fire too. Got to be that way. In the end they going to both be better for it. Now later on, when you know both these animals being taken care of in the same good way, they both got the same amount of food and clothes, and they both live in nice houses, then maybe you say, no need keeping them together in the same room no more. See what I'm driving at? When they're equal, treated as equal, then you can say, all right, this one goes here, that one goes there, no reason for them being together or apart. They can choose. Right now, black folks got nothing to choose. They got bad schools to go to, or they got the chance to be bused to the good schools. Least, that's the way I see it. What

they'd like to say is, okay, white folks don't like all this busing, fine, then we'll make a deal. Since you guys got all the power and we guys got none of it, you stop the buses from rolling and fix our schools up so's they end up as good as your schools. But there's no one, *I* know of anyway, dumb enough to make that deal 'cause everybody and their child, little babies even, know what's going to happen with that one. Once those buses stop rolling, they going to forget black schools, black housing, black folks, like they forgot about us for the last three hundred years. Right now they say it like this: 'We got a dollar and we going to share it with you.' 'Fair enough,' we say. 'All right, you take a penny and we'll keep the rest.' 'A penny? That all you giving me?' 'That's all. You taking it or leaving it?' 'What choice I got?' 'None.' 'Gimme the penny.' "

Willie Christmas leaned forward on the couch and looked down at his clasped hands. He seemed to be holding something precious. As he spoke he never glanced up, and for the first time on this one afternoon, he appeared unself-conscious, not at all embarrassed by his small quarters.

"You got a child, like I see near everyday after the school closes. There's that child waiting for his mamma to come for him. He ain't taking the bus home today. This's a strong child, good child, but he's doing all he can to keep hisself from crying. 'Why you crying, boy?' I ask him. 'Ain't crying,' he say. 'You're crying, boy. Willie can see you're crying.' 'Got to go to the dentist.' 'That's why you're crying?' He's shaking his head up and down. 'You crying just 'cause you got to go to the dentist?' 'Something else too.' 'What's that?' I say. 'I ain't telling,' he say. 'Won't tell me?' 'Won't tell nobody,' he say. 'Got to tell somebody if it's big enough to make you cry.' 'Ain't telling nobody.' 'What you got you can't tell Willie Christmas?' 'I got it,' the boy say. He's just a tiny one too, maybe in the second grade, but he's working there to keep from crying.

" 'Okay,' I say, 'I'll tell you a secret nobody in this school knows if you tell me what you got that's so bad you're about crying.' 'I ain't crying,' he say again but the tears are falling out his eyes. 'What's your secret?' 'All right,' I say, 'but 'member, when I tell you my secret, you going to tell me your secret.

Okay?' He say okay. Now I'm kneeling way down so's he don't
think I'm so big he can't tell his secret to me. 'Well sir, you going
to be the only boy in this school knows my real name.' 'Your
name's Willie Christmas,' he say, 'I know that.' 'No,' I say,
'every body *calls* me Willie Christmas but that ain't my name.'
'Your name ain't Willie Christmas?' He's already stopped crying
like I knowed he would. So he say, 'What's you name then?' 'My
name is Henry George Macon.' Well, sir, this little boy starts to
laugh. There he is laughing and there I am kneeling, see, in the
entrance hall they got in the school. Pretty soon we're both
laughing. He's going to be sitting in the dentist's office in thirty
minutes but he's laughing 'cause I don't look like nobody named
Henry George Macon. 'Henry George,' he say, 'isn't one name, it
be two names.' 'Henry George Macon,' I say, and he laughs all
over again.

"Now I say, 'I told you my secret, you got to tell me your
secret.' 'Well sir,' and he's still laughing, 'my secret is that two
boys told me I was a nigger baby and I shouldn't be in this
school.' Boy's telling me this and he's laughing. He don't feel bad
no more. 'Well, don't you take that stuff from them,' I tell him.
'You ain't no nigger baby, you are a big black boy, just as good
as every child in this school, good as every child in the world.
Let me tell you something else. Things going to be different for
you. You going to a good school and that's going to be good for
you. You going to finish school and get a good job someday like
your daddy.' 'I'm going to be an engineer,' he say. 'That's right.
You going to have a job and make a lot of money and have a
nice family.' 'I'm going to be like you, Willie,' he say. Now he
practically got me crying. 'I think that's fine,' I say. 'You can be
like me and you can be like your daddy. But most important, you
got to be like *you*. You know what I mean?' He shake his head.
He don't understand. So I tell him, 'You in school 'cause your
mamma want you to be in school, ain't that right?' He shake his
head. 'And you going to the dentist 'cause your mamma want
you to go to the dentist, ain't that right too?' He shake his head
again. 'Now see,' I tell him, 'those are two very good things.
That means when you grow up you got a good brain and good
teeth. All you need to know is nobody in the world can make you

feel no good just by calling you a bad name. No one going to beat you that way no more. You understand?' Well, he shake his head, but I ain't so sure he got what I'm telling him."

Willie Christmas had begun to smile. The deep furrows in his brow disappeared and his face seemed younger. " 'What's your name, boy?' I ask him. 'Joe Clay,' he say. 'That's your real name?' 'Joe Clay,' he say again. 'What do the teachers call you?' He say, 'Joe.' 'And what do the children call you?' He say, 'Joe' again. 'Everybody in the world calls you Joe Clay, do they?' 'Yes sir,' he answer. 'Well, that's the first step,' I tell him. 'You keep your name. Long as you got that name, you know who you are, and who your people want you to be. You keep holding on to that name of yours, Joe Clay, and ain't nobody going to shove your name around or keep you from growing up to be a good strong man. You think you can remember all I'm telling you?' 'I think so,' he say. 'You sure?' He shake his head like before. 'You remember my name?' I ask him. He smiles at me, you know. 'Willie Christmas.' And I smile at him too, you know."

5

THEY COULD LIVE THEIR WAY,

WE COULD LIVE OURS . . .

THE SOLUTION SEEMED

PRETTY SIMPLE

Harry Bingham is quickly approaching his fiftieth birthday. Except for his service in the Army, he has spent all of that time in the Boston area. The middle of three children, he was born and raised in the Dorchester district. His father was an automobile mechanic, his mother a part-time seamstress. The family lived in an apartment, on the same floor actually with his father's brother's family. The Bingham children attended the neighborhood schools, all of them completing high school, none going on to college. All found employment and eventually moved away from the old neighborhood.

By watching out the living room windows fronting on Mt. Vernon Street, the Binghams could practically see their beloved neighborhood change. The first sign that things were happening came when Mt. Vernon and several nearby streets were opened to truck traffic during the night as well as the day. Then several businesses closed down. At first the close-out sales provoked

amusement, everyone assuming that the Jewish and Irish merchants were merely playing the old game of seducing customers with rock-bottom prices. No one paid much attention until they realized that no new merchandise was being stocked, stores were indeed closing, and some of the buildings were scheduled to be torn down.

And then there were the Negroes, a fact that bothered Harry Bingham's father Jack Bingham more than anything else. "They're getting closer," he would tell his wife, staring out of the living room windows. "Every day they're getting closer. You see that? They're moving. Real quietly so no one should know what they're up to, but it ain't going to be long before we'll have to move. There won't be a safe building inside five miles of here. First, the big businesses, then all the drug stores and butcher shops. You'll see, Violet," he would warn her. She only shook her head as if to say his daily predictions sounded exaggerated and foolish. "Okay, don't listen to me. You just keep an eye on the Jewish families. If they stay, I'll admit I was wrong. But you just watch and see how they're going to start pulling out now. The Negroes are coming in real quietly and the Jews are pulling out just as quietly."

"You make it sound like it was all being arranged somewhere," Violet would reply.

"Okay, okay, okay," he would say stoically. "We'll see. We'll see."

Sure enough, young Harry and his brother and sister were seeing more and more black children in their schools. They were seeing them in the stores too, their stores, and on their playgrounds. In the beginning there weren't that many, a handful at most, but then suddenly they seemed to be everywhere. What made it worse, Jack Bingham would announce in front of his children, "is that the Negroes specialize in large families. Where we got two kids, three kids, four at the most, they got eight, ten, sometimes fifteen. And they talk funny," he grumbled to his wife. "That's probably the worst of it. They talk so damn strange even if you wanted to pick up a conversation with them, it would be impossible. You need a translator!"

"It's just 'cause they're not city-bred," Violet would try to

settle him down as she worked at her sewing. "They come up from all those little dingy southern towns, they haven't ever gone to school, they have no culture, what do you expect them to sound like? Their life hasn't been so easy, you know. You forget that."

"*Their* life hasn't been easy," Jack would yell at her, accentuating his disbelief. "*Their* life hasn't. . . . What the hell do you think *my* life has been, for Christ sake? You think we're *rich* or something? You think all these years I've worked, and all that little stitch work you do has added up to anything? What the hell do you call this apartment, a *castle?* Three little bedrooms and a living room and kitchen. That's your idea of a successful life?"

"I'm not like you. I don't happen to find all that much to complain about it."

"*You* don't find all that much, but *I* do. *I* find that much. Goldsteins upstairs? Huh? They staying around?" he glowered at her.

"I wouldn't know."

"You wouldn't know but I would. They're leaving. He told me yesterday. I saw him downstairs. They've seen all they want to see. The neighborhood is going to *them*. To *them,* Violet. Not to us. I told you. Watch the Jews. Watch 'em. And they're moving. Businesses are gone, Jews are on their way out, and I got news for you, I'm already talking to people about places where we could go too."

Every night, it seemed, Harry Bingham lay in bed listening to what sounded to him like the same discussion. He imagined his father peering out the window as if able to see the transformations in society taking place, and his mother sitting in her chair, working at her sewing so that she could give each child a small allowance. Then he would close his eyes and make himself think about what he was learning.

Everything his father said about the Negroes was true. They were increasing in number, showing up everywhere, and in their sneaky way trying to take over. They were also beginning to scare him at school. He spoke about this to his friends, but no one could figure out what to do. Several teachers too, were upset by what was going on, like the new styles being brought

into the schools, the "new language," the fights and the talk of
gang wars. They planned to move out of the neighborhood,
where they had lived for years, and they talked to parents about
the advisability of letting youngsters walk around by themselves
at night. Maybe adults should walk to school with the children
as well.

"It wasn't like the old days," Harry's father would tell his
family at the dinner table, "when you could trust a policeman,
believe in the man's honesty. Everybody now is either on the
take or knows somebody who is." Then he would look
pleadingly at his three children and warn them never to forget
their background and what the family should mean to them.
"Those people," he would lecture them, pointing over their
heads in the direction of the living-room windows, "are going to
try to change our lives. They're going to try to push us around,
get us to leave, but we're not going to budge. We're going to lead
our lives like the law says, and we're going to remain decent
people." But at night, after Violet had put the children to bed, he
would pace up and back across the living room and announce to
her that they were leaving. "In fact, it's probably already too
late."

"Don't you think we should wait?" his wife would ask.

"For what? What would you like to wait for? For your
daughter to be attacked in the street? For your sons to be beaten
up some day after school? And how about us? You think *we're*
safe down there in that jungle? Five years from now you won't
even be able to walk from one house to another. And you think
the city cares? They care about us much as I care about them.
By the summer, Violet. You get ready to be gone by the summer.
This is it!"

Jack Bingham never made it out of his Dorchester neighborhood. After suffering two massive heart attacks in quick
succession, the second occurring while he was in the hospital,
he died. His oldest son and a nurse were with him. Harry, who
was thirteen, was waiting outside in the hall with his mother
and sister.

Immediately, both boys went to work to supplement their
mother's income and everyone lived with the goal of leaving

Dorchester as their father had wanted to do. Harry finished high
school and worked in a factory for less than a year before
entering the Army. He saw some action in Europe, but most of
his time was spent in Army bases in the northeast and south. It
was in Georgia that his father's words came back to him and
began to shape his future. What he saw there made sense to
him. There was no reason for black men and white men to live
or work near each other. They could live their way, and we
could live ours, he would say time and again to his Army
friends. The solution seemed pretty simple.

Three years after his discharge, Harry married Irene Purcell,
and in time they had two children. After trying different jobs, he
settled on the insurance business where he became quite
successful. After twenty-five years as a salesman he has all that
he wants, and from his home in a community fifteen miles
southwest of the old Dorchester neighborhood, he has developed what he calls a stable picture of what's happening in
America.

"The problem comes down to this," he says, adjusting his
position on the metal lawn chair. "The Negroes just have never
had anything. They've never been trained or brought up the way
we were, so it's really not their fault they're living in the
conditions they do. You can't blame them, see, for what's
happened. They've had their tough years too. But where they
make their big mistake is in asking that they get things for free,
for nothing. There's not a living soul wants to just *give*
something to another man. It doesn't work that way. Never has.
You have it rough, you got to work that much harder. There's no
alternative to that. But they want everything handed to them.
They want to make me feel that they got it coming to them. Well
sir, they don't. None of us has anything just coming to us. They
want it, they're going to have to work for it.

"What their main goal should be now is to prove to this
country that they can hack it, make it on their own, you know
what I mean? You don't go asking the government to build you
places to live when you've destroyed the old places. You ever
drive around Dorchester? You know that old neighborhood
around Caldwell and Mt. Vernon streets? You see what those

people have done to that area? That neighborhood used to be elegant. The rich used to live in those neighborhoods, and now, for Christsake, it looks like they fought a goddam war over there. Garbage is piled up all over the place, cars are left in the middle of the street, never moved, windows are broken, doors are falling off. I'll tell you the honest-to-God truth. I wouldn't let my kids even drive around over there. They ask me every once in a while to show them where I grew up. You know what I tell 'em? I tell 'em it's a restricted area now, you can't go over there. Colored people have wrecked it. They've wrecked it same as if they came in there with all that building equipment and tore them buildings down. And then they got the nerve to turn around and say they got something owed to them? I say, let them clean it up first. Let them fix up their streets and their homes. Let them make their own schools better. The city can help. I got nothing against that," he smiled, "now that I'm paying my taxes out here, and then we'll see what's owed them.

"I mention schools. Why do you think people like ourselves come out to a place like this? It's a very simple reason. You want nice homes, that's number one. Number two, schools. Number three, good neighbors, people you can trust. You don't have to know them, you just have to trust them. I'll tell you the truth, I don't see how people survive in the city anymore. I drive in there on a call or when I've got a meeting, I can't wait to get out. That's why we come out here. You pay for it. Don't let anybody fool you. You pay right up the old nose for every stick of grass. But you're not going to beat this for comfortable living.

"Okay, so now, while I'm busting my you-know-what to make it possible for the four of us to have a life out here, I got to read every day in the paper that the Negroes back there, they want the same thing. They don't want to work. They don't want to fix up their own back yard, if you get my meaning, but they think their children should be able to come to school out here. Any school they want. Well, I don't care what anybody says, that idea has to be unconstitutional. You don't live that way over there with your drugs and your booze and those divorces, and all that rioting, and then send your kids out here to *these* schools. Who the hell, I'd like to know, gives anybody the right

to think they can just take advantage of these places people out here have been working to keep going? Where do they come off with all this legal talk, all these words they throw around you see in the newspapers everyday?

"You know when they had their best idea? Separate ways of life. Yessir." He was nodding his head and sitting upright in the chair. "Best idea yet. I saw it in the south. We here, them over there, and no guarantee from anybody that we have to meet somewhere. They got their little neighborhoods, we got ours. They got their schools, we got ours. They got their businesses, we got ours. You don't need to go mixing up the races, which is another thing that gets me. All these show-business types thinking it's so nice to be marrying a colored man. What the hell kind of ideas are they trying to plant in these children's minds? That it's all right to marry one of them? What are they, born yesterday? You think the colored want to marry us? It works both ways you know. We don't want them, and they don't want us.

"What the hell you got living in this country, Irish, Poles, Jews, Italians, Germans, Portuguese, huh? And a helluva lot more. You don't see all of *them* complaining. They stick together in their neighborhoods, marry their own, go to their own church. What's wrong with that I'd like to know? What kind of trouble they cause anybody? And don't think those people have it so easy. I know about them. I lived with them in the old neighborhood, and I worked with them, still do. We got a Swede, an Italian, an Irishman in our office." He was rubbing his eyes and searching his memory. "More too I can't think of. We got Jews working there. There's no problem. You never hear any one of them walking around saying they got something coming to them *free!*

"I got a guy in Chelsea I sell life insurance to. Real nice fellow, doesn't have much money. Guy buys a little term insurance from me. Once a year I go over there and we sit in his living room. You know what he told me, what is it here, not more than two, three months ago? He's got eight men working construction with him. They're a crew, like. They stay together." He

shrugged his shoulders. "They're all Polish so I guess they like to stick together. They're not doing anybody any harm, so why not. You know what this guy, Michaels is his name, he changed it, probably from Michaelowsky or something, you know what he told me? The Negroes on the jobs with him want special training. Okay, so he gives them training. Huh? But that's not enough for them. They got to be *paid* while they're being trained. That's what he said. These guys got to do their job and in between, instead of resting or getting a cup of coffee, they have to train these colored guys. Now, you want to tell me that's fair? I told the guy, why don't you just open up a school? He said if he opens up a school the next thing you know all their children will want to be bused to it."

Harry Bingham fell back in his chair and roared with laughter. Then he raised his right hand as though he were about to take an oath. "I swear to God, that's what he said. Can you imagine the nerve of those people? Who trained those Poles? Who taught *them* how to do their work? You know damn well, nobody did. They just went and learned. They didn't ask nobody to pay them. When they knew how, they went looking for a job, like men, and they got their jobs, not because they were owed, but because they *worked* for 'em. That's all there is to it. You work for things in this country. Nobody gives you nothing unless you're rich. Then they give you plenty. But the rest of us work. What do you think happens to us if I can't work? What do you think we did when my father passed away? Nobody gave us a cent. We got a little insurance money that *he* had to pay for all his life, and we all went to work. Even my kid sister helped out, and she was always kind of a sick little thing. But she worked, and never complained. Not like *they* complain.

"That's another thing, you know. Have you ever heard so much complaining come from so few people? You go back in history and think about it, you won't find anybody who does so little and complains so much. That's the thing that really gets me: they get what they want. They think they're owed, and by God they get it!" He pounded the arms of his chair. "I tell you, they get it every single time. They want housing, they get

housing. They want busing, they get busing. They need money, they get money. I'll tell you the truth, when I started working for them, I thought the insurance companies had the best racket going. That's the honest-to-God truth. Before I knew the business all I could see was getting money for doing nothing and having all the odds on your side. But I want to tell you, when I see what these people are trying to pull off, and *pulling* off, they got insurance beat a mile. By a mile, my friend. All they have to do is yell loud enough and they got everybody in Washington running around trying to find ways to help them. I never saw anything like it in my life. You make enough noise and jobs open up, schools open up, banks open up, the whole works. For Christsake, if I yelled like that my neighbor over there would call the cops.

"I guess it goes back to my father. 'Course, a son's going to think his own father is the greatest man that ever lived. You know how that is. But guys like him, they saw what was happening in this country. Saw what was happening *to* the country is more like it. They didn't have the power to change it, or stop it, but everyone of their predictions came true just exactly like they said it would. Every one of them. I remember my father, standing up there looking out those high windows we used to have, talking to my mother, as if it were yesterday. He saw the problems brought by the Negroes moving into neighborhoods like we lived in. And he saw way beyond that to what was happening in every city in this country. The man didn't have more than six, seven, eight years in school, but he could see more than a guy who's gone to school for twenty years! He could tell you where it was good to live, and where it was bad to live. We just followed his orders, you could say, even though he ain't around to see how we're doing. Not a day goes by I don't think about him, listen to him giving his lectures. I just wish he could know his grandchildren, not just my two, but Bill's three and Kathleen's two. The whole family.

"You have to wonder what all these changes mean, and where all this yelling for this and that is going to end. I'll tell you the God's honest truth. I think this thing with the Negroes took

years off my father's life. I think it killed him. If they had just let us be on Mt. Vernon Street where we were living, not bothering anyone, not asking anything from anyone, I think that man would have been alive on this earth right now. Like I say, you have to wonder."

6

YOU DON'T HAVE ANY PLANS,

DO YOU, DARLING,

OF TAKING *OUR* CHILDREN

OUT OF SCHOOL AND BUSING THEM

INTO THE CITY?

Talking to their neighbors in the suburban community where they lived for fifteen years, one got the impression of a couple united in lifestyle, philosophy, and attitudes. To speak with Nell and Ben Armstrong themselves, however, was to hear disagreements on almost every controversial subject, and some uncontroversial ones as well. Many of their discussions turned into intense arguments, and one wondered about the invisible fibers holding these two people together.

Nell Patterson met the young man who would someday be her husband when she was sixteen. At the time, her family lived in a southwest section of the city. On the first day of her junior year of high school, in walked Ben Armstrong, a new boy in class. His family had moved from Terre Haute, Indiana, when his father

was transferred. It was Ben's sixth move in sixteen years, but happily, it was the last his parents would make.

Both Nell and Ben claimed they didn't find each other particularly attractive at first, but in late October of their junior year, he accidentally met her shopping, and the way she acknowledged his presence made him feel that perhaps they could be friends.

They had many good times together, going to movies and sports events, and soon, if their classmates' perceptions were accurate, they were on their way to becoming the lovebirds of the high school. Once they might have denied it. Two dates, they would have said, and everybody has you married. But by Christmas, they were firmly together, and they would never again, through school and college, date anyone but each other.

After graduating they went on to college, Ben to the state university a hundred miles away, Nell to the local community college, their eyes on careers in accounting and secretarial arts. But the separation was too trying. They felt an urgency to be together that was never satisfied by weekend meetings. On New Year's Eve of their first year in college, they decided to get married. No one was surprised. Their friends had predicted marriage, even in the high school yearbook under Nell's photograph. Their parents too were pleased. Each youngster had become a member of the other's family, so marriage seemed the logical next step. All four parents wished the wedding might be postponed until Nell and Ben were further along in their studies, but then, if it was to be, why not immediately?

The wedding ceremony took place in late July at the church near their old high school, followed by a reception at Nell's home. It was an ideal day; everyone said it was the most perfect wedding they had ever attended. After a brief honeymoon in a resort town near the ocean, Ben went to work for a month in an accounting office, getting a feel for what would become his career. That was almost twenty years ago. Time slipped by so quietly no one seems able to recapture the feelings of the birth of the three children, Ben's growing success, the moves from the

small apartment on Cedar Avenue to the slightly bigger one on Crescent Drive, to the generous home they rented on Sumner Boulevard across from the park where Nell took her babies to play.

If the disappointment felt by Nell's parents about her decision to leave the community college after only one year could not be clearly recalled, neither could the rejoicing when Ben announced that he had been made a partner in his accounting firm and was already hunting for a house in the suburbs. What Nell and Ben Armstrong could recall is that for years they lived out the love affair exactly as the inscription in their high school yearbook had predicted. As they reflected on their lives, there were only happy times, satisfaction, good health. The only sadness was felt at the deaths of their grandparents, but the youngest was in his mid-sixties, so it was not as if they had died prematurely.

The three Armstrong children, two girls and a boy, ranging in age from seventeen to twelve, were attractive, bright, never a problem to their parents and grandparents. "Not a perfect life," as Ben would say, "but so close the difference doesn't matter."

What began as two individual families raising children and then watching as a daughter in one married a son in the other, went on to become a happy, settled suburban family, a lovely combination of generations, a testimony to the beauty of family life. Except for one issue, the circumstances might well have been described as perfect, notwithstanding Ben Armstrong's proper insistence that perfection in family matters is never achieved.

Three years ago, Nell Armstrong, casually looking about for some part-time activity, discovered a group of women working on a metropolitan busing program. Not one to keep up, as she said, with local and city politics, Nell nevertheless had for some time been intrigued by the problems in city schools, especially in those communities where black families lived. She never pretended to understand the political and economic complexities of the problems, but a rather simple sentiment rose up in her when she read about these families or saw them in films on television.

They needed help, she thought, in areas of health and housing, but these were matters for the government. Finding good schools for these children was something else.

For months her desire to do something went unfilled. Always she found herself musing about the subject rather than involving herself in some form of work. Then the opportunity to sit in on planning meetings at the neighborhood school arose, and the sheer closeness of the school made it impossible for her to refuse this chance.

Some twenty years after her own graduation from high school, Nell Armstrong found herself seated around a table with seven women her own age but all experienced in community action programs in education. Their project was one in which city and suburban students might be transferred to one another's schools and communities. There was no sense, the women agreed, for the suburbs to keep out of the turmoil that school desegregation was causing. It was too easy looking down one's nose at the city, pretending that suburban families had nothing to do with segregation.

At first, Nell found the weekly planning meetings interesting, if not wholly stimulating. While she never admitted it, the mere gathering of the women satisfied her needs for companionship and intellectual excitement. The women were highly intelligent, all of them college graduates, a fact which early on seemed intimidating. Their capacity for managing family and career responsibilities as well as civic obligations dazzled her. Gradually, she became absorbed in the work. The women were rounding up volunteers and making contacts with school officials in the local community and the city. As one of the women said, their little group was "taking off."

The increased activity frightened Nell. Would there be enough time left, she wondered, for the children and Ben, for her parents and in-laws? When would she shop? How would she be able to sit home waiting for repairmen and service calls when the group needed her more and more each week? They couldn't expect her to walk out on her family in the evenings! Yet the group was now proposing regular Tuesday night meetings. And if she was anxious about the increasing responsibilities and the

commitment it implied, she was also feeling accepted, needed by the other women. Sensing her apprehensiveness, they reminded her that she was the only city-born one among them, the only one who had a feeling for the problems they were addressing. Besides, what else was she doing that could compete with their integration project?

Ben and the children offered only encouragement at first. Ben hesitated when she told him about the regular weekly meetings, but Nell assured him that her first allegiance was to the family. He questioned the position the group was taking. What was the point, he asked, of suburban women getting involved in a school problem fifteen miles away? What difference could it make in the operation the city was developing? While his resistance seemed minimal, Nell found herself prepared to combat his every point. She cited statistics and told him of the ideas the education group had been discussing, and mentioned the people who had offered support, a list that included rather prominent men and women in the community, doctors, lawyers, university professors, ministers.

"Sounds like a swanky crowd," Ben would say, half joking, half serious. "Even if you nice ladies can't integrate those schools, we'll at least be ten steps closer to getting into one of the swish country clubs. You don't have any plans, do you, Darling, of taking *our* children out of school and busing them into the city?"

Nell would smile. Her ability to recall entire discussions of the educational group was uncanny. She could hear Beth Sizer or Bonnie Pettit answering her husband.

"No," she would answer. "We're not taking anybody's children out of any school. At least not yet. We've played with the idea, though."

"Well, if you have to play," Ben would respond smartly, "play with somebody else's children. Not mine!"

"If you aren't part of the solution," Nell would say provocatively, "you're part of the problem, Darling."

While both could sense a growing bitterness in their talks, Nell assumed it was because of Ben's displeasure at her leaving home two evenings each week. Occasionally he would ask the

children whether they minded their mother's absence. Twelve-year-old Elaine said it seemed different but didn't mind it. The older children, seventeen-year-old Laura and sixteen-year-old Tim barely noticed; they were too busy with homework and other activities. "Well, *I* mind," Ben would tell them in the half-serious, half-joking manner to which the children rarely responded. "I think I'm beginning to mind a lot!"

After seven months with the educational group, Nell felt deeply committed to the work which occupied her as much as twenty hours a week. The telephoning, mailing, planning, and endless discussions with city and suburban officials had become a part-time job. Never in her life had she been a member of such a group, never had she received such gratification from her associates and from a constantly growing number of friends. A tangible benefit was a sense of competence—a belief in her ability to do worthwhile work and to be knowledgeable about the requirements of the work. She told a friend: "I never thought of myself as smart in any way. I was always the nice, polite girl who never gave her parents or teachers any problems. The nice old middle-of-the-road kid nobody had to worry about and probably nobody noticed. That was the goal a lot of people believed in, in those days. Don't make trouble, get through school, marry a nice man, have children. If you're lucky, you might even wind up with a big house in the suburbs. That's what my parents wanted for me. It was just expected that they wanted more from my brothers. They wanted a lot from Ben, too. Good old Nell never let them down.

"But I never minded it that much. That was my problem. I didn't know there were things in the world, ways to experience what was going on, that I might have liked if I had known about them. Like, in all the years of our marriage, when Ben and I were at a party and he'd be in the middle of a conversation, I didn't mind not being able to say anything. I didn't feel bad or dumb or anything. I just knew my role was to keep my mouth shut. So I did. There might have been times when I wished I could enter in some way, but mostly I knew I didn't have any ideas worth bringing up. So I sat, like the proverbial bump on the log. I remember once in a while asking Ben, do you mind

that I don't talk at these parties, 'cause lots of the other women did. But he always said he thought that without saying anything I was one of the smartest people there, that most people just talk and don't have anything to say. I believed him. I thought he was telling the truth. I didn't feel patronized.

"But all that's changed now. I know what I say is just as important as what anybody else says. I *feel* that way, and that's all that matters. I know when people start talking about busing and school integration and metropolitanization, and what suburbs are doing about all the problems, I have something to say. Any way the discussion goes I know I will have something to contribute. In the meetings there are always people asking me what I've found out about something, or what I think our group should do. I don't remember once ever being called on in class because someone thought I had anything interesting to say. They'd surprise me, to find out if I'd actually read the book, but nobody believed I knew anything valuable. I doubt they even knew I had a brain. Sad to say, that includes my parents, and my husband.

"Here I was all those years, telling my daughters how important it was to be well-educated. They'd ask me, how come we live in the suburbs when their grandparents still live in the city? I'd say because the schools are better here and your daddy and I want you to be in the best schools, and all along, if they paid even the slightest attention to me, they saw a dumb, uneducated mother without the slightest idea in her head other than what to cook for dinner or where to buy food so you can save five cents.

"The meetings changed that. I hope a lot comes of all this, too. But if absolutely nothing happens in this town, if it turns out that not a single black child goes to school in this community and not a single white child goes to the city to be with their kids, then at least I can say *I* have changed. I really have, you know. More than I dare tell anybody right at this time. Even my own children."

If the educational work had become a part-time job in March, by June it was full-time. Discussions and programs were held almost every day, and it was commonplace for meetings to be

scheduled three times a week. Ben became antagonistic, his temper strained even more by incessant telephone calls. Nell was either on the phone or away at some meeting. Many calls were from men, something which troubled him, and he questioned her about each new name. Nell found him alternating between bitterness and childlike jealousy in which he related to her as his mother. The jealousy especially irritated her and she began to despise playing mother and wife. The sense of openness and freedom she felt with her colleagues only accentuated her distaste for family roles. She was rarely irritable with Ben and the children; she met her responsibilities, even enjoyed their evenings and weekends together, but the investment of her feelings in the family seemed less intense. She found her typical ways with the children to be remarkable. How could she have treated them as if their every breath or swallow was more important to her than the protection of her own body, her own well-being. As she herself said, she didn't feel separated from those who had always been closest to her, she was just no longer owned by them. She would remain a good wife and mother, but to be competent in these roles did not require that she be owned by the people she served. She expected little from the children, but Ben would have to change.

It sounds, a friend told her one brilliant September afternoon driving home from a conference on metropolitanization, like she was giving Ben an ultimatum.

The word surprised Nell. "No, I don't think I'm doing that, although his attitude on integration is beginning to make me a little sick. It's starting to bother the oldest children as well. In fact, it really *is* making me sick. We've found something we'll never agree on. He is totally opposed to busing in all forms and absolutely will not support the group's projects. Fifty crumby little kids coming into this town sends him up the wall. And the thought of some of our precious children going on a bus to be with black kids after school, not even during school hours, makes him go insane. He won't even talk about it any more. It's like, you bring up the subject of racial integration and he gets a chemical reaction. It takes over his whole body. And he keeps going to the children for support. Even Elaine. Can you imagine

this grown man trying to convince a twelve-year-old that she should hate racial integration the same way he does and for the same reasons?

"You know that lovely little family named Armstrong with all their wonderful liberal attitudes and charming ways that used to live in our house? Well, they don't seem to live there anymore. Or if they do, I haven't seen them in a long time." Nell Armstrong looked furtively around for cars that might have sneaked into the lanes adjoining the one her long blue station wagon was in.

"It's getting awfully bad," she went on. "Worse than I thought it would. It's at that miserable point where you want to look for allies, even in your own home. It's a ghastly temptation. I despise it in Ben. It's childish, and when you think that the major issue is racial integration, as perfectly crazy as that sounds, it's unbelievable. I don't want my husband telling my children why they shouldn't be going to school with black children, how if you bring black children into their schools they won't be getting as good an education as they should be, as they *used* to before these other kids came.

"Here you have a country not only debating the merits of busing, but thousands of people possibly willing to kill to get their ideas across. Look what's going on in these cities where busing programs are going into action, or just being planned. Look how people are getting their ideas heard: by hitting, killing, turning over buses. Imagine all the people looking at us from Europe and seeing white Americans having a war with black Americans. But in this little crazy suburb that no one outside this state has ever heard of, Mrs. Armstrong is fighting with Mr. Armstrong over the same question, racial integration, and the arguments are getting so vicious their whole marriage is beginning to feel it. So now you have the fate of all these black children to think of, and the fate of my three children too. That's what it comes to. I'm beginning to lead two lives: Nell the school integrator, and Nell the family integrator. I wish to God someone could look into the future and tell me whether I'm going to win either one of these battles."

Ben Armstrong was beginning to awaken during the night, thinking about his wife's work with what he called her phoney liberal friends, and found himself drinking more than he ever had. At lunch, when friends would listen, he released the anger that never seemed to subside.

"Every damn night of my life it's the same thing. School this, racial that, busing, busing, busing. Suddenly she's an expert. You raise a simple point, an objection—no, you're wrong. She's got the answer. She knows the way it should be done. Excuse me, the *only* way it can be done. You think people in this country are debating busing? Not us. I just sit there and listen. According to her there's nothing to debate. I don't mind a good argument, even between a husband and wife. People who don't argue, I don't know, I don't trust them. They're too calm. You even mention the word busing and you're going to get an argument. You have to. But where I draw the line is when you bring the kids into it. Parents have to teach their children. But in something like busing you don't teach them. You lay out the facts and let them decide. But she's brainwashing them. She's telling them that with busing there's only one position to take. Then in the next breath she's going on about freedom of speech and the good old democratic system. This is what I've been putting up with now for a year. We don't have discussions anymore, we have lectures in political science, and the students, that's me and the children, we don't ask questions. We're just supposed to sit there and agree with everything.

"Well I won't take it. I'm not making any claims about a man is master of his own house. I haven't once raised the question of how come I work and she's out doing all this *volunteer* stuff. I do my share, I don't question what others are doing until they infringe on my rights. And brother, these are my rights. I'm not concerned about any black kids coming to this suburb or that suburb, I'm concerned about whether I have the strength and the stomach to put up with what's happening in *my* house, in *my* living room where all these people come for their meetings, and in my bedroom, goddammit! Your wife wants to work, she works. She wants to do volunteer work on some project, like schools or hospitals, fine. These women do fantastic work. But

my opinion on racial busing matters just as much as anyone's, including hers, and *I* don't want this busing, not in the city, not in the suburbs, not in the country!

"These black people know *exactly* how to get white people to jump up and dance for them. They can make an appeal like nobody. You don't see these suburban ladies doing anything for the Indians, do you, and God only knows those people have it far worse than any black person. But no, a black person opens his mouth and the Nell Armstrongs of the world are jumping through hoops. The country's become a goddam circus with phoney white liberals jumping through hoops like a bunch of trained dogs. She's a goddam trained dog. She never had an idea in her head about what was happening in her neighborhood as a kid. She never heard of the town we're living in when she was eighteen. Neither one of us knew anything. She went to grammar school, high school, college for about a year, that's all, all of them less than five miles from where she was born. And now, to listen to her, you'd think she was this famous professor, a political scientist at least, making all these pronouncements. You and I, my friends, we're the dummies. I hope you've heard that. We're the racists you know. We're the ones that stand in the way of progress. I'll bet you didn't know that. Oh yes, we're the enemies. We're the ones who have to be convinced because the way we lead our lives, making money for our families, that's the biggest obstacle to the missionaries. See how much I've learned? You guys didn't know anything about this busing thing. You just *thought* you did. But we're dummies! Racist dummies!"

The men laugh and lean back heavily in their chairs. One sips at a drink, the other lights up a cigarette and brushes specks of tobacco off his wrinkled grey suit.

"Oh yes," Ben Armstrong is saying, "if the communists were supposed to be the enemies in the McCarthy witch hunt, then little old us, poor slobs who went to Korea, we're the enemies now. What I would like to say to my wife is that no one I know, not one, is anybody's enemy. Everybody's just a product of their environment, coupled with a little luck and hard work. There are men in this restaurant now, *and* women, who started with a little, some with a little more, some with a lot maybe, but they

kept going. That's what they wanted apparently. Nobody in the world, with the exception of a few maniacs, want people to be poor or have their kids going to a rotten school. I don't know anybody who wants harm to come to anyone else. They merely want to lead their lives, not get in anyone's way, not let people get in their way. That's asking very little, isn't it true?"

The men nod. "You go to Korea, Ben?" one of them asks with surprise.

"No. You know what I mean. Nobody wants trouble. For God sakes, men our age have seen enough violence to last for the rest of the world's history. So it happens that I don't want my kids to be face to face with violent situations. I want them to have a nice life in terms of what I can give them. All I can give them is a start. If they want to rebel, take it out on their mother and me, that's their problem. I gave them a start, what they do with it is out of my hands. You know what I mean? You know how many clients I have setting up wills, leaving their kids money after they die? Everyone, right? Everyone leaves their kids dough. Why is that? Because they're not rich. They haven't got that much to give them, so the kids have to wait for the insurance. But the rich man starts giving right away. Why not? I'd do it too if I had the capital. I'd love to watch my kids have a good time with a little money in their hands. Not now. When they're a little older. But why do they have to wait for the old man to die. Let 'em enjoy it.

"So now a kid of mine comes to me in twenty, twenty-five years and he says, 'Dad, I'm really furious with you.' 'What'd I do?' 'Dad, why didn't you send us to an integrated school, you know with a lot of black kids in it?' 'There were black kids in the school you went to,' I tell him. 'Ten, fifteen, that's all. How come you let us grow up in a segregated neighborhood?' Okay? That's what he says. You know what I tell him? I say, 'I got two points for you. That's all. Two points. Number one, I did the very best that was available. You ate good, you slept every night in a bed that was warm and dry, you had the right clothes, you had a great time on vacations, you went to the best schools in this country. The best. That's number one. Point number two, hindsight doesn't cost a nickel. If you thought it was such a

lousy school and there should have been more black children in it, can I ask *you*, how come you didn't raise that with me twenty-five years ago? And I'll throw in a third point too,' " Ben Armstrong grinned at his friends, " 'since it ain't costing you nothing. You loved every minute of the luxuries that were given to you. Every minute. If you're angry about it *now*, when you're forty years old, I'd say you never grew up at all and that's the saddest thing I can say. When the time was at hand to make decisions about school, your mother and I chose the best school, black kids or not. It wasn't our role to be worried about racial integration and segregation. Our role was to take care of each other and you and your sisters. Where the hell your mother went wrong in those days I'll never understand!' "

Ben glanced up at the men, a look of confusion on his face. It seemed that he had vaulted himself forward in time and was surprised to find himself again in the present. Or perhaps the expression of confusion had nothing to do with time. Perhaps he had just made some crucial decisions.

Sixteen-year-old Tim Armstrong is a tall thin boy with fine brown hair that he constantly pushes back from his eyes. There is a fresh quality of his skin that makes him look as if he has just bathed. His parents claim he has part of his brains in his hands, his finger dexterity being extraordinary. He does beautiful wood carving, is an outstanding table tennis player, sculpts, sews, and as a child even convinced his grandmother to teach him to knit. He mastered the basics of weaving in a short time and has learned plumbing and electrical work. When he was twelve he managed to disassemble a small television set and then reassemble it. To everyone's surprise it not only worked, but one station came in more sharply than before. For that job his father paid him five dollars. With the money he bought a model of a schooner which he built in less than a week. The model sits on his father's office desk. It is a beautiful piece that one would attribute to a professional model builder, certainly not to a twelve-year-old.

His seventeenth birthday in February of his junior year in high school marked one and a half years that his mother had

worked with the educational group. Tim occasionally spoke about her efforts, but mainly he overheard her conversations and snatches of the weekly home meetings. How much thought he gave to her activities and what the entire family called her "new politics" no one knew. It was his oldest sister, Laura, a freshman at college, who seemed to be her mother's strongest supporter. Almost every week something else came in the mail from her, an article or newspaper clipping on the subject of racism or school desegregation. Once a large poster arrived announcing a march for desegregation. The march already had been held and Nell telephoned Laura to say the next time an event of this sort took place she would like to go.

As far as anyone knew, Tim Armstrong paid little attention to all the talk about racial desegregation in his home. When the subject came up at the dinner table, as it always did when his father was absent, he listened politely to his mother, but rarely spoke. Nell was upset by the fact that only she and Laura maintained interest in the busing and metropolitanization programs. Elaine and Tim were old enough to appreciate the seriousness of school desegregation. It affected them more than it ever would her, she told her friends, although it was hardly in her own children's behalf that she worked. How a boy like Tim, who was so sensitive and thoughtful, could let the issue of integration pass him by was beyond her. Perhaps, she would say, this was the curse of living in the suburbs.

"The young people are so isolated from anything as real and important as busing they don't get interested in it. Maybe that's the reason why black families have it so bad, because rich white families have set up lives where they think only of themselves and their children and let black families, and especially the children, suffer. Tim doesn't even read about it. He doesn't even look at the newspapers. We can be watching television when it comes on and I see him turn away. They'll show films of busing and *that's* when my nonreading son suddenly picks up a book. You don't need to be a psychologist to figure it out. He and his father despise me for this. The two of them, they're the same blood, the same flesh. They don't know whether to hate *me* or the black kids. They share a narrowness, I'm sorry to say.

They're both alike, living with blinders. They're out for themselves, each of them with his little talents. My husband knows
nothing but figures, my son knows nothing but his models and
building. To get them interested in what's happening in schools,
including his, is like running into a stone wall. These people are
right when they say in their speeches that you don't work at
changing the society, you change the minds of the people in
your family. Well, I've always got Laura. She's got good values.
She won't end up with blinders, and she won't go through all those
empty years sitting at parties without a single worthwhile thing
to say. And Elaine's too young still to know how she'll turn out."

All of this would be said with resignation and a trace of
sadness. The family's fate was becoming clearer; she felt the
inevitability of accepting what befell her. "Everything has its
price," and, "With every deal there's a trade-off," had become
her favorite expressions. She acknowledged that she had
learned both from Ben. What went unmentioned in her conversations with friends was the worsening condition of her relationship with her husband. The marriage was disintegrating. Away
at school, Laura could feel tension in the phone conversations,
although the letters from her parents contained no hints of the
problem. Ben had grown close to a small number of men who
knew all about his hours of moroseness, silence, and angry
tirades against his wife. One of the friends, a lawyer, promised
Ben he would be around to help if "things got that bad."

A marriage everyone had viewed as ideal was unraveling
seemingly over the matter of busing. By Tim's seventeenth
birthday, Ben refused to have the topic mentioned in his home.
In outbursts of fury, he called the black children in Nell's
program niggers, and her colleagues phoney nigger lovers. He
screamed at her for using his hard-earned money and tenuous
status in the community as means for improving the lot of
people she knew absolutely nothing about. He accused her of
being caught up in a fad and of being utterly disloyal to the
white working-class families in the city, the very families she
knew as neighbors when she was young. She was "as phoney as
a three-dollar bill and as politically sophisticated as a four-year-
old." Elaine had better sense and understanding than she did.

In retaliation, Nell accused him of being a racist of the worst order. He was a self-interested money-crazy man who cared nothing about people's feelings and life circumstances, only on how he could save rich men money on their income tax. He was exactly the kind of person who, because he could never care about anybody else's suffering, the integration movement had to pass over. There was no sense wasting time with people who could never learn and never change. "Still," she said, "I feel a lot more sorry about the state of the schools and those families than I do about what's happening in this house."

"Then move there, go rescue them!" Ben would shout. "For God sakes, if you love them so much, be one. Marry one. Maybe that's what's behind it all. Have an affair. Get yourself one of those beautiful football players. But do me a favor. When you tell your children you're having a big romance with O. J. Simpson and you're leaving your husband, let me be there. I want to see their response. You better invite your precious daughter in from college to hear about it too."

"Poor Ben," Nell would say softly. "Does everything a white wants to do for a black have to come down to something sexual? You can do better than that. Don't you think it's a little late in the game to start bringing up the oldest stereotypes in the book!"

"I'll tell you something, Nell," Ben would answer, livid with rage and wanting to hit her. "I didn't realize any of this was a game. I actually took it rather seriously, our marriage. I never looked at it as a *game*. I'm sorry you did."

"I didn't mean that our marriage was a game."

"Then busing's a game?"

"Don't play lawyer, Ben. You know what I meant."

At last he would calm down, as though catching her air of resignation. "I'm sorry, Nell. I haven't understood anything you have said or done for the last year and a half. I don't know what this busing thing means to you. I didn't stop you although I thought it was wasteful and the most hypocritical nonsense I have ever seen. But, you want to do it, then go ahead, with my blessing. But without *me*. Okay? Without *me!*"

"That's your proposition?"

"You got it, baby."

"Are you actually saying, Ben, it's marriage, the family, this home, or my involvement with busing?" She could not have sounded more incredulous.

"That's exactly it." He smiled at her. "All the lady has to do is to make a decision. Either the little bus with the little blacks, or little Ben with the money. You think on it, okay? Go to bed and think on it."

Then they would hear the sound of the living room clock. The silence from the study meant that Elaine and Tim had turned off the television set in order to listen to them.

"I've thought, Ben."

By late March, Ben Armstrong had moved into an apartment in the city. Both he and Nell had arranged for attorneys to settle the complexities of their divorce. Neither felt an urgency about a settlement but accepted its inevitability. The physical separation lessened their anger, they even laughed together occasionally on the telephone.

"It's really the busing that brought us down, isn't it?" Ben would ask.

"It really is," Nell would reply kindly.

"The world's out there screaming, everyone's at each other's throat, and our family goes quietly to hell."

"It wasn't so quietly," she reminded him.

"How the children doing?" he would ask, although he visited regularly with them on weekends.

"The children?"

"You *do* remember the children, don't you Nell?"

She would become slightly perturbed. "Yes, Ben, I remember the children."

"So how are they?"

"Today they're fine, that means tomorrow they'll cry. Okay, you happy? They're destroyed by this."

"Am I happy?" His voice would be barely audible. "A thirty-year-old man dying of cancer with one minute to live is happier than I am. Honest to Christ. He's a happier man."

"I'm sorry, Ben."

"I hope to God that all the black kids you're so worried about are happier than I am."

Laura Armstrong was distressed by the news of her parents' separation but not surprised. She said she felt it coming and assumed they would wait until Tim entered college. Elaine, at thirteen, was frightened and sad. For several months her school work dipped and she became short-tempered, a rare quality for her. Tim Armstrong evidenced the deepest hurt and anger. At first he vowed that he would prohibit his parents from getting a divorce. Then he claimed that if his father moved out, he too would leave. If his parents had no desire to live with each other, then he had no interest in living with either of them. In the end, as his parents listened patiently to the children express emotions they never believed the children possessed, it was Tim's words that hurt most.

"I'll stay with my mother until college 'cause that's the arrangement. But when I leave, I'll leave both of them for good. With money or without, I can't consider where either of them live as my home. Maybe I feel sorry for them. I don't have the faintest idea why they had to be so cruel to each other, but we got hit in the crossfire. They talk about us now, but they didn't think about us then, otherwise they might have worked it out differently. I admire my mother for the work she's done and how she's changed her life. She's grown up more than any of the rest of us. She's educated herself like nobody I've ever seen. But I remember what she said about me. She was disappointed because I wasn't involved with all her busing programs. I think it's great what she does, but she didn't have to forget me or look down her nose at me while she was doing it. She's guilty of the same thing she accused other people of. She was like a bad teacher, giving up on me. I wasn't turning out like she wanted, so she gave up on me. But how could I get so involved with her busing when my father was being left out of it? She was saying, if you're for busing, you come on my side. If you're against busing, you go on your stupid father's side. How could I win?

"My father is just as bad. He laughed at her for her work. He looked down his nose at her like she looked down her nose at

me. It's all right to be involved in politics, but you can't start feeling so superior. She doesn't have any special claims. My father though, should have listened to her. He couldn't grow up. He's still Mr. high-school big shot. He hasn't changed in twenty-five years. If his friends don't agree with him, he goes out and finds another group of friends who will. That's really childish. Worst of all, he's a bigot. She gets too carried away, thinking no one else has the right to disagree with her, but he's a bigot. He hates black people. I never saw that my mother loves them so much, but he hates them. He'd cross the street to avoid them. I know he would.

"So, I guess they got what they wanted, otherwise they wouldn't be where they are now. She's working for busing and he's probably running around looking for girls my age. Isn't life wonderful? She's wrong, you know, if she thinks poor black families are the only ones in this country with problems. Rich white families have problems too. Plenty of them. Maybe what the old Armstrongs can do is bus me and my sisters from my mother to my father one day and then back to my mother the next. Maybe I'll invent a new thing, busing for family integration!"

7

TWO MORE BOYS ON THE BUS

Cassie McDonough's mother Ellen got the news first unofficially by phone, then two days later officially in the mail. Cassie himself, who is eleven, barely remembers the details. He remembers walking home from school on a spring afternoon in 1974 and finding his mother fretting in a way that he had never seen. He didn't speak much with her; he merely watched her as she telephoned her friends, pacing about the small kitchen and almost pulling the phone out of the wall. That night, his father too began what Cassie calls "fretting," the same way his mother had that afternoon. They told him not to listen and sent him to his room. "You'll find out soon enough if the letter comes," they said. The letter came. It was the official announcement that Clarence Charles McDonough III had been selected one of a group of students to be transferred starting in September. Cassie McDonough, from the South Boston district of Boston, was going to be bused to school.

If Ellen McDonough was upset by the news, her husband Clarence, a tall handsome man with reddish curly hair and a long straight nose, was outraged. "They did it to me," he yelled one evening when I visited their home. "They went and did it to me, those goddam sons of bitches. I told you they would. I told you there'd be no running from 'em. You lead your life perfect as a pane of glass, go to church, work forty hours a week at the same job, year in year out, keep your complaints to yourself,

and they still do it to you. They're forcing that boy to go to school miles from here in a dangerous area, to a school no one knows a damn thing about just so they can bring these other kids in, kids who don't belong around here, don't want to be around here. Someone's got to explain it to me. I'll listen to anybody, but someone's got to tell me how this Garrity guy, this big deal judge, gets all this power to move people around, right the hell out of their neighborhood while everybody else in the world comes out of it free and equal. It's a goddam joke, busing my kid half-way around Boston so that a bunch of politicians can end up their careers with a clear conscience. You know why they're busing? Because the kindly old mayor of this city wants to be President, and if you want to be President you get yourself involved in national issues. So who does he pick on? The rich? Sure, the rich. He picks on the people right here, this street. What the hell does he care about us for? What the hell does he care about South Boston for? We don't vote for him, he ain't losing no votes by busing our kids around the city."

"You going to fight it?" I asked.

"Yeah, I'm going to fight it," Clarence McDonough replied sarcastically. "And after I win that, I'm going to run for the Pope!"

During the month of August, I met regularly with Cassie McDonough. He was wearing his hair longer now than he did a year ago and his voice seemed to be getting lower and sonorous. In September, a few days before the start of school, he was confused and frightened. At times when we spoke there was anger in his voice, but mostly he was unsure how to think about this new adventure. He had lined up friends who would be going with him to the new school, and had spent time figuring out how to remain friendly with the boys who would still be at the neighborhood school. Three days before school opened, Cassie and I met at a local spa for a sandwich. He was frightened, and his appearance, for the first time in our three years of friendship, was disheveled.

"I've been fighting," he said. "Kid I know called me a nigger lover 'cause I'm going to school over there, so I punched him out."

"You win?"

"Not really. Nobody won. Maybe I won a little. I just hope that being in this new school doesn't mean I got to do a lot of fighting. I don't even know if there's going to be more of them or more of us. My mother says there will be more of them which is weird 'cause I ain't never been with so many of 'em before. Walking around here and going to stores and stuff you see colored people, but going to school with 'em, that's different. Eating with 'em, in the cafeteria, you know, at the same tables, being on the same teams with 'em, sitting next to 'em. Like this one kid told me that, like, colored kids get talking this strange way and you can't understand 'em. I figured that could be too, 'cause how do you know if you can talk to someone when you ain't never talked to 'em before. Then, when they dress different than you, and have their hair different from you, how you going to be friends with people like that? I don't have nothing against 'em. How could I? I don't even know 'em. But I seen them all around and they're different. All you got to do is look at 'em and you can see that.

"And another thing. They don't live over here. *We* live over here. They live where they live. My dad says it isn't so different over there but it isn't as nice. They don't have lots of money. Lot of their fathers don't work so they don't have lots of money. We don't have lots of money either. Maybe that's how we're a little alike. But we look different to them too, so they don't like us and we don't like them. But that's okay for two groups, you know, who don't have to see each other. But when you have to see each other, then you might get a war. And if I have to fight in a war then I'll fight over here where *my* friends are, not over there where *their* friends are. That only makes sense. You go where you have the best chance. They beat up white kids over there. So if they don't want us, and all they're going to do is beat up on us 'cause they don't want us over there, then I can't see why the government's forcing us to go there. Maybe they got kids around here who want to go there, and colored kids over there who want to come here. If they do, then the government should let 'em. But if they don't want to, then they shouldn't have to."

I spent several minutes explaining to Cassie the reasons for

the forced busing program. I spoke about school desegregation, the fact that black children his age had never been given fair opportunities in school, and how those people making the busing decisions were not punishing the white children. Cassie heard me, but his thoughts were elsewhere.

"I've been thinking," he began, "ever since we found out about the busing, you know, about going to school with colored kids, everytime I think about this new school—I don't call it *my* school yet—all I think about is colored boys but never colored girls. And I also never think about what the teachers are going to be like. I thought all the teachers would be white but maybe they aren't. But I never think about learning anything over there. My mother says the whole thing is unfair. She says it's like a big experiment, and everybody's going to lose. I hope I don't lose my teeth in some fight. Some kids maybe are going to die. They got kids, littler than me, carrying knives and guns. So some people really could die. Boy, would my old man go crazy if some kid from around here dies. He's always saying the government doesn't care whose kid dies, just so it isn't one of their kids. I don't want to die. Those other kids might not care about it, but I do. I want to go to school around here and if I have to fight around here, for fun or 'cause some guy starts something, okay. But I don't want to fight just to be alive. And especially not for no experiment!"

Two of Cassie McDonough's friends were far more bitter about their assignment in an integrated school. One week before the start of the busing program, Joey Billingham insisted he would quit school before he would let anyone send him anywhere. "They can put a gun to my head," he said, "and I wouldn't go. That school is three miles from my house. I wouldn't go, wouldn't go three feet to no school on a bus. I walk to the school around here or I don't go. Nobody's busing me just so some niggers can get a better deal. I didn't set up the schools. I didn't make 'em like they are. No one I ever knew had anything to do with it. Niggers don't like their schools, let *them* change 'em, but they don't have the right to tell me what to do. Kids don't got any rights anyways. The only right we got is to go to school near where we live. If they think they're going to change

that, they're out of their minds. I ain't moving a step. I ain't going no three miles on a bus just so some nigger kids get it better. Why do I have to have it worse just so's they can get it better. I don't see that nothing's fair about that. I ain't going!"

Jack Griff, who palled around as much with Cassie's brother Ken as he did with Cassie, said he would now have to carry a knife to school. "Everybody knows what's happening," Jack told me as Cassie and Joey listened. "Everybody in the city's rooting for the niggers. One minute they don't give 'em nothing, next minute they give 'em everything, including *our* schools. Maybe I'll go, maybe I won't, but if I'm going, I'm going protected. There ain't a nigger kid in this city goes to school without a knife, or a gun too maybe. Every one of 'em carries something. That's the truth. You ask 'em. They'll tell you. They come armed so we're coming armed. People who voted for busing, all they wanted was a war between them and us. They'll get it too, 'specially if one of them starts something with me. Them kids have no right going to the same school with us. If they didn't learn their lesson before, we'll have to try all over again. They don't belong around here, not healthy and going to school anyway."

The day following my talk with Cassie I visited the home of Francine and Ronald Dearborn. Francie is a woman in her mid-thirties, black, the mother of three young boys, one of whom, eleven-year-old Claudell, was preparing to attend a school located in South Boston. The Dearborns, too, had been chosen to participate in the busing program. During the week prior to the start of busing, Francie's friends and relatives stopped by her cheery four-room Roxbury apartment, some of them bringing food, all of them wanting to be in touch with her, and with Claudell too. All three sons had been especially quiet during these days, none of them wanting to talk much about what everyone in the house was calling Claudell's school trip.

Ronald Dearborn, Claudell's father, spoke little about busing. He read the morning and evening editions of both Boston newspapers, and he waited, somewhat surprised by how little the school had prepared his own child for the busing program.

On several weekends, always during the day, he drove around the area of Claudell's new school, inspecting the streets and homes, and seeing the small neighborhood businesses. "It's a long way," he said, "even by car. Let's hope they keep those buses running fine. I'd hate to think what would happen if they broke down some night over there. If white folks don't look kindly to having black folks attending their schools, then they sure won't like to see a bunch of black youngsters parked outside their home all night."

Francie told me that in years past her husband might have uttered these same words and laughed at the thought of white parents up in arms over the presence of fifty stranded black children. Now, since the busing program and Claudell's participation in it, black children stranded in a white neighborhood was no longer an amusing image. "Ronald's not fearing for the boy's life," Francie explained. "He and I are just plain fearing. You have to take steps like this, it may not be the best way or the easiest way. But you start like a baby: small steps, careful easy steps, your parents watching with their arms out, ready to catch you, *if* they can reach you when you fall. Ronald's not worried about the falling. When you're black you know all about falling, and what you don't know this country teaches you mighty fast, even when you go to schools where everyone is black like we did. Falling's easy. It's like they say, it's the bump when you hit. That's what we worry about. Busing's a fall, and you have to hope that no one, not one of ours, not one of theirs, gets their head split open.

"It's an experiment," she sighed, using the same word Ellen McDonough had used and passed on to Cassie. "They don't call it that, but everyone knows what it is. You manipulate people, bus them here, bus them there, measure how *we're* doing, measure how *they're* doing, count the casualties, maybe even find out—heaven forbid—whether any of the children are reading better or talking better or counting better than they did a year ago. When the experiment's over, folks making the experiment decide what it means. It's just as simple as that, except for one thing. Those who liked busing in the first place, are going to decide the experiment worked. Those who never did

like the idea, they'll say it never was any good to begin with and it still isn't. So it's an experiment that only fools get to be a part of. I say fools not because they're dumb, but because they all know how it's going to come out. Those folks over there, they know, just like folks over here know. We all hear the same stories, read the same newspapers, listen to the same shows. We all care for the lives of our children. That part of it everybody knows. So the only part of the experiment my husband and I really care about is, will those folks in charge be careful with the children? Before they guarantee me that Claudell's going to end up in a better position, I want them to guarantee me that if I put him on that bus every morning, Monday, Tuesday, Wednesday, Thursday, Friday, some very responsible human being will make sure that he comes home safely every afternoon, Monday, Tuesday, Wednesday, Thursday, Friday. When that part's taken care of, then we'll discuss reading scores, racial desegregation, America's efforts at doing something worthwhile for its minority people. Anyway, Claudell says he wants to talk to you."

Claudell Dearborn wasn't so certain that September afternoon whether or not he did want to talk to me. Dressed in bright blue pants and matching sportshirt, and wearing a wide gold band high on his right arm, he looked at me as we sat on the front steps of his house with an expression I had never seen. I'll talk about my feelings, he seemed to be saying, but I'm just not sure any of this is doing any good for anybody.

"See over there," he said, pointing to a filling station part way down the block. "That's where the kids from here going to meet on school mornings. Parents drop us there, then they got another group of people going to walk us to the bus and ride with us. That's our protection. White folks going to do it too, they said. Makes you think you're some famous person. When I was a kid my dad took me to this theater somewhere, you know, and somebody real important came in. I think it was Martin Luther King. Anyway, this man walked in there with a whole lot of people walking all around him, protecting him like. Now they're doing it for us. Makes me scared thinking about what we need all that protection for. I know what it is, only I get scared thinking about it. You can know all this stuff in your head, but

down here," he patted his stomach, "it don't care about what you *know*. My stomach says, 'Look out, man. Keep a look out for everything that's going on, and everybody too!'

"My mom says this is the way it has to be. She says children will be all right, only they get their ideas from their mothers and fathers. She's trying to make me feel better. I know they got kids over there waiting to see us walking into their schools. They call 'em their schools too. They got it in their heads they *own* those schools, and they aren't about to go renting them to us just 'cause a judge says you got to let them other kids come in. They're getting ready to keep us out of there."

"You know that?"

"For sure I know that, man. You think they *like* all this? They didn't *ask* for it. They're taking their orders same as us. And somebody's going to get hurt. Even the littler kids. All you got around this city now is a bunch of old folks telling young folks what's going to happen, and young folks looking at each other like to say, 'Let me out of here, man. I never asked for none of this.' That's what they're saying. 'I ain't never asked for this to happen.' Least that's what I hear."

"Don't you want to be bused over there, then, Claudell?"

"Sure I do. It's better over there, least that's what everyone keeps saying. Besides, even if it ain't, it ain't fair that one group of people get to do what they want, and another group's got to sit around and pick up the pieces nobody wants. My dad says black folks pick up the pieces. He says, their folks eat the chickens and us folks eat the pickens." Claudell looked down at his hands folded in his lap. "Busing's just got to be, man. Got to be. We got it coming to us. We got to open up ourselves, spread out. Get in to this city, man. Move in to all those places we can't go at night, you know. Go to good schools, live in good places like white folks got. *You* got all that stuff. My folks don't, so they want it for me and my brothers. That's why they're busing us. Anyway, I been scared before. This ain't no first time for me. You guess they'll have lots of police around there in the schools?"

"I imagine so."

"I guess they have to. Hope they watch out for *us* like they watch out for *them*."

During the autumn months, I visited with the McDonoughs and Dearborns almost weekly. Both the boys, Cassie and Claudell, were keeping records of their experiences, writing down some of their thoughts about this special school year. Both said writing helped them to understand things a bit better. Their parents too, were eager to read these personal notes.

By November, Mr. and Mrs. McDonough were members of two community organizations opposing busing and attempting to pressure the existing powers to reduce the scope of the following year's busing program. If the news accounts were accurate, the next year would bring even more communities into the program. Both of the McDonoughs felt uneasy about having Cassie hear their arguments and complaints. They felt it important that he not have his school day, already trying enough, complicated further by the rantings of his parents. But it was impossible to keep their feelings and what they themselves called their prejudices from him.

"There's lots of parents who stick their noses into their children's business," Ellen McDonough told me. "People like us always thought it best to leave the teaching to the teachers. When it comes time to vote, you vote, but when the voting is done, you mind your ways and live by what the people have asked for. That's how we felt 'til the busing thing came along. But those days are gone. Now we have to keep an eye on things. I don't give up worrying about Cassie. I don't know what happens to him two seconds after he leaves that door. I don't know what the teachers are planning, or the Mayor, or Judge Garrity. If the parents in this community don't look out for themselves, no one will. The days of voting and sitting back are gone. We're going political. I got a whole new way of looking at this country now, and this city, and this government. When it comes to your children you don't let politicians run your lives. We'll be looking out for ourselves, police or no police, *Boston Globe* or no *Boston Globe!*"

Indeed it was the Boston newspapers that continually received the hatred of the McDonoughs and their neighbors. The editorial stands, the cartoons, the accounts of events seemed to present a powerful case against those, like the McDonough's, opposed to busing. Moreover, whenever I visited this one South Boston community, I was invariably reminded of the distinctions between the rich and the poor, the city families and the types in the suburbs, the shanty Irish and the lace curtain Irish. But I never once heard the McDonoughs express a desire for violence or personal injury. They wanted the forced busing program stopped; that was all. When a black man was dragged from his car and beaten in a nearby neighborhood, they were shocked. "No white person in this country," Clarence McDonough told me the day after the beating, "has 100 percent decent feelings about the colored. Everyone of us has some feelings that maybe we wish we didn't have. Maybe I'm even a bigot. Maybe I am. But I don't go for beating up an innocent man. The people that did that are animals. They have no right walking the streets!"

Cassie said he talked with some boys who had been in the crowd when the man was dragged out of his car. "All I could think of was that maybe *they'll* start doing that to *us*. All they have to do is stop one of the buses, come inside, pull us out and beat us up like they did over here. They could do it to get even. They'll have more cops in the schools now than they had before. There'll be more cops than children going to school, but otherwise it hasn't been so bad," he said, with surprise in his voice. "I'm learning some stuff. Our teachers are pretty good. Our homeroom teacher, she's all right 'cept she spends all her time taking attendance. Lots of the teachers don't care who's there and who isn't, but old lady Prisely she's got to know everything. Sometimes she'll take attendance twice in one day, once in the morning and once after lunch. She's always afraid some of the kids will skip out after lunch, you know. Lot of 'em do too. Like we got kids in there who skip out one day and then you never see 'em again. We even had a teacher do that. But 'cause of the busing they're all counting who's there. But they teach you a lot, some of 'em. Some of 'em shouldn't be teachers.

They even tell us they don't like it. They say school would be great if it wasn't for all the kids. We say it would be great if it wasn't for teachers who say things like that. I can't see why they want to teach if they don't like kids. They could get other jobs . . . or maybe they couldn't. Some of 'em could get other jobs 'cause they're *real* smart. But some of 'em couldn't get other jobs 'cause they don't know nothing about nothing. Not even how to teach. They're only in the school 'cause their brother or father or somebody's the principal.

"We got new books in the school, and a lot of those other kids aren't as dumb as everybody said they were. I thought, you know, that the teachers would be spending all their time helping *them* instead of *us,* 'cause they needed extra help. That's what I heard. But they're as smart as us. Fact, two of their girls are smarter than any of us. One of 'em," he smiled, "this big fat girl, she's smarter than everybody put together. I could really respect her too, 'cause she's smart. She was the first one of them to speak in the class. Know what she said? She said, 'My name is Janice and I don't want nobody to call me colored. I want everybody to call me black.' She wasn't mad, she just said it like she was telling us how she wanted us to call her."

"So you'll call them black people now?"

"Sure, if that's what they want. I told them to call me Cassie too, like the kids here call me. So you know what they call me?"

"What?"

"Cassie." He was smiling broadly. "They tell us, we tell them. It ain't so bad like I thought it would be."

"You still scared going there?"

"Sure. None of that's changed. There's fights almost every day. Sometimes everything's fine almost the whole day, then somebody starts something and man, does it get tense. Some of the time you're sitting there trying to concentrate, you know, and some of the time you're like a night watchman in this big dark place thinking you just heard some sound that ain't supposed to be there."

Francie Dearborn looked forward to my visits to her home with an eagerness that grew with each week. The television and

newspaper accounts of episodes related to busing couldn't be complete, she insisted. There were far more injuries than anyone dared report, far more trouble than anyone dared confess. I always told her I knew no more than she did but she would not accept this.

"You're the one who told us of the boy in that one high school who they put in a locker and threw out the window. You know the details 'cause you can go to those places. Even when they integrate the schools, part way like they're doing, the schools still belong to you white folks. No one's going to tell *us* what's really happening. We read in the paper there's some outbreak here or some business with kids in the halls. They tell black folks, nothing going on, no problems, but they tell *you* a boy is put in a locker or held in a steam shower. I can't stand not knowing, or feeling that folks are lying to you. Most days now (we were approaching the Christmas vacation) are pretty calm, at least at Claudell's school. But I don't know, last Tuesday here I was watching television while I was doing my work, and all of a sudden on the noon news, the man's talking about something going on right near where Claudell goes. I called the school. I even called the police. Nobody knows. Nobody tells you nothing. I'm like a mother waiting for her son to come home from a war somewhere. Is he going to be all right? Is he going to come home with a limp, with a bump on his head? Will he be here when Christmas comes?"

"But so far so good," I said quietly.

"So far, beautiful. Claudell really likes his school. I don't even think he misses the kids from around here. Have you heard the latest? He was invited by John Doherty's family to go to a movie for the Doherty boy's birthday. Two of them are going. I mean two of us," she laughed. "Mr. Doherty's taking six boys to a movie. He called here, you know, and asked our permission. We thanked him and asked Claudell. He said yes, so we said why not. And Mr. Doherty will bring them home." Francie's eyes widened. "There are days when the sun sure shines. Saturday these kids will go to the movies together and in South Boston they'll probably have to close the high school, they got so much trouble. What in the name of the good Lord, that great colorless

Lord in the sky, is wrong with people? The sun shines one minute, then the war starts up all over again."

Claudell's notes over the months of September, October, and November contained references to just about everything he was doing in school. Indeed a fascinating diary was developing. He never let me actually see the notes, but preferred to read them to me.

"I don't want you to see how bad I write," he said sheepishly on the last school day. "I'll just tell you, okay?"

"Of course."

"I think someone will be murdered in my school and I think it will be a black girl. My favorite teacher is Mrs. Levine but I don't tell anybody. Even though she's white, she's smart. I think the black children think she's smart but you feel strange saying it 'cause you want the black teachers to be better.

"Most of 'em are about the same, 'cepting that you can't always go to a white teacher and tell her your problems. You can't be sure what they'll say. And you can't always go to the black teachers 'cause they're always so busy. They ain't got but a few of 'em anyway. They're trying but they got too much work to do. We had one of 'em come to our house to talk to us before school started. He was real nice. That's Mr. Cranston. He came and told me about the school. He said he liked it and I would too. He didn't have to come neither. He told my father he wasn't getting paid for it or nothing. He just wanted to on his own. I went to see him once and he's all right, 'cept he's got so much to do. I thought there'd be a lot of black teachers but there ain't. They said they'd get more, but the school says a lot of things that never happen. Like they had this one teacher who you can really tell hates black kids. She can't even stand to look at 'em. I think she's taught in the school since they opened it. Fact is, she probably built it for herself. Some of the older kids told the principal she was really unfair. White kids knew it too. Everybody hates her, man. Everybody. So the principal, he said they'd get her out of there, put her in another school. But they never did. She's still there. My friend Sandy, he asked was she coming back next year. She told him it ain't none of his business but she was. She's coming back. That type always comes back.

"She ain't the stupidist though. The stupidist person in the school is Mr. Archery who is like an assistant something. All he thinks about is kids running in the halls, smoking in the bathrooms, talking when they ain't supposed to. So he noses around like an ugly old dog, sniffing around, you know, always hoping somebody's getting into trouble so he can arrest them. You should have seen me the other day, man. I'm running somewhere, outside the gym, you know, and out of the corner of my eye I see Archery. I couldn't stop real quick so I start running in place pretending I'm into doing these exercises. The dude walks right past me. I'm afraid to look at him, man, but I'd say he was smiling. Sylvia Backham, she saw me, she started to laugh and all, watching me making up exercises. I'm going to the movies on Saturday. John's old man, he's taking a group of us." He had changed topics without a pause. "We told him we were up to see a Bruce Lee, but they got some other flick they want us to see. Makes no difference to me, just as long as I get something to eat, I'll watch anything.

"I wrote this thing too on playing basketball and how they made some of us take off our shirts which is okay, you know, but lots of time they let the girls go walking through there. And another thing, they ought to fix that gym or open a window 'cause it's always smelling in there, man. You take a deep breath in that place, you like to blow away. Lassiter, he smells the worst, man. Everybody knows it too. My mother talked with his mother about it. They talked about putting him in a bath with Ajax cleaner."

Claudell was beginning to giggle. I was starting to laugh too, and thinking about how in the midst of the turmoil surrounding desegregation I was hearing old-fashioned, eleven-year-old schoolboy talk.

"My mother said, 'Put the Ajax over that boy and rub it in good.' But Lassiter's old lady, she says she's going to put him down with Drano. 'If it clears up the sink,' she says, 'it'll take out the stink.' Out of sight, man. They'll be busing me to the school and Lassiter to some laundry and dry cleaning place." Claudell exploded with laughter. "You see some dude opening

up his laundry somewhere and out pops Lassiter, all fresh and clean. Good-by, ring around the collar. Hello smell."

There have been, in these last months, many scenes and experiences which these two boys, who do not know one another, have described. Cassie continually refers to his parents' notion of the lack of freedom, the breaking up of his neighborhood, the special treatment shown black children in his school. Yet he confesses he sees no changes in his neighborhood and has witnessed no special treatment of black children in his school. In fact, he admires their courage and feels sorry for them when he sees them entering the school in the morning through a rear door near the gymnasium. He argues frequently with his friends in the neighborhood about going to school with black children.

"I tell 'em I'm learning a lot of things that you can't read about in books. It's like, when we're not supposed to be learning we're learning anyway. That's one good thing about the school."

By his own admission, Cassie thinks less and less about busing, being reminded of it mainly when he hears discussions among people who oppose it. Also by his own admission, he has stopped using the term colored to describe black children, and has noted that he no longer speaks about "us" and "them." He prefers to think of us and them as referring to us students, them teachers. But the feeling of being scared at school has not wholly subsided.

Claudell too has recognized that what he still calls the experiment is going fairly well. He sees unfairness in the treatment of black children but realizes that often white children don't understand that an injustice has just been committed. "Lots of times," he says, "I feel sorry for them. Sometimes it ain't their fault. It's some teacher's fault, but the kids don't understand." Claudell believes he's learning more in school than ever before, although he says that some teachers let some of the kids get away with things they shouldn't get away with because people are afraid that small incidents might turn into giant explosions. "Most folks walk around in that school real uptight. Everybody's afraid of everybody. Everybody thinks everybody's

going to start something. You go blow your nose or ask to go to the bathroom and they look at you like you're going to start a war."

Like Cassie, Claudell's fears have never disappeared. Unlike Cassie, the bus ride to and from the school, while filled with laughter one day, boredom the next, is a time when frightening events occur. On three different occasions I have been on a school bus with Claudell that was pelted with stones. Claudell reports that his bus has been stoned eleven times. Lying on the dirty floor of the bus one afternoon, listening to rocks clanking against the metal sides and hoping the windows wouldn't be broken, I heard Claudell ask me: "You scared?"

"You better believe I am. Why, aren't you?"

"You kidding me, man? I'm scared all the time. Second I see this bus I'm scared. I don't need no rocks out there to tell me I'm scared."

"You be on the bus tomorrow morning, Claudell?" The children were still lying flat on the floor.

"Sure. Will you?"

There is so much more to say about these two boys, these two families. The richness and complexities of their lives cannot be captured in a few pages or found in descriptions and citations involving the desegregation of two schools. No one claims that these families represent anyone but themselves. No one claims that their views in fact reflect upon all the issues connected with the autumns and winters of busing. It is questionable that one can end with a feeling of hopefulness, although it would be inaccurate to say that the families I have called the McDonoughs and Dearborns are despairing and utterly pessimistic. Certainly the boys, Cassie and Claudell, are not pessimistic. If not genuinely hopeful, they are at least hoping. Cassie has spoken several times of a wish that his school would be awarded a prize for the best school in Massachusetts. The prize furthermore, should indicate that his is the best school because black children and white children go there together. A short time ago, Claudell Dearborn dreamed that his school was given an award by the President of the United States. In the presentation of the award, the President said that Claudell's school was the best

school in the world and that Claudell and his friends were the best students and the bravest students in the world. Claudell and a white boy whose name he didn't know, received the award for his school.